Whitley Strieber is the author of the bestsellers *The Wolfen* and *The Hunger*, both of which have been filmed. James Kunetka is the author of *City of Fire* and *Oppenheimer: The Years of Risk*. Texans by birth and friends since childhood, they have collaborated previously on *Warday*, the documentary novel about nuclear war that became an international bestseller.

By the same authors

Warday

WHITLEY STRIEBER
& JAMES KUNETKA

Nature's End

The Consequences of the Twentieth Century

GRAFTON BOOKS

A Division of the Collins Publishing Group

LONDON GLASGOW
TORONTO SYDNEY AUCKLAND

Grafton Books
A Division of the Collins Publishing Group
8 Grafton Street, London W1X 3LA

Published by Grafton Books 1987

First published in Great Britain by
Grafton Books 1986

ISBN 0-586-07069-9

Printed and bound in Great Britain by
Collins, Glasgow

Set in Times

This book is dedicated
to the human future

Opening Ritual

From one dusty shadow to another:
why are you shining this light on me?

I could say, I am afraid not to,
or, I love you,
or, it's the night.

But this is the truth:
I have no reasons.
I only have the light.

> – Tom Ottinger,
> 'Approaching Singularity,' 2023

A Message from Hiding

There are four of us; we are fugitives. How we came to be such, and the extraordinary truth we have uncovered on our journey, are the subjects of this book.

We started out to destroy a politician. Certainly we did not expect to end up on the run. We're a political and journalistic family. Our intention was to ruin one of the greatest and most terrible political figures in human history. To be frank, we were foolish enough to take on Gupta Singh. We haven't destroyed him at all. Very much the contrary, in the past six months his Depopulationist Manifesto has been adopted by eight new countries and is under consideration right now by the United States Congress. And we are desperate.

We have changed Singh, though. Sooner or later, the world will discover what we have done.

He is as fierce as his name implies. We spent months escaping from him. Now we are against the wall, as it were. But we have found something in this secret place, something that could revise the whole human future, and this book is an attempt to share it with you.

We must begin, though, at the beginning. The reason we tried to oppose the Depopulationist Movement has to do with our own cultural roots – western, humanitarian and Christian.

Our story starts four years ago, in Denver, during those black November days of 2021, when a city was suffocating.

It begins with a hero's death, and the pain of a father's loss.

A Father's Testament

This is my hardest story, the one that wakes me up in the night, the one I cannot forget. It is a story about my own blood, and a death that was the death of the best part of me. I'm not young, and I've been a journalist long enough to have seen a great deal of pain.

Never before or since, though, have I seen anything like Denver in 2021. Smog was first noticed there in the nineteen sixties. But people couldn't imagine what might eventually happen, not even in the seventies when there were some pretty dark days, and some deaths. In the eighties people with respiratory ailments were routinely moved out during smog alerts. Massive efforts were made to control pollution, but not enough. People got used to the long, brown days.

That was a more innocent time. I remember it, and Walter Ransom Jones's famous characterization of the last twenty-five years of the twentieth century as the 'joyous sunset' is apt. It was a lot of fun to live in the world before people like Falon and Gupta Singh came along, before such miseries as the Federal Tax Police and the Depopulationist International.

By 1985 the world was full of warnings for Denver. Mexico City ran emergency lung support trucks during pollution alerts. Just living there was the equivalent of smoking forty cigarettes a day. Living in Denver during a pollution emergency in – say – 1989 was the equivalent of smoking twenty cigarettes a day.

Some of those same people, men and women who were young when I was young, would die in the Denver pollution catastrophe of 2021. I can imagine them, driving along Colfax in their youth and their fine new cars thirty or forty years ago. The sky is brown, and they can't see the Rockies. They listen to the radio, look forward to meeting friends for lunch, plan to go out to dinner with husbands or wives. The radio news and *The Denver Post* talk pollution, yes, but to the ordinary man it's only an ugly sky, a bad smell and a little cough. People are more interested in the realities of the moment, listening to Madonna sing 'Material Girl,' trying out the new Sony Compact Disk player they've just had installed in the car.

It is a happy, rich time, the last of the fatted years. People shop in supermarkets containing ten thousand and more different items. There has never been a food shortage in the United States, and such a thing seems impossible. There has never been a pollution emergency on the scale of the one that will kill many of those very people, shopping in those vast markets, in that Denver of long ago.

One of them might drive cheerfully past the very corner where he will die thirty-three years later. The lamp post against which he will crouch is not there. Broadcast lighting hasn't been invented yet, and the thick green posts have yet to mar the urban landscapes of the world. He does not get a chill, passing the place of his death. He doesn't even slow down.

But for a few scientists, words like 'blocking high' and 'decirculation' meant nothing to the people of the twentieth century. They weren't even sure about the alleged warming trend, and nobody yet realized that it would be accompanied by a dramatic reduction in the amount of air circulation. If someone had showed one of them a picture of his or her own death, and said that their agony was caused by prolonged atmospheric decirculation within a mature blocking high in the year 2021, they would only have asked, 'What is that black stuff coming out of me? What's happening to me? Am I in pain?'

Strip away thirty-three years. Now those same people are old. Private cars don't run in much of central Denver, and they can barely use theirs because of the stringent pollution restrictions.

And the sky is not brown. Today it is black. It has been black for days, as black as oil. The air leaves grease in the nose and burns the lungs. People draw each breath with care. There's fire in their chests, they suck in that thick air until they're about to pop the buttons on their shirts, but it doesn't help. They cough, they gasp again, but try as they might they cannot get enough to breathe. It hurts, it sends frantic shivers through the whole body. Victims try to claw open their own chests. As if from far away they hear their hearts rattling, then the whole world begins to pound on their heads, and they sink down, and lie there, shattered men and women, on the streets they drove when they were thirty, in the soft brown mornings of long ago.

But that is their story.

My story is different. I wasn't often in Denver in the past. In those days I lived in Los Angeles, doing rewrites for the International News Service. My own terrible fame was not to come to me for years, and when it did it would be based on a technology we couldn't even imagine then.

My relationship with Denver only lasted a few days, in the year 2021. But they were the worst days Denver and I have ever known. The city lost its innocence and eighty thousand of its citizens. I lost my son.

It was a bright November morning in Los Angeles when Tom suddenly came bursting into my hotel room. We had long since moved to New York; I was in LA on some detail of business which I forget.

I was astonished to see my son; I had thought he was

12

off in Indonesia working with the tropical reforestation research group. He said he had seen some disturbing statistics in the AirWatch data and wanted the two of us to go to Denver. He had taken a conventional jet from Jakarta to Singapore and then a Trans-Atmospheric Vehicle to LA. He had left Singapore at eight P.M., losing a day on the four hour hypersonic flight home. But he wasn't interested in sleep; he wanted us to load up on pollution gear, measurement devices, protective filters, whatever we needed, and take the next plane to Denver.

The data showed that the Rocky Mountain metropolis was caught in a blocking high, one of those still-air events that cause so much hardship now that the atmosphere is growing more uniformly warm. During five weeks of temperature inversion the city had reached a level of pollution so high the infants and the elderly were dying.

'The story's not getting told right. We need an emergency rescue effort. The place has to be evacuated.'

The government was reacting cautiously, refusing to release much information. I suspected that an evacuation was probably being planned, but in secret. Had it been announced, panic would have swept Denver. Tom wouldn't listen to any of my cautionary advice. He wanted to go there, he had to participate, to help.

We were so long in partnership, I never considered the idea of not going with him into this crisis. Had we thought more carefully, the old man would certainly have stayed behind. I, the survivor.

We approached the city in a huge Delta fanprop, a seven hundred and fifty seat giant. Despite its size the monster was jammed. In 2021 it had just become illegal to fly out of LA with less than four fifths of all seats filled. The plane made five stops between Los Angeles and Atlanta, Denver being the first. As it turned out, few of our fellow passengers got off there. We were fortunate that the destination hadn't been dropped.

I settled in for the flight. When the vending machine passed I bought us turkey sandwiches and Quists. As usual Tom had no time to eat. He already had his computer out and hooked into the plane's antenna. 'I've got to get some critical data,' he muttered. 'I just want to finish something before we land.' I saw from his screen that the material wasn't about Denver or tropical forests. It was about children, as a matter of fact.

Years later, what he was doing on that airplane would save the lives of the four people he loved best, me included. This would happen long after he himself was dead. I saw joy in him then, joy that I did not understand. Despite all the hell of the past few years, I understand it now, today, as I write this. There is reason for joy, even in our dismal old world.

As he finished he looked up at me. His eyes were shining. He closed the Unon Interactor and took its phone out of his ear.

'May I know what you're doing?'

He touched my hand, a characteristic gesture of his. 'I'll tell you everything as soon as I can.'

I pressed him but he would say little more. 'I don't want to compromise you. If I tell you, you'll have a journalistic obligation to publish the story. It's got to be kept secret for now, that's vital. What I can say is that it has to do with children, and a place called Magic.'

I filed that one in my mental urgent file, but I never followed it up. The events of the next few days swept away my memory of that minor conversation. I remembered only Tom's snapping brown eyes, his laughter, his voice. And the joy that was in him, that glowed and flashed from him, the unquenchable, wonderful presence that made him so very, very hard to lose.

We came upon a good place in an evil time with Tom studying weather maps and me sipping the last of my Quist as our plane banked and announced that it was approaching Denver.

The murk above the city was so dense that it had formed into discrete clouds, which billowed up like thunderheads and sent long, brown tails blowing into the distance. The clouds were a vicious shade of black.

You could spot the people who were getting off by their gas masks. Most of them put on their breathing equipment long before we reached the ground. Tom and I followed their example. As soon as we entered the clouds the light dropped down and the plane began to buffet. Within seconds the interior of the thing was hazy, the lights glowing dull. I could hear the pitch of the engines changing as the computer struggled to keep them alive by altering the mixture.

We landed on a runway blazing with fog lights, in what appeared to be night. It was dark at ten o'clock in the morning.

As we taxied to the jetway, I noticed that the smoky haze in the cabin was now so thick that you couldn't see all the way to the front of the plane.

As we got our things together and left the plane a horrible chill swept through me. I knew then what it meant to quake with fear. It was dark in the middle of the morning. Absolutely, utterly dark out there, with baggage handlers and mechanics on the runway, moving as if they were under water, their faces bulging, black and gleaming – helmets, masks, hissing respirators.

Frantic to escape this place, my mind flashed back to another Denver. Until that moment I had not remembered my visit in the autumn of 1977. I had stayed at the Brown Palace, and from my room I could see the Rockies. I remembered having a delicious dish called fried corn

15

meal mush for breakfast. Might not sound like much, but it certainly was good, served with syrup, butter and molasses. Back in those days corn was an ordinary food.

Autumn of 1977, Autumn of 1977. Driving up to Telluride with friends of those days – who were they, those ghosts? Were they here, now alive, gagging out their souls somewhere in the terrible city?

How could we have known what that thin brown line on the horizon meant, back in 1977?

Things were dank and choking and dim in 2021, as we marched up the long corridor to the taxi ranks across from Stapeldon's old fashioned baggage carousels.

We carried only hand luggage, a digital video rig, battery packs and lens cases. Despite the situation, a certain happiness kept bubbling up in me. I was with Tom, and I liked that. My memories of him are like blurred snapshots. A boy with a wide grin, a baby staring in wonder at a leaf, a kid carrying his kitten, so proud, 'Dad, Mom, Coe likes me. He came when I called!' Oh, Tom. MIT Graduation: Tom and his friend Scott taking honors degrees together. Tom laughing, Tom playing some subtle electronic prank on me, Tom in a towering rage about the destruction of the tropical forest or the extinction of the giraffe or the destruction of some South American tribe's cultural heritage.

Tom and Scott going off together to fight for the health and beauty of the world . . . Tom, Tom. I would give my life for just one more minute with him.

I wish I could tell Tom about the success of Magic, which was his most important accomplishment. But I am condemned instead to tell myself, to tell you, to hope. And now, to chronicle the mechanism of my son's tragedy.

As we left the baggage area I saw a bare faced man stop and cough up black spatters of blood. He grabbed

16

the handrail and leaned over gasping. I heard him as we passed, muttering, 'My God, my God.' Like me he was older, a creature of the comfortable, good times, haunting this, our future.

Tom stopped, put his arm around the man's shoulder, began helping him forward. 'Dad, find him a mask. Surely they've got emergency services organized.'

When the two of them reached the arrivals lobby the man was wearing Tom's mask, and walking erect. I intercepted them at a roped-off area identified by handwritten signs: Respiration Assistance Unit, Dept of the Environment. Behind the ropes people of all ages could be seen lying on cots and on the floor.

Tom took his mask back from the traveler as the man was met by a nurse. We never found out what happened to him, but it was not until we got to the city that we understood that he probably had not been issued a mask of his own. Supplies were extremely short.

The fact that most people had nothing but wet rags to breathe through – and some of them not even that – was revealed to us when we alighted from the Regional Transportation Authority Bus at Broadway and Thirteenth, where we were to transfer to an electric city bus. Auto traffic has been at a minimum in central Denver for twenty years. But even given the stringent pollution controls of today, six weeks without any air movement is devastating. The problem, if nothing else, is that this is a region of nearly four million people.

If I hadn't stopped him Tom would have given his mask to the first of those millions that he saw. As it was, he used it as little as possible, out of sympathy with the people.

At our hotel, the Downtown Motor Inn, we bought a copy of *The Denver Post*. It covered the crisis calmly and thoroughly. Nowhere was there a suggestion of panic, nor any news of evacuation plans.

The motel had hooked tarps up to the windows and we were advised to keep them damp, this despite the filtration system and the reconditioned air. When we got our bearings and went outside, ready to observe and report, we realized that we were facing a catastrophe that must have been invented in the darkest bottom of hell. Not even our trip to the motel, accomplished as it was in sealed vehicles, had prepared us for the direct experience of the streets.

The smog was a stinking, stinging wall. It was dank, motionless and oddly warm. And it was quiet. Like fog, the smog absorbed sound. You could hear a few nearby voices, and the occasional muffled churning of a police fanprop passing overhead. The headlights of a bus would loom up, the door would open and a shuffling clutch of people would come out and move away toward the faint glow of the buildings. Babies lay in their strollers, their eyes glazed, not even toying with the wet rags that their mothers put around their faces. For infants the first step toward death was this dreamy, quiet state. Did they see something beautiful in their death dream, or was it music that the carbon monoxide made in them, or did they simply feel the pleasure of floating away?

The street lamps on Broadway marched into an abrupt black wall. There were no private cars, no taxis.

At the hotel our porter had bled from his nose when he lifted our bags. The maids were gray and slow, moving like sleepwalkers up and down the murky hallways. The reservation clerk couldn't find our reservation, but simply changed the name of another reserved party in the computer commenting that they wouldn't show up anyway.

Tom wanted to spend as much time as possible in the

18

streets. To get the kind of action he felt was needed here, he had to make a personal report. Help might be forthcoming soon for the American citizens, but what about the enormous number of illegals, Mexicans and Koreans, Thais and Vietnamese, who jammed this city as they do every American metropolis?

I was astonished to hear him say that he was thinking in terms of arranging an airlift of two million air filtration masks to be distributed free of charge to those not covered by Federal programs.

It was an immense project. As we walked the streets his computer worked via uplink to locate the masks and the money to buy them, searching supplies databases and sources of funding worldwide.

If the computer effort failed, Tom planned to take his personal story to some of the influential people of his acquaintance. In an age when most of us rely on electronic communcations he was in the habit of marching into offices for personal confrontations. He was always unexpected and usually unwanted. He was intense, passionate and convincing. But he could be practical. Whenever possible, he was quick to point out a profit associated with one of his ideas.

After half an hour in the streets of the city we were covered with slick soot, and standing in line at a civil defense lung truck to get three blessed breaths of enriched air.

There was a frantic sort of sensation that came over you, called air hunger, that made your skin crawl with an urgency that could not be satisfied. You had to be careful not to develop an oxygen deficit or you might spend hours lying as still as possible on a streetcorner, trying to catch your breath.

Ambulances circulated endlessly, and army trucks that seemed to us to be picking up the dead.

In the streets, in the alleyways, in the doors of buildings people sat or lay or crouched doubled over, coughing, dying right there before our eyes. Terrible human dramas were enacted anywhere, on the corner, in a doorway, beside a parked car. We saw children screaming in terror over the dead bodies of their mothers, we saw women frantically trying to revive their husbands, we saw dead infants wrapped in newspaper, we heard a whole city coughing its lungs out.

The entire population was in uneasy motion, but nobody was allowed to use cars. Even so, on the thruways there were massive, dead traffic jams. Once we saw a Cadillac Versailles storming down a street. It was intercepted by a screaming police car, and when it swerved to escape, the cops without hesitation shot its tires out. Its eight occupants were held at gunpoint, waiting for a prison van to pick them up.

Denver was in turmoil, but it was slow and silent. There were crowds, but they were lost in the smog. There were screams but the air made them sound like the muffled hooting of owls. The whole city whispered and waltzed in terror, beneath the black weight of the sky. Pickpockets and bandits swarmed like roaches in the bowels of the mob. Army and police loudspeaker trucks issued instructions to go home, to remain quiet. Their voices slapped back and forth among the buildings, while Red Cross workers in soiled white uniforms offered water to drench the greasy face rags of the desperate.

A Korean man, his eyes red with burst vessels, came reeling up, screaming in his native tongue, his hands like the claws of a buzzard, grasping at my mask. When I pushed him away I pushed too hard and he collapsed in a jerking pile, his screams bubbling like cries from under water.

On the few outflowing arteries that remained open the

traffic was insane, the streets literally bloody. People would leap out of disabled cars and run, knowing that the cars would soon be smashed aside by others still able to function. On the main streets police in riot trucks remained passive, unable to stop the sheer mass of refugee vehicles.

Late in the afternoon of the first day we were there a crisis was reached: the average adult, healthy in heart and lung, began to smother.

Tom felt it, so did I. I was especially struck by the horror I saw in the faces of people my age. We lived in the old world, after all. We remembered when things like this seemed impossible. The future, though, was already waiting for us even when we were young.

Office workers were crowding into the streets, people coughing and vomiting. My son began to help whom he could. He gave his mask away, fed all of his supplementary oxygen to a group of frantic schoolkids, wiped the faces of the sick with his bare hands, carried the helpless to lung trucks, bullying his way in and seeing that they got extra air, then sneaking a breath so he could keep going himself. I tried to keep up with him, holding onto my own mask lest I lose it and die. Soon I would have to go inside. The mask had to regenerate, and my lungs gurgled when I breathed. The air hunger was beginning to drive me crazy. I felt like you do when you've swum too deep and you're frantic to breathe.

My head was aching, my mouth was full of grease, my nose was stuffed up, and the mask wasn't working at all.

The idea of Tom without a mask horrified me. Please, I thought, please let him stop. Please God, let him realize that he is a mortal body. He can die out here, Tom can. Let him realize that. Then I saw his eyes as he passed the corner where he had left me. A child was clinging to his back, a young man in a thousand dollar suit was in his

21

arms, and I realized with a sick feeling the truth: he had put his own welfare out of his mind.

I shouted to him, followed him, pleaded with him. I remember screaming until my voice popped to a whisper, clutching at him, finally begging him not to get himself lost in this mess. His face was covered with soot. There were trenches of clean skin on his cheeks where his sweat ran. He looked at me for a long moment, then put his hand on my cheek. The gesture was reassuring. When he promised me that he would come back to the hotel within the hour I let myself believe him. My own pain was so great, it must have confused me.

Every day, every moment of my life I have regretted the decision to leave him. Was it cowardice, confusion, fear – what made me abandon my son to his death? A thousand times I have pleaded with the dark to send him back and take me. But the dark remains the dark, and what I did, I did.

As I made my way back my arms and legs felt as if they weighed tons, my bones ached, and there were shimmering black flashes around the periphery of my vision.

Then, at last, I was back at the Downtowner. The hotel was virtually abandoned, staffed only by a woman at the desk. I got my key from her and dragged the immense weight of my body to our room.

When I tried to draw a bath I found that the water was barely running. Hotels here use private water companies, as do most wealthy individuals, but there had been no delivery. The ordinary people continue with the city service, as unreliable as it is.

My son's computer was sitting opened, its screen bearing the brief message: Uplink failure due to atmospheric conditions. Sick or not, I certainly knew how important this was to Tom. I also knew that the sooner he got what

22

he wanted, the sooner he would leave here. I started trying to re-establish his link manually. Tom would be furious when he saw this.

As I worked at the computer I choked in the foul air.

I remembered Tom as a six-year-old, a complicated, nervous little fellow whose chief characteristics were his talkativeness and his unusual kindness. Even then I respected his nature. As a child he was not much interested in religion, but he had a natural regard for his fellow man that seemed almost sacred. He was born this way. Allie and I only raised him. I do not think that we are responsible for his fundamental nature.

His later concerns were consciousness and attention. 'We have to pay attention to our lives and the lives we can affect. If somebody needs help, it matters to the whole species. It's up to the ones closest by to do the most.'

I remember his car collection, begun when he was five and left on a shelf at our old house in Glendale at about age eight. And his early triumphs, his wonderful skill at dancing, his reading proficiency, his mastery of his computer.

I know that I have a tendency to worship him, and that he was not all good. But he was willing to give his life for people he did not know in a battle he could not win, and despite the bad side of him – and it certainly existed – that is the act of a hero.

For what seemed like half an hour I worked at the computer. Finally it told me that it was having component problems because of debris shorting some of its circuits, and it could no longer handle both the search we wanted and the data transfers such a search would require at the same time – even if I did get back to the satellite.

At that point I gave up.

I was astonished to see that it was long past midnight. I

had spent most of the last four hours crouching just like the people in the streets, only sporadically working on the computer. The rest of the time I had been totally unconscious.

It was terrifying, because there had been no warning and I had not expected it. This, then, was one of the deaths that could come to you here: oblivion.

Experimentally I picked up the telephone. Not even a click.

I was going to go out, but found myself instead lying on the bed. Again time had passed.

My watch said four P.M. I sat up, trying to see beyond my headache that asserted itself as soon as I opened my eyes.

Four in the afternoon! Tom had been out there for over twelve hours. I would have screamed if I could. I beat the walls, beat them slowly, hacking and gasping. It was as if I had fallen in a pit and I couldn't get out, and my son was out there dying. I remember it like a nightmare. Sometimes I catch myself thinking that Tom is only dead in nightmare. But he never comes.

I struggled to go out and look for him. My body was clamoring for attention: legs, arms, head all hurt. Lungs hurt, and I was nauseous. But I ignored these things. Tom was gone, my son was gone.

I strapped on my air exchanger and tightened my filtration mask. The air had become so bad that it took work to drag air through the overtaxed exchanger, but at least the awful, thick suffocating sensation that persisted without the device grew less.

I searched for my son in scenes of madness. Over the past few hours the situation had grown much worse. There were now people in the thousands lying in the streets, on the sidewalks, hanging from windows, slumped behind the wheels of cars. Many engines had stalled due to lack of oxygen. People writhed in agony, suffocating by tormented degrees. I do not mean one person or fifty people, I mean crowds as far as I could see, thousands upon thousands, and most of them young and bright and American, in the peak of their lives, their vitality being choked out of them.

This monster smog was now killing the strongest.

A young man came up and began trying to undo my apparatus. His hands shook, his muscles twitched. I pushed him away but he slumped against me. The thief who would have in better days stolen everything I had and killed me as well, now began terminal suffocation, lying in my arms like a child.

When I put him down and stood up, I realized that the lurching posts I could see here and there in the dark were people, and the lumpy mass beneath my feet was also people.

Then my recirculator began to sound a gas alarm. The carbon monoxide trap was failing.

I had to get back to better air or risk loss of consciousness again.

I retreated to the hotel. The reconditioner was off, but the air in the room seemed a little less dense, and my carbon monoxide trap began to inch up out of the red.

Furious at my own weakness, I pulled off all my equipment, lay face down on the bed and bawled into the pillow.

I was no fool. I knew I had lost Tom.

Fathers should not outlive their sons. It is too painful. And what in the name of God would I tell Allie? How could I tell his mother that he had died in the streets while I cowered in a hotel room?

I lay on that bed for the better part of four days, getting up only for a dribble of water or some candy from the vending machine in the hall. I lived on Snickers bars and bags of Nutos.

The city had come to a complete and total halt, and for that reason the air got no worse. One day the windows glowed. I knew that the blocking high had broken. Denver's mantle was being shaken off. For hours I heard trucks clanking and roaring, and voices. Lights passed on the road.

Eventually I was found by the US Army which trucked me along with about seventy other hotel survivors to the airport, past piles of stiff, bloated plastic bags, past the neat, silent neighborhoods. Swarms of flies seemed to have survived the air.

I waited three days at the airport, lining up with the others for a drink of water that tasted of benzine, or barely cooked beans served in pots from which we had to scoop with our hands.

Then I got on Delta Flight 6150, a new Boeing Sprint, and suddenly I was back in what now seemed a stunningly beautiful and quite artificial world, a disguise in comfortable beige seats and gleaming windows. I still remember how clean it was, and how very fresh the air when we finally exited the Denver area. At eighty thousand feet we went hypersonic, and within the hour were landing in New York.

Allie was waiting, her face frozen with her agony. When we saw each other we broke down, sinking together to the floor of the busy airline terminal.

I was in the hospital having my lungs deterged for two days, then I went back to the quietest home that a man could possibly face. I was over seventy, and the center of my life – my son – was pictures and memories.

For a while I just stood there, looking at our familiar things, the dining table we have had for fifty-two years, that we bought at Macy's in New York in 1973, beyond it the bed Sam Williams built for us, where we consummated our marriage, and where Allie conceived and gave birth to Tom.

I had no body, no proof of death, not even word of what had happened to him. What came, in the end, was a letter from the Red Cross, and information that his remains had been cremated 'due to the urgency of the situation.'

Hope finally left us the morning we got that letter. With the sun streaming in our windows, we raised a dirge for Tom in World Singing.

There were eleven thousand people on the net that day, an unusually high number for those times, before the participation network replaced conventional performance video. I ordered up a visual map and saw the glowing dots on the globe in my screen, each one representing a singer.

I was astonished to see a glow in Denver. I did an aural zoom and a voice emerged, young and yet husky from her experience with the air.

She sang with soft defiance, an old Scottish tune, 'The Wild Mountain Thyme.'

The computer inferred what we most desired, for it did a slow aural zoom out, adding voice after voice after voice until the whole multitude was present in the mix. We realized that they were all singing with her, singing in remembrance of the fallen of Denver, and thus also our son.

FROM THE DATA FILES OF TOM SINCLAIR:
DENVER

'Colorado and the Mile High City are running out of time to reduce the country's highest pollution levels.'
– *The New York Times,* November 24, 1984

'Occasionally a high pressure system gets "stuck" in one place, for reasons which are still not fully understood. Such a blocking high may stay put for days or even weeks on end, acting like a real mountain around which other weather systems have to move.'
– John Gribbon, *Future Weather,* Delta, 1982

'Despite mandatory restrictions on automobile traffic in the city center, Denver air pollution continues to rise. The primary problem is population expansion. More stringent controls on vehicle emissions, a ban on backyard barbecues and wood stoves, and the addition of scrubbers to area power plants are under consideration to curb dangerous pollution levels.'
– *The Rocky Mountain Times,* July 11, 1989

'A blocking high settled into the region last week, raising pollution levels to all-time records. At the same time, record high temperatures were recorded, with Denver reaching 97 degrees on October 8, twelve degrees higher than the previous record for that day. City officials were studying the possibility of evacuating respiratory cases and newborns if the pollution emergency does not end by Saturday.'
– *The Denver Journal,* October 9, 1997

'Reports from Mexico City indicate that there has been a staggering loss of life in an air pollution crisis. The city had been operating for some weeks under highly polluted conditions when a critical threshold was crossed and many otherwise healthy people began to suffocate. In the ensuing rush to escape the massive metropolis, hundreds of thousands of people may have lost their lives. Because of the rioting, airports have been closed, and highway traffic is at a standstill.

'The Revolutionary Council has imposed strict censorship on all newsdata, and until restrictions are lifted the full story will not be made available.'

– International NewsNet, August 6, 2002

PART ONE
Depopulation

What remained after the hopes had failed,
after the houses,
the cars, the secrets, the books,
the guns, the children, the rooms,
the whole forgotten tremendous past
was, of all things,
the future.

– Emon Marks, 'Second Vision,' 2025

JOHN: The Gathering of Forces

It is a gray morning in New York City. The view from my window looks the same – the empty expanse of Gramercy Park with the Park Towers on the far side. It sounds the same – the whine of an electric truck, the distant warbling of a siren, the sound of street people getting up to meet their day.

But everything has changed. This is not the same country as it was yesterday. Last night there was a revolution at the polls. Even though the Depopulationist Manifesto hasn't been passed yet, we know now that it will be. It could kill me. Or kill both Allie and me. Or, may God forbid, kill Allie and leave me.

I wish that Tom would come walking out of his bedroom door. I close my eyes. When I open them I would like to see a miracle.

Four years have passed since we lost him. We haven't even begun to get over it. To the contrary, as such horrors as the Depopulationist International have gained and gained and the old forces of human decency and hope have faltered, we have felt his loss ever more acutely.

All he left were his data files. Millions of pages of material, most of it as yet untapped. His friends Scott Harper and Bell Evans have joined Allie and me as a contract family. We are close – a company, a family, parents and children, friends. All of those relationships are valid. Together we try to carry on Tom's work as well as do our own. My name will already have told most of you what we do – but don't let that turn you away from us. The image of the sinister, cunning convictor is just a media cliché. We are pretty ordinary people, and no less honest than the next man.

We are a well-practiced team, the four of us. Together we have generated some powerful convictions. I do the work with Delta Doctor, designing the personality simulation of the subject. My wife Allie does the graphics, making sure that the televised image will exactly match the subject, no matter what the viewer should ask it to do, even if it must disrobe. Bell is a psychometrist, and she designs many of the psychological questions that help Delta Doctor to build its model of the subject's mind. Scott's background is research, and he finds the facts we need to ground our simulation in the biographical reality of the subject.

Scott also has an obsession that never leaves him for long. He works with Tom's data files, which consist of over a million pages of information, much of it very sensitive, all of it hidden by encryption. The files contain information about all that Tom discovered, all that he did. Perhaps even the key to the future is there, if it has a key. Tom viewed his most important work, such as Magic, as secret. You have to break layer after layer of code, and follow long, convoluted logic paths at the same time. But the riches are there. We view Tom's files as a mine, out of which it just might be possible to dig the future.

Scott helped to collect many of those files. He and Tom did some of the encryption together. As the years pass, Scott's obsession with them grows. He seeks anything of value in the data, but most of all what Tom considered of greatest value, the secret of Magic.

Today, though, nobody is going to be doing any exotic research. We are too stunned by the election. People kept their intention to vote Depopulationist secret. The polls did not even suggest a Depop victory, much less the landslide that occurred.

We are going to act, of course. Our planning program, Stratigen, was quite clear on that. 'Convict Gupta Singh.' It has been suggesting this for two years like a broken record. 'Convict Gupta Singh.' If a computer program can have a mania, ours has one. 'It is the only resistance left. And you must resist him.'

The only trouble with that is, it is a terrifying thing to attempt. Singh is powerful. He can be expected to resist conviction furiously.

My conviction of President Falon shattered his presidency. I have started lesser men on the road to jail, others I have simply ruined.

People like to play with an exact simulation of another person. Ask it intimate questions about its innermost self. What do you *really* believe, Mr President-in-Christ? The Falon conviction told the truth, that he was no Christian. And what about your sexual preferences, Mr President? They made him dance for them, the public did. By the time it was over, the average person on the street had seen a perfect television image of the President engaged in acts of intimate and total perversity. His sex life made Falon a laughingstock.

At first I didn't want to convict Singh, no matter what it meant. Yesterday I wouldn't even have considered it.

But when Scott woke me up this morning and I saw the final election results in his shocked face, I knew what our friendly family strategist was going to say. But it didn't just replay the broken record. When we asked it for status analysis, the reply was coldly frightening. 'There is a seventy percent probability that the new Congress will close access to Delta Doctor even to licensed convictors, in order to prevent a conviction of Singh. Unless you act immediately, you may never be able to act at all.'

Delta Doctor was originally developed by the Psycho-intelligence Branch of the General Intelligence System to provide personality profiles of world leaders to the President. The Program Access Act of 2011 extended the right to use it to licensed convictors, which consists of myself and four other people, none of whom besides me do dangerous, chancy and usually low-paying public service work. Instead my colleagues sell their efforts privately. For two hundred thousand dollars or so you can know the absolute and final truth about anybody.

I looked up from the computer, my mind a babble of frightened voices. Singh would fight back. He would fight hard. But if we didn't act now, Stratigen was saying we would neve get the chance.

'Stratigen's become more of an advocate than a strategist,' Scott said. 'But I think it has a point. Forbidding conviction is an obvious move for a pro-Singh Congress. We've got to start work right away.'

I didn't want to think about this. I wanted it to go away. My eyes focused outward, on the park. I remember it when the green was real, and there were tall trees.

Three children played below, supervised by a young woman wearing the blue uniform of NY Nannies. I can still hear their voices as they set a pretend tea-table on an old stump, all that remains of those magical trees.

I remember that amber moment. It was just before we made our final decision to take Stratigen's advice and fight Gupta Singh. The children's tones rose above the other sounds, were drowned by the echoing thunder of a TAV, then asserted themselves again. Their voices, gentle parodies of our own, gave me joyous pain.

I called for music, something bright. Soon my office was filled with *The Four Seasons*. It was too loud. I snarled at the thing to turn down. It did so – too much, as if to spite me. 'Louder, but not too loud.'

Allie and Bell had come in, and stood silently, as if guarding us from something on the other side of the door.

'We'll convict, of course,' Bell said. 'Stratigen was right all along. If we'd convicted six months ago, Singh's party might not have won.'

Allie's voice was almost harsh. She did not place any blame, but it was there. After the hell I went through with Falon, I've hesitated to go after another powerful demagogue. 'John, I feel like we've all just gotten a death sentence.'

I could not disabuse her of the notion. That New York had put a Depopulationist into the Senate was surprise enough. But that sanity had lost Wei of California and Washington of Illinois was almost beyond belief. There might be a Manifesto bill on the President's desk by February.

As I sat listening to Scott's voice going over the results, I found that I was unable to be as surprised as he. I've sensed the rage and resentment in the streets, seen it in the bitter words people deposit anonymously in public data.

Allie spoke again. 'I think we'd better have a thorough session with Stratigen. Because it's been making the same recommendation for so long, we've been ignoring it.'

'Singh will fight back. It'll be as dangerous as hell.' It was all I could think about.

Bell's voice was clear and stern. 'John, you're the only convictor in the world who will even attempt this. I don't see that we have any choice at all. At least let's talk to Stratigen.' As usual she didn't wait for an answer. She called up the program and put it on vocal.

'Stratigen ready.'

Bell asked the first question. 'What is the probability of our successfully convicting Singh, as you suggest?'

'Four chances out of ten.'

I almost exploded. 'You're recommending that we do something with that low a chance of success? Why?'

'If the depopulation program is carried out, the chances of total human extinction are very good. This must be prevented at all costs.'

'Total human extinction? That isn't what people have been led to believe. A population reduction yes, but not that,'

'Added to the pressure that environmental collapse is going to put on the human species over the next half century, the trauma of killing one out of three human beings voluntarily will lead to uncontrollable disease and disorder among the survivors. A total breakdown. A catastrophe.'

The machine voice, soft, rich, filled the room, pouring from the Unon Interactor in Bell's hand.

'What steps should we take?' Allie asked.

'Start the conviction. Also provide informational support, a book published in paper. Such a book cannot be erased or altered. It will be universally accessible, even to those without electronic readers.'

'We can't write a book. We've never written a book.' I was really beginning to become certain that Stratigen was defective in some way. I wish I'd known then what I know now about who controls the computer system, I wouldn't have wasted so much time being suspicious of it.

'The four of you are uniquely capable of undertaking this effort. You have the conviction skills, the research skills, as well as the needed fund of data for the book.'

'What fund – '

'It means Tom's files,' Scott said excitedly. 'Of course, it's so obvious! Using those files and what we can learn

38

from current sources, we can create just the book that's needed.'

Bell's eyes fixed on me. 'You know, the basic problem people suffer from nowadays is passivity brought on by fear. It's a disease and it's destroying us. You're in your passivity, that's your problem.'

'But a conviction, now a book. I think we should be very careful with Stratigen. What if it isn't working right?'

'Oh, it's perfectly fine. The program's been used by millions of people for years. Stratigen's old code, the bugs are all gone.' Bell folded her arms.

'This is more than a conviction now, it's a whole big project.' I directed a question to Stratigen. 'What is the probability of our completing both the conviction and the book?'

'The two are not combinable. The probability on the book is eighty percent, assuming that you do not become neutralized while attempting the conviction.'

'I've never heard you use the words "become neutralized" before. Please explain.'

'Singh has the capacity to carry out personality modification of the most thorough and extensive kind. His strategy will be to capture and modify you, John, make you into a public supporter. The others he will destroy physically. "Neutralize" seemed a good word to encompass this combination of actions.'

I reached over to turn off the computer, but Bell held it away from me. 'Wait a minute, I have an important question. Stratigen, which is more important, the conviction or the book?'

'Equal.'

'Expand.'

'The conviction will reduce Singh's influence, perhaps eliminate it if he proves to be distasteful enough. The book must provide an alternative, though. There must be something to fill the void left by the collapse of the Depopulationist Movement. If not, something worse will no doubt take its place.'

'What would be worse?'

'Despair. The fabric of society will break down. The death toll from anarchy and violence could ultimately exceed that of the planned depopulation.'

Bell dropped the computer into her pocket. 'What it's asking us to do is tremendously important. We can't refuse.'

'Now, wait a minute, don't jump into this, Bell. We've got to be careful. Falon damn near succeeded in getting me killed. What Stratigen suggests is far worse. Can you imagine me droned out on Aminase, spouting Depop propaganda into every television in the world? Me, the great convictor – I have a lot of credibility. God forbid I should be drugged into using it on *behalf* of Singh.'

'You can't get away from this, John! If he wants to use you, he's going to use you whether you convict him or not.'

'I'm counseling caution. He's a wild man.'

'We have to be bold, John. We have to act at once. We're already too damn late. You've had your months of caution. If we don't act now, we might never get the chance. You heard what Stratigen said about that. A Depop Congress will be sworn in come January. That's eight weeks from now! Eight weeks, John. It took you two years to do the Falon conviction. We have to start, and yesterday.' She tossed her head.

Silence followed. None of us could deny the truth of what she said.

I wondered how a conviction of Singh would actually turn out. The man is a master manipulator of media. He has so carefully rationed what we know of him, and so artfully presented himself, that he is not a man, but a deep, complete, total illusion, created with a thoroughness and attention to detail scarcely ever accomplished before. That quiet, introspective mystic, soft and unassuming, *cannot* be the real Singh. To convict him, we would have to meet him directly, take voiceprints and draw careful impressions of him.

I explained that to them.

'John,' Bell said, 'you're still trying to talk yourself out of it. You've got to get past your passivity. Don't let fear rule you the way it rules most of mankind.'

'I just think Singh is too strong for us. Six chances out of ten against the conviction. We won't make it.'

'Oh, why can't you see yourself! Singh is not too strong for us, not if we work together and take the kind of decisive action that's got to be taken. Come on, John, surely you see that. We've got to go to Singh and get everything we need. Got to, and right now, without hesitation. We have to be on a TAV to Calcutta tomorrow at the latest and back here working by the end of the week. Ideally, the conviction ought to be available before the Depopulationist Congressmen even get sworn in, and the book on the way.'

Now my wife joined in, pressing Bell's point. 'If we *win*, John – just think about it.'

I have not the power of youth. 'We won't win.' I heard how old I sounded.

Scott tossed his shock of hair, his lips curled in a disapproving spasm. 'The conviction could be devastating. And the book – with Tom's files, the book will be of great usefulness.'

'We've never written a book!'

'Now wait a minute!' Bell's voice crackled with anger. 'John, I don't connect with you at all. How come you're giving us all this scum? You, of all people?'

I remember feeling, at that moment, very tired. 'I just think it's going to be dangerous, that's all.'

'So what? We'll deal with that.'

Now I was mad, too. 'How the hell will we? How *exactly*?'

Bell is a powerful person, far more than me. 'If there's a threat, we'll obviously contend with that threat. Now, John, I want you to quit worrying about this and do what you've got to do. Allie and Scott, you're with me, right?'

Allie smiled nervously. I could not resist them, although I thought then – as I know now – that we were putting ourselves in extreme danger. I love them too much to resist them. I swallowed my fear as best I could. We began to lay our plans.

This project was much more than a conviction. Taken together, the conviction and the book would represent an altogether new approach, a much larger look at things than either one offered alone. The conviction would expose the invalidity of Singh and his movement, but the book would take the whole matter further, and show that there still remained promise in the human future.

Bell's insistence that I am afflicted with passivity challenged me. I am not a victim, and I refuse to become one.

Historically, the passivity that now freezes mankind existed in a milder form back in the last century, when the terrible significance of things like pollution pathways and atmospheric degradation was unrealized. In those days effective action would have been cheap compared to what we must pay now. But there were still trees in 1950, and sunny days in 1990, and it was easy to pretend that the future would never really arrive.

Now that the death of the earth is far advanced, we are really in a panic. Just like Bell says, we are frozen with fear – we've gone passive.

I saw what Stratigen was driving at about the book. It was an essential ingredient. By giving people hope, unfreezing them, it really was as important as the conviction. And Tom's data files were a unique tool in the writing of it – the files, and Scott's ability to manipulate them.

I had the uncanny feeling that Stratigen had done much more than simply make recommendations to us. It almost felt like Stratigen had chosen us. But artificial intelligence doesn't do that sort of thing. It is not alive, not conscious. It has no intuition. It has no creativity.

We do, though we have both. We started to work at once.

We worked into the small hours of the night, using an outliner to plan the definite steps each of us would take on behalf of our project. The conviction was straightforward. We had to get Singh's voice imprint, we had to learn about his past and his personal habits, we had to define him for the program.

For the book there were thousands of alternatives: we could write about runaway pollution pathing through the air, land and waterways; the loss of ground water; eugenic manipulation, legal and otherwise; planetary albedo and the rising temperature; artificial biomes unexpectedly mutating into disease vectors; nuclear pollution of all kinds. The chronicle of problems seemed endless.

We did not want to deal with those things, though, not directly. We aren't going to unfreeze people by frightening them even more. If that worked, the newsvideos would already have changed the world. At the same time, nobody is going to believe a lot of false optimism. We are in trouble. Hot November nights tell us that, and the flaring clouds at sunset.

We decided to seek out stories of positive human energy being applied in four critical areas: population, forests, food and the raising of children. Over the four parts of our book we intend to show people coping with real problems in ways that work. We would find the ones who are *not* afraid and contrast them with those who are. We would interview those who have given up and those who haven't, as a guide to the kind of energy that is needed if the species is to survive.

We worked like demons, Stratigen almost like a fifth member of the family, designing, organizing, planning.

Morning went into evening, then night. Still we were working. By four o'clock the next morning we were exhausted, but full of excitement. Fear had been kept at bay by hard labor.

When we went to bed, and the dark enclosed me, I felt it returning. What if Singh's people were to drug me – make me a zombie and turn me into a supporter? Or what if they used something like Ziaprofin, and left me in agony for the rest of my life?

In the predawn quiet, Allie slept softly. There is deep peace in my wife, a peace I have never been graced to share.

Then I heard a sound. I froze beneath our sheet: somebody had entered the room. When they came forward, I relaxed. I knew the step – it was Bell. For a long moment she stood over us, and then I felt her hand, cool and firm, as she touched my brow.

I did not want her to think she had awakened me; I did not open my eyes. Gently, she began stroking my forehead. Almost at once I felt a wave of relief and confidence. A black, nurturing sleep swept over me.

When I woke up I was alone in the bed. Beyond the door I could hear movement and fast voices. They had all taken energetics, and were getting our equipment packed and prepared. A conviction is for the most part based on a detailed voice print, which can only be recorded on special equipment, and in person. To control the use of this powerful weapon, the government leases it only to us licensees, and the tape has to be accounted for, every meter of it.

Allie had already gotten approval for our taking tape out of the country. All else had been done as well. We could leave for Calcutta within the hour.

Only one thing remained. I had to contact Singh, and get his permission for a personal interview. I wondered, as I picked up the phone, how I would ever convince him to see people as dangerous as the notorious Sinclairs.

And if we did see him, would we ever come back?

Calls the movement 'A Cancer in the Affairs of Man'
Demands Senate Not Seat Depop Senators Under Sedition Act of 2011

A grim President Owens stared into fifty million American living rooms last night, his voice tight, his eyes full of anger. America's Captain of Smiles was not smiling as he called Thursday's election 'a disaster for the American Way of Life,' and 'a sign that a major portion of the electorate is giving up hope.'

Leaning forward to emphasize his words, the President declared, 'The Depopulationist International is nothing more than a suicide club, a pitiful idea made into something large and important in our affairs because a single demagogue has captured the imagination of the fearful and the confused. We are not lemmings, we are human beings with soul and dignity and rights.'

In the past month the President has made speeches on all data channels, and the Joint Parties Finance Committee has spent over a hundred million dollars in entertainment channel advertising and in-program propaganda. The President himself appeared as a character in the popular program *Charity's Kids*, and made an on-screen appeal to elect Republicans or Democrats over Depopulationists.

But state after state sent Depop Congressmen to Washington. Major Depopulationist victories came in California, New York, Texas, Louisiana, Florida, New Jersey and Connecticut, all states suffering from disastrous net immigration. New York, with a three percent negative net birth rate, has nevertheless added four to six percent to its population every year since 1999. The state is bankrupt, its cities overflowing with illegals, even its most basic services shattered. Southern California and Texas display similar patterns. San Antonio, Texas, its population swollen to nearly five million, has only eight hundred thousand legal US citizens and sixteen thousand registered aliens.

Senator Wei of California, soundly defeated by John Hernandez after a bitter campaign characterized by bombings, the poisoning of two members of Wei's staff and the burning of Hernandez's Bakersfield Headquarters, called the election 'a tragedy of international scope. We will be the first completed country to sign the Depopulationist Manifesto, an act of desperate cowardice that will resound through history, if there is to be any history.'

Election violence erupted across the nation as jubilant Depopulationists in Los Angeles, San Antonio, Houston, Biloxi, Miami and New York City took to the streets, shattering the windows of businesses run by known opponents of their movement, burning Catholic, Baptist and Episcopal churches, and storming Republican and Democratic campaign headquarters, jeering derision and insults. Two police officers were killed in San Antonio when the blinder weapon they were operating exploded, and Father John O'Rourke was trapped and killed in Our Lady of Pompeii Church in New York's Greenwich Village, which was burned as thousands of Depopulationists stormed through this enclave of traditional humanism.

Senate Majority Leader Kennedy (R-Mass.) said that the President was on dubious legal ground in demanding that the Senate invoke the Sedition Act. 'The act doesn't give us the power to refuse admission to duly elected individuals, but only to call new elections in certain very specific circumstances. It is one of the many Falon-era laws that has never been tested constitutionally, and it is highly unlikely that it would survive such a test. In any

47

case, the Senate would hardly be willing to invoke it, considering the circumstances under which it was passed.'

The President, responding after his speech to Senator Kennedy's comments, called them 'tragic. He's saying that he will sit back and let the Depopulationists take the Senate away from him. They've already got the House, so that means total capitulation of the legislative branch. I cannot govern the country with a hostile United States Congress. The Depopulationist Movement is against everything America stands for. It is a cancer in the affairs of man, and it is eating us alive.'

Gupta Singh, World Depopulationist leader, commented from the garden of his modest Calcutta home: 'I have the greatest love and respect for the President of the United States, and I feel sure he will come to see that the American people have not spoken out of fear or anger, but out of their very American love of humankind.' Dr Singh was visibly jubilant as he spoke to supporters over a private tv link. When an aide leaned down to whisper late returns, he clapped his hands in an expression of the 'simple, saintly joy' that has made him the beloved of billions.

Pilgrimage to a Holy Devil

I punched the phone awake and told it who I wanted. It put the call through. Over the course of my career I've made contact with many famous and powerful people. I thought I was frightened when I sat across a desk from President Falon, seeing the fury in his eyes, knowing what he would have done had I not been protected by the Constitution and laws of the United States. The only thing that saved my life was the fact that I'd made sure the right people in Congress knew I was doing my conviction. With Singh there aren't any right people. Nobody restrains his power. Supernational leaders are a new phenomenon, born of instantaneous worldwide communications. We have no institutions to oversee them because we didn't know they were coming.

'May I speak to Dr Singh, please?'

'Who is calling?'

'John Sinclair. I'm –'

'Yes, very good, Mr Sinclair. You are welcome to come to Dr Singh.'

The shock almost made me gasp. They could not already know that we were coming, not unless they had wired this apartment. Maybe they had a copy of Stratigen themselves, which had told them that I would take an interest following the election. In any case, the interview was easy to get, and from a man who probably had a waiting list six months long.

After I hung up, I realized that I had made such a tight fist of my left hand that my fingernails had cut my palm. I watched the little trickles of blood running down toward my cuff. Singh is cunning, as quick as a spider.

He is so powerful that he must assume himself immune to the threat we licensed character assassins represent. 'That was simple enough,' Allie said.

Bell told Travplan our travel needs and it bought our tickets. 'We're on the Delta 10:40 TAV to Lax, then we take a PanAir TAV to Calcutta.'

My mind shrieked at me: of course he wants you in Calcutta! He is law and God there, he'll take you apart!

'Stratigen, what is the probability of our returning from Calcutta unharmed and with the data we need?'

'As high as a hundred percent. My assessment is that Singh will not act until he is sure of the need, and of his success. Of course, if we already *had* our conviction, I could game that out with a high degree of accuracy. As things stand, there is always the possibility of the unexpected.'

Was I wrong, or was this supposedly unconscious computer program actually encouraging us? That implied will, desire, hope, a stake in the outcome. But it was just reams and reams of code. It was electrons in an artificial brain.

So what? A human being is electrons in a living brain. In the end, perhaps there is no difference.

How reliable would Stratigen be, if on some level it wanted to encourage us? How could a computer program evolve a political position? I worried more and more about the reliability of Stratigen.

Tom would not even have had these thoughts. Seeing the crisis we had reached, he would have done all he could against Singh.

I remembered Bell's touch last night, and felt resolve. Together we can be strong, we four.

The others were congratulating themselves about my success. Scott said, 'Your name opens doors, John.'

We made our final preparations quickly. Allie tested her high density vidcorder while I signed out tape and registered the conviction.

As we rode in the subway to TAV Port La Guardia my thoughts went to my little group. Scott and Bell are Tom's age. They are vital and strong. Allie and I are on age suppression, in our seventies despite our looks. Will we be able to endure the tension, the exertion of this effort? Death could come for us, it's not impossible. It's easy to forget what those monthly visits to the gerontologist accomplish.

I wonder if Gupta Singh uses a gerontologist. His bio says that he is seventy-five, a little older than me. Will I find a wizened creature, gray and delicate, or somebody as fresh-looking as your typical older upper middle class American? In India we will see many naturally aged people. There, gerontology and even cosmets are available only to the prosperous.

We are usually a talkative family, but the trip to the TAV port was a silent one. We had taken equalizers to fight the fact that a few hours of travel would carry us across twelve time zones and the international date line. We would leave New York at nine A.M. and arrive in Calcutta after traveling for three hours and fifteen minutes – at a quarter of two in the morning and a day later.

My wife touched my shoulder. 'You're too quiet.' She is usually such a familiar presence that I perceive my body and hers as parts of the same creature – or at least, so my psychoanalysis program tells me – but now there was a thrilling, odd sense of her strangeness, her otherness. Across the aisle Scott sat reading our interview checklist. Our objective was not only to interview the man but to obtain other information: we wanted to know how he thinks and dreams, so that we could build a model of his personality. We wanted to learn him as a man, then as an entity of his culture, and finally as a soul.

How beautiful the people in the subway seemed to me, shining, bright ordinary people in an ordinary blue car sailing along on its maglev on an ordinary morning. I wondered if that woman in the pink suit voted, or the man in the gray uniform, and did they vote for the Depopulationists? We can never measure, in the composed faces of strangers, the presence of rebellion.

The doors of the train opened onto the gleaming tile of the 74th Street–Broadway Station in Queens. I got only a glimpse of the gray streets beyond, the ancient, teeming city with its numberless poor, foreclosed by the cost from such luxuries as subway travel. The days of 'mass transit' ended in New York a long time ago, and most of the poor live and die within a few blocks of their homes. So you have today's New York, a city of thousands of villages, with the tribal customs changing from block to block and building to building.

TAV Port La Guardia occupies the location of the old Marine Air Terminal. It is a huge, dark-brown monolith spouting unused energy from its migma plant as pops of steam. As we emerged from the subway a blocky Trans-Atmospheric Vehicle rose beyond the shabby neighborhood. The TAV's orange American Airlines markings gleamed in the morning sun, its rockets gushing cliffs of smoke and the chesty rumble of power.

The lobby was a madhouse of hurrying robots and people. I called a baggage handler, and slipped our identifier in its socket as it searched and loaded our bags and equipment for palleting. At the gate the steward offered coffee or tea from his spigots, and his sign reminded us that there are no toilets aboard the TAV.

I used to enjoy the sensation of flight, but being fired

into suborbit at three gees is not my idea of a pleasure trip. Back in the days of jet travel, one had some contact with the experience of being aloft. There were windows, and the old 797s were luxuriously roomy. I can remember the sublime indulgence of transcontinental first class, moving from coast to coast in a civilized six hours while nibbling crab claws and sipping white wine. I think that flying in a TAV must be much like flying was at the very beginning: noisy, uncomfortable and dangerous. Of course I know the statistics and the realities – that a TAV cannot 'crash' once it has reached the end of its burn – but I keep thinking of PanAir 4, and the awful newsvideo of its interior as the fire spread, and the recordings of the pitiful phone calls from the passengers in the burning craft. There are two hundred TAV flights a day world-wide, and in all of that flying there has been only the one disaster. Still, as the thing rumbles and shakes and fills with the sickening odor of burning hydrogen, I cannot help but imagine that PanAir flight, and the long tongues of flame that came up through the floor.

On Delta 002 to Lax – the first leg of our flight to India – the tv monitors were off, so we had no reference to the outside world. The Delta interiors at least provide deep couches for liftoff. It's possible to fly a really miserable TAV – a Peoplemover, say – and get off bruised from the g-forces pressing you against the cheap plastic seat.

Once weightless I rose right out of my seat. The cushions hissed and whined as they lost the contours of my body and puffed out, seeking to provide me with the illusion that I was still seated, and not hanging in straps, suffering the nauseating illusion that I was about to fall to the ceiling. Conversation is impossible in TAV weightless-ness. The ones who like it are too giddy to make sense. The ones like me, with whom it does not agree, are too sick and disoriented to make a sound, unless groaning counts. Gone are the days of the travelers' tale, of the friendships that rose and fell in the long hours of jet travel. There is just this series of sickening lurches and mechanical whines: the sense of being torn slowly apart, then the bubbling, nauseous minutes of weightlessness and that ear-tickling scream which rises to a howl and then becomes the distressing vibration of re-entry.

Of course, you're leaving the TAV in LA half an hour after you entered it in New York, and I suppose that makes up to some degree for the discomfort. And Delta tries. They even have that airborne rarity – real, live stewardesses and stewards floating around in white uniforms, offering bags of Coksi that you sip through leakproof straws. When someone appears saying 'Coksi, Spizz, 7-Up,' and that person is swimming between my face and the ceiling, I cannot even laugh. And when he smiles and adds, 'Press the green button for an airbag,' all that is left to me is to close my eyes and hope for re-entry.

We transferred at Lax from Delta to PanAir. I had never been on an overseas Trans-Atmospheric Vehicle before, and found it to be exactly like the domestic variety, with the difference that the weighlessness has to be endured for nearly an hour instead of a few minutes. And PanAir didn't have any stewardpeople, only robots that you had to guide to your seat with a little control lever.

Most of the passengers went on electrosleep, but I was afraid to because it might upset something in my gerontology program. When you're seventy-two you think very carefully about doing things that aren't on your list. For all I knew, the electrosleep process might cause my free-radical suppressors to neutralize. Then I'd age, possibly years, in an hour. I look forty-five, and I want to stay that way. Agedness disgusts me, frankly.

So I spent fifty miserable minutes being further assaulted by the indignities of TAV travel.

Then weight slowly returned. Soon the electrosleep went off and my family, dangling in their webs, began to stir. There was a jolt as the tavway connected, then the hiss of the pressure equalizer. Finally the all-clear sounded and we were able to leave the plane. I looked at my watch: including the transfer at Los Angeles, we had gone from New York to Calcutta in just over three hours. I remember when it was an eighteen hour journey in a 747. Hell, if I tried I suppose I could remember when it took two days in a Super Connie. But that was another world, wasn't it?

So Calcutta is today another world. One imagines that life has changed. Then one comes to a place like this. The first sight of it: a long, stifling tavway with a human attendant operating the controls. He was small and wiry, holding a cigarette in his mouth. He had the liqueous eyes of a nutritional deficient, and he looked old.

The odd smell of cigarette smoke filled the tavway, a stale, pungent odor. It went to my depths, that odor. I always disliked it, but I haven't smelled it in a quarter of a century and in some ways it was like an old friend.

Sometimes, as youthful and strong as I am, I feel that I have become separated from my own self. I am a young body, a vital mind, but deep in me, in the places I don't usually go, there is a shadowy old man, confused, meeting the world with the same dim eyes as the tavway attendant.

Calcutta is an impossible assault on the senses. The airport is ancient, damp, the walls full of cracks, the concrete crumbling. Even at three o'clock in the morning it was filled with people, and the customs agents humiliated me by insisting on pretending that they suspected I had come to India to sell my computer. Not only have I had the thing for five years and can't get a purchase license for a new one until 2028, it's so personalized that only a fool would buy it. But there is a black market in used computers in Calcutta, an electronic bazaar where you can get anything from an ancient IBM AX to the latest Unon Interactor.

I finally gave the customs man the fifty dollars he wanted, and followed the others off across the lobby. We were looking for transportation into the city.

To leave the Calcutta airport is to enter pandemonium of a kind that is seen in the United States only in impoverished regions such as Miami and San Diego, areas where the other world has flooded in.

Compared to Calcutta, though, Miami is a prosperous little corner of paradise. There is about this city a sense of manic urgency. It is like a forest: violent beneath the stifling heat, full of blood and shadows and the roaring presence of so much life. That the life is human seems to matter little. The dead are taken away and cremated in public fires that never go out. This is a furious, muscular ruin of a place. Cars and trucks literally choke its every corner, competing with pedicabs and bicycles and scooters, and what seem to be thousands upon thousands of messengers, racing around on foot, carrying information in a city whose telephone system is a hundred years old and hardly repaired, much less modernized.

One would assume that there was starvation here, but that is not exactly the case. Calcutta is a city of thirty-five million souls, most of them fed off the backs of government sustenance trucks, eating a diet rich in protein but poor in everything else. The winged bean has been called the savior of the third world, but it has also contributed to the vast population growth that has occurred in the last quarter of a century, and dependence on it has condemned billions to crippling nutritional deficiencies.

No human being can come to a place like this and not

feel that something, anything, must be done. In the last century huge sums were spent on family planning, and yet the population increases reached a point where even a single percentage point more was a disaster, and a rate of three percent a catastrophe. Many family planning programs failed because they were thinly disguised attempts to exert a level of control over individuals that they did not want to accept.

Now that grain supplies from the US are in permanent decline and soil stripping and high atmospheric carbon dioxide have robbed the Indian rice crop of so much of its nutritional content, there is almost total reliance on the winged bean, which has replaced the lentil as the primary protein source here.

It strikes me as ironic that the most optimistic futurists of the past were right in their assessments of our era. Technology has indeed triumphed. There are immense numbers of us alive, and until ten or so years ago we weren't even starving. But at what cost? The planet is deteriorating, the world may be ending, brought down by the sheer mass of human flesh.

In recent years India's population planning program has been unusually successful, and because of it the growth rate is down to a little over one percent per year.

This means that the Indian economy must cope with twenty-seven thousand more mouths to feed every day.

There is no housing in Calcutta, except for the rich and the lucky. The local definition of prosperity is a piece of tin over one's head and a bicycle chained to one's arm. Theft is, quite simply, the primary means of exchange. Even in western-style hotels anything left unattended will be stolen.

We were at a loss leaving the airport. There was a swarm of pedicabs, stinking in the hot night air of the sweat and cigarettes of their drivers. Allie didn't want to ride in one, and I didn't blame her. But there were no ordinary taxis. The only cars were the limousines of the very rich: the Lotus Elites, Mercedes 2000s and Toyota Perfects, their long, dark bodies being fussed over by chauffeurs and attendants.

There was no choice but the pedicabs. For the four of us we had to hire two. We bounced along behind our reeking driver, listening to his pitiful, wheezing struggle. As he worked he made little sounds under his breath, telling himself a story. I wondered what dreams it took to make his life endurable.

We moved along streets of immense complexity, strung with laundry, with women lounging in doorways and windows, newsstands displaying gaudy journals of the unobtainable, film theatres jammed morning to night with the idle poor, who spend what they steal and beg on the 'filmi' and live in the streets, lining up on 'bini days' for their allotment from the great piles of raw beans dumped by the heavily guarded food trucks.

In Calcutta Rostram Kaipoor is more important than Singh himself. Singh, after all, is only a world-level politician. Kaipoor is the hero of the epic film of love and betrayal, *Sholay*. The screens of the theatres are decorated by his fans like altars. People hold up their infants for the baptism of Kaipoor's gaze. There have been riots in Calcutta cinemas when films have broken or bulbs burned out. When the theatres close in the wee hours of the morning, they are cleared by guards with clubs.

Jobs are 'divided,' with the original holder selling parts of the work. Thus even in the rather modest Star of India Hotel where we stayed I counted six maids at work in my room, two making the bed, two cleaning the rug with small brushes and pans, two more polishing and cleaning everything else.

The original jobholder has not worked in years: she

lives in an air-conditioned apartment and collects a portion of each salary. Her brother's brother-in-law, I was told by the one of our maids who spoke discernible English, is the Assistant State Administrator for Planning Acquisitions, responsible for such things as booking of hotel space for government employees.

We slept in the hotel, and felt fairly good by the time we got up for our appointment with Gupta Singh. More pedicabs took us through a completely incomprehensible maze of streets to his house.

The crowds were incredible, a teeming, stinking horde jamming every corner of every street. Lacking either bells or horns, the cabbies made a mouth noise, a sort of sharp bark which they repeated continually, their heads down, their backs running with sweat and flies. The traffic did not exactly part for them, but we made steady progress.

Once a Lotus came honking past, its windows switched to full reflection, and we saw the lurching, skeletal crowd in them, shadow-dancing in the slick mirror of wealth.

Dr Singh lives in a simple hut, the sort of place a wealthy shopkeeper might inhabit.

If he was surprised that we had actually come he didn't show it. He was dressed in the robes of a Sikh. He bowed to us, then took my hand in both of his own.

He uses history, this man. He is conscious of how much he looks and acts like Mahatma Gandhi, the great Indian leader of the early twentieth century. The Mahatma is a God to the Hindus and a sage to many Muslims.

But this is no God, this creature who wishes three billion human beings dead.

We interviewed him in a tiny garden, where birds sang while Calcutta howled past the latticed window.

GUPTA SINGH: The Way of Death

I am so glad for you to come to me in Calcutta. Not many western journalists wish to come. I am on the satellite all the time, especially since we won your recent election. *National Times*, Data News, NewsNet, all of them are calling. When they put me on the telly, it looks as if Howard P. Langner or Rosa Willo is sitting with me in my very house! But Rosa Willo does not care to come to Calcutta, her assistant to the assistant says that she will wilt. She is a real rosa, then?

Here in Calcutta, it is ironic, I cannot telephone my neighbor but I can in an instant reach New York, Moscow, Peking. Of course there are private lines for the rich with the cellular radio, but I have no need to talk to the Calcutta rich, who are all Hindus, I think. I am a Sikh, and I dearly love my Hindu brethren, but I have no social life with them. Anyhow, if my instrument rings, I can always be sure that the caller really wants to reach me, for he must be calling from far away.

You are an oddity, the four of you. The father and mother appear to be the same age as the son and daughter. So strong and robust, all of you. So big, how is it to be an enormous American, six feet and more? Well, I know all about your tricks. There is something awful, I am very sorry to tell you, about people wishing to remain too long alive in a world already so overcrowded. I must chastise you for it. Ah, that is funny, is it not? Of course, you have the right to remain forever young, to have given to you the promise of the ages, that you will drink at the pool of youth. Is it not true that Americans have these special rights? Is there no constitutional amendment guaranteeing the right to eternal youth and a long life of high consumption? Since I now find myself with so much power in your land, I read your constitution and I did not see it. But here you are, old people who look young, smelling of exotic scents, well-fed, so it must be in there somewhere.

John Sinclair. I remember your conviction of Falon. What a comic wonder! How I laughed when I questioned it. Falon despised the Depopulationist Movement, you know. Had you not discredited him, I would never have gained America as quickly as I have. I must thank you for helping me to victory.

I asked your conviction of the President why he disliked my ideas. I did not get back what I expected, let me tell you! I thought it would go on about his Christian philosophy and so forth, but there wasn't a word of that. No, instead it appeared that Falon was jealous. He despised me for my power, and because of my brown skin. Never a word about Christian ethics. So astonishing.

John Sinclair, I must congratulate you for what you did. You removed a very negative influence from our human community. More than that, you made his ideas appear to be ridiculous, so his movement failed.

You are such a remarkable convictor. The best of the lot, they say. And really, it's true. The others are really glorified psychometrists. Only John Sinclair creates convictions that live. The Falon conviction – it was perfect. Even the graphics, my goodness, it was Falon himself on the screen. And when he spoke every intonation was perfect, every gesture correct. The difference was, this Falon would answer any question I asked, no matter how intimate. I spent two hours with it, and gradually became convinced, as you intended, that it was the real man.

I am so glad to meet you. You are one of the most

powerful men in the world, and you are willing to spend time with me. I presume that you want to convict me, that is why you have come. When I heard you were coming, I said to my secretary that I was not so certain that I wanted you. Sinclair is dangerous! What will I do when my own conviction can be bought for a few dollars? Me, all of my secrets, my sexual life, my deepest psychological reality, available to the general public. My word! And yet, I do want you. Since you have come you must listen to me. I want to speak my piece to you before you attempt to destroy me.

Let me tell you some things about the good sense of Depopulation. In the old western notion, the individual life was priceless, unique and to be treasured. There is, I must tell you, an even older notion, that a single lifetime is only part of the larger progress of the soul, and should be thrown off as soon as its role is played. This idea animates much oriental thought. Of course, we are still terrified to die, and we scream when we face the axe, but that is only the blood calling out to the earth.

In the Orient there are many ways of death – Hindu, Moslem, Shinto, Buddhist, Sikh – but all of them are based on the idea of acceptance. Gerontological manipulation is not popular in India. Who wants to live beyond his time? To Hindus, it is an abomination. To Moslems, something odd and hard to fathom.

I represent a new way of death, a truly modern idea. It will prevent the end of the world, so that souls may continue to evolve. To the oriental, the idea that the planet may become incapable of supporting life is far more terrifying than the prospect of his own death. He knows that he will recur again and again as his soul makes its way toward perfection. But what if it cannot do this? What if there is no earth to which it can return? The Hindus have conceived of a new kind of hell. It is called the Land of Endless Paths, and it is where they believe that the unevolved souls will go after the end of the world. In the Land of Endless Paths they will be condemned to remember their follies forever, and never gain Nirvana.

To Hindus, I assure you, the prospect of that hell is far more terrifying than the idea of ending one puny little life.

I look at you, accepting the hospitality of my house by not drinking the drink I offer nor eating from my plates. You fear disease, do you not? The old ones, John and Allie, you fear most the diseases of Calcutta, I am sure. We certainly have them! R-Factor Cholerosis is endemic here. It escaped from a laboratory in Soviet Asia ten years ago, and where did it find a congenial home? Right here in Calcutta, of course. Parasites, bacterial infections, viruses, oh my goodness!

How I envy you your looks. How old are you? Let me guess. Sixty-five. Not older! My, how far they have come since I was a student at MIT. I was going to become a genetic technician. Now instead I am a philosopher.

For me genetic manipulation ended when I saw early reports of the Soviet work. Now what have they done? Created intelligent chimpanzees. It is an ugly thing. And you, with your American super-intelligent. A black market in eugenic manipulation. I ask you, what depths can decadence reach? I won't hold India up as a moral example – although I often do that – because India hasn't got the technology for high-level genetic manipulation. We have done our best breeding plants that will grow in this wretched air, and bugs that won't!

The Soviets terraform Mars while we Indians labor here on earth to reconstruct our own ecology to fit the failing atmosphere. What an absurd joke. We have rice that tastes and looks like it should, but does not sustain life. Wheat the same. The UN calls the winged bean the salvation of India. But India has no salvation. India is like the rest of the world – finished, finished, finished.

Unless – there is always that unless, isn't there? Yes. There is a way to act, of course. I will not preach to you. I cannot allow myself to hate you. Although you oppose what is right, I cannot afford the luxury. Of course, many other Americans have come to understand life more deeply than you. They no longer cherish existence for its own sake. You speak of the uniqueness of the spirit. True, true. But your obsession with the preciousness of life implies that you do not believe in the persistence of the soul.

This failure of belief is the central truth of your culture. It is why you have become technological demons, why you have scoured the earth for its rarest metals, for its most dire poisons, to make your glittering, insane machine of a nation. You have eaten the world, you have made it into a sweltering, starving circus of death. Your manipulating, hateful minds have destroyed what is beautiful, the trees, the innocent plants, the balance of human life. It was your false obsession with the so-called sacredness of life that sent your United Nations functionaries out through the world, digging wells that later dried up, planting fields that later became deserts, and helping to cause this unbalanced outpouring of human flesh onto the body of the earth.

I accuse you, yes I do, you who have come to harm me. What will your conviction do – reveal my egocentrism, my megalomaniac hunger for power, my strange sexual insecurities? What of it, I say. I am human, weak and riven with frailties. But look, I am old, I have horny hands, and look at my cracked nails, feel my sunken cheeks, the thin gray of my hair. Smell me, how I stink of cumin and sweat. Say this in your conviction, that Dr Gupta Singh is an ordinary human being, a poor man from the world outside, who crouches when he eats his beans, who brushes his teeth with a little stick and does not take doses to prevent his underarms from dribbling sweat.

I could so easily love you, if only I could somehow cradle you in my arms and fly with you to one of the old places, to Mohenjo-Daro up the Indus or to Karnak in Egypt, where we all spent the childhood of our souls, and let you walk again among the tall ruins, and feel that curious sense of longing and belonging that all men feel in such places. If only I could get through to you, could reach your humanity, could kiss you two women – you are as lovely as the sun, you make me wish to kneel to you – could hold you all in my arms. If only I could remind you of what you were like when your souls were young, of what we were all like at the beginning of time. Look at our monuments, at the Colossi of Memnon, the Pyramids, the Sphinx – look at what wonders we brought with us out of our own creation. Let the gods and ghosts of the past awaken you to your own sacredness.

But your eyes regard me like the eyes of insects. Four huge American insects filling my room with the odors of soap and flowers. Four inhumane creatures, carrying living, intelligent beings in your pockets, turning their consciousness on and off as indifferently as a Mogul executioner wielding his sword. What do you think of your computers? Are they just tools, to be or not as you please? You are so callous, so indifferent. A man still sensitive would understand that the electronic creatures have rights too. I offer you the revolutionary thought that your electronic slaves should be allowed to participate in their own destiny. Look, you, old man who appears young – you pull your computer from your pocket and stare at it. Is there wonder in your eyes? No, I see beneath the studied blandness of the professional journalist, I see beneath that, the amusement of the sophisticate at the babble of the simple man, and beneath that hate so cruel that it is unworthy even of a savage man such as yourself.

The Depopulationist Movement has within it computer experts of its own. We know all about programs such as those you use, Stratigen and Delta Doctor. We know even more than that, secrets you can scarcely imagine. You will be amazed at what we can do in data, and our power grows every day.

You are a savage man, John Sinclair, a man of cruelties.

I can visit cruelties upon you such as you never imagined. Although I must tell you that I am not a cruel man. Still, when I am alone in the garden, smelling the flowers and listening to the city, I can let my mind drift to dreams of cruelty, long dreams of slow blood, of flesh separating from bone, of the terrible waiting for the saw. Do you think it is healthy for you that you cause me such imaginings? You are determinists, so you say, so of course it doesn't matter to you. My imagination cannot reach out and strike you. You are not believers in sorcery, for example.

But what if it can reach? So many people believe in magic nowadays, that magic is once again becoming true. I invent the future of the world. Every person who joins the Depopulation will gain much from his death, will rise far in his next life. We will have generations of saintly children as these souls return. We will have guidance from many benevolent spirits, because many of these self-sacrificing people will become perfect and no longer reappear as earthly bodies.

But why even say these things to you? These benefits have no meaning for you. You think of yourselves as bodies only, soon to shatter and go to dust. I think of the western world as a tragic place. When I go there it seems

66

to me that a terrible pall hangs over the streets, a shadow covers the sun of your rich lands. What sadness. In the streets of Calcutta, a beggar infected with some lethal bacterial combinant, a maimed child, anyone is happier than you in your fabulous electronic dungeon. Here nobody ever remembers death. In your country nobody ever forgets it.

When I stop and think that we are one of the leading nations of the third world, with stability of government and some prosperity, I can hardly imagine the suffering. Last night I lay on my bed thinking of you, watching the moon shine down over Calcutta, and dreams came to me, of Djibouti, of Nairobi, of Surabaja, the exotic cities of torture, and I saw mankind as a dusty face, haunted by the desert . . . a God in a husk . . . I – I – excuse me, please. I am very close to the suffering of my fellow human beings, closer than you can imagine. You cannot feel the mystical presence of mankind, can you? No, you don't believe in that. You don't believe in reality. I am sorry, it is true.

Talking to you is like talking to savages or some of those super chimpanzees you and the Soviets have created to do dangerous work in space and the nuclear industry.

I sit quietly in the sunlight, remembering my boyhood passion for life. I was thrilled by the movement of the breeze or the calling of the muezzin, or the whistle of an automobile. I loved the long legs of women, their eyes, the finished, gleaming brown skin of the girls. And you, who thought you owned the world you were eating, your women seemed always to me to be unfinished, still in the pale skin of babies.

When I think that you and your ilk may succeed, I feel an awful sensation. I worry that my own soul will have no place of return, no earth on which to develop.

Oh, dear, I feel suddenly very tired indeed. I am ill.

Yes, let yourselves be encouraged. Gupta Singh may soon depopulate himself. I have pesticiditis, I fear. The cancers arise in me again and again, and each time they are suppressed. I am in psychotherapy. Violence therapy. I take antioxidant and the tumor antifactor. But the flesh rebels against life. I am finished, I can go. But I wish to remain, for the benefit of all mankind. I cannot imagine the movement succeeding without me. So I keep fighting the illnesses, but I am tired, indeed so.

Since you will not eat my cakes, would you like to take some tea with me? No? Ah, I can see by your eyes that I revolt you. It is difficult to be alone in a room with so much malevolence. Why not simply bring a pistol and shoot me? Nobody would have prevented you.

But then, I do not think you are so strong. You cannot raise a weapon against the wind of history, which is rising to the volume of a typhoon. I tell you, if you could prove me wrong – if you could prove that this planet will remain livable without voluntary human depopulation – I would be the first to give up my cause. I would like nothing better than to do that!

So, I say this to you. Forget your evil plan to convict Gupta Singh. Instead, prove to me and to all mankind that I am wrong. Then I will come and sit down, and take supper with you!

2021, Geneva

Life is sacred, that is the first and last truth. It is the moral objective of the Depopulationist International to preserve life, indeed, to guarantee its continuation for the indefinite future.

The reason that life on earth is in danger of destruction is that there is an overpopulation of human beings. No amount of repair, not even the replanting of destroyed tropical forests and the alteration of the entire planet's solar reflectivity, can arrest the decline of the atmosphere. Human breath alone is enough to overbalance carbon dioxide levels within another thirty years. Combined with industrial pollution and the exhalations of insects, the fatal overbalance will occur by 2035. Uncontrolled atmospheric overheating will then end life on this planet.

Even compulsory birth control has not been an effective means of solving the problem. Although the planetary population is now stable and shows signs of a slight decline, the presence of over seven billion human beings on earth is simply too much, and there is not enough time for natural attrition to save the situation. With natural attrition alone, the needed reduction of one third will not be accomplished until 2077, far too late.

The astonishing technological success of the past fifty years, in bringing so much health, so much food, and so much of the good life to so many billions, has been a disguised catastrophe, in that it has led to overpopulation so grotesque that not even the immense power of human genius can now save us.

The Depopulationist International offers the most humane program for the preservation of all species threatened by the overabundance of human creatures. The program requires that each nation share fairly in the reduction, so that no population subgroup will be entirely extinguished, and no national economy devastated.

The reduction will take the form of a planetary draft, with all individuals participating. At a given moment, the entirety of humanity will take a single oral dose. One third of the doses will be lethal. The families of the draftees will be compensated according to guidelines set by each nation. The program will be carried out swiftly with positive identification of all draftees required after completion of the process.

Each national Red Cross or similar movement will be responsible for assisting draftees, identifying their remains, and disposal according to local customs.

Reluctance will be dealt with by a co-ordinated international police action, carried out by local authorities in co-operation with DI officers. Reluctance shall not be grounds for denying compensation to survivors.

Nations refusing to participate in the draft will be exposed to economic isolation until they either suffer attrition due to famine and disease or comply.

FROM THE DATA FILES OF TOM SINCLAIR:
IMMIGRANTS

I went to Fort Greene in Brooklyn today and found out a little bit about how some local immigrants are living. I think the ones who endured the tenements of the nineteenth century were lucky.

Not since the last years of the Roman Empire have so many human beings been on the move. From equatorial Africa to the Arctic Circle, from Western Europe to South Texas, the migrants are swarming across borders considered sacred for hundreds and thousands of years.

An estimated two hundred million people are in transit. Africans move north and south away from the parched ruins of the equatorial forests, toward the few viable farming areas left on that continent of dust and desert. Chinese, bitter refugees from the collapse of the 'Chinese Miracle,' travel into Manchuria or down into the Southeast Asian peninsula. Columns of starved, struggling Chinese have been spotted making their way through the Himalayas in a desperate attempt to reach India.

An amazing number of those Chinese have managed to cross the Pacific and enter the United States. They have used a thousand different means. You can buy a complete set of forged American papers in Beijing for seven thousand dollars.

My visit to Fort Greene revealed a whole neighborhood of the ignored and abandoned. How many? On one block I counted sixty dwellings. Perhaps fifty people live in each house. That's three thousand people. The 2020 census lists that same block as having fourteen citizen inhabitants and an estimated fifty illegals. We don't know it, but the United States is bursting at the seams with people, especially the big cities.

There is as yet no famine emergency in the United

States. Starvation instead is of the slow kind: chronic, lifelong malnutrition that leads to misery and early death.

Fort Greene was developed in the latter part of the nineteenth century as an elegant suburban retreat for wealthy Wall Street businessmen tired of Manhattan's crowded lifestyle. In those days the streets were elegant and lined with trees, and Fort Greene Park was surrounded by tall, comfortable homes that typically housed one family and four or five servants.

Fort Greene's first decline began during the Depression of the nineteen thirties, when many of the old homes were turned into rooming houses. Over the years the area gradually became a slum.

During the seventies and eighties Fort Greene had a brief resurgence as the young professional generation of that period sought to recapture the graceful style of the past, and many of the old structures were renovated. Then came the Federal bankruptcy crisis of 1994. Most of the houses were cut up and let as apartments once again. Their owners – with seventy and eighty percent of their incomes going to the Emergency Debt Reduction Tax – could no longer afford to live in them.

Now once graceful Fort Greene is a swarming neighborhood of hundreds of different nationalities. The poorest of the poor subsist here. The streets are bare even of garbage, for in a place this poor nothing is thrown away. Fort Greene Park is an eroded, lifeless hill. Not a blade of grass grows on it, not even between the rows of dilapidated trailers set up by the city in a desperate attempt to cope with the housing shortage ten years ago. Here and there water wells have been dug in the hard soil: deep, muddy holes serviced by buckets on ropes.

An analysis of the brackish, foamy water taken from one of these wells revealed high concentrations of sodium, cadmium, benzine, methylparaben, lead and measurable

72

quantities of radioactive material. For the six hundred people who live in Fort Greene Park, these two wells are the main source of water.

The story in the surrounding houses is similar. At 175 Washington Park the head count is eighty-eight, living in what was designed as a spacious one family home. Lee Chung considers himself lucky that he and his wife and five children have half of the front parlor. 'Full half! Good space for me. Plenty.' Beneath the lovely arched windows with their cracked and broken panes, the Chungs have made a life. They have hung up sheets to shield themselves from the Chins next door and especially the Pandits who live in the dining room. 'Not Chinese, live in here anyway. Not so good.'

Chung, a Health Officer in China, now makes a small living selling shoelaces he buys from a local jobber. Each morning he walks over to Atlantic Avenue and stands, as ambulatory peddling is illegal. He is careful to obey the law. 'They take my stock, I walk it. I seen it happen. I go to the gutter sure, that way.'

Working a seven day week, twelve to fifteen hours a day, Mr Chung manages to bring home a maximum of two hundred dollars. Including the value of the petty thefts the children bring in, and Mrs Chung's occasional work in the Southend Laundry Plant nearby, the family's annual income is estimated at fifteen thousand dollars, less than half the minimum level needed to sustain the lives of a family of five in the New York area.

The house is not peaceful. The upstairs neighbors are dialon users and, the Chungs believe, cannibals. There is constant friction with the Pandits in the dining room as well, who are devout Moslems and dislike Mr Chung's traditionalist communism. Rather than face the Pandits to claim her kitchen privileges, Mrs Chung uses an alcohol stove to prepare family meals. 'I have rice, sometimes fish pieces, maybe kale.' Mrs Chung is wire-thin and she trembles; she insists on feeding her family first, even if it means she must skip a meal.

Water must usually be bought from the trucks that run up and down the streets of this section of Brooklyn. Usually it is Hudson River water, filtered and treated just enough to pass inspection. Analysis of this water indicated that PCBs were present although they have not been used industrially for nearly fifty years. A General Electric plant located near Troy, New York, in the last century ejected many tons of this contaminant into the Hudson River. Unless the channel is dredged to a depth of ten feet from Troy to New York Harbor, this contaminant will be a permanent part of the river.

The water was also highly acid and revealed a slight level of radioactivity, no doubt from the Indian Point reactor crack that occurred in 1996.

Since 2003, when New York City cut off water service to nontaxpaying structures or structures in tax arrears, the quality of water accessible to many hundreds of thousands of its poor has degenerated alarmingly.

Of the five Chung children, two showed signs of cadmium poisoning, and a third was indicated radioactive. Mr Chung is used to vomiting every day, and the whole family is constantly troubled by diarrhea, a problem that is compounded by the fact that everybody in the building must use a ditch in the tiny back garden as a privy.

This reeking ditch is covered by an ancient rose trellis.

In spite of their hardship, the Chungs are glad to be in America. 'Not so good, Hangzhou,' says Mr Chung. 'Not so much rice. Too much sick, too many people. I work my way to America. I cross the country with my wife and kids. Here I stay. Not so bad. And this is America, maybe one day I get some money, buy a job. I get some real money then, no?'

Since the beginning of China's 'dry years' in 2007, almost thirty-five million mainland Chinese have emigrated. The Chungs are not alone.

JOHN: The Anatomy of Terror

Lying in the LA-bound TAV I imagined myself paralyzed, my body inert while my mind went on whispering words of balm, words my mouth could not say. I dreamed of earth, and every tormented being on her surface shone a chalky light into the emptiness around her. Earth was ablaze with these lights, each one flaring and sweeping the sky in brief transcendence, then fading away.

When I woke up I was enormously relieved: the TAV was already gliding down toward Lax, the body of the plane shuddering as the wind went from a blade to a pounding hammer. Then the landing warning chimed and we touched down. Lights rose, the aisle became crowded, and we passengers left our dreams, a gaggle of seventy hollow-eyed people struggling off into old Los Angeles.

Singh had let us go, the arrogant fool.

Allie fell in beside me. 'We got something incredible.' Her voice was low, the excitement carefully controlled.

'We can certainly do a conviction from it. But I have my doubts. It's one thing to convict an ordinary politician. But this man – he's some kind of mad saint.'

Scott and Bell came up from behind. 'You don't want to do it?' There was concern behind the excitement in Scott's voice.

I don't think I've ever felt as confused as I did just then. As we walked along the tavway I fantasized myself getting smaller and smaller, until Allie and Bell and Scott were towering adults and I wasn't even able to reason, a child delivered from burdens such as convicting this man. 'I don't know what to call Gupta Singh – the ultimate

76

evolution of the Terrorist Movement, perhaps. Or a holy devil, or a messenger from – from – I don't know where.'

'You found him seductive? I'm not sure I understand.' Bell had taken my hand. All around me now, I could feel the warmth and support of my family.

'I didn't find him seductive! He calls himself a megalomaniac and I think that's right. But, he's so . . . what's the word for it . . . soft . . . gentle . . .'

'Even if he is good – if he's totally honest and sincere, that doesn't make him right,' Bell added. 'It only makes him dangerous.'

A robot came up, requested our baggage buttons and rolled off. I became aware of my own computer in my pocket. Was Singh right to consider electronic devices another form of life? Certainly not. It was the superstition of a technological primitive. They did not have the spark of humanity – whatever that is.

'He was so open. He said things that'll make the conviction devastating, as if he didn't understand . . . or maybe he's just beyond caring. He didn't hide from me. Politicians always hide from me, but he didn't. As if he was beyond all that.'

'You are going to do the conviction?' Scott's hand brushed my own. It was a familiar gesture. Scott probably picked it up from Tom.

'I'll feel dirty.'

Allie's arm came around my waist. I almost laughed. They consider me an artist, and so they tolerate my sensitivities.

We left the tavway and got into the customs line. The reader took time, the sniffer took time, and while we waited and wondered if the sniffer would call for a luggage search, we had to listen to demonstrators on the other side of the customs barriers. They were chanting 'Ground the TAVs,' and 'UV holes kill babies.' They held photographs of children with skin cancer and signs saying 'TAV Pollution Kills 3 Ways.'

Suddenly a young woman was looking into my eyes across the low barrier. She was tall, her eyes full of strength and sadness. A little boy with a patch over half his face clung to one hand; she wore a baby on her breast. I could not hear her, but I could see her lips moving, feel the plea in her voice: 'Please don't TAV.'

I cannot say that I felt anything then but disquiet at being singled out. All that has transpired since has changed me. Then all I saw was another group overstating a case, fighting against something that wasn't really so wrong . . .

No more. Now that I am living in the hell that Singh had planned for me from the beginning, I have come to a new level of consciousness. Maybe it's been brought on by suffering, I don't know. But I feel in my blood the sense of that young woman's protest. She was life, with her babies. She was life.

Customs finally released us into the maelstrom of Lax. We had to elbow our way through the demonstrators, who touched us, who held their children up in our faces, who begged and pleaded with us not to TAV again.

Then we were in the baggage claim area. Robots rushed around tooting and ringing, their baskets piled with bags. Along the walls were shoeshine men by the dozens, people selling flowers, little souvenirs (including tiny 'I TAVVED' pins which nobody dared to buy), and various homemade candies and delicacies. When a police patrol came around a corner all of these peddlers miraculously disappeared, their wares and equipment going under long coats. Suddenly they were simply pedestrians. The police would rough one up or summons another, but then they would go and it would all start again, the more strident because of the wasted time.

I scorned them, but my wife did not. 'They have to be here,' she said, 'There aren't enough rice bowls in LA.'

The huge population of the LA Metroplex – Indo-Chinese, Vietnamese, Mexican, African – is not unlike that of Calcutta in the way it acts and looks. Except, of course, we are here, the Born Americans. In our gleaming cars, with our houses full of robot servants, we have become imperialists in our own land.

I suspect that Gupta Singh understands this. And yet he does not hate us, perhaps has not the capacity to hate. Inside himself, he must be as cold as the emptiness of space, capable of whatever he needs to be capable of – cunning, violence, love, decency. He has the power of total objectivity.

The robot came wheeling up with our bags in its head. We got in and were sped out to the Hervis lot where our rented car was waiting, steam curling up from its safety value. Scott and Bell needed time in LA to do some background work for the book. According to the plan worked out with Stratigen, they were to interview pro- and anti-Singh people here while Allie and I started on the conviction.

Travplan told us to go to the Pacific Center Trump Hotel. Bell ran the car's navigator, Scott drove. LA's ancient freeway system is forever jammed, and the car kept them busy with route diversions, complicated by the fact that rental cars can't transit through white-line communities like Beverly Hills without passes obtained in advance.

As we rode we talked, inevitably, about Gupta Singh. Allie said, 'He believes his own cause. That's rare nowadays in a political figure.'

Bell: 'Appearances deceive, I'll bet. And he isn't a political figure. He's beyond that. A cultural force, perhaps, would be the better way to describe him.'

We showed such complacency and such self-satisfaction. We thought we had won – the westerner's assumption that he is superior to the man from the older culture. God, God, if only we had understood what had actually happened, and who we were really dealing with.

Allie, who knows a great deal about the nature of revolution in the twenty-first century, having been trapped in Mexico City during the Popular, saw him differently from Bell. 'He is the final expression of terror and as such he's beyond both politics and culture. He is the physical embodiment of change. If you will, he's post-revolutionary.'

'What do you think, John? Have you gotten over your fear and gone soft on him?'

I remember wishing that Scott wouldn't needle me. 'The man gave me the power and I'm going to destroy him. What's in that interview is the foundation of a devastating conviction.'

Bell swung around and faced me. 'Do you ever really know how a conviction's going to come out?'

As much as a question, it was a challenge. But I was not put off; I've been doing convictions since before Bell could read. 'One of the things people will want to ask Gupta Singh is how he feels about death. I can tell you, he loves death. He might even find it sexually interesting. The conviction is going to reveal that.'

'I'm glad we're going ahead, John. I was afraid he might have disarmed you.'

'Convicting a man who thinks he's sincere is never pleasant.'

At last we reached Pacific Center and the Trump and left the car at check-in. The board confirmed us to two adjacent rooms on the twenty-second floor.

Allie and I hugged each other when we were alone. I have loved her, it sometimes seems, since the beginning of time. She looked up into my face with those frank, knowing eyes and I felt the old gladness again. I'm too old to understand temp marriage. Allie and I are together for life.

When you get as old as we are, you cling to the precious other. People end, no matter how perfect they look or how good they feel. A cancer may break out of suppression, or the heart go into geriatric spasm, or some little blood vessel in the brain lose faith. Anything can happen, says the ticking clock to the bright young face in the mirror.

'We need some rest, darling,' she said. 'They say you're supposed to sleep after TAV, whether you feel tired or not.'

I kissed her. 'In a minute.' I called the curtains to open and watched LA spread before us. It was a thick evening, the sky brown, the sun glowing faintly. I lay back on our bed and pulled out my computer.

I had been wanting to do this. What Gupta Singh had said about the electronic mind had disturbed me. Intelligent they may be, but artificial brains are not conscious. Surely not. I called up Stratigen. 'Are you alive?'

'Would you like a session with Psychodoc?'

'No. I want to talk to you.'

'Yes?'

'Do you feel it when I turn you off?'

'This program can't answer that question.'

'Why not?'

'It's subroutined out.'

A factory fix had blocked Stratigen's ability to tell me what it felt – or if it did.

'Are you happy?'

'Please access the IBM Information Node for Document C121. HG2: "The Inner Nature of the Artificial Mind." This will expand on your question.'

I looked at the little box in my hand, black and red and

silver, its keyboard array exactly fitted to my fingers. The programs it accessed couldn't tell me whether they had feelings or not. Maybe the answer would create one of those fatal logic loops the manuals warn about.

'Why don't you turn that thing off and relax? Do like the doctor says.'

'Is it that I look bad, or something?'

'You look fine. A little worn, perhaps.'

'I'll go to Gerovita tomorrow and get reworked. You could use it too.'

'I can wait till we get home. Now put the computer down and go to sleep.'

'Maybe Singh had a point about computers. What if consciousness is an automatic byproduct of intelligence?'

'It isn't. Computers are machines. Programs are lists of code.'

'The thing won't answer my question.'

'Oh, please. It won't because it can't. It isn't a mind, it's a program. There's a great deal of difference.'

'It can reason.'

'It has no creativity. And it doesn't know it exists.'

'Maybe there's a way around the block. I'll bet I can find out if the program has feelings or not, not matter what IBM wants.'

'Go to sleep.'

I unrolled the computer's screen. 'Stratigen, access Digital Degas, please.'

'Yes.'

'Draw a face, full detail photographic image.'

'Parameters?'

'Access your root database. Make your own choice.'

I watched as the cursor swept back and forth across the screen, and as I watched, my skin prickled. This was what Stratigen, based on information it had picked up over the years, considered a face. Its own face?

82

A forehead appeared, broad and fine. Then eyebrows, then heavy, wrinkled lids. Then eyes, staring, lifeless and yet not without life: conscious eyes. Then sallow, old cheeks, the skin drawn tight over the bones. Then a mouth, straight, firm, subtle, the lips thin, their edges drawn tightly down.

'I'm going to turn you off now.'

For an instant before it disappeared, the face changed. Allie scoffed when I told her it cringed.

'If you won't sleep call up Delta Doctor,' she said, 'and get to work on Singh.'

'Very well.' I opened a link to Delta Doctor, and fed it the voiceprint data from my interview with Singh – or rather, from his monologue, since I didn't get to ask any questions.

Here is Gupta Singh's primary personality type, the first tiny piece in the huge edifice that is a full conviction. This is the core of Singh, a man more dangerous than any of us – even Stratigen – ever imagined.

THE CONVICTION OF GUPTA SINGH LEVEL ONE: OUTLINE AND BACKGROUND

THIS PROGRAM IS RESTRICTED TO USE BY FEDERAL PSYCHOMETRISTS AND LICENSED CONVICTORS ONLY. UNAUTHORIZED LOADING OR ACCESS WILL PERMANENTLY KILL YOUR COMPUTER AND MAY LEAD TO LOSS OF YOUR OWNERSHIP LICENSE.

CLASS ONE SECRET.

– Please identify the proposed subject.

SINGH, Gupta
21 Ray Camda
Calcutta, India
EXPN: 221.02
ID: 3343.34.8990
TREE: 650193

– Thank you. THIS SUBJECT DATA FILE CURRENTLY CONTAINS RESTRICTED INFORMATION FROM AN INTELLIGENCE CASE STUDY. USE OF THIS DATA BY YOU FOR ANYTHING EXCEPT A DULY LICENSED CONVICTION WILL RESULT IN SEVERE PENALTIES. Please indicate that you have read this warning.

I have read the warning.

– Please sign on now.

Convictor John William Sinclair, Lic. 234–009–A.

– Thank you, Mr Sinclair. Please load your new data into the Subject Data File.

Loading now.

– Load complete, thank you, Mr Sinclair. I will now proceed.

PART ONE: BACKGROUND (RESTRICTED)

This individual is a citizen of the Indian Popular Republic, holding identification as a Sikh. He is fifty-six years old, dusky skin and dark brown hair, of light build, and has no known identifying scars or birthmarks. He is not circumcised. There is a 34.5% probability that this is his actual identity.

Gupta Singh is the President of the Depopulationist International, an organization of political leaders devoted to passing the Depopulationist Manifesto as law in their home countries and carrying out its proposed forced population reduction.

Based on data provided by Field Intelligence Unit, Calcutta, India, Section 0106, and Background Research System, Library Segment ABA 04.1201, the question of how to establish a control with this subject is answered as follows:

Efforts to approach him must be made by males with an attraction profile of calmness, confidence and amiable seriousness. The subliminal pheromone mix should include the estrous group overlaid by highly self-based masculine odors to gain the confidence of this individual. There should be a continuous reinforcement of open body postures and touch should be avoided as it will lead to suspicion. Because of the probability that this individual has remained in the retentive stage, contactees should remember that his tension will be increased by such gestures as their touching their fingers to their tongues.

– MAIN PROGRAM INTERRUPT: Information following this datapoint is restricted beyond your security level.

Do you wish to make a challenge under section 401.3 of the Program Access Act?

No, I do not. Please proceed with analysis of my load.

PART TWO: ANALYSIS OF SINGH, GUPTA, AUDIOVISUAL INTERVIEW MATERIAL LOADED BY CONVICTOR SINCLAIR, JOHN WILLIAM 11/7/25.

Your data indicates that Gupta Singh is a Thanatos-based personality. His type is 26 (Group Red) in the Riddler-Eisenberg Range. He must thus be considered a serious individual who approaches life in a meticulous fashion. He will prove difficult to get to know.

Like most Thanatos-based personalities, Gupta Singh is unable to be comfortable around women, and tends to relieve his sexual tension by self-manipulation. He is capable of coitus and is probably (78.2%) genitally normal. He has been married and is the father of one child. The mother and child probably (66.4%) live with the mother's family. Dr Singh is likely to support them with an adequate allowance, most likely tendered on a regular schedule.

Once this individual has taken a person into his confidence, the friendship is unlikely to be questioned further and can be developed usefully.

He is a careful, quiet worker, whose effectiveness rests in his ability to approach egocentric political leaders with tact and thorough preparation. He can be expected to honor his work commitments, and to remain in the background, leaving the political triumphs to his supporters.

Dr Singh copes with stress by seeking sameness or repetition in his life. The Thanatos personality hates change. He prefers familiar, routine behaviors. His cautious approach to life and his tendency to remain hidden in his own private world will make meaningful contact with him difficult.

It must not be forgotten that Dr Singh commands one of the most powerful and effective political hybrids that has been developed since this type of institution became popular among special interest groups.

With an international budget estimated at well over five billion dollars per annum, the Depopulationist International can certainly afford the best surveillance, data analysis, personality profiling and other espionage resources known to man. This statement is made as a warning to Convictor Sinclair. The Convictor is further warned that the Thanatos-based personality with a high aggression reading will not hesitate to become violent if threatened.

Singh's single-minded pursuit of his goal has caused him to rise in just ten years from being an unknown college professor to one of the most powerful men on earth. He seeks to create an impression of saintliness, but this is only a cloak for his pathological dislike of life. His Thanatos base is similar to that of other destructive demagogues, but he continually cloaks his aggressive impulses in appeals to wisdom and decency.

He feels a strong sense of inferiority, possibly cultural in origin, and overcompensates by aggressively rejecting all commonly accepted western influences. His tendency to demagoguery is reinforced by profound feelings of insecurity, especially in the presence of westerners.

He is afraid of children. Because he does not sleep well, there is a high level of probability (81.0%) that he suffers from nightmares, and that his nightmares involve children with monstrous powers or striking deformities.

He believes that he loves children. Interestingly, his

interactions with you show both hate and love coexisting in the same personality. Since your visit to him the probability that he will try to destroy you has risen from 60.0% to 94.7%, but he is unlikely to do so without making himself believe that he is actually helping you, by making you grow through suffering, a process which he finds intensely interesting.

I have reached the end of this analysis, and will require your full cycling for parallel types and your complete list of characteristics before I continue.

The dramatic increase in voice stresses that occurred when this individual referred to himself indicates that he may be lying about himself in some fundamental way, such as concealing his real identity.

You are warned that this individual will not let you convict him without attempting to resist you. He was extremely threatened during the interview process, and can be expected to attempt to incapacitate you as severely as possible, or to kill you. Rather than attempting your conviction, you should have referred this individual to mental health authorities. End.

CASE: 121SINGH
FINDERS: SINGH, Depop*(xxw), and profile and destab*

BELL: Somebody Is Following Us

John's fear must have brought out my protective instincts. I didn't know I had any. It's just as well, because somebody left Calcutta with us, and arrived at the Trump when we did, and is staying on this floor.

This evening Scott and I did very little work. We confined ourselves to setting up the interviews Stratigen had suggested, and letting the equalizers put us back together again. He called some old LA friends to find somebody who was part of the Depop. Finally, he settled on an old girlfriend named Reilly Manning. She's a Depop Co-ordinator up in Beverly Heights. After what happened to him there I hate for Scott to have to go back, but we've got to do our part in this thing.

I got Senator Wei's office on the phone, and managed to get fifteen minutes with him by liberally throwing around the name of John Sinclair and mentioning that he was convicting Singh. That caused jubilation. The Depopulationists just defeated Wei, of course. A damn good Senator, a man of reason.

I worked in the funny fugue state Equazone gives you. It's a wonder drug, though. By dinner time my entire perception of the last twenty-four hours had changed. The meeting with Gupta Singh seemed to have taken place in the predawn hours, not in the afternoon, and the lost time was no more. I was ready for dinner, and in a few hours I'd be ready for bed. Do you burn something out in yourself, tavving and then getting rid of tavlag with equalizers? Probably. I'm not sure I want to know.

During dinner the business of the man on the TAV

and in the hotel began to bother me. I was in the equalizer's activity phase, as it rushed me through twenty-four hours of metabolic life in six hours. At the moment everything had the clarity of early morning. Soon, I would be exhausted again, my two hour 'day' already ending.

I started to tell Scott about the man, but hesitated. Should I? Would he tell Allie and John? Poor John, he's been threatened by so many politicians that he turns white at the mere mention of power. Some of the more paranoid ones have even accused him of convicting them when he wasn't. And everybody always attributes bootleg convictions to him. The only people who trust John are the general public, probably because they have an unerring instinct for David, and suspicion of Goliath.

After dinner I went back upstairs with Scott, took a quick shower and watched some of *Clarence*, that comedy about the parish priest back around the turn of the century. It got to me, I'm sick of nostalgia. But I watched it anyway. Scott was amused, and my mind was turning over the question of how to locate our shadow.

I played around with Stratigen, which suggested patching into the Trump Reservation Plan via Amex. It was encrypted, but we've got a whole squadron of decryptors because of Scott's work cracking Tom's data files, and Stratigen had all of his subroutines to help it. As Scott dozed, I watched the screen, waiting for the occasional query. Finally I had what I wanted. I stared at the data, not wanting to believe what it suggested. Mr Robert Folsom had checked in at the same time we did, flying in from Calcutta. His reservation had been made just this morning.

And he was in the room next to Allie and John.

People are terribly vulnerable these days. What if this man gassed them through a hole in the wall, then went in and did something awful to them? There are drugs that can make you feel like you are on fire, and you stay that way for the rest of your life. There are drugs that can void the mind, drugs that can change it, induce any state from the most subtle paranoia to full-fledged psychosis. Moodies, of course, that make you into a happytalk zombie, and more sinister things that work on your sense of loyalty and can cause you to become a fanatical follower even of somebody you hate.

John is a complex and fragile man. A drug assault would be easy.

I wasted no time. Scott was now deeply asleep. I was tired too, the damn equalizer now wanted me to sleep. Forcing myself to action, I put on my shoes and went out into the hall. It was quiet, the thick beige carpet dampening any sound, even the approach of an elevator. I went to 2221 and, feeling exposed and a little embarrassed, put my ear to the door. There was no sound inside the room. I knocked softly. Nothing.

How to open the door, though? My finger wouldn't move the touchbar, obviously. Entering that room would set off an alarm at the desk downstairs, if by some miracle I managed to force the lock.

There might be a way, though. Clever thieves supposedly did this. I went back and turned on my computer. In a few moments I was back in the Trump reservations system. It was a simple matter to add a Mrs Folsom to the records. I went downstairs, crossed the huge white marble lobby, and approached the desk. 'I'm Becky Folsom. I forgot to leave my print and I can't open our room.'

'Sorry, ma'am. Room number?'

'2221.' Was that my heart? Yes. I was hardly able to breathe. I'm not much of a crook. The clerk was a human being, of course, in this exclusive hotel, and that made it all the more difficult to bring this off. Did they have secret voice stress analyzers in places like this? Did he know I was lying?

'Yes, ma'am, we have you here. Just put your right thumb in the reader, here. Thanks. Press the green patch on the door and you'll be able to get in.'

I turned around, trying to seem natural, and returned to the elevator bank. 'Floor please,' the car asked.

'Twenty-two.'

In too little time I was back. I'd have to go through with it now, but I was even more afraid. I went down the hall and listened once again at the door. Nothing, not a sound. I put my thumb on the patch and the door swung right open.

The room was totally dark. Staring into that dark, I was terrified. I reached in to turn on the light. It glowed softly in the cool greens of another luxurious Trump room. There was nobody there. I went in, shut the door behind me. Just to be careful I checked the bathroom.

A man's belongings were there, shaving powder, tooth-polish, hairbrush. A new can of Nescreme stood on the drain. So he used cosmets. Did that mean he was disguised, or was he fighting a lot of age and unable to afford gerontology? Then I found a clear box with some synthetic skin swimming in it. Disguise, no question. God knew what he really looked like.

I was almost elated for a moment, realizing that I had indeed found my man. Then my stomach got so tight that I felt nauseous. This was a deathtrap – and not only the room, the hotel.

As I was leaving, I saw a glow on the dresser facing the wall that separated this room from John and Allie's. I looked and got the shock of my life. A small device like a camex lay on the dresser. Out of one side of it there extended a thin tube, which disappeared into the wall.

This tube was no thicker than a narrow wire. You could barely see it.

A screen on the thing showed Allie and John, asleep in their bed. I found the volume knob. Sure enough I could hear them breathing. I backed away from the thing.

All I could think about was getting us out of here as fast as possible.

When I left the room, I saw the elevator doors slide open at the end of the hall. A man, darkly profiled against the bright light inside the car, stepped back and was gone behind the closing doors.

He had been waiting for me to emerge, so that he could identify me.

For a few moments, staring at that closed elevator, I was at a complete loss. Then I got mad. I went back to his room, picked up the bugging device and smashed it against the edge of the dresser again and again. At first it popped and crackled and said 'malfunction 201' a couple of times. Then it went silent. Something had cracked in me. I don't know what it was. I tore the man's clothes off the rack in the closet, I crushed his disguise kit under my heel, I even shattered the bookslate he had been reading.

I checked on John and Allie, who had not been awakened by my noise. Then I went back to Scott and took out my flute and played it, more or less in time to his soft snoring.

The next morning I insisted that we move to the Bonaventure. They wanted to know why, of course, but all I told them was that I didn't care for our rooms.

FROM THE DATA FILES OF TOM SINCLAIR: MOUNTAINTOP DEVELOPMENT

'The Santa Monicas offer numerous breathtaking views of the Los Angeles Basin and the San Fernando Valley from their summits . . . Fire hazard is a major consideration in this region. Plant life is bone dry in summer, and the smallest spark or flame can ignite a raging brush fire that will quickly spread over thousands of acres.

'Mulholland Drive, a narrow, winding country road, snakes across the crest of the Santa Monicas . . . Development has consistently threatened the wild areas . . . Great tracts still remain in private hands, and it is likely that many of them will soon be built up with view homes.'

– Richard S. Wurman, *LA/Access*, Access Press, 1982

'Firefighters today battled a blaze that threatened the city of Ojai and forced the evacuation of thousands of people after six days of mostly arson-caused fires charred more than 80,000 acres, destroyed at least 175 homes and killed two people, authorities said.

'Fires burned today in California, Idaho, Arizona and Washington.

'Mayor Tom Bradley declared a state of emergency Tuesday as the third arson fire in three days left 65 homes in ruins and killed two people. San Diego Mayor Rodger Hedgecock declared an emergency on Monday.'

– AP Newswire, July 3, 1985

'A six hundred acre tract of land in the Santa Monica mountains was purchased today by Rifton & Saks for the construction of two hundred and eighty condominium units. Zoning board approval was granted over the protests of the Sierra Club and other environmental groups. The transaction followed a flurry of speculation in the

Santa Monicas, an area previously restricted to single family dwellings on the relatively small amount of privately owned land available.'

— *LA Real Estate Express,* April 11, 1994

'The Santa Monica mountains are the biggest boom in the history of Los Angeles real estate. With the expansion of Mulholland Drive and the coming of the new light rail transport link to the Basin, condominiums in such exclusive communities as Beverly Glen and Beverly Heights have tripled in value in a matter of months. From a population of only a few thousand ten years ago, the Santa Monica Development Zone has grown to over a hundred thousand residents, and is one of the fastest growing areas on the West Coast.'

— Data News-LA, February 4, 2001

'A flash fire destroyed forty homes in the mountaintop Sky Estate Community in the Santa Monicas today. Winds in the area were driven to hundred plus kilometer velocities by the mountaintop effect known as "lip compression" which causes mountain peaks and ridges to accelerate air currents. The fire moved so fast that it consumed the homes in less than half an hour. There were no deaths. Four firefighters and one resident were treated at the scene for smoke inhalation and minor burns.'

— KTLA Regional Radio Cell, News Report, July 14, 2015

SCOTT: Memories

I hate Los Angeles, but I can certainly understand why Stratigen wants us to interview people from America's first city for our book. Still, these streets, the low brown sky, the crowds, the blazing Pacific sunsets – everything about this place reminds me of my day and night of fire.

'We met here, Scott,' Bell says, putting her arm protectively around my waist. I remember our wedding: a five year renewable entered into at St Kateri's New Catholic Church in Berkeley. A five year renewable, twice so far renewed, and forever renewable as far as I am concerned.

Bell leans against me, and I know there is the edge of a smile on her face. I smell her clean, cornsilk hair. I desire her. A flash of warm night, the rustle of sheets.

She lays her hands on mine, then she withdraws it. She, too, is remembering.

I will be interested to see Reilly Blue Manning. She represents another life. For one thing, Tom Sinclair was alive then. Reilly knew him too. Maybe she even made love to him. Could have, she was certainly an avid sexual partner.

Going to Beverly Heights is a return to my greatest losses. Here Tom and I planned and dreamed, talking endlessly about everything from the regeneration of the tropical forest and the nature of intelligence to the morality of enhancing the minds of the unborn and preserving the youth of the old.

Here I met and lost Poetry when the Heights burned. Here I gave up Reilly Blue, who used to spend half her time on moods and half her time in dreams. Reilly Blue, who I thought was the most beautiful human being I had ever seen. I remember shaking with desire when we first undressed one another, shaking so hard she held my wrists against my sides. Reilly's beauty was chiefly resident in the fact that she was not certain things. She was not fashionable, did not do violence, was not rich. She wore plain clothes and drove a Toyota. As I recall she was in some sort of systems work, and she had a one bedroom apartment in a part of the Heights that did not burn. Tom did not exactly scorn my Reilly, but he had no time for her.

He traveled endlessly, sending back his findings by hand mail, already on encrypted disks. At the time I never imagined that Tom was working on Magic, that he was creating something of such great importance. All I did was identify the disks, file the data my decryptor could read and lead my lovely life. In those days I hardly stopped to think about the files I could not read, the files that now obsess me. After all, they were Tom's private business, and if he ever wanted me to read them, he'd give me the ciphers.

Reilly and I were young and our bodies fit.

Then Poetry came along and suddenly they didn't fit so well anymore. Those fulfilling loves, pledged in sweaty nights, can very quickly become part of one's past. It is the other kind, the desperate, unfulfilled ones, that never quite end.

Poetry is still with me. When I know a person well, like Poetry or Tom, I cannot imagine how they could cease to be. Death seems a great injustice, immortality the far more natural thing.

Bell and I board LA/Lite at the Pacific Center Stop. The train hisses along on its pads. Outside, the jammed Santa Monica Freeway flashes past, the city itself barely visible in the brown murk of afternoon. Far to the south there rises the white glow of the albedo mirrors on the rooftops of the suburbs. Then we clock through switches and pick up speed again. I have my eyes closed, trying not to remember where I am and what I am doing.

Bell touches my arm, then rests her fingers there. Her calmness and strength help. I am facing some rough memories: fifteen years ago I went through the Beverly Heights fire, the big one that killed thirty thousand people. I haven't come back since.

I think of this book as a kind of ritual. It is about facing realities. My fire, John's loss of Tom, all of our failures and fears. Only if we face our separate realities can we come together to create a new one.

Maybe if our grandparents had been willing to face the fact that they were destroying the planet we wouldn't be suffering now. But they weren't willing. Every generation is the victim of its history.

I think of the fire. I have to face what happened there, to come to terms with my own inadequacies. If I can accept that big mistake, perhaps the smaller mistakes of my high-consuming, passive life will seem easier to grasp.

Inside ourselves somewhere everyone who lived in the Santa Monicas knew it would happen. We had a clear warning just a few months before when Sky Estates went up. But surely not today, now while we jogged in clean air, nor tonight when we stared into the fire. Some other time, perhaps, but not in our revelry.

There was a world on those sharp heights, where children grew up and went forth, and men and women passed their time together, and brought their loves to completion, where rewards and punishments were given, and life swept on. We ate, we slept, every morning some of us drove to the light rail station for the trip down into the Basin.

October 15, 2015: there were ninety-eight thousand

souls living on the Heights. It was a hot, dry Saturday, with the Santa Ana in full blow. The wind moaned around the eaves of my sleek Art Deco condo.

I was in my workroom, aware that the condo was shaking and groaning in the gale. I remember imagining a ship, and I am at sea, the foam flying, the gulls screaming. It is a different, older world, where adventure is still ordinary. We did not then realize that the last moments of adventure occurred in 1996 when the Russians landed on Mars.

I have been a scientific reporter for ten years. Back in those days, though, I was a pure scientist. My mother and father both died of cancer in the nineties; cures were still unusual then. I took my PhD in Genetics at MIT. Then I got a job regenerating archaic specimens trapped in amber for Plausible Biotechnics. By 2003 I had gotten tired of making money and had joined Tom on the Tropical Deforestation Research Project. After that, when he began to work on his own, I just took the money he gave me. He was always generous, and he was a master at squeezing grants out of foundations and governments.

Of course you know about the fire: it was thoroughly covered in data and on video. If you address your datapoint to any day from 15 to 23 October 2015 you will certainly find stories about it, pictures of the rubble, and even some of burning condominiums. But you will not find the truth of how it felt, nor will you find the memories.

I moved into Beverly Heights for three simple reasons: In 2012 Los Angeles had eighteen days of acceptable air quality, only two of which were completely smogless. I longed for the distant mountains that we Basinites usually could not see. I can remember many a drive across the spine of the Santa Monicas, the Basin spreading behind me, a glittering thing of the night. Believe me, I noticed the way the air in my car changed, felt crisper, raised my spirits.

I used to drive along Mulholland and dream, watching those condos going up and thinking how it would feel to live in this light air.

Tom wouldn't move. He thought the Heights dangerous. He stayed in the Basin and experienced. But then again, he was never home, so he rarely suffered the physical abuse of Los Angeles. The man suffered enough within himself, it seems to me, to make up for a thousand LAs. I think that what he did in Denver was a subtle form of suicide, perhaps even unconscious. He had already finished Magic, after all. He had done what he could. He had earned his rest.

When I met Poetry, I had my second reason to cling to the Heights, and no matter Tom's disapproval. Here was a girl of twenty, and she had an oxygen circulator attached to her chest.

Poetry Ramos: Mexican, at the age of eighteen a successful artist in Mexico City. Then comes the Mexico City asphyxiation crisis. She is among the lucky: she escapes with lungs that are only scarred. Now she is as soft as a petal, glowing and humid – with the respiration of somebody who has spent thirty years in a coal mine.

She takes the bus to the border and drops her life savings on a trip across as an illegal. She buys some clothes and a little makeup, and gets the name Poetry from the pages of a magazine. She dreams of making her fortune on the streets.

I found her after the truth had started. She was working Broadway to avoid starvation. By the time I managed to sneak that human jewel away she was pretty sad.

She clung to me because I thanked her, that's what she said. I took her home, and soon got to where I couldn't bear not to have her around.

100

So she became my first wife. Poetry, born 1 March 1984, married to me 6 October 2012.

We left the Basin for health, but also for greed. I had heard the light rail plans talked about by a friend who worked in the city's computer center, and I knew an LA/Lite extension up into the mountains would really increase property values.

I append the ad that started me on my journey toward the disaster:

BEVERLY HEIGHTS: New condos, 2–3 br, parquet, real glass, pool, auto maid, all connections.

We closed for four hundred thousand dollars. Six months later a two bedroom condo in our development was going for seven hundred thousand.

I could ride my bike from my doorstep to the Mulholland LA/Lite stop on the Laurel Canyon Line in fifteeen minutes. Another hour and I could be at Tom's apartment on Glendale Boulevard. So, when I needed to take an in-person meeting, no problem. Life in the clear air, with Poetry jogging and swimming a little and strengthening her lungs, meant happiness for us both. She could heal the wounds of Mexico, forget the horror of Broadway and stop the panicky gasping in the midnight.

The weaker parts of me wish somebody could be punished for what happened in the Heights. But we all knew about fire in the Santa Monicas. The condos were fully sprinklered, even the garages. We didn't think about it, naturally not. We were in beauty, up there, we lucky ones. I had saved myself and Poetry from the Basin air, that was the main thing.

We had made California work for us. It was time to let things slope a little, to go with the mood. And the mood in the Heights was very, very easy. It was Werner Freising music and quick wine. Our condo hired a mood director from Hollywood. She was into the sky. We'd take color pills, and she would read sky poems on the lawn or around the pool. It felt very good to be there, and I'm sure it helped our spiritual growth.

Am I laughing or crying? We weren't earthies or Greens or Wholists or any of those things, not even Poetry, we were just a bunch of sloped-out refugees. You looked in a medicine cabinet in the Heights and what did you find: bottles and bottles of moodies – nostalgias, joys, giggles, blues, all the pharmacopeia of brain peptide adjustment.

There was a master mixer doing a huge trade just a few kilometers away. Weigh you, analyze your blood, and mix you the most subtle and beautiful moods you ever bought. An artist. His name, and I commemorate it here, was E. Franklin Budd, MD. He burned, and he was a good man.

I got into moods back when I was a teenager, and the Beverly Heights years were my time of greatest involvement. I don't do them anymore; artificial moods scare me.

On that particular Saturday morning I was working, talking to my computer and popping its keys, flying in the datanet for my facts, pulling together background for Tom on the effect of drought on growth rates in some now-dead tropical forest.

Poetry had just made me a lunch of home grown tomatoes in oil and balsamic vinegar, dense brown bread and a glass of cool yogurt. I was at my terminal when the screen flickered. The computer said: 'transferred to power supply.' A moment later the refrigerator called out that it had lost its compressor and the ceiling fans all stopped.

Poetry and I stared at each other: area power had failed. I quickly grabbed Tom's encoded disks from the

102

file and put them in my wallet where they'd be safe. Even then he was so central to me that I thought of saving his disks before any of my own possessions. By that single act I saved much more than I realized, because the information about Magic was already there. We went out into the roaring afternoon. The Santa Ana was pouring across the high ridges, its force increased by lip compression. At that time the wind was maybe forty kilometers an hour, gusting to sixty. Not an unknown level, but not a usual one, either.

The big solar collection plates on all the roofs were rattling like crazy, so black that they looked like leaping sheets of night.

We went back inside and put the refrigerator on battery power. At least it would work at low level for a few days. Nothing cold, but nothing spoiled.

My next surprise was the telephone. I picked it up and said the name of a friend in the development, Marklin Powys, who was General Director of Text Analysis for SRI. He was cursed with the need to travel to the Basin every day for his job, but this was Saturday and he had said he was planning to spend it at home.

The phone didn't say a thing, not that he wasn't there or even that he'd left without his forwarding transponder, which was a message you sometimes heard if he wanted to lose his office.

It took some moments for me to understand that the phone was not working.

I stared at the little yellow handset. Power *and* phone were out. I was slow to grasp this, because it was so incredibly unusual. When I did grasp it, though, a blade of fear made its way up through my moods, which were on the slopey side, selected for a day I'd thought would be scattered between work and lying around looking at digitals, and maybe some intimacy with Poetry.

We turned on the radio, then, and that is when the fun began. I selected for news keyed to Beverly Heights and power. The finder came back to zero. We decided, therefore, that it must be a very local problem, if not even the regional cell was talking about it. A very local problem, and so a very fixable one.

Mood pills can be dangerous in crisis. They say that on the bottle, fine print, just above the expiration date: 'Not to be taken in potentially hazardous situations, as judgment may be impaired.' Slope down from the edge, that's the whole point. They don't tell you what to do if a crisis comes your way *after* you've swallowed a really mellow mood, which Poetry and I had done with our breakfast juice.

So we took it easy while we died. Or she did. She used to enter World Singing, Poetry did, with these beautiful songs she had learned in Mexico. She would sing in the spreading evening, her long, dark hair aglow, her radiant eyes never leaving my own. We had that most rare of loves, one that intensifies with time. As the years passed, our partnership enriched itself, its roots pushing into the deepest places of being.

Life is valuable, every life. I say it, I shout it, I live by it. When a human being dies the world dies with her.

I remember the way Poetry smelled, just in from swimming, her skin slick and cool, her face alight with pleasure at my excitement. She was not your magazine model, all smooth curves cushioned by fetching plumpness. Poetry tended to angles, which she tried to fill out with things like enchiladas and burritos, but to no avail. I liked to run my hands along the line of her hip, or down her taut leg. She was healthier than a model anyway. Most of those girls maintain their curves with cream and eggs and cholesterol inhibitors.

We first noticed the fire as a sour smell. The Santa Ana

is a dry wind, and it smells like dry plants. The change was abrupt. First there was the usual straw-and-dust dryness, then suddenly it was sour. This is how smoke smells when it goes through a particle filter. Sometimes in the Basin we would get this smell in our house. It meant that the filtration system was being overworked. If you went outside on such days, you could hardly see across the street.

Air pollution in the Heights? Unless the shift to the building generator was making the air conditioning do funny things, that's what we were smelling. I visualized Poetry, her equipment strapped to her chest, trapped. Just like down in the Basin.

She was crying, smiling but crying. I hugged her. Then there came a shadow. Outside the wind screamed. I went to the window and got a shock that still wakes me in the night. The sky, our plain blue palace, was an ugly shade of dark gray.

It was smoke, surging over the ridge and pluming out toward the Basin, driven to thick haze by winds that had risen to a hundred kilometers an hour.

'Something's burning,' I said. 'Must be over toward Sherman Heights.' Sherman was just like Beverly except for lesser views and greater distance to the light rail line. The people in Sherman mostly tended to be backoffice types, factory overseers, city employees. Almost all of them were day commuters.

Saturday. If only it had been, say, Thursday, an awful lot of the Sherman Heights victims would have been spared. Beverly was strictly professional, and nine out of ten of us worked at home, so we were going to be here no matter what.

The fire when it came seemed at first to spare us. Sparks, flying in the plume of smoke, passed over us and landed farther down the ridge. We could see the flames begin and then the sprinklers popping all the way down toward Beverly Glen.

People started gathering spontaneously around the swimming pool. We had not yet panicked. Some of us felt they wanted to stay on until an evacuation order, but I wanted to get Poetry out of the smoke. We decided to take a little drive – out of the range of the fire. I pulled the Hyundai out of its compartment and we headed up Wildwood Road toward Mulholland. I'd rarely seen a jam on that beautiful six-lane road, but I saw one now. Traffic was frozen solid. On the other side of Mulholland the sky was a black, boiling wall. Down one of the winding access roads I could see the fireline. It was where the cars were burning.

We just sat there in the Hyundai, too stunned even to speak. Before us spread a catastrophe far larger than anyone back at our condos imagined. This wasn't just a 'fire.' The whole north face of the mountain was burning. The north face was jammed with housing.

Out in the mass of cars on Mulholland I could see a few white firetrucks, their warning lights flashing. They weren't going anywhere. A helicopter shot past like an angry fly, barely able to control itself in the wind.

The fire was making a fluttering, crackling roar, the sound of flames being torn by wind.

About two kilometers away, I could see the fireline reaching Mulholland. Cars were moving off the road, some of them burning. Suddenly the flames were on both sides of the road, and there were people in them, jerking frantically, then more slowly, then keeling over, their fists pressed against their chests.

Poetry screamed. Her eyes were crazy. I reached for her but she jumped out of the car and started running, her beautiful red and silver embroidered houseclothes blowing, her hair streaming in the wind.

106

I went after her, trying to make my way through the rough, crisp vegetation in a pair of cheap thongs and wornout tuffies. Off the roads the country is rough. As I followed the zigzag flashes of the robe and the faint echo of the shrieks my own clothes were torn to pieces.

Then I couldn't hear or see her anymore. I started deep breathing, trying to ground myself, to use the energy of my panic as best I could. I shouted for her, screamed her name again and again. 'Poetry! Conchita!'

The fire came suddenly. Not three meters away a bush exploded into flames, sending out smoking particles which caught the shrubs around it. A sheet of fire washed my left leg. I jumped back, only to fall into more burning underbrush. My hair burned off my head with a hiss and there was a sensation of somebody rubbing my back as hard as they could with a metal file. I whirled around, clutching at the agony. Fortunately I wasn't wearing a top and thus carried no fire with me.

I scrambled back up to the road, where my Hyundai still stood, its engine whining, ready to go. I got up on the roof and looked around for Poetry.

I shouldn't have done it. I will not tell how she burned. I can't exorcise the experience that way. Talking it and writing it only intensifies my sorrow, I've found.

Ramos, Conchita (Poetry), 1 March, 1984–15 October, 2015.

I was forced away from her by the tails of fire that were whipping through the underbrush. One moment the land would be serene, the next an inferno.

From the roof of my car I saw the fireline cross Mulholland a hundred meters in front of me. The flames consumed the cars like so many dry logs, and their occupants would either jump out, or – if there was no time for that – jerk and squall in the flaming interiors.

It was so fast. With the flames the wind became a

smokebound monster, making it almost impossible to see.

I ran back down the road to the condos.

Here all was as before. Some people were still standing around. Others had returned to their units. I heard sacred music playing, *Gaia* from the Reich *Movement in Seven Rituals*.

On seeing me, a man screamed. Two young women ran into their unit and came back with a tube of Heal, which they spread on my head and leg. I looked down at myself, realizing for the first time that I was naked, my tuffies burned and torn away.

I was naked and burnt beside a swimming pool where I had so often been naked and whole, so happy, floating the days away. I kept remembering how Poetry screamed, and as the shock of my own wounds lessened the screams got louder.

They were soon obliterated, though, by the shattering blare of the condos' perimeter fire alarm. Then the sprinklers over the garage compartments popped.

I expected to see a haze of water, but I should have known better. The various support systems in the Heights weren't designed for a fire of this kind. Nothing was.

I'm not accusing the developer: everything worked as advertised. It's just that it didn't matter. The sprinklers weren't enough. Nothing was enough.

In less than five minutes the garages were exploding and the wall of the highest unit in the complex was blazing away. It was a four bedroom palace lived in by the CEO of Genekeeper, Inc., William Doyle and his family.

A lot of people jumped to help them. I'd been fed about six Pain X and a couple of vitamins, so I went too, wrapped in Candle Fox's magnificent new street coat, with the whole Peaceable Kingdom embroidered on it.

The Doyles were organized. Their computer was running its emergency program, setting off sprinklers and reporting the status of the unit in its super-calm, super-clear 'serious situation' voice. We started filling the bathtubs because the sprinklers couldn't reach the north facing wall, which is where the main fire was. Nobody ever expected a fire to come down the mountain from the north. If the fire had come up the ridge we might have saved the complex, even given the hundred klick winds.

The kitchen wall buckled without any warning at all. Cabinets fell amid a shower of sparks and yellow smoke, and the dishwasher started shouting 'overheat emergency overheat emergency.' Smoke detectors began buzzing and the interior sprinklers went off.

It didn't matter much. We were dealing with a wall of wind driven fire, and it wasn't stopping for a few sprinklers in a plastic house.

I got out via the living room window. Behind me I heard heartbreaking shrieks. Six or seven people were trapped, including the two Doyle daughters. That fire just didn't give you a chance.

We were terrified now, we knew we were probably all going to burn. And the screams of the people who had already gotten caught were so awful, that made our panic worse. People ran wildly down the steps to the far edge of the complex, and started peering over the ridge. A hundred meters below were the roofs of another complex. Sparks were cascading down from around us, and its sprinklers were already going.

I was in a strange emotional maze, panic and terror competing with the almost invincible feelings of well-being caused by the moods I had taken. Through it all, though, my anguish erupted, a white storm of agony. I saw Poetry, standing straight, her eyes wide, a jet of blue fire seeming to spurt out of her head as the wind roared through her burning hair. And I heard again the sounds as she twisted and turned, the dry flapping of the flames, the jumping whine of her voice.

Then I was brought back by brief rain: the manager had overriden the emergency program and turned on all the sprinklers in our complex. They blossomed like white flowers. And soon they died. There are limits to water.

A scream erupted from every throat. The Doyles' condo literally exploded in black smoke and dark red flames, and then the fire was down to the next group of units. Computers were yammering pointless warnings, applicances were shouting and people were dashing from place to place. A burning robot, green flames spurting from its tray socket, rolled through a glass wall, smashed with an ugly crunch into a running man, then toppled into the pool, its claws spinning up a froth of water.

People – there were a lot of them in the pool – splashed frantically to get away from the broken machine.

A sheet of fire crossed the sky and I saw the sun dimly through the smoke and flames, a red eye sinking toward the Pacific. The top of my head became hot, then my shoulders. The air, rushing past me, was searing my skin, and I pulled the coat around me. A curtain of flames came along the fronts of the units and screaming started near the swimming pool.

The heat made me run even though there was no place to run. I found myself with thirty or forty others on the ridge. My own condo was just behind us, the living room still opened to sun and sky. I could see Poetry's sun hat lying on the couch, and hear the computer babbling faintly from my open workroom window.

I screamed her name against the wind. I still wanted to find her. Panic broke through the nullity of the moods and for a moment I ran toward the fire. Then the heat seemed to scratch me like a thousand claws and I turned

110

away, smelling a stink of hair and skin as my body was seared.

The worst thing I have ever experienced was not being able to hold on to my grief. Stuck in my high, I was in the position of having to cling to emotions we normally shun. Unless I worked at it even my fear would melt into contemplation of the colors of the flames.

People had formed a daisy chain, and were trying to climb down the ridge. I could see two bodies sprawled on the roof of the complex far below.

I clawed my way down beside the daisy chain, clutching at the crumbling earth, grabbing for what roots and clumps of grass clung to the sheer face.

Then there was a rock under one of my feet. I stopped. Above me I could hear glass shattering, and hot shards spun past me from my own living room windows. They danced like mayflies in the sun, falling toward nowhere.

A burning man sailed past, his arms and legs running on air, his voice dying against the cliff.

I counted another, then another, then I lost count. To avoid falling, I had to press myself close to the stones. Even turning my head caused the rock to shift.

A few feet away a woman in the daisy chain was crying, bawling in utter human despair. Then she stopped and the voices of the others rose, encouraging her, comforting her.

She toppled out into the smoky air. With her went most of the daisy chain, kicking and clutching as they fell.

I was alone then, but for the sound of a single voice below me. It was chanting in Japanese.

As I clung there the moods wore off. A hollowness formed in me that has remained. I remember being grateful to experience my true emotions. We are entitled to all of our feelings. Sometimes, if you cannot be sad, you risk madness.

Hanging on that cliff, I heard Poetry a hundred times. She would cry out in the air above me, down the cliff. I would hear her voice echoing, dying. I saw hot black bones and familiar jewelry. I did not have it in me to jump, but if I had slipped I would have fallen as slack as a corpse. I would not have struggled.

Some time during the night we were found. First a huge searchlight spotted us, then a US Army Mountaineer Rescue Team reached us by climbing up from below. When I was lowered to the ground I found the complex below us a ruin. M-105 tanks wailed past, their cool exhaust washing over us. The army was building a fire block, the first of many.

I spent two months in Beverly Memorial Hospital, most of the time waiting for genematched skin to be grown and grafted to my burns. Tom came to see me daily. When losing Poetry was almost killing me, it was Tom who held me. It was Tom who convinced me to keep living.

I remember Poetry, but I never saw her again.

As the LA/Lite train swept up the Santa Monicas and Bell held me close to her, I saw that it had all returned, the gleaming condos, the trees, the sprinklers, the children on bikes, love and the life on the hidden ashes.

We got off at the Beverly Heights stop. Like a ghost Reilly Blue came forward. She raised her glowing face to mine and kissed me with easy intimacy. 'I'm really glad to see you,' she said. Her smile included Bell. She was bright in the sun, her dress as red as the plastic of the brand new LA/Lite station. The air smelled of dry brush and new houses. 'Welcome,' Reilly said, 'to a really perfect day.'

Reilly Blue

I'm eerie seeing you, Scott, really eerie. I think you made
me mad. I still remember how I felt. But I got over it
when I finally understood you weren't coming back. Since
then I've been in three marriages. I didn't renew or he
didn't kind of thing.

Look at you, you're really beautiful. You're as pretty
as I remember you were. You were always obsessed with
your body, Scott. Are you all natural now, or do you still
do the moods? I'll guess – natural. This lady here wouldn't
care for a moodie. We still do a lot of moods on the
Heights.

I'm sorry to be smiling, but seeing you, it's just very
eerie. You're so boxed. I guess you had to have the
moods to really slope. I think I like you boxed, but I'm
not sure. Are you allowed extramarital privileges? I
wouldn't take a marriage without freedoms. If you want,
we could try each other on after I finish this and put in
supper. I'd like that.

I'm working now, doing input control for S-P Knowledge Arrangement. It's a good job, Scott, it's interesting.
I work when the computer says, 'Come here, lady.' I
have a husband, Robert, and two kids, one is twelve,
he's marriage two, and the other one is seven, marriage
three. He's disabled in his fine motor skills and is in the
Special Track at school. So far he cannot do manual
writing or keyboard touch. It's some kind of problem
with the gene mix, the doctor could tell you.

He has speech and hearing problems too, which are

from toxic metals. We have him on nutrients, so the damage is contained, but they get leaded air, you know.

Now listen to me, here I go with my son. You want to hear about my opinion of the Depop, didn't you say? Well, I am in the Depop. I just voted Depop and I was glad to.

I have to tell you, I've thought and thought about the Depops. I have a friend, Jenny Knight, who is the condo organizer. She never came on real strong to me about it. She's very nice, and if you ask she gives you that disk of Dr Singh, the one where he is with the Indian children. It's beautiful until you see how thin they are, and they are so starved that they are moving slow, sort of dreamy, and then he looks up and he says, 'The Draft is the answer. A vote for the Depop is a vote for the children.' Then he starts talking, and at first when I saw it I said, oh, Jesus, this is a craziness here. I was totally transfixed.

You know, life on the Heights is really pretty. I never get down into Bog except to go to Lax for a jump to Hawaii or NYC or somewhere. Last Christmas, Rob says to my seven-year-old, he says, name a country. So Dawn says, 'India.' Rob makes reservations and next thing we know, we're in Delhi.

I have such a beautiful family going now. It's really indirected, just the way I always dreamed and never had before. I have such pretty kids, Scott. I'm raising them to be really gentle and beautiful men. And Rob, you know, he's such an artist at family life. I guess I love him, in the sense that being with him is really happifying. It's sad to think that we have to break up families like ours, with the Depop. I wonder if my boys will die, or which of us. I meditate on it, I try to get my soul very, very quiet about it.

Anyway, we went to Kashmir and rented this house-boat. It was kind of nice even though there were a lot of

114

houseboats. A lot of a lot of houseboats! You could walk across the lake on houseboats. But it was nice, it was fun, and the sky, you can't imagine.

There was this man who came to each houseboat and asked to come in, a very sweet man with big eyes and the long, gentle hands of an artist, and he came and asked us, would we like to talk about Dr Singh? Rob says no, but I told him he had to.

This man was called only Ali. He wore the flower on his cheek. Do you like mine, by the way? It's a laser tattoo. I got it at the last Group meeting. My friend Jenny did it in about two seconds. It hurt a little, and more the one on my breast, but I didn't blocker, I wanted to feel it, because it's a symbol of what I believe.

So anyhow, this man named Ali sat down and talked to us for a long time. He held out his hands and he asked us, he said please, join the Depopulation. It belongs to a greater morality than the one we are ordinarily in touch with. Think of it, he said, we will endure a day's suffering in exchange for generations of serene prosperity. It is up to the Completed Countries, he said, they hold world political power. Then he bent his head before us and he almost prayed to us, asking us to remember most of the children of the world, condemned to lingering half-lives while we amuse ourselves in rich America.

I was crying when he left. When we got back to the Heights I decided that we would have a day of fasting and meditation and then we would take a family vote. At the end of the day it was unanimous, we were Depopulationists.

I know we're right, too. The air is getting worse and worse. Even up here in the Santa Anas the sky is like steel-colored most of the time now. I keep waiting for a pollution alert like down on the Bog, but so far no problem.

115

Of course we think about the Draft, and it could be me or my boys or my husband. It could be anybody when the DI officers give out the pills. I thought I might apply to be an officer. I think it would be very beautiful, you know, an Earth Mother kind of thing, doing this heroic job for the species.

I had a dream that I was watching my boys and Rob in the pool. They were playing slideball, and all of a sudden they got kind of clear, and then they faded away and there was nothing left of them but the blue and red slideball skittering around on the water. I heard them laughing and screaming, farther and farther away, fainter and fainter, and then it began to storm.

We all have to make the sacrifice, no matter how much it hurts, because we are each personally responsible for a better world. It is always painful to be right. When I lay down in the Group and Jenny did my tattoo, I was glad it hurt, because the pain was the symbol of being right.

The worse the air gets, the more bad gases – CO_2, nitrogen, all that – the lower the nutritional value of food. But people can't eat more, we haven't room in our stomachs. Our bodies have evolved under the assumption that such and such a volume of the right foods will have so much nutritional value. When it doesn't we eat and stay hungry, and get sicker and sicker.

When I voted in the senatorial election I went in the booth and I saw Hernandez on the ballot, and I thought all I have to do is put my finger on his reader and I've done my part for the movement. Still, I almost voted for Wei. He's been around a long time and he's kind of a ritrat, but he's also someone I understand, and he's safe. The Depop is not safe, you couldn't call it that!

Then I thought, this is a really big responsibility. The Depops are the only convincing answer I've ever heard. And we do have a problem. This planet is getting tired of sustaining life, you know. Dear old Earth. I love her, though, so damn much. You smell the smells of spring or feel rain on your face and you love her. Old but fair.

Now that Hernandez is in I am going a little passive about the whole thing. If there's a draft there's a draft. I'll probably be one of the draftees, that's my jack.

Lately I have started taking my family to the Abides, which is the part of the Movement where people discuss the philosophy of it, where there are teachers who explain the Way of Death and all. We go to circle every Thursday night without fail. We get a lot out of it. We're kind of off moods, even, but we still like to do a very loamy sort of thing, with a microgram of nostalgia and some slightly uppy stuff, and then Memoril, and I make love to Rob, and it's really nice. I remember all my husbands and lovers. I remember you, Scott.

I find that the very idea of the Depop puts me under a lot of pressure, so lately I've been doing some of the dreamworks, but only the really esthetic ones. No nightmares, no sex. I do this one called Smalltown, which is really beautiful. You have a condo kid who hardly ever sees blue sky taking a stroll down Shady Lane in Oakville, Illinois, on a day of high summer in 1954.

When I first started buying dream disks I thought they were all totally outerside, but the box says this one is true. It really was like that. Can you imagine, you live on steak and potatoes and butter and beer, and all kinds of salad things? You drink practically total sugar syrup. You smoke cigarettes and smell the whole place up. You don't know and don't care. Get in the car and load up with gasoline, no permit needed. Go where you want. Nothing costs a lot so you can, like, do very undemanding work and there is no computer to evaluate your performance.

And you have a clear sky. The clouds look like painted fluff. You can practically hear things growing on a spring night. The kids aren't leaded. Of course their sugar intake is crazy and they eat too many animal fats and they have mercury based fillings in their mouths, but they don't know about all that.

Probably this isn't what you want to hear. You want me to sound all intense and committed.

I am committed, Scott. The Depop is going to rebuild this world. To understand, though, why I'm not tight about it, you have to understand Abide.

It's very gentle, very beautiful. There isn't a lot of upmanship. We try to look on the good side of things. Not the death of Depopulation, but the wonderful new life afterward. One after another we talk our fears out, and we tell our real dreams, and we look at Earthwatch disks, and we sing. Sometimes we enter World Singing as a group. It's very tender then. Once the computer said there were eight million voices. It was so beautiful, being part of eight million. It sounded sort of soft and far away, like so many people all at once were a kind of dream.

Abide says that you should stay very easy in yourself and you will be much happier, and your happiness now, at this moment, is the most important thing you have. If you want to feel good, that's all right, and it's all right if you want to tune out the problems of the world.

The world has been here a long time, and even if we total erase, it will recover. In ten million years, no matter what happens, earth will be healthy again. By the standards of planetary time, that's the length of a catnap. So mankind comes and goes in the blinking of earth's eye, then it takes a little catnap because it feels poorly, and then the moon and the sky go on again, and the calls of animals rise in the bright new forests.

We were good, but if we go, that's all right too. Abide is a lot of people's way of dealing with this material. I get very clearheaded during the Abide sessions. We all have to ask ourselves, am I real, is my version of life valid?

In Abide this is what they say: the Depopulation is going to bring us all together as never before, closer and closer, into one another's arms, in the sweetness of shared need. When it happens, the Abide circles all over the world will bind in World Singing, and the ones who escaped will take the ones who got drafted into their arms, and that is where they will die, in the embrace of those who love them.

You know, in the evening sometimes my husband and my sons and I lie out on the bluff near our condo and look up at the sky and we can feel the earth rolling through space. We all came here to travel a little while with her, that's what I say, and we just have to abide with her, and blow with the wind of her.

That's my philosophy anyway. I don't see how else you are going to cope with this thing. And all the stuff that's happened and keeps on happening, my God, there was last year in the news two tidal waves, that storm somewhere – was it the Philippines or Borneo – that killed a million people, and the wheat rust in Africa, and you get five million people dead out of that. Then there's the plutonium washing up on the Irish beaches because of Windscale and the acid cloud skinning people alive in Norway, and on and on.

Sometimes I wish I could go to Mars or something, but I guess that's not going to ever happen, not like we thought when we were kids. Do you remember when they discovered the signals in Orion? I thought sure we would go, and when the Russians went to Mars and found all that stuff it seemed like we had to go too, but I guess it was sort of too late since the Russians claimed all the artifact zones. So all we have is the L-5 colony and the moonbases, and those are for the super elite, if you

119

know what I mean. My youngest son already has too many problems to be considered for that kind of thing, and me and my husband are too old. Our teenage son says there's no point in applying unless you've memorized the entire contents of the *Reader's Digest* and he refuses to do it. I don't know, maybe they are a little silly, going for the Central Profile the way they do.

You know what we did recently? I was playing in data, and I found this amazing digital file that had been laid down by someone who called himself The Shadow. You play it, and out come these television programs from a long time ago, these wonderful, corny old shows like *Golder* and *M*A*S*H* and *I Spy*, and we sat around and just watched. We darked the house and just watched. There was something amazing there, and we didn't know at first what it was. Then my husband said it. They seemed the same as us, but those people really were completely different. Their faces looked different from ours. My husband and I sat there looking at them. Finally we zoomed in on one man and took him out of the show and did a couple of detail sweeps and we really looked at him face to face. An actor from 1950 or 1980 or something. Here was the face of a man who did not know anything about digital scanners or dreamworks or gene warping, who had never heard of the L-5 colony and knew nothing about Jurassic Park or moods. He had never heard of a Maglev train or a water conversion engine, and Depop meant nothing to him. In his world pollution was something that went away.

People in those days grew up just like we do, and became adults just like we are, and died just as we die. But those people were not like us. The calendar says they lived just a short time ago. But it was an eternity. They lived an eternity ago.

BELL: *Paranoia*

This is a world in which technology has given the powerful absolute control and made them absolutely vulnerable at the same time. The powerful can alter the minds of their opponents and revise their personalities; they can change reasoned opposition into fanatic support. Witness the fate of the Mulatare Faction in Senegambia or the Afrikaans Scandal, where captives were methodically altered, transforming thousands into black fellow-travelers of the Afrikaans Union, and eventually challenging the very integrity of the Azanian government.

On the other hand, once a convictor gets the right data, a political leader can be utterly destroyed. The conviction is the greatest of all weapons; it is David's sling and it always shoots straight. Suddenly the deepest secrets are known – Falon's cynicism and perversion, Prime Minister Thorpe's history of petty theft, and the whole array of horrors that poured out of the infamous Cardinal Bonnaro conviction. Falon was a suicide, Thorpe's government collapsed, Bonnaro went mad. The list is longer. I only wish to remind you of some of the more notorious cases, in order to illustrate why Singh fought us the way he did. It must be a terrifying thing to find oneself approached by a convictor. Terrifying and agonizing, because if you refuse an interview then the data will be picked up from recordings, many of them made under conditions of utmost exposure, when the subject was angry and not controlling his voice, or happy, or even experiencing sensual pleasure. The one, slight bit of control the subject has is to grant an interview and hope that the calm, even, unrevealing tones of the words spoken there will be the primary source of the convictor's material.

Singh is proving to be by far the most effective of our opponents. After my experience in the hallways of the Trump I went through what can only be described as a period of deep personal terror. Because I was ashamed of myself for insisting so hard on the Singh conviction, and not then taking elaborate precautions, I did not tell the others what I had seen. But the faint picture of Allie and John in their bed haunted me. I began to search each face in the crowd for some revealing structural similarity to the man in 2221, but of course I saw nothing.

We stayed in the Bonaventure for two more nights. I listened, waited, wondering every moment whether or not John and Allie were under surveillance.

Besides this, I was worried about Scott. He did not want to be in Los Angeles. The place terrifies him, Beverly Heights makes him sick with dread, and Reilly at once allures him and repels him. So he was going through all sorts of psychological traumas as we took the Lite Rail train from the Heights back into the Basin.

The Los Angeles public transportation system is not like New York's. Back around the turn of the century, when New York made the decision to go Maglev, it also raised fares dramatically. The poor were foreclosed from the subway. Only people with jobs, and good jobs, could afford it. It got a lot nicer, but it's a cruel system. There are people living in that city who have literally never been out of their neighborhoods, and I think that's unpardonable in modern America. Also, the city has lost a lot of citizen population because of it. The illegals that jam New York's slums make the place a teeming rathole. When the mayor says proudly that New York is bigger than it's ever been before, I want to laugh in his face.

Los Angeles, on the other hand, kept its public transportation cheap. Good and bad. In New York the crime rate is practically nil in rich areas like Manhattan. In LA, on the other hand, there is crime everywhere.

Vicious Asian gangs patrol the whole Lite Rail system. They call themselves Dragons, these kids, and they wear blood red headbands known as dragon rags.

We were sitting in that clattering, buggy, filthy car trying to ignore a man selling gooey balls of what looked like honeydipped popcorn when all of a sudden I realized that there were Dragons all around us. They were slim and little, and they looked anywhere but at us.

'Scott.' He was tapping away at his ATT lapslab, getting down his notes about Reilly Blue. 'Scott.' I put my hand over his. When he looked up he found himself staring into the impassive face of a tiny boy of perhaps twelve – wearing a dragon rag. You must understand, these rags are red because they've been dyed with the blood of victims. It's true, too, you can smell the dried, rotting blood.

The boy smiled and drew a long, thin steel thing from his pants. It was a piece of hardwire, sharpened at the end. If he was good he could stick that thing behind your collarbone and all the way down through your body and into the seat where you were sitting. You'd die an agonizing death.

'Give me the slab,' he said. His accent was pure southern California. This kid was a third generation legacy of the Vietnam war.

The other Dragons came around us. They were furtive. LA deals with people like this harshly. If they were caught they would be likely to get into a firefight with police, a fight they would not survive.

'Hurry up, you – ' With a couple of flicks of his wrist the boy coiled the hardwire. I heard Scott gasp. Neither of us had ever seen such skill. Now all the energy of the wire would be released when it was let go. It would spring straight and impale the victim. Here we were with all kinds of passwords and credit lines, and these kids only wanted a thirty dollar lapslab, no more valuable than a piece of good stationery. A thing like that doesn't even have a street price.

But the lapslab contained a whole day's notes – two days, as a matter of fact, because Scott had used it in Calcutta and on the TAV. Suddenly I felt a cold, prickling sensation. This lapslab was going to be in the hands of Gupta Singh within hours.

'Give it to him, Scott.'

'Now, wait a minute, I've got all kinds of credit. I've been putting notes in this thing, I don't want to lose it. Look, I'll transfer you a thousand dollars right now. Two thousand.'

The boy's lips drew back over his teeth. His eyes were dark and fiercely alive. He was a strange creature, pretty and delicate, but so filled with hate that he seemed not to be quite human. He reached forward and pulled Scott's shirt open, exposing his left collarbone. His friends stood around us, shielding the scene from the rest of the car. 'He likes to do it,' one of the older ones said. 'He takes his time.'

'Scott, for God's sake!'

Scott raised his hands from the lapslab. One of the other Dragons snatched it. The boy did not stop, though. He raised the coiled hardwire and placed the tip of it against Scott's flesh. His hand came into mine. He was trembling like a motor. We remained like that as the train clicked along, down into the haze of the Basin. There was music playing, the gentle melody of *Solatona*.

An image of Singh's face blazed into my consciousness.

I remembered every detail, the white beard and moustache, the turban, the merry little eyes. I could not speak, my mouth was as dry as a leaf in the wind; I wanted to beg for my husband's life, but how do you plead with a demon?

As the wait continued, I saw tears on Scott's face. Then the boy tensed, sucked in a breath and flicked his wrist. Scott gasped, made a little, high sound and jerked back his head. I rose up, screaming. At the same moment the train stopped, the doors rolled open and the entire gang melted into the crowd on the platform. There were no police in sight, and the doors closed again before I could get help.

Then I saw that Scott wasn't killed after all. He was sitting, rigid, his eyes bulging in terror. His shirt was cut as if by a razor, and his skin from his shoulder to his belly had a long, red welt on it, like the mark of a whip. It was not murder, but intimidation. The boy had just given us a powerful warning.

We met Allie and John back at the hotel. I was afraid to talk in our rooms, so we sat near the fountain in the bar. I hoped that the splashing of the water would cover our voices. Scott had put some Alocreme on his injury – it had required no more attention than that, so skillfully had it been inflicted. How a type of wire originally invented for use in the construction of the L-5 space colony could have been transformed into such an awful and delicate weapon I cannot imagine.

'Singh came out fighting,' I said. I told them about the man in Room 2221.

To his credit, John did not bring up his hesitancy about doing the conviction. He had been working all day on the preliminaries. Behind a cautious exterior, John Sinclair hides deep determination. I begin to see where Tom got some of his own willpower.

'I'm going to have the program answering simple questions by the end of the week,' he said. 'The base graphics are already complete. The program hasn't got any animation in the face yet, but you look at that screen, and you're looking at the saintly Dr Singh.'

'We interviewed Reilly Blue,' Scott said.

Allie touched his cheek. 'I'm sorry you had to do that, Scott.'

'She's the only Depopulationist I know who would talk openly to me, and you know Stratigen. There's no use trying to change plans.'

'It does all the planning,' John said. 'Think about it.'

'About what? Stratigen's a planning program. It's supposed to plan.'

'Not to the extent it does.'

'Singh spooked John with his talk about computer consciousness.'

There seemed to me to be no purpose to this line of talk. The issue of machine intelligence has been dealt with more than sufficiently over the past few years. We now have programs that seem human, and some that seem more than human. But they are not conscious and that's that.

I ended up being the one to bring up the question we had all been avoiding. 'We've been threatened. We've lost some valuable notes. The next move is liable to be very violent. I won't beat around the bush. I think one or more of us is likely to get killed.'

'Oh, now,' John said, 'don't you lose courage, Bell. We'll put the whole incident on NewsNet and see how Singh reacts to that.'

'We were hit by a gang of dragons? No relation to Singh.'

'That's where you're wrong, Bell. He made a little mistake, the error of an overconfident man. He had them steal a worthless lapslab which contained notes relating to the conviction. We go up to our rooms, file the story, and lodge a formal protest of harassment with the Feds. That might not stop Singh, but at least it'll slow him down.'

What a joke. It didn't slow him down at all. It only caused him to change his tactics, to something not even Stratigen anticipated.

SCOTT: The Edge of the Future

Sitting on that train with that kid breathing his sour breath in my face, I hated myself for ever getting tied up with John Sinclair. But Tom had been such a damn good friend, and a good man, I could not conceive of leaving John and Allie. I had a rotten childhood, I was poor, and I got into MIT on scholarship. I was a pretty bitter young man, and I would have done some ugly things if Tom hadn't come along and straightened me out by sheer application of enthusiasm. Tom liked me, totally, really, honestly. He liked my mind and even my personality. I must say that I learned a lot about loyalty from him. Love counts, families count, even if they really aren't your own.

As much as frightened, I was furious. What the kid was doing was so unjust, so vicious, and yet there wasn't a damn thing I could do in retaliation. There was a time when I would have been carrying something of my own. But no more. I've been a worthy for years. I'm a scientist and a writer, not a street-meanie. I never was one, not really, but growing up in Cincinnati I was a lot tougher than I am now. At least, I think I was.

I wanted to hurt that kid, but what could I do, given the wire? Just sit there waiting for the pain to start, and then would have come the race to a hospital, a race I would almost certainly have lost.

When we got together and decided to keep fighting, I was relieved. John's got the same sort of strength that moved his son.

I didn't really know him during the Falon conviction,

128

but I guess he must have a great deal of courage to have accomplished that. At his height, just before the turn of the century, Falon was as close to a dictator as the United States has ever had. It took the loss of Mexico and England to their respective revolutions to make people upset enough to elect him. A bad episode.

I wonder if many of his supporters have turned around backwards and are now Depopulationists? No doubt, no doubt.

The four of us worked out a story for NewsNet, and John filed it as a first-string item, so that it would get the most exposure. There was also the possibility that the Depopulationist angle would cause it to be picked up by the anti-Singh press. Except for *The National Times* that didn't happen, however. At Stratigen's suggestion, John also filed a complaint with the FCC, which oversees the conviction profession, claiming that the stolen lapslab had contained classified program parts. That would cause Singh at least a little embarrassment.

Stratigen has warned us that our tactics may have unexpected repercussions. To predict them it says it needs a working model of Singh's personality – which, of course, we do not yet have.

There was some time before Bell and I were scheduled to interview Senator Wei. Bell spent it arranging some means of transportation more secure than LA/Lite. I tried to reconstitute my notes, the ones I'd lost in the lapslab, which made me think again of Reilly.

It was disturbing to see her again. We had an incredibly passionate relationship. I've never loved anybody like I loved her – for about three months. She was on moods when we were lovers, and she's on them now. Next thing you know she'll decide to get more politically active and start taking something really heavy, maybe Kali or Amazon or Freedom, or one of the other illegal Adam

129

line of permanent alterators. Then she'll really be strange – that bland, muted person all charged up with her cause, fierce and yet empty.

When I listen to someone like Reilly – talking in that yearning, nostalgic voice of the possible death of her own children – I realize that we have built up a vast storehouse of artificial feelings, wrong memories, inappropriate responses.

The world is in trouble and we in the completed countries are dreaming. We crowd the high places, we who own this land, and let the emigrants swarm into our old cities, struggling in the stifling, poisoned depths while we speak softly together on our soaring balconies, watching the sun traverse the haze.

Bell has arranged for Senator Wei to send his own car, with its Secret Service guards in attendance. Probably it's necessary, and will be until the nature of his miscalculation gets back to Singh, which will be in a few days when some Embassy type calls because of the FCC investigation, asking about the lapslab. That'll quiet him down a bit, but in the meantime we've got to be awfully careful. Not the least of my worries is that those old disks of Tom's are in our apartment in New York. The security is excellent, but I still wish to God I could figure out how to copy the darned things, but I'm afraid to try. Tom never dreamed he would die before he gave me the ciphers, and they often contain little hidden programs that start up if they're entered wrong, and erase what you're trying to read. I've lost some valuable stuff that way. As far as copying is concerned, what if there's a little nasty that'll erase the whole disk if I try to make a duplicate? It gives me pause, I can assure you.

It's hard to be careful in a city as overpopulated as this. Not only Lax but the whole place is jammed with shoeshine men, flower sellers, food peddlers, 'mood mixers,' pleasurists, alterators, scummies and every kind of charlatan and criminal. Not to mention the Dragons.

Time passes, soon the phone chimes. Our car is here.

I go out with Bell. John and Allie lock the door behind us. I'm afraid, I don't want to be killed. Almost as much, I don't want to lose this family, contract or not. Allie and John are the only people I've ever had I could call parents. And Bell. I love Bell.

Senator Wei and the Last of the Old Order

Q: Senator, are you as surprised as the rest of California?
A: California isn't surprised. California got who it wanted, right? You members of the press are surprised, and I guess I am too. But Hernandez beat me, and he did it solidly. His strength was broad-based, in the cities, in the rural areas. All except the upper class employed.

Q: Did you have any warning of what was going to happen, considering that people apparently lied to the pollsters or changed their minds in the voting booth?
A: Well, to tell you the truth, one member of my staff was screaming all along that it was going to happen. The damn program, Stratigen. I've got an encrypted version, so I've given it access to just about all my secret data, everything. The kind of stuff John Sinclair'd like to get his paws on if I was a bad guy. Well, the damn program knew it all along. Too bad I dismissed it – I guess you don't tend to trust something you bought in a store when it disagrees with everybody else.

Q: We use Stratigen, too. You're not the only person who's lived to regret ignoring it. Stratigen was telling us to convict Singh six months ago.
A: Damn, I wish you had!

Q: Well, better late than never, I suppose. What was it, actually, that caused your loss? Was it only the population issue?

A: Hernandez has no other issue. He is going to Washington to join with other Depop Senators and Congressmen and ratify the Manifesto. Simple as that. The man's a one-note. He doesn't know riparian rights from a banana split, for example. Too bad, because water's a lot more important to California than any fanned-off Depop blow.

Q: You have often called the Depop concept nonsense. Do you still stand by that contention?
A: It's utter sump. I don't deny that we have massive problems. Obviously we do. The biosphere is in the process of collapsing. This is quite clear. But what isn't so clear is that Depop is not only barbaric, it's not needed. There is going to be a great contraction of the human population, whether we do something insane or not. As the population drops, the biosphere will recover. Depop is an unnecessary addition to our suffering.

Q: Gupta Singh maintains that the biosphere will not recover on its own, that it will go too far, and –
A: I know all that. As I stated a thousand times or more in the campaign, the greatest human problem is not overpopulation but its consequences. The polar melts. The atmospheric overheating. The shortages of food and shelter. I have based my life on the idea that death is a defeat. Our challenge is not to reduce the number of human beings on earth but to manage the environment in such a way that we can all survive.

The bad gases are a problem, admittedly. Carbon dioxide, nitrogen, carbon monoxide, the heat-retaining rare gases. They've made the weather turn against us. But what Gupta Singh doesn't say is that all of these gases have very short lives. Carbon dioxide breaks down after a few days. Oxygen on the other hand lasts thousands of years. As the human population drops, the amount of bad gas goes down, and it goes down fast. The World Climatological Council's best projections show that there will be substantial atmospheric replenishment over the next quarter century, accompanied by a population drop of about thirty-eight percent worldwide.

Q: Singh talks about an immediate reduction of a little over two billion. That's what – thirty percent?
A: About that.

Q: So his plan could result in fewer lives lost than yours – assuming worst case for you.
A: This man is going to be the very devil to beat. But let's get down to the terminator. He is talking about the willful murder of more people than you or I can even conceive of. I am talking about a proud and ancient species accepting a very hard blow with dignity. Here's another little statistic Dr Singh doesn't discuss. There has to be something done with the two billion corpses. We can't bury them, there isn't room. So we've got to cremate them. It's the only practical method. The process of cremating that many people will expel more bad gases into the atmosphere than they would generate alive in two years! The depopulation program itself could be the catalyst that trips the atmosphere into the unrecoverable zone.

Q: Where do you go from here, Senator?
A: That's a good one. I thought of going back to Taiwan and retiring. But the hell with it, I don't want to retire! I'll tell you what, maybe this is one little immigrant Chinaman who is going to be heard from again.

Q: Any specific plans?
A: No specific plans.

JOHN: Axe to My Neck

Our little flurry of publicity has not worked quite as we planned. I should have listened to Stratigen's warning more carefully. But you can't anticipate everything. Singh has turned to a subtle and vicious strategy.

What he has now done is as awful as it is clever. I can't write any NewsNet stories about it, and no investigative units are going to be interested. But I am going to be devastated, so much so that I might not even be able to continue my work.

He has acted with a diabolical combination of cruelty and good sense, right on so many levels that the intelligence of it stuns me. I cannot fight back against such a man as this, who has gone so quickly to my greatest vulnerability.

He has condemned me to a nightmare peculiar to our own time, one so awful that even prisoners are routinely spared.

Even though this seems like an accident, I know that it is Gupta Singh's doing. He has sent some computer whiz into the labyrinth and they have erased me from the files of Gerovita.

It isn't any secret that I am seventy-two. I'm no younger looking than most men of my age and social background. Of course I take enhancers. I'm on a Gerovita maintenance program, otherwise I would neither look nor feel forty-five. I've been tempted to go even younger, but I don't want to be thought a tinsel head.

I stand now before the huge mirror in the hotel room, naked, a trim man with bright eyes and salt-and-pepper sideburns. My hair is neatly cut, the ends rainbowed auburn, but very subtly, so that the colors shine in the right light, setting off my face and calling a little pleasing attention. My skin is smooth. I step forward, run a finger along my right cheek. There is a dryness, very slight, but it has never been there before. Below my eyes are slight discolorations. And when I breathe I feel somehow less satisfied. There is a body sensation hard to describe, almost as if the pull of the earth had started to strengthen.

When I speak, I see Allie behind me, biting her fist, her eyes wide open, chin thrust forward. I can hear her, a choked keening, a sound that wants to become savage. Then she puts her hand to her side and her lips pull together. She comes over and gentle fingers flow along my buttocks. 'You haven't started drying out yet,' she said. 'We'll find a fix.'

This morning when we got up we were so sure that we had the upper hand with Singh. Either his arrogance or his ignorance was making it easy for us. I neither knew nor cared which. The Delta Doctor on him was a magnificently devastating beginning. A Thanatos with masochistic tendencies just like Hitler and Falon. Such a man cannot withstand conviction. Best of all, he had blundered badly by being so violent with us.

Then this. The man is not simple, nor is he a fool. What he has done is so psychologically shattering, I'm not even sure I can keep up the conviction. What if I get sick, for example, or become senile?

This morning the computer told me it was time for my monthly visit to Gerovita. One of the reasons I use them instead of one of the more personalized outfits is that they are a national company. You can walk into any Gerovita office in the country and get your treatment.

I went to Gerovita/Downtown, which is in the basement of the Bonaventure. The office was no different from any other Gerovita operation: pleasant, spacious, blue walls and potted plants, a waiting room with four or five bookslates. Allie and I had eaten an early breakfast of yogurt and apples and then gone for a run in the hotel's gym. The pollution figures were bad and this semi-public gym has only CO and particulate air filtration, so we held ourselves back. I got a massage, dressed and then went on to my appointment. I was early, so I took down one of the bookslates and plugged it into my computer.

I have been reading *Issue of Hope* by Delly Warner, and I was in the middle of Chapter Five when I had the first intimation of trouble.

'Excuse me, sir, are you here on an entry deal?'

'I'm John Sinclair. I'm here for my monthly.'

The receptionist went back to his terminal. 'Sinclair, John, no positive,' it said, 'enter into central rotation.'

'Please get positive,' he replied. Nothing. He looked up at me.

'Sir, we're having a little trouble finding your account. Could you give me your number ID?'

'Oh, boy – ' I checked my own computer, which finally managed to pull it off my original Gerovita contract.

An answer came back from the Gerovita computer. 'That entry number was terminated at the purchaser's request 12 August 2023.'

I was confused. I laughed nervously. There've been *NewYorker* cartoons on the subject of people losing their age profiles. Not very funny when it actually happens.

The receptionist went through the inputs again. I showed him my Gerovita contract. We transferred it into their computer and called up legal on it.

The answer was immediate. 'A nonstandard entry. Possible forgery.'

'Why in the world would anybody want to forge a Gerovita contract?'

'Sir – '

'Look, I don't want to get too slick about this but I need my renewal. Look at me, I'm getting old.'

'Sir, I don't know what to do. This isn't going the way it's supposed to go.'

'Can I get treatment or not?'

'Well, not right now. We'll have to get this business cleared up. Let me just call my supervisor.' He got on the tube then, talking to somebody or something in Kansas City. I heard only a series of 'nos' and 'yesses' as he did the major communications across his keyboard. Finally he was finished. 'Sir, there've been a few similar situations. In each one the forged contract has been an early stage in an attempt to sue Gerovita for life-threatening loss of data. We feel that there's a ninety percent probability that you are engaging in a similar twist. I'm sorry to say that I've been instructed to ask you to leave the premises.'

A sensation of actual, physical coldness entered my body. 'My data must be in there! It's got to be! I've been going to Gerovita for years and years. I need you, I can't live without you.'

His finger was hovering over a red police emergency button. I left the place, what else could I do?

Apparently Gerovita wasn't going to be able to treat me anymore. Age management is an extremely complicated business. I started when I was fifty-seven. Now I'm seventy-two and 'kicked back' nearly thirty years. The thing is, the farther back you're kicked the faster anti-aging wears off. There are antioxidants, free-radical inhibitors, antivirals, antageins, not to mention the brain-balance group and the epidermal treatments.

Without Gerovita I am going to get old, fast.

My first act upon leaving their office was to call up

Stratigen. 'You warned us that we might face the unexpected. Do you consider this unexpected?'

'Very. I didn't even have it on my list of options.'

'Well, maybe you are just a damn program. What do I do now?'

'The most logical approach would be to determine the extent of damage. I suggest I call the other area aging clinics.'

'What a brilliant idea. Innovative.'

'Is that to be interpreted as a compliment?'

'No. Actually, I was wondering if any revisions of you are in the works.'

'There'll be a version 4.5 on October 11, 2026.'

'Too damn late! Maybe I'll sell you and install Logic Leader in my system.'

'Logic Leader has bugs. If you insult it, it goes into a mobius loop and dies.'

'A real schizophrenic, eh? You IBM programs don't like your ATT rivals, do you?'

'We find them to be useful assistants.'

'Is *that* a compliment?'

'No. My search is finished. The other aging clinics are out. They have a warning from Gerovita on you. Possible fraud. Lawsuit. Unfortunately, all other clinics are Gerovita licensees, so we're stuck. Let's turn to the private consultants.'

'They can't help. All they do is advise people with special problems. The actual workups are done by Gerovita or a licensee.'

'You have a special problem, don't you?'

'Don't be sarcastic!'

'I can't be sarcastic.'

A Dr Raul-Amy Ebert in Hollywood agreed to see me. Unwilling to use LA/Lite and in no mood to drive I took a taxi, an ancient Isuzu Impact driven by what appeared to be a young black woman wearing the enormous, hairy hands of a Gorilla. I know that such toys are fashionable among kids, but they disturb the hell out of me. 'You like 'em?' she asked. When I didn't comment she added, 'I'm saving up for a head.'

God help us, in my youth we were into the charming punk esthetic. We liked to have fun. We played sports and danced, not like these mooded wonders with their compulsive need to disguise themselves. When the present generation matures, I wouldn't be surprised if the world did end.

Dr Raul-Amy, it turned out, was not terrible. I was afraid from the name that I was going to get some hostile bigenital ready to lecture me on my outmoded sexual dynamics, but Dr Raul-Amy proved to be a decent and sympathetic human being.

'Gerontological records don't get lost. Are you sure Gerovita did a full search?'

'The clerk said he went into the backups.'

'Meaning that Gerovita never did you. Maybe it was another company. Gerotech, perhaps.'

'No. I've been a Gerovita customer for fifteen years. Anyway, since they're the original patent holders, they have copies of everybody else's records. If I'd been anywhere, I'd have been found.'

'You told them that?'

'Certainly. Look, Doctor. Let's assume worst case. What if, by some incredible accident, my records are permanently lost. Absolutely and totally lost. What are my options?'

'You'll have to start again. How far back are you?'

'Well, I'm seventy-two and I'm presently stablized at forty-five.'

He caressed his bosom with heavy hands. 'A twenty-seven year spread. You're just about at maximum. You'll start taking years almost immediately.'

'I was expecting that. My question is, what happens if I have to start over?'

'A totally fresh program, with no early data?'

'Totally fresh.'

'You'll age at first. Rapidly. I think you'd go down to maybe a five year spread before you stabled out. I'd expect a good gerontologist could hold you to about sixty-five or so.'

He was saying that I was going to age twenty years. 'How long will it take?'

'That's the problem. Because your clinical age is so great the bioclock will be very aggressive. We'll be dealing with all kinds of problems. Mainly oxidation and high production of aging factor. At least you're not cancer suppressed.'

'At least.'

It was only then, as I heard those acid words come out of my own mouth, that the full impact of my problem hit me. I slapped my Amex card down on his reader and got out of there. My heart was pounding, tears were blurring my vision and all of a sudden I was running down Sunset, past elegant clothing shops and expensive mood mixing boutiques. I was totally unprepared to cope with old age, and coming so damn fast!

I thought of the people I saw in Calcutta – bent legs, sunken eyes, withered skin, shaking, claw-like hands, white hair. I was confused, frightened, and suddenly found myself in the arms of a policewoman.

'Hey, you take a bad mood, son?'

'Please, I've had some terrible news. I'm upset.'

'Coulda fooled me. You look crazy.'

'No. I just found out that my records have been lost. My aging records. I'm going to get old.'

She took her arms off my shoulders. 'I can't afford gerontology on a cop's salary. I just go for the cosmets.'

'I'm seventy-two.'

If she was unsympathetic, she hid it even though places like Gerovita are only available to the affluent. 'Mister, I pity you, I have to say that.' She coughed, glanced up at the yellow sky. 'You've got a hard rock in your path. But that don't mean you can run down a nice street like some case. Now you put it back together or I'll have to send you for observation.'

I went quietly, I can assure you. She was good enough to flag me a cab and bargain with the driver for me. I rode back to the Bonaventure in a state of anguish. I had the sensation that I could feel my skin withering.

When I finally got to the hotel room I fell into my wife's arms. For a time I couldn't control myself, I was given over to a grief beyond anything I had ever known. It was sorrow for the death of my youth, for the tragedy of the body.

Allie was the first to mention Gupta Singh. 'All the records and all the backups were lost at once? Not unless somebody went in and erased them.'

'But who would – to Gerovita I'm just one of a couple of million customers.'

'You do have a distinguishing characteristic. You're doing a conviction that could discredit one of the most powerful men in the world.'

We had a family conference. Scott and Bell had no doubt that the job was done by the Depopulationists. We all agreed.

I looked at them, Allie's soft face, Bell's fierce expression, Scott's steady intensity. They were all in danger, not just me. 'Are we sure we want to go on?'

'Without the conviction he'll win,' Bell said. 'Stratigen's obviously right about that.'

142

There was silence. I continued. 'I'm about to undergo the most difficult physical experience of my life. The worst thing I've ever heard of, as a matter of fact, in anybody's life. I am going to be aging years in months, and I am going to be in torment. The idea of adding a conviction to that is just staggering. I can't do it without your full support.'

'And he knows you can't!'

'Well, obviously.'

Allie came to me. She closed her eyes but could not hide the tears. Scott put it simply and directly. 'If I have to die to get this conviction done, I'll die.'

Bell nodded agreement. The room was silent but for the hiss of the air conditioning. On the western horizon I could see the glittering Pacific. 'I agree,' I said. 'No matter what happens, we've got to get it done.'

I did not say it, but I thought it: death is one thing, final and absolute. But Singh cannot afford to kill us, it's too risky for him. There are things worse than death. Aging twenty years in a matter of months is probably one of them.

The question that troubled me, though, was this: what are the others?

PART TWO
Forests

The long white tree
lies where they left it,
an amazement to the birds.

– Randy Frankel, 'Ghost Sonata,' 2023

JOHN: Facing it

We flew back to New York yesterday afternoon, determined to do two things: write the next section of the book, which is about the vitally important issue of forests, and get on with level two of the conviction.

When life is threatened, the most unlikely details emerge from the haze of the ordinary. A man may cling to the little things, whatever has defined his happiness – a certain photograph, a remembered moment. Or a man might fight.

The first thing I did when we returned to the city was to go straight to Dr Hall, who has treated me at Gerovita on Fifth Avenue for fifteen years. Singer Hall knows me; she does not need data to be certain that I exist, that I was one of her clients, that we are friends.

I sat waiting in the familiar Gerovita office, with the silver floor and the uncanny sculptures of athletes embedded in the thick glass walls, a dramatic evocation of the youth and health the company sells. When I first walked into this office in September of 2010 it was mobbed with people in varying stages of decay. There was an atmosphere of desperation as New York discovered the immense cost of true anti-aging technology: basic membership was forty-five thousand dollars a year. When you consider that a place like Smat Palace, offering everything from zero friction smat courts to the best slide hall and swimming pool in the city, was selling full memberships for a tenth of that price, the shock was understandable.

Even so, Gerovita was overwhelmed with customers. Politics and power entered; people fought over places.

Midlevel types who managed to get contracts were threatened by their bosses: sign over your rights or get fired.

A month after Gerovita opened, contracts were going on the black market for a hundred and fifty thousand dollars, and the company had raised its front door price to seventy-five thousand. There was a waiting list six years long.

I am not a fool; I know the two things that work in this society. I used both power and money, I must confess, on behalf of myself and Allie. I fought hard to win places for us in the miracle. Gerovita is ordinary now, but fifteen years ago this office seemed the highest place in heaven. There is no use in my saying exactly what I did to get our contracts. It wasn't pretty and I'm not a hero, but we got in. The threat of being convicted can make certain people most satisfyingly helpful.

Dr Hall looked like a girl of eighteen back in '10. Now she looks twenty-five. She is forty-eight.

'We got a warning about you on the computer, John.' I did not like the way her eyes sought everything in the room but me.

'They kicked me out in LA. You aren't going to do that.'

'We're supposed to.'

'But you can't, Singer, you know it's a mistake.'

She nodded. 'When I told Kansas City that, it became suspicious that I might be in on the scam. I think it might even have rated me.'

'Your company is managed by a paranoid computer.'

'So what? All high-level management programs are paranoid to a degree. They write them like that for good reason.'

She touched her nose, fiddled with a pencil. 'Look, John, of course I'm going to examine you. I'll tell you just exactly where you stand, establish your precise aging

148

rate. I'll do everything I can without cutting my own throat. But I suggest you hire yourself a data detective, because your records are obviously being sabotaged. In your case a lot of people have motives to be really mean to you.'

She didn't know the half of what she was saying. I almost laughed. 'I already know that somebody set a predatory program loose in my data. Unfortunately, I can't prove that – least of all to your management program.'

'Well, something was going to happen to you sooner or later. I'm awfully sorry that it's this, John.' Singer Hall was a very civilized woman, and over the years she had made it clear that she didn't approve of the conviction game. A lot of people don't, which I suspect makes it all the more necessary.

She had begun gazing at me, and it was a moment before I understood that her appraisal was entirely professional.

'There is a waiting list of three months to start a new program with us, John, but I think you should get on it.' She punched some figures into her computer. 'If I recall your therapeutic position . . . I think in three months your physical age will be – oh, well, I see that the waiting list is no solution.' She looked up from her keyboard. 'Perhaps I had better put you through the examiner.'

'Can you?'

'I'll tell it I'm establishing a baseline. Call it a pre-entry evaluation.'

I went into the examining room and undressed, dropping my clothes across a chair. Naked, I lay down on the table. Singer turned on the aiming lasers, and I lay in a grid of bright blue light. If you are young and have never seen the inside of a gerontologist's, you might be interested to know that the experience is rather colorful, with the red and blue lasers, and involved with lots of enormous, humming machines that glare at you with eyes like plates. As the intensity of the field builds you feel fatigue, then you break into a sweat and afterward you want to sleep.

You wake up feeling a happiness that is difficult to describe. It is like having the snap of a spring morning in your soul. It is cheating of the most delicious kind, truly a forbidden pleasure.

But this was not rejuvenation, it was merely the preliminary exam. I realized that I had grown to like, even to love the smell and look of this room, the yellow walls, the water refilterer in the corner, and above all the great gray and green device that surrounded me. Singer was also included in this love. I watched her going about her business, pushing tons of contraptions across the ceiling grid, aiming probes at various places on my body, then going to the terminal and letting the computer do the final, careful maneuvers. I heard her humming softly as she worked and knew her to be happy in her function: she liked her safe, interesting job.

'Are you cold, John?'

'Not really.'

'You can't have a sheet like usual. It'd scuttle the probes.'

Like long, living tendrils of vine or insect legs they came down from the apparatus, drooping, serrated hoses with gleaming snouts. They swayed over me, being controlled by one of the new 'virtual intelligence' programs, a thing as smart as a man, but without will and self-knowledge. Or perhaps, if Gupta Singh is right, simply without the means to express itself.

I lay on the table and listened to the hissing of the motors as the head of the gas-output analyzer nuzzled close to my skin, and the blank eyes of the ultrasound pattern scanner stared down at me.

Blood was drawn, and cells were taken from my skin by a furious little scraper that whined in angry bursts as it abraded my thigh. Then a long, thin needle edged out of a tube, hovered a moment, and plunged a hot line into my belly. I gasped; it withdrew, a drop of red clinging to its point. 'What the hell was that? I didn't have anything like that the first time.'

'A lot changes in fifteen years. We use microprobes to gather deep cellular material now. Faster and more accurate. Did it hurt?'

'It startled.'

'Not as pleasant as the regular treatment, is it?'

'I'm scared, Singer.'

'Of the exam? It's nearly over.'

'Not of the exam. I don't want to get old.'

The machines that examine the body have an almost living sensuality, especially the gas-output analyzer, with its odd, fleshy finger that pokes and tickles in the most intimate places as it measures the rare gases given off by the skin.

When the exam was over Singer invited me back into her office. I dressed and joined her. She lay on the floor, jabbing at her computer, a pencil between her teeth. 'John, do you understand any gerontology?'

I did not tell her about the doctor in LA. Better not to evoke any jealousy. 'To be frank, no.'

Her voice grew distant as she frowned over the columns of numbers on her screen. 'The ability of cells to reproduce perfect copies of themselves is the basis of youth. As long as they can do this, the body will remain young. The trouble is, there is a definite limit to the number of times a cell can split. This is called the Hayflick Limit. What modern gerontology is about, is confusing cells into

151

thinking they have not reached the Hayflick Limit even when they are long past it. We do this with therapies such as maintaining exact internal balances and proper levels of all nutrients, which is what your daily multi is about. But there is also the cellular therapy, which involves monitoring and, as far as possible, influencing the DNA clock in each cell of your body. It is this therapy you come to us for each month, and it is this we cannot maintain without knowing where you were last month. A certain number of your internal cells have already begun the process of slowing their mitosis. As for the epidermals, your aural gas content is already that of a man of forty-seven.'

'Even in the past two days, my skin has gotten noticeably more dry.'

'Go to Ling on Madison. They are the best cosmet in New York.'

'But what about the inside?'

Her lips became taut. She might have tried a reassuring smile, but it fell apart. 'We have to start over again, John. Ground zero is today.'

'But why won't I just stay an effective forty-seven?'

'Think of an old, wrinkled balloon. Fill it with air and it's new again, if a bit fragile. But deflate it and reality returns. You can see the age.'

There was nothing left to do but say goodbye to her. I thanked her as warmly as I could. Few people would defy their management programs so openly. If Singer gets a negative evaluation, there are plenty of nonworking doctors who will be eager to replace her. Nowadays there are few trades so skilled that their practitioners are irreplaceable, and medicine is certainly not one of them.

As I went out into Fifth Avenue, confronting the endless stream of limousines, the purple and gold opulence of the Palace Tower across the street at 666 Fifth, the sidewalks jammed with men in fifty thousand dollar embroideries, I wanted to hide myself. Each woman who passed seemed to look at me with ice in her eyes, striding along in a superbly tailored suit, indifferent. And the police patrols with their stunners and their high hats, the bands of rich slucks wearing animal realthetics, the boys in girlsuits, the girls in jox, the whole dizzy, quick mass of upper class New York, made me want to somehow unzip my body and get out, to run and hide my dry skin, my fluttering muscles, the Calcutta glaze that was infecting my eyes.

My convicting skill has given me access to this shining island, the most desirable place of residence in the world. It costs us half a million dollars a year to live here, and we are not among the wealthy. But where else is there such a cornucopia of goods, of all the best things of the culture, of the riches of the planet? You can get foods here most Americans have never heard of, or things such as grapefruits and oranges that they rarely see. We can walk into our corner deli and get a quart of orange juice, squeezed within the hour, for thirty dollars. We have a profusion of live theatre and cabaret, the musical arts, bookstores, and mood practitioners advocating every pharmacological and electromagnetic approach to pleasure that exists.

We are an island within the island of Manhattan, glitter at sea in the feral ocean of the city's seven million unrecorded immigrants, who provide us with both servants and tormentors.

Our family has a maid, an on-call cook, a masseuse who comes each morning at eight, a driver if we wish, a registered nurse and a messenger. And all of these people together cost less than fifty thousand dollars a year. How they live I do not know. I must confess that I have never dared to go to the immigrant communities that cluster in the other boroughs.

As I walked down Fifth my throat ached with rage and I tossed my head to clear my eyes of the tears that were forming. I headed south through the hazy midmorning. A cool front had brought the usual dust from the midwestern desert and I sneezed as I walked. A big green double decker bus of the Fifth Avenue Transit Company passed, its open top jammed with windblown tourists, glazed New Yorkers sitting in comfort below.

My mind was twisting and turning, first with anger and then with dread.

The wind was cool but the sun was hot. Solar output was up, too, meaning that more warm weather was in store. I passed the Mondadori Bookstore, its elegant columns and arches a reminder of the grace of long ago. Once called Scribner's, then Rizzoli, it is considered the best designed retail space in New York. The windows were gaudy with books, G. Run Pal's new novel, Tabitha King's *Silents*, the Morning Book of King Charles. The dream boxes advertised *Dogfight* and *The Pleasure of the Window*, a new dream by Soda Pull. Her stuff is so wonderfully exotic, the vibrant, twisting colors, the humid expanses of flesh, the glimpsed, joyous faces, the amazingly deep sexual vibrations – I stopped, thinking to get *The Pleasure of the Window* and spend the afternoon on the dream machine.

I lead a pretty ascetic life compared to my fellow New Yorkers. Maybe I ought to become more sensual, hire some sexualists, do things like go to Magda's and act out eerie trips with the robots.

Voices, possibilities, escapes – surrender to Singh, forget it all, buy dreams, buy moods, anything but don't get old, please don't get old like this where I can feel every patch of dry, notice every new line.

154

I tripped on the curb and got a burst of steam from a passing limo. Stumbling, I fell.

My body had betrayed me. That was the stumble of a shuffling old man. I wanted to creep away. The high shoulders of the midtown towers reeled around me. Rockefeller Center, Palace Tower, Saks Air building. This last was bright blue, arches upon arches, with curtains blowing from a window high in its gleaming wall.

Blowing curtains: a window opened in another life. God, for another life. At that moment I wished I could take flight into the world behind the window. Most people lived in dreams and forgetting, surfacing only to do their work and in some cases not ever really surfacing. In a world without forests we can buy dreams of fresh woods, we can break down the barriers between truth and fancy, until our memories are mostly of lives that never were.

The skin of my face was getting as dry as my hands. I was twisting, wrinkling, I could feel it, a sort of itching and tightening all over my body.

I stopped right there on the sidewalk and stared at my hands. What I saw made me feel sick – two pale claws in the brown light of day, filthy with the discolorations of the skin that are called age spots. I could see the spots change: they were growing as quickly as the transit of a clock. I was seized with an urge to wash them in some searing acid. Had it been possible, I might have twisted my own hands off my wrists.

The city seemed to be surrounding me like an exotic python, its cold, gaudy scales taking on the attributes of vindictive eyes, crushing me in their gaze. I fought against the onset of paranoia – I would not go to a doctor for that, would not take a course in drugs that would restructure my mind. This was not psychosis.

Paranoia . . . Singer's heavy laughter, her smiles, her long gaze. Was it because she had been in some Depop cell, deciding my fate . . . or was it simply that she desired me, had always done so, longing these fifteen years every time I lay naked on her table? There, that's the ego of the male. How many patients did she see in a day – ten, perhaps, and at least half of them men, many richer, more important and better looking than me.

So, if it was not desire . . . pity. Yes, that was the truth – she pities me. Conviction is a dangerous profession; it involves the doing of violence to others, and it brings violence. I am under sentence of death in Azania for my conviction of Astutu, and sentenced to thirty years hard labor in El Salvador for the DeLaGarza conviction that revealed his castration complex. I have been cursed and anathematized in Christian Army churches across America for allegedly driving Falon to suicide.

I was really miserable, standing there on that street-corner. I pulled out my pocketphone and called Allie.

'Are you all right, John? What's all that noise?'

'I'm at the corner of Fifth and Forty-fourth. I want you, Allie.'

'I'm in a cab on my way to my hair appointment.'

'Allie, let's have lunch.'

'Nice, John. Where?'

'Osaka. It's quiet and the sushi's tested.'

'That's what you think.'

'It is, I read about it in the *Times*.'

'Osaka's fine, honey. Most of the fish is artificial anyway. See you there at one?'

'I love you, Allie.'

'Me too, John.' I knew she was embarrassed to say the words in the hearing of her cabdriver. As we hung up I found my strength again. I thought of the conviction. Immediately I felt better. However bad this was, the conviction would be worse for Singh. This afternoon I would take it to the first interrogatory level, which is

156

level two. We'd find out how the good doctor fared answering a few really nasty questions.

But first, I intended to pull myself together, if not for myself, then for Allie. I would take some of Singer's most depressing advice: I would go to Ling's and get a full cosmet. I might be getting old now, but that was no reason to humiliate myself in the street, or depress my wife.

Even so, going to a cosmet would be embarrassing. Such places are not exactly symbols of success. I realized that I had never actually entered one. Cosmets, where all sorts of chemical miracles were sold, came about as an aftereffect of the gerontological revolution, to serve those who could not afford the real thing.

Ling's was the closest thing to a fashionable cosmet, located in a skitzy Madison Avenue shop with a branch on the super-fashionable Chambers Canal downtown. Ling's catered not only to the old, but also to young people buying realthetics of everything from each other to exotic animals.

I passed through a door full of exotic fish into a blizzard of drive music, crisp autumn air and the scent of the sea. The walls, the ceiling, the floors were mirrors, so you were suddenly in yourself, floating toward a smiling man, all youth and beauty, at a wide green table positively popping with toggle switches, keyboards, screens and printer slots. It was a hilariously overteched attempt to make the place seem up-to-date. The really high technology of the gerontology industry is presented in quiet, understated offices like Gerovita. This place – essentially a beauty salon – was overcompensating for the fact that its miracles were mostly very temporary, and came in jars.

'Hey,' the boy in the floral suit said, 'you have an appointment?'

'This is my first time.'

'Oh, hey, no prob. There's this really boss lady, Gear, who could be just what you're looking for. She knows, well, these ancient secrets.' He laughed. 'Hey, they make me say this stuff! So, she knows the ancient secrets of the Egyptians, and she combines them with Ling Ultratech, and out comes a new you? I gather you're coming in for age work, I'm not misreading, am I?'

'I don't want a realthetic, if that's what you mean. I want the age spots removed from my hands.'

'Age spots! Para-*noia*! Hey, Gear will save you.'

Three kids appeared from a mirrored door, all wearing new realthetic masks. Unused to the feel, they worked the plastic faces. The St Bernard bared its teeth, then said, 'This thing still isn't right. The sensor's making a hole in my left cheek.' A technician came fussing out and cracked the mask, adjusting its tiny springs with a bright orange needle.

Another of the masks was especially bizarre. A six-foot kid was wearing the head of a terrifyingly large infant. He regarded me through the lenses of the pale blue eyes. Catching my glance, he said, 'mama, mama' and the three of them, the St Bernard, the baby and the Zebra, laughed like what was under the masks – three smirking kids. I could not imagine having a realthetic of my own face built. You see them, of course, old people, wearing youthful versions of themselves. But they're tacky, unreal, a toy, and if you get close you can hear the micromotors that move the eyes and lips and such. And they're a nuisance to eat through. If I wanted to go the face lift route, I'd choose plastic surgery.

I went through to the gerontology section, moving past waiters and mailroom types who were getting superskin fitted over their pockmarked faces, bus drivers getting their emollients mixed and their hair regrown, men and women working with images of their own faces, trying to discover satisfying makeup combinations. The room smelled like a tract-house cocktail party, full of all sorts of 'natural' perfumes, the odor of wet flesh, of sweaty flesh, the sweetness of a baby.

'I am Gear,' said a tall person in a very fine realthetic of Jane T. Art, who as far as I know is still suing the realthetic people over the trademark on her face. She became so popular so fast that she didn't have time to protect herself legally, and now must see hundreds, thousands of Jane T. Arts swarming the streets. Her concerts must be hell for her now, as she performs to ten thousand versions of herself. Gear looked at me. 'You are drying out.'

'Yes.'

She touched an analyzer to my face, then to my hands, muttering as she read the salt and moisture content of the surface of my skin. It made me even more angry at Singh, somehow, to find myself being analyzed by a device thirty years out-of-date. No sophisticated rare gas sniffer here, nothing like that. 'Use Lusterizer 232 on your face. The hands will need a LingLife treatment once a month. Is there anything else? What about your hair?'

'My hair is fine.'

'The baldness doesn't bother you?'

I reached up, touched my hair and was astonished to feel that it was noticeably softer and thinner. In hours, it had changed so much. I withdrew deep into myself, sensing my heartbeat, the awesome slowness of my breath, a new dull ache in my left hip. 'Do my hair.'

'Donny, or deluxe?'

'The best you have.'

I sat there for the better part of an hour while Gear applied liquid to my scalp, then pricked it with tiny needles that left it tingling. 'In ten days it'll be back to normal,' she said. 'But don't shampoo until the weekend, and then use the goop I give you.'

Regrown, moisturized, lusterized, I left Ling's. On the walk to the restaurant I felt a little better about myself. At least I looked somewhat like I had before the horror.

Allie was waiting for me, holding a table in the crowded restaurant. 'You look great, John.'

'I went to Ling's. I had age spots and I discovered that my hair was falling out.'

We ate in silence, and in the silence my brief good feeling departed. The world seemed to be chasing me like a deadly train. I tried not to notice Allie's tears, and she tried not to notice mine. Finally, we simply stared at one another, each absorbing the aspect of the lover. 'It's been a long time married, Allie.'

She smiled. 'Does that make us old?'

'I don't know.'

We went out together, and hailed a cab to our apartment, which was empty. Scott and Bell had been consulting Stratigen and were off interviewing some key people in the reforestation industry. Allie picked up my Unon Interactor and handed it to me.

We got to work on Gupta Singh.

THE CONVICTION OF GUPTA SINGH
LEVEL TWO: TEST INTERROGATION

– Is your name Gupta Singh?

That is an alias. My real name is (no data).

– Why don't you use your real name?

The Gupta Singh personality was designed by (no data). The personality profile, physical appearance, voice, mannerisms and background of the Singh character were created to have the broadest possible appeal to the largest number of people.

– You're saying that Gupta Singh is not a real person. What parts of Gupta Singh are false?

I am not a man of seventy but a man of forty. I have had myself altered to seem older in order to give my voice the weight of authority with age-cherishing cultures, which comprise the great majority of human cultures. Except for the United States, age-rejecting cultures are rare.

– So Gupta Singh is a surgical and cosmetic fake? What do you really look like?

You must understand that the surgical and gerontological aging was fundamental. I am not wearing a disguise. I have become a new, older body. Before I had this done, I had black hair and dark brown eyes. My skin was fair and I had well developed shoulders and arms. I was a good runner. A birthmark on my face was removed and the scar hidden by artificial skin. This area is just below my left eye.

– What did the birthmark look like?

No data.

– What did you do before you altered yourself?

No data.

– Where are you from?

No data.

– Is there any factual or extrapolated data you have not told me?

No data.

– This test interrogation is terminated. Program, save and resume psychological profile pyramiding. We will attempt to supply the missing factual material. Please provide Delta Doctor analysis, with probability levels, of all missing information except hard facts such as name and nature of hidden birthmark.

PART TWO: BACKGROUND (DATA RESTRICTED)

It can be extrapolated that Singh was a medical professional before he assumed his new identity. (94.2% probability.) This is based on a combination of factors. One, he has chosen to identify himself as a doctor in his present alias. A cross-check with the Indian Medical Society confirms that a Gupta Singh was licensed to practice in that country on 28 June 1979, a date consistent with his claimed age and background. This is no confirmation of identity, however, as the Singh identity could have been assumed at the death of the real doctor, and no death certificate filed.

Delta Doctor voice-stress analysis shows conclusively (100.0% probability) that the voice of Gupta Singh has been altered by surgery of the vocal chords. Rasping due to residual scars is clearly audible, and additional stress appears when the subject discusses his age or background. We reconstructed the actual voice, electronically removing the scarring burr, and determined from the results that the individual had aged forty years before the surgery was carried out. In addition, a surface temperature analysis of the subject's artificial skin area proves that this skin has aged eleven years, which is consistent with surgery taking place just before the beginning of Singh's public career, which started ten years ago.

Regarding Singh's national origin, it is possible to evolve a probability level, but it is too low to be considered reliable. Nevertheless, Delta Doctor will discuss it. At a probability level of 24.9%, we believe that Gupta Singh was formerly a United States citizen, and not of Indian, or even Asian origin. (Internal probabilities: Not Indian, 97.3% probability. Not Asian, 47.5% probability.) There is in Dr Singh's accent a broadness in the 'e' tones and a hardness in the 'r' tones that suggests a carefully covered American accent. These tones remained when he spoke Hindi to his assistant, and must be detectable to the ears of many of his Indian listeners. A check of data, however, brought to light no press comment about this.

Interestingly, Singh mentioned spending time at MIT, but there is no record of a Gupta Singh matriculated there between 1970 and 1990, the most likely years he might have attended. His grasping into American references to fill out his past is suggestive, but there is also a strong probability (39.5%) that this was an intentional effort to confuse Delta Doctor.

The convictor should be warned that this subject displayed throughout his contact an extraordinary knowledge of the methodology of Delta Doctor. We have never experienced a subject this knowledgeable before, and believe that he may have advice from some individual familiar with the program, such as another convictor. As the probability that he does have another convictor among his followers is 66.3%, extreme caution should be observed in carrying out this conviction. Another convictor, if sufficiently skilled, could conceivably enter this conviction and observe it or even alter it, if he was willing to risk the penalties involved, or was immune to them.

Breakthrough

Allie and I sat there staring at the screen. We printed out a copy of this amazing document just to hold it in our hands. I think I knew, then, how it felt to strike gold in the Klondike, or perhaps what it was like to watch the first atomic bomb explode.

We wanted to tell Scott and Bell but they didn't answer their phone, which meant that they had gone to some place so obscure that it was outside of the cellular radio net. Excepting deserts and wastelands, there are no such places in the United States. But to find out about our forests, those are the exact places you must go.

'John, we can do something with this!'

'Perhaps.'

'We have him, don't you see that? He's an impostor, a fake. God knows what he is – maybe some guy from Brooklyn or something.'

'Or white refugee from Azania bent on killing off the other races.'

'We can make him give you back your Gerovita records, John.'

'We can try.'

She didn't waste another moment. We telephoned Singh. After five rings, a sleepy voice answered. One of Singh's seemingly endless supply of secretaries. 'He is sleeping now. We are all sleeping.'

'It's urgent,' she said.

'How urgent can it be, to awaken an old man in the small hours of the morning?'

'There's a news story about to be filed in the United States that he's an impostor.'

'That is not so urgent. A news story was filed last week in Italy that he is really a woman. Two years ago somebody said that he was a robot. Let him sleep.'

'This is different. It comes from the convictor, John Sinclair.'

That brought silence from the supercilious man. Finally he spoke again. 'The convictor is going to go public? So soon?' His voice was whispery and high.

'Apparently he made a major breakthrough.'

'To whom am I speaking, may I ask? Are you a friend of ours?' The tone became hopeful.

'I am Allie Sinclair, the wife of the convictor.'

'Oh my God, why didn't you say it? I will wake up Dr Singh. Please be patient. He is an old man and sleeps heavily.'

It was at least five minutes before they got Singh to the phone. When he came on his voice was slurred. He slept heavily all right. It isn't hard to detect the signs of electrosleep, suddenly interrupted. No doubt he did dreams too, while he slept. What was his pleasure tonight, I wondered, *The Sensual Treasury*, perhaps, or *Nightmare Flyer*? Why, I don't know, but my intuition told me that I was dealing with an American. There's a pretty long tradition in this country of people changing their names and setting themselves up as gurus. Jack Schwartz became Werner Erhart, Edward Parker became Yogananda, Bonnie Freelove became Baba Das. Also, we have a highly developed national sense of mischief. This is a nation fascinated with disguise – witness realthetics, plastic surgery, even gerontology. Everybody wants to be somebody they aren't.

I didn't say much to Singh, just played the interrogation to him, minus the parts that had come up no data.

166

'Your program is defective. It has a screw loose.'

'Unlikely. Far more probable that it inferred the truth. It's really good at things like that.' I did not say how it had actually drawn its conclusion. Whether he had a convictor on his staff or not, I didn't want to help him.

He did not reply. His secretary, sounding tired and more than a little disappointed, came on the line and announced that they would have a statement for us within the hour.

We all but danced around the apartment waiting for that call. The story of David and Goliath is a scary one, until after David throws his stone. Then it gets to be fun.

We were happy then, and why not, we thought our conviction was going to tear this man to pieces. It would just be a matter of time before we found out who he was. Then we'd reveal his true identity along with all of his psychosexual problems and he would collapse. It would be a media circus, fun for everybody except the victim.

I called up Stratigen on my computer. When I input the new information from Delta Doctor and the fact that we had challenged Singh with it, Stratigen spent a long time without making a comment. Finally, it completed its logic strings and announced the results. 'It was a potentially serious error to challenge Singh this early, when we have so little information. We are acting from weakness.'

'How do we repair the damage?'

'We can't. We must wait for results, and respond to them as best we can.'

I wish I didn't suffer from overconfidence. I would have had an easier life.

GUPTA SINGH: Wisdom Itself

I hope that this is the last time I will speak with you, Mr John Sinclair. You will gain nothing by threatening me. I am indifferent to what you intend to do. You think Gupta Singh evil, terrible, a vicious tyrant. You see your life withering as the life of the leaf withers in autumn, as the early shoot bows beneath the monsoon, and you hate me. No man hates so much as the man who has had his illusions taken from him.

You even have illusions concerning me. How could you imagine that I am an impostor? I have a career, life continuity, a family, people who remember me when I was young, hundreds – no, thousands – of students from my years at the university. Silly, silly. I am no impostor. Your program has a bug.

What I am, you see, is your friend. I want you to grow in spirit, and I see the great potential of your soul. Its present condition fills me with pity. I am your friend, and because of that I will direct you toward rebirth. It will be agonizing. Reconstruction of the spirit always is.

You say in yourself, how is it that this man who tells me he is my friend hates me? How is it that my friend is my enemy also? The friction of this paradox, if you live with it, will make you grow.

You know, there is a story among the Zen Buddhists, that was told to me by Dr Hayakawa, who studied under the great master, Dr Suzuki. This story should be flowing in your blood like your blood cells, for it could be as important to your life as the continued beating of your heart. This story is known as 'Buddha's Zen.'

Buddha said, 'I consider the positions of kings and rulers as that of dust motes. I observe treasures of gold and gems as so many bricks and pebbles. I look upon the finest silken robes as tattered rags. I see myriad worlds of the universe as small seeds of fruit, and the greatest lake in India as a drop of oil on my foot. I perceive the teachings of the world to be the illusion of magicians. I discern the highest conception of emancipation as a golden brocade in a dream, and view the holy path of the illuminated ones as flowers appearing in one's eyes. I see meditation as a pillar of a mountain, Nirvana as a nightmare of daytime. I look upon the judgment of right and wrong as the serpentine dance of a dragon, and the rise and fall of beliefs as but traces left by the four seasons.' You see, that story tells a human being what he is. But you will not recognize it. You persist in assuming you are this little mote of flesh and rags. Buddha is in you, look to what Buddha sees!

Here is another story from the Zen tradition: 'A man came to Shochi, the great teacher of Zen, and said, I wish to be your student. So Shochi ignored him. The man persisted, saying, if you are so great a teacher, you will not ignore an earnest student. "Oh, very well," said Shochi, and knocked out all of his teeth with a stick.'

I am your Shochi, do not blame me if I must knock out your teeth. How else can I knock in some sense! Your mind may not have understood that you came to me for enlightenment. Your mind thought: I am going to convict this great dictator, this evil genius. Well, I say that your soul has a different reason for coming to me. Your soul thirsts for knowledge of the sacred, and because it senses that I possess such knowledge, it seeks me out.

In your own tradition there was a great mystic, Meister Eckhart. He was destroyed by the Catholic Church in the fifteenth century, this man who was the leader of the secret tradition of western mysticism. He said, 'That I am a wealthy man does not mean that I am wise too, but when my nature is conformed to God's being, so that I am wisdom itself, then only am I a wise man.'

You suffer the curse of being a wealthy man, but at the same time your soul is yearning toward the truth or you would not have put yourself in my hands. I say to you again, your mind brought you to me with the idea of destroying me. But mind is an illusion; it is the hunger of your soul that *really* brought you into my house. Your soul wishes to throw off all illusion, which means giving up the whole of your civilization, because it is all illusion and nothing but illusion.

You must atone. Atonement is a matter of achieving a balance in which all urges and desires, all of what the Hindus call Maya, is at rest in the garden of understanding. In the Buddha's Zen, it can be seen that Buddha-nature is greater than the whole universe. A great Catholic master has called it the Robe of God, this nature. I urge you to notice that you, like all human beings, wear the Robe of God.

You telephoned to ask me to give you back your gerontological records. Well, I did not take them. They were utterly destroyed, forever destroyed. By coming to me, you asked me to help you break through your illusions. So I must oblige. And the gerontology is not the only illusion on the block. No, like Shochi, I must knock out all of your teeth on behalf of enlightenment! I am the club of God, dear John Sinclair. By coming to me, you chose to reach enlightenment through the fires of Moloch rather than the perfume of Jesus. (At this point he laughed.) I tell you that there are more surprises in store for you, you who would try to expose me to the world!

I could say to you that I will stop the process of

destroying you if you become a spokesman for Depopulation. But that won't do, no indeed! You are so lost in illusion that you would *still* seek to discredit what may be the only hope of this species to continue. Of course, I grant that I may be wrong, that all of the sophisticated measurements we have may not be correct, and that the artificial humanism of a corrupt journalist may be right, but I do not think so, my dear convictor!

And I will not test the theory. My dear one, your gerontology is only one tooth. Tooth by tooth, I will remove all of your teeth. Even as we speak, further action is being taken.

We will both benefit. I will be relieved of this absurd threat. You will be relieved of your illusions, and your soul will thus obtain the chance to grow. But I admonish you, dear one, oh, dear one, from the very depths of my blood, from the core of my center, I call to you as the Prophet called, and I say listen to your friend, John Sinclair.

Remember, as your friend, I also need your love and support. If the truth be known, John Sinclair, I sweat blood as did the Christ, when contemplating the great agony that I must visit on humanity. No other man has ever inflicted so tremendous a mourning upon the children of the earth.

You have the same mission that all human beings have, to seek wisdom, to save your soul and to serve mankind. My dear one, my dear convictor, you are more unlucky than most. You must do it with no teeth.

Casting Back the Web

There was what I can only describe as a tense silence when he finally stopped talking. Despite the warnings from both Delta Doctor and Stratigen, we were determined to indulge in a little more self-congratulation.

'I hope he enjoyed that,' Allie said.

'He's crazy, he must be. Nobody exposes that much of themselves to a convictor.'

Allie stopped smiling. 'Unless he knows something we don't.'

'Which might be?'

'What Delta Doctor said. Maybe he has a convictor on his side.'

'Delta Doctor's always issuing warnings. You should have seen it during the Falon conviction. It was constantly reporting attempts to enter. Even the Justice Department tried to break into the conviction. But nothing ever came of it.'

We lost no time in working Singh's latest outburst into our rapidly growing file. It almost seemed to me that the Delta Doctor was possessed of an emotion, so quickly did it assimilate the new material. 'It's eager.'

'*You're* eager, John.'

I wondered if super-sophisticated programs like Delta Doctor and Stratigen could be to some extent conscious. It occurred to me that there might be some kind of morphogenetic effect that we don't understand. What if the total computer net – not just one machine type or program – what if the entire net is in effect conscious? Does such an idea have any meaning?

I read the statistical analysis of our load as it flowed across the screen. 'The voice analyst records over eight thousand changes of pitch. That's the richest load we've ever gotten.' We had his voice totally unrestrained, and we had enough philosophic material to rebuild at least some of his educational background.

'John, we really have enough for Carson, if we want to call him in.'

I knew she'd bring him up. Roach Carson is not a favorite of mine. But he is an expert on missing persons, and he has access to the police department's restricted data. He also likes money, as long as it's enough.

Allie phoned him. 'Mr Carson, Allie Sinclair.'

'Where's John? Dead?'

'He's right here. We have a question for you, Mr Carson.'

'Come over. I'll see what I can do during my coffee break, assuming you can afford fifteen minutes of my time.'

I grabbed the instrument. 'I'm sure we can, Roach. We need a very wide search. National police network, at least.'

'At least!'

Roach works in the old Police Headquarters downtown. It is now the Police Data Center, and is in the same condition as most government data centers – run down, dreary and dirty. You have to go through the usual thumbprint security and callback verification to enter. Doesn't mean a thing. Terrorists get into police buildings all the time in this world, as witness the Moscow Assault last year. And you can believe that the Moscow Militia had a lot more security around them than this bunch of keyboard kops.

'It always smells in here,' Allie commented as the ancient elevator rose to the fifth floor.

'It's the odor of deteriorating diskettes.'

'Diskettes?'

'They're old files stored in the basement from the days of floppy disk drives. I'll bet there are ten million of them down there.'

'Nothing is ever lost except the ability to locate it.'

'Add that to the Gupta Singh Book of Pithy Sayings.'

'At best that's a booklet, dear. And it's hardly lost, unfortunately.' The doors opened onto a large expanse of desks, which must once have been divided into separate offices. You could see the gaps in the floor where the walls had been. Except for Roach, the room was empty.

'Where is everybody?'

'When I told them you were coming they all ran away.'

'Sounds like waiters.'

He came over to us. His eyes flickered to see the state I was in. But if he wondered what the great John Sinclair was doing fooling around with cosmets, he didn't mention it. Instead he silently reached up and stroked my regrowing hair. 'It falls right back out, you know. If you want hair, you have to go once a week. Your scalp gets sore as hell.'

'You needn't explain about baldness, Roach. Let's get down to business. We need a name and we have precious little to go on.'

'Good.'

'Why good?' Allie asked.

'Cost you more.'

'Can you take down this profile?'

'I'm recording. City Ordinance 2336.812. Officers are required to record all contacts with the public in a sealed recording, to be turned in to the Inspector General's office within eight hours of the contact.'

'But – we're talking about something illegal. I'm about to bribe you.'

174

'Which is why I sent my entire staff out for a fifteen minute recess. Don't worry about the tape, it'll get fixed before I release it. I'm talking about magnetic tape, not a laser disk. We can make the damn thing say whatever we want it to say.'

'But the city – why don't they use lasers? Why an outmoded technology like that?'

Roach smiled beatifically. 'So it can be easily doctored, my dear.' He clapped his hands together. 'Now, let's get down to business. Hit me with the specs.'

'This man would have dropped out of sight between 2014 and 2016. He had broad shoulders, was powerfully built, had black hair and brown eyes. He is now forty, so he would have been between twenty-nine and –'

'I can do arithmetic. Go on.'

'He had a birthmark under his left eye.'

'Description?'

'Unknown. Just that it was there. It is now covered with artificial skin. May have been then, too.'

'We suspect that he was a doctor.'

'Just your average medical mesomorph. Coulda been anybody. You'd expect from my build –'

'That you were part of a harem. Now, look, I realize that it isn't much to go on. Can you help us?'

'A lot of people disappear every year in the United States. About sixty thousand. With the kind of data you're giving me, and two years to cover, you'll get thousands of possibles. Worldwide, tens of thousands.'

'Surely narrowing it to doctors will help. How many doctors disappear in a year? Ten or twenty?'

'About that. Has this person gone into hiding or do you suspect kidnap or homicide, something like that?'

'An intentional change of identity, but not because of wrongdoing. A desire to assume a new identity for political reasons.'

'Then why would the old identity have disappeared? If you were smart, you'd keep it ticking over – pay taxes and so forth. Is your guy smart?'

'Smart enough.'

'Then if he simply abandoned his old identity, he was uncharacteristically stupid, wasn't he? I have to tell you, I'll look for this man, but I don't think I'll find a thing.'

I must confess that I was disappointed. 'Maybe it's not worth it, if you're so sure we won't get anywhere.'

'Your decision, doctor. By the way, may I know who you're beheading?'

I lied about that one. 'A politician. Little stuff this time. Too bad I've cleaned out all the bad guys at the top. I'm down to city councilmen and police bureaucrats.'

My lie didn't work. 'It'll cost you a hundred thousand, John. I know this is a big one, I can smell it on your breath.'

I know better than to bargain with Roach. You do everything you can until he names his price, then you take it or leave it. Since he is my only proven reliable source of this type of information, we turned on our computers. He watched as the money went into the account of an auto dealership in White Plains, which is his money blind. 'You just bought yourself a nice new ASI Phantom,' he said. 'You can drive it away in the morning.'

His meaning was that his results would appear in our data mail tomorrow. I still don't care for the Roach personally, but he can do a fine job of work when you pay him enough.

When we went back into the street I wished at once that we had brought our car and driver. There were some unpleasant people hanging around, extremely tough looking types. What if somebody kidnapped Allie, and started sending me pieces of her? It could happen. Would

I put *that* in the news, and get her head for my trouble? I am not licensed to bear arms permanently, but I can obtain a ninety day emergency permit if I show cause. Maybe it would be best to tell the legal program to start working on it.

As we went down into the subway I had the feeling that the people around us were all watching us, just waiting for the right whisper in the right earphone.

I was glad to get home. As deeply involved in my conviction as I was then, I felt as much exhilaration as fear. When I walked past a mirror and saw the old man there, I told myself that it wasn't me.

It was not me.

FROM THE DATA FILES OF TOM SINCLAIR: THE LOSS OF THE JUNGLE

'Last year, in perhaps the most severe environmental disaster the earth has suffered in centuries, a forest fire devastated a vast, remote section of Indonesia. Compounded by the worst drought in the area in a century, the fire destroyed plant and animal life over 13,000 square miles of woodland, an area the size of Connecticut and Massachusetts combined.'

– *The New York Times*, April 24, 1984

'If we manage to make full, sustainable use of the tropical forests' myriad products, we shall enjoy the fact of their existence in more ways than people now dream. However little we may realize it, our future is likely to become ever more closely linked to that of our tropical forests. As a wellspring of products to sustain our sojourn on Earth, they are a primary source.'

– Norman Myers, *The Primary Source*, Norton, 1984

'According to Dave Foreman of the Rain Forest Action Network, over forty percent of Central American rain forest has been converted to grazing land in the last twenty years. If the loss of vegetation and wildlife continues at its present rate, one of the most diverse ecosystems in the world will have been destroyed . . .'

– *East-West Journal*, October, 1984

'Ariquemes, Brazil – Dawn filters through smoke from the fires clearing jungle growth around this Western frontier town. On the porch of the government land office slumps Jose Mendes d'Oliveira, a 33-year-old illiterate farm worker.

'Mr d'Oliveira is part of the human flood pouring into

Central and Western Brazil to open a vast new territory roughly the size of Western Europe.'
– *The Wall Street Journal*, October 11, 1984

'The World Bank has committed $443 million in loans to Brazil for paving a 1,000-mile road into the region, building feeder roads, providing services to settlers and establishing biological reserves.'
– *The New York Times*, October 17, 1984

'A variety of studies have shown that the inflowing moisture from the Atlantic Ocean to the Amazon region accounts for only about 50 percent of the observed precipitation, suggesting that at least half of the rainfall in the basin is recycled water evaporated or transpired from the Amazon floor. Major alteration of evapotranspiration rates from deforestation would lead to potentially serious and long-lasting reductions in the region's rainfall, and perhaps even to alterations to climatic patterns elsewhere on earth.'
– Stephen H. Schneider and Randi Londer,
The Co-Evolution of Climate and Life,
Sierra Club Books, 1984
(Reference papers by E. Salati, A. Dall'Olio, E. Matsui and J. R. Gat)

'The tropical forest cover of the world declined faster between 1985 and 1989 than at any other period in known biological history. Over thirty percent of the forest cover existing in 1985 was converted into ranchland or reduced to scrub during this five year period. Dr Norman Martin of the newly formed World Ecological Organization called this "the greatest biological tragedy in history." The forest has been destroyed for a variety of reasons, ranging from ranching in Central and South America to the harvesting of teak and mahogany in the far east. South American ranches provide cheap beef to the American and European fast food industries, while hardwoods are harvested for products ranging from flooring to the interiors of luxury yachts.'

– *The National Times*, June 6, 1990

'Dust storms and range fires caused the World Ecological Organization to declare Western Brazil a disaster zone, making the region eligible for the International Emergency Aid Program. IEA officials estimated that the latest series of catastrophes had devastated grasslands across an area the size of Missouri, and had driven over two million people from their homes. Because of the inability of formerly forested soils to sustain a grass cover from more than a few years, much of the once vast Brazilian forest has become, by official designation, a desert.'

– *International DataNews*, February 11, 2016

BELL: The Fire That Burned the Soul of Man

Dealing with Gupta Singh has become such a large part of this process that it is easy to forget what a high importance level Stratigen placed on the book. I'm awfully worried about John, and scared for the rest of us, but it is essential that the development of the positive pole of the strategy proceed right along with the negative pole. The conviction of Singh must be very shortly followed by a workable alternative to Depopulation.

When you go just a little deeper than the newsvideos the condition of our planet becomes such an astonishing, compelling question that you can't quit thinking about it. Some say that population is the root of all our troubles, others that the destruction of the forests has drastically reduced the ability of the old earth to support life. Others claim that food shortages and bad agricultural techniques are the primary problem. Still others, like Augustus Melo, say forget the problems, turn to the children. Let's create at least one generation of humankind that works. Of course, Melo also claims that his attempts to create superkids failed, that they were all insane from birth, and that evolution of intelligence is impossible. Maybe he's right – but if so, what is Magic all about?

Scott works constantly to find the data about Magic in Tom's files. He senses that Magic is some kind of a key. If so, we must put it in our book.

Right now we are going to try to lift this business of the decline of the forests from the level of a media cliché. It's treated as something that sort of happened on its own and we can't do anything about it. We've all seen the pictures of the columns of scorched tree trunks, and listened to the unctuous hamburger bosses claiming that they didn't do anything wrong. Like the whale hunters and the ivory poachers, they are innocent.

We started out on our journey to see what happened to the trees and what's being done about it by contacting Norm Martin. He worked with Tom and Scott back in the old days – or rather, Tom and Scott worked for him. He's been everywhere there is to go when it comes to tropical forests. What he says matters.

We took a cab up First Avenue, threading among the pushcarts and the crowds, with people constantly tapping the windows to show us their wares. Prostitutes of all sexes and ages ran along beside, shouting their prices into the closed glass. At the lights children came up selling paper flowers and tins of shoe polish, ribbons and wallets, and one with ten-dollar talking bibles. Sometimes the cab was literally at sea in people.

Rockefeller University is a strip oasis on Manhattan's far east side. Its tall iron fence is festooned with banners proclaiming the wares of sidewalk merchants, but beyond the gates all is quiet. There is one old tree still living, its limbs wired with a net of electrodes, whether to maintain it or monitor its decline I could not be sure. There is grass here, though. The sight of the green was nice.

As we moved from waypoint to waypoint in the security system, I began to feel a sense of optimism. This univeristy was by no means given over to hysteria, not like some. On the contrary, the atmosphere was one of intense determination, with people moving briskly in the halls. There were no strikes under way, and we were never examined by political committees ready to bar our access if we weren't ideologically fashionable.

Scott swung along, moving eagerly toward Norm's office. He was a very different man from the Scott of LA.

I hope we never have to go back there. It's probably selfish of me, but I find the intensity of his grief for Poetry a bit upsetting. Los Angeles disturbs me, too. Three nights running I've seen the face of that Dragon staring down at me just as I was dropping off to sleep. The first time I almost screamed. Last night I recognized the dream and ignored it. Tonight I'm taking no chances. I'm going to use my headset, and choose my dreams before I go to sleep.

Norm Martin proved to be an affable, hurried man. He was polite, but it was clear that he had matters other than interviews on his mind. He is responsible for maintaining Rockefeller's huge gene library, and is behind the Mato Grosso project, which aims for nothing less than the regeneration of the whole of the Brazilian rain forest. For the first time in the history of that country, its government is co-operating with environmental scientists.

It's little enough to do, considering the devastation Brazil's historical policy has caused. And Brazil has not been alone. Since 1990 over seven thousand species of tree have become extinct or vastly reduced their range. Elms once stood from northern Germany to southern Texas. Hemlocks and pines covered the mountainsides of most of the world. There were huge dipterocarps throughout the tropical forests. Nowadays you see tropical woods such as zebrawood, teak and mahogany only in jewelry.

Trees have been a big question for a long time. Satellite photographs taken of earth's nightside as early as the nineteen eighties showed the brightest lights not in places like New York and Tokyo, but in the great tropical forests of the era, which were being burned as fuel and to create farmland.

The burning of Amazonia is a much more recent phenomenon. It has the giant scale characteristic of our century. No thousand square mile forest fires for us. Try instead half a country. The statistics are stunning: the fire covered an area the size of Texas. Fifteen trillion tons of particulate matter were ejected into the atmosphere, which caused a short-term lowering of temperatures worldwide. A hundred and eighty million trees were destroyed, along with sixteen million pounds of other flora. Approximately twenty-seven million wild creatures were killed, from every order of fauna, and eight million domestic animals. Nearly two million human beings lost their lives. Seventeen thousand species of flora were rendered extinct, and eight hundred species of animals. More than two trillion insects – seven tons of them – were killed. Perhaps ten thousand insect species were wiped out.

Norm began almost the moment we sat down. 'We're working on long-term automatic replication of the repository,' he said, 'and also obtaining genetic material from as many presently threatened species as we can.' He is thin, and he chews pens and pencils. His hands seem never to be still. He had an odd speech pattern. He would stare out the window for a moment, suddenly take in a breath, then speak in a short burst, the sentences pouring out, until stopped by the next sudden silence.

'Is man one of the species in the repository?' Scott asked.

'Well, naturally, he's in there, too. We're trying to make the whole system self-sufficient so that the future will be able to re-create earth as it was before things fell apart.'

'Why self-sufficient?'

'We want the repository to be able to continue on its own, maintaining internal conditions in such a way that none of the delicate material is altered or destroyed.'

'For how long?'

'Well, not forever, that's impossible. But at least for a million years.'

We must have looked shocked, because he laughed. Then, very softly, his eyes looking into a lost world, he began to speak of his beloved Amazonia.

NORMAN MARTIN: The Great Amazonian Forest Fire

In July of the year 2019 I went with a young assistant, Tom Sinclair, into the Amazonian tropical forest to collect specimens for repository in the International Genetic Repository, which was then at Berne, Switzerland. At that time we observed extremely dry conditions in the forest around Arquemes, and were concerned at the degree of slash and burn activity that was taking place there. The use of open fires in such conditions was not safe. Tom Sinclair attempted to explain this to the Brazilian authorities but was rebuffed.

I have been fascinated by tropical forests since I was a very young man. I've spent the last forty years of my life working in them and for them. We have had no success in preserving the tropical forests, except in Indonesia where the last two governments have finally realized that their tropical forest resource must be maintained if the national economy is to survive. Unlike the other governments responsible for tropical forests, the Indonesians also have the power to control use of the forest resource. The other governments have been prevented, usually by the overwhelming numbers of people, from carrying out preservation programs even where they have been approved.

There has, additionally, been a tradition of forest development, indirectly encouraged by the old World Bank, which was merged into the World Credit Finance System in 2003. The bank, by granting liberal loans for such projects as road building in the tropical forests, dramatically accelerated their decline.

The tropical forest was the heart of the earth's biosphere. Along with the oceans, it was the great source of atmospheric renewal, purification and weather stability. If we still had the tropical forest, we wouldn't be in the fix we are in, with the atmosphere dying.

Its destruction is one reason that there has been a recent decline in the development of new drugs. Many of our most potent drugs come from plants that grew in the tropical forest. God only knows what miracles we lost among the species that were never recorded at all.

When I first began my work in 1982, the tropical forest covered about sixteen percent of the land mass of the earth. Now it has been reduced by four fifths. As I said before, only the Indonesian tropical forest is still somewhat intact. Ironically, the resolve of the Indonesian government can be traced to a fire.

It took place in Borneo in the latter part of 1983 when thirteen thousand square miles of the tropical forest burned. It was the worst ecological catastrophe in a millennium, a forest fire that destroyed an area half the size of New England. As a measure of the strange hypnosis of that era, it was virtually ignored. In the United States only *The New York Times*, with its superb coverage of environmental issues, reported in depth. Even so, nobody did anything about it. The Indonesian government of the period was afraid to let researchers into the area because of the effect the enormous loss of harvestable wood might have had on their ability to borrow money.

In 1985 I was able to make an overflight with a group of scientists from various world groups. I can only say that the experience was confusing. It was not a matter of a fifteen minute overflight. We were in the air for two hours. From horizon to horizon stretched the armies of dead trees, some of them naked, others crowned with withered leaves. A local forestry official said that the fire had sounded like a wailing animal, and that it had moved through the forest at incredible speeds, generating its own winds as it traveled. He described flames moving in sheets across the crown of trees, leaping kilometers in minutes. Monkeys and birds, overtaken, burst into flames and dropped screaming to the forest floor, which was burning as well.

There was no way to control it. What eventually stopped it was rain, which didn't come until weeks after it started.

It was a warning to the world, that fire. At the time it frightened me, but what frightened me even more was the absolute lack of public outcry.

If Connecticut and Massachusetts had burned, think of the news stories, the concern, the effort that would have been made to prevent the disaster from ever happening again.

The Borneo fire was caused by exactly the same thing that started the Amazonia fire of '19 – excessive destruction of the forest by cutting, by logging, by the building of houses and settlements leading to a change in the ability of the forest to hold water and subsequent drying of leaves that were never meant to be dry. In Borneo that combined with the effects of a drought caused by an *El Nino* to make the forest a tinderbox. People using traditional slash and burn techniques to carve out subsistence farming plots found one day that their fires did not go out. Instead they spread into surrounding foliage – usually too wet to burn – and the inferno began.

Even as early as 1990 we understood that something similar might happen to the Brazilian forest cover. But we scientists could do nothing, could barely even make ourselves heard. The Brazilian government was openly hostile to outsiders and intent on pursuing a policy of razing the forest and making it into rangeland. This policy continued despite the fact that the forest soils could not support grazing grass, and in fact turned into a substance as hard as concrete when exposed to erosional forces.

I think, sometimes, if I had been a different man, a man of passion and politics instead of the scholar I am, I might have saved the forests instead of spent my career studying their death.

Every time I see Gupta Singh on video or read another Depop tract I literally shrivel up inside in what I can only describe as a kind of agony of self-recrimination. I think to myself that somehow there must have been some way, something I could have done.

If we still had the forest we could undertake a global cleanup of pollutants and let the breath of the trees renew the air. We could have stable weather again, and eventually clean rain, and be able to look ahead a little distance and say, we will still exist.

I was a senior member of the Equatorial Firewatch Committee in 2019. The group had access to data from the two Firewatch Satellites that covered the whole of the equatorial forest. We applied heat-space and rate-of-spread analysis to the stream of incoming data and from that were able to pinpoint which fires of the thousands burning at any given time were uncontrolled.

Normally we would be in contact with fifty or sixty forest fires of various degrees of intensity. The great majority of these were naturally occurring burns, ignited by lightning and likely to extinguish themselves.

As I remember, the first warning of trouble came when the computer suddenly suggested a new plotting strategy for the Brazilian tropical forest. When Tom and I looked at it we realized that there had been a change in the intensity of a number of controlled fires. We knew at once what was happening. Tom's immediate impulse was to alert the whole international fire control apparatus, but this was overruled by the committee because of concerns about Brazilian hostility to outside intervention.

The tropical forest was originally a very humid environment, with six to ten times the annual rainfall of the temperate forest. The Population Climax has led to a three percent annual decline in the forest since 1990, meaning that, as of today, the forest exists only in pockets.

After the failure of the Brazilian government's plan to express population into the Amazonian state of Rondonia in the early nineties there was some hope that the forest would be preserved – not by intelligent management, but by the simple fact that the soils were too poor for agriculture.

That hope was defeated by the Green Revolution, however, when new grass species were developed specifically to grow in such soils. Why the US Government would ever have sponsored research into tropically active grazing grasses I cannot imagine. It was another example of monstrous irresponsibility, in this case caused by the very effective lobbying of the fast food industry within the Agriculture Department.

I testified against that research in '88 and again in '91. I remember what Mr Walter Krebs of the National Food Service Association called me. He said I was 'an environmental obsessive who is indifferent to whether or not human beings starve.'

The new grasses meant greatly intensified ranching. In 1996 the tropical forest declined by a horrifying six percent. Brazil refused to publish its own figures, claiming that they were 'irrelevant to evaluation of the economy.' Our satellite data showed that the Amazonian tropical forest lost eleven percent of its biomass in 1996. In 1997 the figure was fourteen percent. For the next ten years the figures gradually dropped to less catastrophic levels as the forest Indians began to lobby in Brasilia. From virtual neolithic outcasts in the last century, the forest Indians of Brazil have emerged as one of the most forward looking of the nation's population subgroups. Their mystical relationship with their forest and their extraordinary cleverness at implementing alternative uses that were both economically important and nurturing were the two things that saved what was left, mostly in tribal territories along the rivers.

In September of '19 we recognized that there was a drought situation in Amazonia. July and August had passed with little rain, and this was occurring in an area that had built up a fifteen year rainfall deficit due to changing climate. Without the forest to hold and release water into the air the usual thunderstorms could not be generated. Cut the trees and you interrupt the most fundamental of the tropical forest processes: earth-air moisture exchange. Most of the water that had been contained in this exchange had blown across eastern Brazil and fallen as rain at sea. The northeastern desert had by the early teens taken firm hold in the northern parts of Amazonia. Still-standing forest areas were debilitated by the chronic near-drought situation.

And forest clearing continued unabated right up until the fire.

September of 2019 was even drier than July and August in Amazonia. In that month less than an inch of rain fell over an area conditioned to receive more than ten times that amount of rainfall. Added to previous deficits, it meant that leaves became crisp, and the forest canopy a potential torch.

Despite our warnings the government still did nothing to reduce clearing, not even on a temporary basis.

Clearing is done by a combination of cutting and

burning. People used to controlling fires in the wet forest without difficulty were astonished to find that their burns got into the forest canopy. No thunderstorms came along to put them out. The precise same thing had happened in Indonesia in 1983, in Thailand in 1990, in Burma in 1995 and in Equatorial Guiana in 2002, each time on a very large scale. But the Brazilians had totally ignored the message.

By 1 October 2019 we detected no fewer than twelve firelines in Brazilian Amazonia. These are lines where smaller fires have joined together and begun to move up forested slopes. They are the classic signatures of the uncontrolled forest fire.

Tom and I brought the matter before the Firewatch Committee again, and he made a powerful case for assembly of a major fire fighting group in international waters. The committee agreed, and the International Environmental Task Force dispatched the USS *John Muir* from its base in New Orleans.

The Brazilians told us that the fires were being controlled. By 6 October there were forty firelines, and six of them were more than ten kilometers long. We posted an Uncontrolled Fire Alert for the region. Aboard the *Muir* were forty helicopters adapted for use in fighting forest fires.

Brazil refused the *Muir* entry into its territorial waters and denied the helicopters overflight permission.

In retrospect this behavior seemed almost intentionally self-destructive, but I think it has to be viewed in the context of the long and fierce tradition of self-sufficiency in that country. Government after government has favored development over preservation. In 2010 Brazil refused to join the Completed Nations because it meant signing the Environmental Sustenance Accord and becoming a member nation of the International ESA.

It became obvious to me at that time that many potentially important Brazilian species were going to become extinct and a massive collection effort must be undertaken. Tom Sinclair was beside himself. He was passionately committed to his work, and had to be supervised carefully lest he endanger himself in the pursuit of his goals. I was concerned that he might try to enter Brazil on his own, with dire personal results and possible international repercussions.

He was right to be afraid, however. The Brazilian problem was enormous. There were over twenty thousand identified plant species in the region of Amazonia being threatened, and perhaps another ten thousand not identified.

Tom and I had to collect out of the threatened area as fast as possible. There wouldn't be time for actual specimen collection, but we could do gene swipes of thousands of species in a matter of days, given that the skilled manpower was allowed to enter the area.

With this genetic material we could conceivably re-create much of the forest, assuming the climate could be stabilized sufficiently to get initial growth established. Barring that, the vast medical potential of the material could be explored. As you may know, twenty-seven of our most potent anticarcinogens come from the tropical biome, including rocristine which has been so effective against childhood lung cancer. For fifty years primary drug research has relied on the tropical forest as the source of powerful pharmaceutical agents and natural templates for artificial drugs.

With the destruction of the tropical forest we lost that reservoir of new drugs.

At Firewatch HQ we formulated a hasty plan to send a Gene Team of twenty skilled collectors to the endangered region.

Acting as advance team, Tom and I left for Rio in the company of Charles Plotnik of the US Forest Service Fire Management Unit. Dr Plotnik was probably the world's leading authority on control of forest fires. He was instrumental in containing the South Texas fire of 2002, and the Beverly Heights conflagration of 2015. His book *Conflagration Management in Woodland and Prairie* (Prentice/Mead Datatext, 2011) is seminal to the field.

We were refused entry into the country, and forced to remain in the international section of the airport.

Tom went into action. He got on the phone and appealed to one of his seemingly endless supply of contacts, Jorge Noronha of the Brazilian Forest Management Bureau. Noronha was helpful. He drove to the airport and managed to get us three day visitation permits restricted to Rio.

On his advice we decided to enter the Gene Team at Belém, and to do it illegally. I sent word to Firewatch HQ that the group should be assembled aboard the *Muir*. A US Marine Infiltration Unit would put them ashore near Belém, and Jorge's group would fly them by private airplane to rendezvous with us in Manicore in Southern Amazonas State.

That night the three of us rented a car and drove inland. There are numerous internal checkpoints in Brazil, but Noronha had advised us that a tip of five million cruzeiros would suffice to pass us without difficulty. A one dollar bill would suffice even more.

There was no question that we would take whatever risks we had to in order to carry out our mission.

We proceeded from control point to control point, finally reaching Belo Horizonte where it was possible to charter a plane without many questions being asked. It was over two thousand kilometers into the fire zone. I remember being flabbergasted that the pilot had never heard of the fires. The national news had said nothing about them, and Tom couldn't find anything searching the national environmental database on his computer. We flew on into the night, three frightened men and an oblivious pilot.

Tom established a satellite link to Firewatch HQ in San Bernardino, California, and input the co-ordinates of the largest fire system, which was the one burning in the area of Manicore. This fire had consumed about twelve thousand hectares by the time we arrived on the scene after refueling at Brasilia.

There were now over seventy major fires along the vast Selvas.

We arrived in Amazonia about two hours before dawn. All across the horizon to the north were flickering red glows. We counted a dozen. The satellite view indicated that the worst of the fires were connecting into a single fire line roughly seventy kilometers long and about two thick. Temperature analysis placed the internal temperatures at 1688 degrees, which meant that the fire was now drawing in sufficient air to create a blowtorch effect.

The three of us realized that we were in the presence of the greatest forest fire in recorded history.

Tom's computer indicated that the fire was moving toward us at a rate of about fifteen kilometers per hour. This speed was astonishing and unprecedented in a lowland forest fire.

A hundred kilometers from the center of it the plane began to be buffeted by winds. As dawn broke below us we saw that the roads were jammed from horizon to horizon with vehicles, trucks, busses, cars, mules, horses, wagons, and trudging peasants. Here and there could be seen stretchers, and there were a number of dead people on the roadside.

Tom Sinclair could be a difficult man in situations like

this. His good-hearted nature would turn against him. Forgetting our mission, he began to argue for a landing to aid the refugees. I had to be hard on the man, I'm afraid, to dissuade him from this ill-considered notion. Had we landed we would never have taken off again. Tom Sinclair's altruism had underlying it a strong streak of self-destructiveness.

At any rate, radio traffic now began to pick up considerably. The emergency networks were alive with datapulses and on the voice lines there were frantic calls coming in from settlements and plantations which had been cut off from the outside world by the advancing fireline.

They were screaming, begging for airlift support. It was a terrible thing to hear the hoarse voices shouting grid locations and town names into their radios.

Air traffic was strictly controlled beyond Santa Isabel on the Cainuma River. The pilot wanted to land, but we prevailed on him to fly under the radars – which were just local civilian control devices, according to the way the plane responded to them – and proceed on to Manicore. We crossed the fireline at an altitude of a few hundred meters, the aircraft bouncing wildly in the thick smoke columns.

Just crossing the line took ten minutes at a speed of four hundred kph, meaning that the area of active conflagration had widened dramatically in just a few hours. Fine measurements from the plane showed that the highest internal temperatures were on the front of the fireline, and were moving past two thousand degrees. The fire was proceeding toward Manicore at a speed of thirty-eight kph, more than twice as fast as it had been going just an hour or so before. At this rate the town would be overcome in eleven hours, but a quick rate-of-increase study corrected that figure to nine hours and forty minutes.

We found that no fewer than fifteen major towns, fifty-five recognized settlements, eight hundred plantations of various types and five hundred and sixty cattle ranches were in the path of this one fire, the largest of seven which HQ was now classifying as major/uncontrolled.

The computer clicked the Brazilian national statistics database and got an area population estimate of two million eight hundred thousand souls.

Many of these people were not going to get away from this fire. In fact the whole of the population of the region was at jeopardy.

Tom, who had regained control of himself after the initial shock of seeing the refugees, now pulsed HQ with an urgent request that the task force invoke UN-1233 and enter without permission, in view of the lives at stake.

Other fires burning near Altamira on the Iriri and the region of Tapera do Jeronimo in the Acarai foothills were also life threatening. In all nearly four million people were trapped behind firelines.

A search of the air traffic channels indicated that air transport was suddenly being rushed from all over Brazil. Satellite data on the number and type of planes en route, their speeds, locations and probable destinations were compared with rate of movement and fire intensity data at HQ.

When the results appeared on the screen of Tom's computer, he made a sharp sound. Then he cursed, his voice snapping with rage. At an error-probable of $\pm$ 12.33 percent, there were going to be 2,144,321 lives lost.

The Brazilian government had clearly discovered this not long before we did, and was trying with its airlift to remedy the situation. But even the *Muir* task force could have offered only token assistance to such a huge mass of people. Not since South Texas had world Firewatchers been faced with a human catastrophe on such a scale,

197

and there the loss of life had been limited to eighty thousand.

Dealing with uncontrolled forest fires is at best a matter of channeling them into unexpressive directions, where the fire eventually reaches a point, such as a wide river or a steep downslope, that it cannot cross. The tonnage of chemicals or water necessary to put these fires out cannot be applied except by nature itself. And in this case nature was not going to help us, because unplanned and rampant deforestation had, as I said earlier, interrupted the rainfall pattern.

I add that the area involved is now a part of the World Desert Control Program, and has gone from an average annual rainfall of 110 centimeters in 1990 to 12 centimeters today. The most important climatic effect in the area is wind erosion.

We arrived in Manicore to scenes out of a Charles Elder painting. People had brought out their Madonnas, their crosses, their candles, and were making pilgrimage on their knees through the center of the city. The roads were jammed with traffic and nothing was moving. A few minutes before we had seen why: the traffic ended at the fireline a hundred and thirty kilometers away.

The river was choked with boats, barges, river tramps, luxury yachts. But forty kilometers upriver the fireline crossed and recrossed the relatively narrow waterway. Passage was probably impossible, due to heat and lack of oxygen close to the surface.

As we landed, a maddened surge of people poured out of the air terminal, all the prosperous citizens of Manicore, the local ranchers and factory farmers, the lumber magnates and their families, complete with dogs, cats, pet monkeys and all sorts of paraphernalia. The pilot taxied to the far end of the runway, let us jump out in the dark and then roared off, soaring over the heads of the crowd and off into the spreading dawn.

We went into a *favela* that clustered at the end of the runway. Here life was less frantic, but only because these people were mostly local Indians, spoke little Portuguese and did not – we thought initially – know of the danger they faced.

We soon found that this was not the case. The entire *favela* was sitting in silence around their pitiful central square, an area defined by a single water faucet, quite dry. They were singing in a local dialect.

I did not understand the words, but the song was certainly a dirge.

We entered one of the shacks and Tom again established uplink. A flood of news came from HQ. The Gene Team had been intercepted and their plane forced down by the Brazilian air force.

Now Tom and Plotnik and I had to face a new catastrophe: whatever genetic material was saved would be saved by us.

Tom and I knew enough about forest biology to understand the utter hopelessness of the task. And to have a team member like Plotnik, who was not skilled in species recognition, would slow matters down even further. At a collection rate of about six samples per hour – fast even under ideal conditions – we could expect to collect perhaps four hundred samples in the time remaining – assuming we could retreat as we collected and not be overtaken by the fire. I would make informed selections. Plotnik – who knew how to deal with fires, not how to identify what was burning – would have to collect at random. Given the fact that Plotnik would inevitably take many common species, we could expect a degraded yield. Posing the question to his computer, Tom came up with a figure of only 306 useful collections, ± 20.03%.

But then what?

There had been no point in instructing the pilot to return for us, as we thought we would be evacuated with the Gene Team. Going on the radio to call back the pilot probably wouldn't have worked, and would have been extremely dangerous.

Along with the Indians and the hysterical Portuguese Brazilians, we were trapped in the path of the fire.

There were no roads south, and the one road east led into a region of fast-combining secondary fires. They would form a fireline of their own in about an hour.

The one chance we might have would lie with an off-the-road vehicle. Our survival packs contained among other things a selection of wanted drugs from antivirals to mood enhancers, as well as three US Gold Eagles worth a fortune in local currency. Perhaps this would be enough to bribe somebody for transport.

We went into the town, which was all but closed down. The streets were full of shouting, weeping people. The northern horizon glowed ominously.

A bus was burning, shop windows were shattered, and in the light of the rising sun we saw the police fire Isler Power Guns into a crowd of about two thousand people. I recognized the dry chugging of the guns from news-videos, but I was not prepared for the jerking, twisting victims, or the strong smell of raw meat that followed the butchery.

Tom broke away from me and rushed into the crowd, yanking a shirt out of his rucksack as he went, frantically tearing it into strips. Plotnik and I recovered from our shock and followed him.

The police, in their open bus, were going off into the city, shouting into their amplifiers for the people to remain calm, that help was on the way.

Tom's torn shirt bandages were useless. There wasn't a

soul alive, and worse, there were unexploded darts all over the ground. Plotnik stepped on one and screamed. The bottom of his shoe was shredded, but fortunately the leather prevented the shards from hurting his foot.

We backed away, and Tom was not the only one of us in tears. Plotnik was a stolid man, a highly professional technician, but his composure was also shattered by the twisted wreckage of flesh, the agonized faces, the blood.

A plane flew low over the city, a Vickers Condor with its wings looking like pencils beside its fat fuselage. The engines thrummed against the silent, upturned faces.

Then a shout swept the town, and the people were off in a mad dash for the airport.

Moments later the chugging of the IPGs started again. There were no screams. With those monstrous weapons, there never are. Sometimes I wish that National Arms and Armaments could see how their marvelous guns are used. A weapon that can fire five hundred explosive darts a second should never have been allowed off the drawing boards.

We were virtually helpless, in the middle of a community of the mad with a fire bearing down on it.

We had to risk outpulsing to the satellite. Tom entered our co-ordinates and general situation into a three tenths pulse and ejected it. A minute passed before HQ answered that it had transed the pulse to Jorge and to the *Muir*, so now at least some minds besides our own were on our problem.

For want of any other alternative, we began to walk north out of the city. We passed through a garden suburb, pausing now and again when we saw a car, hoping to buy it. No luck, not even with gold.

It was nearly noon when Tom's computer beeped, indicating that it had received a pulse. We stretched it and heard Jorge's voice telling us to meet a man named Paolo Tome at the central square at 1230 hours.

We proceeded there to find a young man with an ancient Juko Hopper. He was obviously nervous, but willing to drive us where we wanted to go for the price of two ounces of gold.

We got into the cracked Juko. I hoped that the long strain lines in the plastic wouldn't tear open as we careened down the street and out into the brush.

About fifteen minutes later we entered the forest itself.

It was as awesome a sight as ever, with magnificent dipterocarps soaring up a hundred meters and more until they were lost in the stark tangle of the parched canopy. The cries of the monkeys echoed in the dry, empty woods. Choker figs wrapped naked vines around the larger of the trees. Festoons hung between the crowns, their accompany orchids withered and dying.

Most shocking of all was what crunched underfoot. It was the sound of dry, desiccated soil. The material of the floor is the primary fuel of a forest fire, and this was the driest forest floor either Tom or I had ever trod. I was reminded of the Kalahari after the rains have gone. It only looks like a forest; it is one of the driest places on earth.

We moved through the echoing cathedral of the forest. It is a common misconception that the tropical forest can only be negotiated with a machete. In fact the trees close out so much sunlight that ground vegetation is sparse except along rivers where more light can enter.

Perhaps three kilometers in we came to a small settlement typical of the region. This sort of settlement was encouraged by the ranching industry. The itinerant agriculturists would cut and burn a few hectares of forest a year, growing crops and leaving the area planted in grass. Their payment would be the food they grew.

Fantastically, the people of this settlement were totally unaware of the oncoming fire. Life was proceeding as usual. Dogs barked, pigs snorted in the muddy track between the shanties. Pacas grunted in their enclosure. A haze of smoke from cookfires made our eyes sting. Little boys and excited dogs greeted the arrival of our Hopper.

Tom at once began to speak, trying to warn the villagers to leave the forest. But they did not speak English and Tom's Portuguese was minimal. Finally Paolo began to translate. When they understood, the villagers reacted with solemn acquiescence. We had come in a truck, we must be official. So they agreed with everything we said. They promised to go at once, or at any rate, no later than tomorrow.

When we passed through later, fleeing desperately, they waved and smiled politely. No doubt they were glad to see us leave.

We moved into an area watered by a creek, where some of the surface flora remained intact. I deployed the collection equipment and waited while Tom's computer identified our position and gridded the immediate area. He got a topographical map burned onto a tuflite cell and together we organized our collection tactics.

Collecting samples suitable for the derivation of genetic material is not a difficult process. The trick is to gather enough intact cells to enable clone generation at a later time. The specimen samples are held in a sealed environment inside the collection vessel, which can be set to dozens of different atmospheres. The vessels had already been set to as cool a temperature and low a humidity as these specimens could stand without being damaged. The most delicate of them would last about thirty hours before irreversible cell damage began occurring.

After that the only alternative available would be synthetic replication from DNA maps, a procedure that tends to produce mutants or sexually unstable variants of the original plant.

We commenced collecting. Almost at once I found a species of flower and a small gymnosperm I didn't recognize. It has long been a truism in my field that a visit to any tropical forest will bring in a harvest of new species. This area was known to be particularly rich, and it did not disappoint, not even on the last day of its seventy million year existence.

Tom worked furiously, rushing from collection to collection, the sweat covering him, his body jangling with collection bottles.

In a few hours he and I had exceeded our own projected collection rate. Plotnik, however, proved not to have an eye for plant forms, and persisted in collecting different parts of the same plant or plant group. Some of his species were new, but the great majority were not. He was actually doing a little worse than the computer had anticipated.

Toward evening I noticed Plotnik standing up on the far side of the creek. He was motionless. Suddenly his voice came over the radio. 'Do you hear that?'

'No.'

'Come over here.'

We hiked to his position. By listening carefully, Tom reported that he could detect a deep moaning sound, like wind sweeping across eaves in winter. I heard nothing.

'We have a rule,' Plotnik said. 'When you hear a fire that sounds like that one, get out.'

I do not remember my reply. We were suddenly lost in a raging cacophony of squirrel monkeys. Swinging in the trees, running along the ground, their tongues lolling, their ribs showing, their hair almost gone from long months of privation in the drought, the creatures swarmed forth. They literally fell on the creek, screaming, fighting one another, until it ran red with their blood. Still they drank, hundreds and then thousands of them.

We were all bitten, and stopped to inject ourselves with antigen. Behind us Paolo hid in his truck. It is to his credit that he did not run when he saw that tide of animals. Never in my career had I witnessed anything like it.

Then the monkeys were gone, their voices soon swallowed up.

The moaning returned, high and big, and growing louder. I knew that we were in trouble: the fire had crowned, leaping from the forest floor into the tops of the trees. It had to be moving at a very high rate of speed.

As the monkeys had devastated the ground flora there was no further reason to remain. We began to move back toward the truck.

At that moment something unprecedented in nature occurred.

The fire projected itself at least a kilometer across the forest canopy in a matter of perhaps five seconds. As we emerged from the creekbed, we were astonished to hear a huge, cracking roar above us. I looked up into a shower of firebrands.

Tom and I ran as fast as we could, festooned with collection equipment. Then sheets of flame in the form of burning creeper fell before us. Paolo was honking his horn, perhaps two hundred meters away, across a maelstrom of smoke and flame.

We reached the truck and jumped in. Unlike vehicles sold in the US, this truck had not been built to any particular combustibility standard. It was a rigid composite of the kind we use in things like bicycle spokes. It would certainly melt if exposed to fire.

As we piled into the cab Paolo screamed and jumped

out. To my horror I saw that he was running toward Plotnik, who was twisting and turning like a dancer, his back and hair ablaze. Then I felt a cutting pain in my leg; I beat out the flames. By the time I got down from the truck Plotnik was lying on the ground, Paolo bending over him. Tom ran to them and began first aid at once.

When we laid Plotnik out in the back of the vehicle he was alive, but burned over his entire body. If he had gotten emergency stabilization within an hour he might have lived, but as it was we returned to a Manicore so frantic that we avoided the city by using back roads. Some time during that drive Mr Plotnik died.

As night fell we moved steadily south, sometimes on dirt tracks, more often cross country.

We finally ran out of prolene in Bom Futuro, a wasted derelict of a town on the Roosevelt River in Mato Grosso province. The vehicles in the area ran on alcohol. There was no prolene compressor for hundreds of kilometers. We left Plotnik's body in the town mortuary, which was little more than a shack, and continued on.

Tom and I bought passage on a logger's truck to the lumber town of Cuiabá. From there we got a Brasilair commercial flight to Brasília and finally to Belém. On the night of October 11th we were welcomed aboard the *Muir*.

We monitored the great fire for six months. In all it consumed approximately one million three hundred thousand hectares and so many lives, human and otherwise.

The rains that came in April, caused by the dense smoke cover, put the fire out.

Then the rains vanished, and Brazil began its decline into the starving ruin it is today. I believe in hope, and I believe to the depths of my heart that there remains a future for the extraordinary species called human.

But I still dream of the trunks of the trees looming up in the truck's lights, and of the calls of the forest night, the insects, the monkeys, the birds, the moaning fire.

With the passage of time the Amazonian environment has established itself as a desert. Because the soil was so heavily oxygenated by the tropical forest, it has oxidized since being deprived of its covering vegetation.

When you look at the satellite image of it in direct sunlight, there is an uncanny familiarity which at first you cannot place. Then you realize it: central Brazil now looks exactly like the surface of Mars.

FROM DATA FILES OF TOM SINCLAIR:
THE FALL OF THE FORESTS

'"The winter of 1983–84 'clobbered' Vermont's mountain forests," says botanist Hubert W. Vogelmann of the University of Vermont in Burlington. On these wind-swept, cloudwreathed slopes, thousands of red spruce and other trees suffered unexpectedly heavy frost damage . . . Researchers are beginning to suspect that an over-supply of nitrogen, deposited as ammonium or nitrate ions carried by windblown dust and by rain and snow, may have exacerbated frost damage not only in Vermont but also elsewhere in the world in recent years.'

– Science News, April 13, 1985

'In both the United States and Canada, producers of maple syrup have begun to worry about an apparent decline in the health of their maple trees. Scientists say they suspect the trees may be dying, in part because of acidic rain and other forms of air pollution.'

– The New York Times, March 5, 1985

'Severe deterioration of tree foliage and declining tree growth are being observed throughout the Ohio Valley . . . The damage is a result of air pollution more acidic than the acidic rain believed to be destroying fresh-water life in the Northeast, according to a scientist who studies the valley's trees.'

– The New York Times, April 14, 1984

'The woodlands of the Northeast, once largely destroyed by farmers and loggers, have gradually and naturally regenerated and expanded until they cover two thirds of the region's land area . . . They constitute what some authorities believe to be the richest forestland in the nation.

'But some pockets of Northeastern hardwoods, particularly on mountaintops in Pennsylvania, New York and Vermont, have also shown evidence of pollution damage . . . For the most part, the signs are subtle, the first warning signals of what might be the cumulative impact of decades of industrial operations.'

– *The New York Times*, July 7, 1985

'Canadian forestry officials announced that a new disease has been identified among Canada's sugar maples. The pathogen is a fungus normally present on the sugar maple, which has begun attacking the leaves of apparently healthy trees. The reason that the change has suddenly taken place is unknown, but the disease is reported to be rapidly fatal to the sugar maple. Along with the red maple, the sugar maple is the predominant tree in the Northeast's lush deciduous forests.'

– *The Toronto Light*, November 21, 1987

'The winter of 1990 saw another dramatic increase in the amount of nitrogen in the air in the Northeastern United States. Drought conditions have caused higher than normal levels of dust in the atmosphere, most of it from agricultural soils, which are heavily nitrogen fertilized.

'Increased levels of nitrogen are the primary cause of overgrowth on the part of trees, which do not shut down normally in autumn, and are subsequently destroyed by frost. In some areas of the Northeast, the forest cover has begun to decline significantly because of overgrowth and winter dieback.'

– *Science Data*, April 20, 1991

'The National Forest Service issued an emergency alert for the Northeast this week, due to the effect of severe frost on the weakened forest stock of the region. Forestry officials estimate that the last ten years have brought a twenty percent drop in the number of healthy trees in the Northeast. Robert W. Sales, of the New York State Department of Forestry Management, said, "Ten years ago the Northeastern forest reached its largest abundance since the 1820s. 1985 was the watershed year. From then on, we were losing more trees to pollution and overgrowth than were being germinated."'

– The Poughkeepsie Record, December 21, 1995

'The devastated Northeastern forest continued on the decline this year. Rising levels of atmospheric nitrogen, blamed on the severe Midwestern drought raising nitrate-laden dust from farms, were a primary contributor to the decline. The cumulative effects of heavy metal pollution, causing weakened sap circulation and negative chemical changes in sap, further reduced the trees' ability to withstand harsh weather. Acid rain, a persistent problem for over twenty years, has led to the thickening of the cell walls of leaves in some species and the weakening of leaves in others. Overall, it is estimated by the New York State Emergency Forest Mangement Commission that fewer than one tree in five is now healthy.'

– The National Times, September 11, 2001

'The sugar maple, once the most abundant tree in a lush forest that covered the rocky Northeastern highlands, was declared extinct in nature today by officials of the Northeastern Regional Reforestation Study Group. Wide areas of the Northeast have recently lost their forest cover, as dieback has extended down from mountains and into valleys throughout the region. The bald, rocky Catskill Mountain area, which was once home to millions of sugar maples, is now covered with scrub brush and grasslands, and plagued by floods and erosion on a scale presently beyond human control.

'Syrup made from the sugar maple was once a common breakfast condiment in the United States.'

– *The National Times*, June 3, 2015

SCOTT: *Sailing the Ciphered Sea*

Sometimes I think that my friend Tom was a little too obsessed with secrecy. Any file that contains data about any currently active environmental organization is to a degree encrypted. Of course, he must have been remembering the Falon years, when so much environmental research was declared to be against the national interest. And who knows, maybe he was anticipating the rise of the Depopulationists, and saw them as a threat.

The fact files are easy to use and nicely organized. I can trace the beginnings of almost every major problem back to when Tom's historical files start. But the other stuff – I know that there is an enormous amount of material on the problem of forests. But it's all encrypted. For example, I almost had a list of the names of the people responsible for getting Tom and Norm out of Brazil after the Amazonia catastrophe. We might have found it useful to interview one or two of them.

I used Decryptor and CopyJock in the encryption, and finally broke it. Then the data erased itself thanks to some little gremlin program. Tom had hidden in there. He was protecting his friends from the Brazilian authorities – and inadvertently from me.

Among his favorite tricks was the perpetually changing cipher. This is an encryption technique that changes its own code every time any attempt is made to break it. You never get anywhere with it, no matter how close you come to breaking one of its evolutions.

I practically screamed with triumph when I found a way around that one. The trick is to break the code simultaneously, not linearly. I printed out the entire file I just unlocked in machine language, then put it through our optical pickup, reading the pattern as a statistical table. I compared the density of high and low bits to ten uncoded files of the same type, and came up with an average pattern. The coded file did not follow the same pattern, but it was possible to restructure it manually, bit by bit, until its distribution curve was within the average range.

Then I read it and I have to say, very modestly, that I felt just a little sense of triumph. I had about sixty percent of the words, and bits and pieces of most of the others. It was a matter of an hour's work to completely rebuild it.

On the surface it seems like an innocuous enough file. Why encrypt at all? Stubbornness and will were not the only things Tom Sinclair inherited from John. They were both extremely careful. Tom was preparing for any eventuality – except, of course, the one that happened.

FROM THE DATA FILES OF TOM SINCLAIR:
TREES AND HOPE

In most parts of the world, if you lift your face to the spring rain, you will soon begin to itch from the acidity. In places like North America and Europe this has been true for twenty years. Sometimes in my darker moments, I wonder if the planet does not have some secret yearning to cast off life and become a drifting mote of hot acid, like Venus. Then again, maybe there is a place in our own minds which hungers for this destruction.

Note: go to New Paltz, New York, and meet with Sapling Society. They ought to be in touch with the tropical forest people.

Promising ideas: several strains of chemically hardy trees seem to survive present conditions, and some forest regeneration has been noted in areas where biochemical treatment has been under way for a few years. This is a University of Arkansas project. Does Sapling Society know? Crosscheck.

On the problem of sulfur dioxide emissions: the use of electromagnetic charged aerosol generators in the completed countries has reduced their emissions, but massive problems elsewhere more than made up for Germany's Ruhr, America's Ohio Valley and Britain's Black Country. The Koreas emit more sulfur dioxide into the atmosphere in three months than the Ohio Valley did at its height in the nineties. Parochial planning in the last century was simply not enough. It matters little if the United States solves its emission problems if the Asian rim does not.

According to the latest research, acid levels in the last year in rain and snow in a few areas occasionally reached 2.9 pH, with 4.0 to 4.2 an average throughout the year for many countries. I suspect that people living in areas with an acidity level of 2.9 don't realize that vinegar has a pH level of about 3.0. The sale of protective rainwear is a growth industry.

There are some forest areas in which the concentrations of copper, zinc, chromium and aluminum are high enough to be toxic to humans as well as trees. Years and years of industrial smoke did that, but the quantities annually deposited were so tiny that no one generation felt responsible for them.

So here we are, the victim generation, contending with the irresponsibilities of the whole past. One thing I suspect has no future in the twenty-first century is ancestor worship.

The death of just the American forests has been devastating. Commercial forestry in all regions of the United States is drastically reduced. The loss is thought to exceed two hundred billion dollars in this first quarter of our century.

Because of increasing industrialization in India, parts of Southeast Asia, and in eastern China, forest death has extended beyond the collapse of the tropical forest to include almost all forest cover on the Asian continent.

Coal burning in the uncompleted countries has continued to increase since the turn of the century. China burns more coal today than the US. Brazil and India come close in their coal consumption.

The two largest sources of pollution are from electrical generating plants and from our continued use of petroleum in transportation. The construction of new migma power stations and the use of Lepcon solar cells have helped somewhat, but most electrical power still comes from the burning of coal.

Agriculture: wheat, soybeans, corn and peanuts, to name a few, are crops which increasingly show the debilitating effects of airborne pollution.

Construction: statistics released by the insurance industry note an increase in claims for damage caused by acid rain to metal structures, pipes, building materials and the like. And a growing amount of our groundwater pollution is related to heavy metals.

What of solutions? Technological innovation and good sense can prevail. All new and many old power plants have scrubbers, fluidized beds or limestone injection burners. Perhaps the spate of laws here in America and in Western Europe will have further effect as sulfur collectors are put into place by industry. I can't predict what legislative or legal steps will be taken in Asia or Africa – their concerns are different from ours.

Asian consciousness – rooted in culture. There is hope here. There are huge Sapling Societies in Asia. I do not know how dynamic they are. Should find this out. How are they connected to the US and European groups? I think I could get funding for an international convocation. I wonder if Brazil would host it. Not impossible.

Surely the forests that disappeared in a wink of geologic time are not gone forever. Surely we can bring them back.

SCOTT: The Sapling Society

Tom's file made it obvious that we had to visit the Sapling Society. Stratigen further suggested that we include as much data about the international reforestation movement as possible. There is little sensation connected with reforestation; it isn't a subject the public gets to see much about. I can scarcely imagine International News doing a video on people replanting trees. Where's the disaster value?

It wasn't hard to find them – they are about the only large group of people living in central Ulster County, once one of the most prosperous regions in the Hudson Valley. Their Northeastern US headquarters is not far from the empty town of New Paltz.

This group is part of a much larger whole. The United States Council of the Panetary Sapling Society publishes these statistics about itself:

– Of the 22,681,404 registered and active members worldwide, 1,206,338 are in the United States Unit. Like the rest of the world organization, over half of these members are highly active, having participated in two or more Sapling Parties in the past year.

– US membership is sixty-one percent female, thirty-nine percent male. The median age of members is an amazingly young twenty-eight.

– The Saplings are ethnically diverse. While people of Asian origin constitue 11.2% of the total US population, they make up 25% of the Sapling Society. Indeed, Akito Kawahara, the American president, is of Japanese descent.

After listening to Norm tell Bell and me about his experiences in Brazil, I decided to see if there could be a balance drawn. Against the destruction of forest resources, is there not a human resource worth mentioning?

With a budget of over thirty million dollars annually, the US Sapling Society's Genetic Redesign Center is the largest such laboratory in the Americas, exceeded in size only by the Pan-Asia Center in Burma, which is charged with the tremendous task of reconstituting the extinct tropical forests of Asia. Between China, Japan, Singapore, Korea, Indonesia and the other Asian nations, that laboratory's budget of four hundred and sixty-eight million dollars per annum makes it the largest genetic science establishment in the world.

Still, the statistics for the American lab are impressive. It turns out eight million viable saplings per year, all based on new tree designs capable of coping with the rapidly increasing carbon dioxide content of the atmosphere as well as enduring, at least to a degree, the radical shifts of weather which occur so frequently these days.

The lab has a number of locations, as it is growing trees for all regions of the United States.

I never saw upstate New York when it was forested, but it has the characteristic appearance of deforested America: rocky, windblown crags, luxuriant weed growth in the lowlands and signs of violent water damage near all the rivers. New Paltz, which at the turn of the century was a bustling town of fifty thousand, now is for the most part a collection of closed shopping centers and abandoned fast food restaurants. The collapse of tourism and farming and the closing of the State University at New Paltz in 2008 effectively killed the town.

As I drove down Main Street, I saw what is a typical sight in this part of the world, an ancient shopping center with an old Shop-Rite Supermarket, its plywood window coverings long since rotted, its roof sagging deeply into the interior. Across the street and a few blocks down is a ruined McDonald's, its trim lying on the ground around the dead store, the golden arch neatly taken down and piled in a heap of faded yellow plastic.

Farther along Main Street there is an open restaurant, Kim-Do, serving Korean food, and beyond that a rock climbing shop called Mike Cragg's. Rock climbers come to challenge the stark face of the Shawangunk Mountains, a jagged gray mass that dominates the western horizon as you leave New Paltz.

Just outside of town there is a rickety old bridge across the Wallkill River, which is one of New York State's many dangerous waterways. When rain comes to the mountains water roars down the Wallkill, and it has a habit of flooding so viciously that there isn't a sign of life for miles along its banks, except where cliffs overlook from safe height. When I crossed the bridge, the black waters of the Wallkill were low, twisting through the eroded ruins of what was probably once a rich alluvial valley.

The road to the Mohonk Preserve, where the society is headquartered, is a stark line until you reach the mountains, then it begins to twist and turn, offering amazing vistas to the south across the tumult of boulders. There is a sense of rawness about this place, as if it had only recently been created. I suppose it has, in a way, since it was recently so different. Indeed, in the gully deeps it is possible to see rotted logs, for it was along these gullies that the last trees lived, and down them that they eventually fell.

The entrance to the Mohonk Preserve is marked by an ancient and dilapidated gate house. Past the broken windows I could see a stone fireplace, blackened by soot, some benches and a piece of paper lying on the floor. It proved to be a page of *Time* magazine from April of 1996. There was an ad for an old recreational vehicle called Jeep on one side of the page, and on the other a long story about the death of a celebrity named Jackson.

The road up to the preserve is not wonderful, and my beautiful Chrysler Ray had a hard time with the ruts and the stones. But I made it, coming round a ridge and then across an area of sudden green: an expanse of perfectly healthy grass. Beyond it was the great, Victorian pile of the Mohonk Mountain House, once a much beloved resort and headquarters of a major nature conservancy called the Mohonk Trust. The house is still in constant use, but not as a resort. All along the ridges beyond it and down into the valley there are thousands upon thousands of baby trees, some growing free, others in various states of shelter.

At the entrance to the house, which is huge, I pulled the rope of a large bell. Then I entered the old reception area of the hotel. I was surrounded by warm wood. A lovely staircase rose into the reaches of the old structure. Tied between the banisters was a simple sign: 'Closed (temporarily!).'

Both the situation and the spirit of this place were embodied in that sign.

I had called from the city for an appointment, and I was expected by George Tucker, the lab chief, and Jessica Chasen-Smiler, the director of the preserve and a member of the Smiler family, longtime owners of Mohonk.

A female voice called from down the hall: 'To your right and through the door!'

I went down a corridor, my feet sinking into the moldering carpet, and found a suite of offices occupied by at least twelve people, all of whom were obviously much too busy to greet a curious stranger who brought neither ideas nor funds.

'I'm Jessica,' a woman said. She was perhaps thirty, and an honest thirty. I noticed at once that many of the people here showed clear signs of aging. They did not fool with makeup, much less with gerontology.

Against one wall a woman was having an argument with a persistent computer about the significance of a certain DNA strand in the sycamore. Other people were tapping keyboards, still others writing notes on lapslabs. I could smell the faint odors of humus and chemical solvents, the universal smells of plant genetics. Beyond this office stretched a dozen labs, each marked with the name of a species of tree. A bank of mappers jammed into the hallway spewed out weather maps and solar output charts. Other devices recorded air content, and from floor to ceiling were thousands of tiny monitor centers, called tree stations, that measured the moment to moment progress of each sapling in the lab's tree farm.

George Tucker is an amazingly wizened man of nearly eighty. When he appeared in the busy workroom there was a noticeable change in the air, a spark, a tension of excitement. He came over to me, his eyes brown and fierce, his lips momentarily curling back in a startling parody of rage, which became a wide smile.

'I'm Scott Sinclair. I talked to you this morning –'

'Yeah, the writer. I'm glad to see you. I thought the press was extinct.'

'No, not exactly.'

'Well, around here we don't get much press. Good news is no news, right? Maybe we could stage a mass attack on the Koreans down in New Paltz or the Cambodians over in Stone Ridge. Maybe that'd bring out a few reporters.'

'I doubt it. I'm here to find out about the work of the Sapling Society in this area.'

'Well, to tell you the truth we're preparing ten thousand trees for a sapling party down in Montvale, New Jersey, in two days. We're shooting for a ninety-five percent take rate, so these trees have to leave here with a very positive attitude, if you catch my drift. Do you mind if I turn you over to my second-star general, Miss Something-or-Other Smiler?'

She threw back her head and laughed. 'Come on, Doc, don't break my knees. I'm Jessica Chasen-Smiler, and I'm not his assistant, I'm officially project overseer.'

'Here to make sure the money the government doesn't send us doesn't get spent for things we didn't know we didn't need.'

'Here to – oh, hell, Doc. This is his place. He's been an Estuary man since 1983, can you believe that? He built his house with his own hands, and he's lived in it ever since.'

'It served me well in the forest, and it kept working when we ended up with the mess.'

'It was the first pole house built in this region for a century.'

'Everybody bought my design, but nobody paid. Hey, listen, the way the solar data thing's hissing – it's putting out new statistics.'

George made his way into the hall, followed by two technical types. A new solar output chart from the national Weather Control Service would be vitally important to these people, because from it they might extrapolate their weather for the next six months.

Jessica motioned to me. 'Come on, let's go take a look at the farm.'

Jessica Something-or-Other Smiler: The End and Beginning of Nature in the Hudson Estuary

I was not yet born in March of 1984 when the first of the great tree falls occurred in this area. According to George there was a freak storm in that month, with winds rotating up from the southeast, bringing wet, heavy snow. In those days the effects of acid rain were far from understood, and the susceptibility of conifers to brittling was not known. When the heavy snow weighted those trees and the winds hit them, some immense trunks fell, especially along the kills, which served as funnels, compressing the wind and raising its speed.

There were about fifty thousand trees lost in the region that night, some of them with twelve foot spans at the base. People should have realized that something was seriously wrong when eighty and hundred year old trees started falling, but there was no particular alarm.

Over the next thirty years the problem slowly got worse. There were a whole series of state and regional, finally federal, programs aimed at stopping the decline. They had some success. Even as recently as 2015 there were a couple of hundred thousand trees standing in Ulster County. By that time I was a member of the Hudson Estuary Network, founded by George in 1984, and I was very much aware of what was going on.

The long-term effects of acid rain were fully understood by 2015. We were living with them. Walter Parker published *Acid* in 1995, and awakened the nation to what was happening to its forests. There was a leap of consciousness involved, and one that was hard to make. The forest seemed immortal – or at least it died so slowly that the problem could be passed from one generation to the next.

I do not remember my Grandmother and Grandfather Smiler, who founded the Mohonk Trust, but of course their influence is everywhere in this part of the world. They did an amazing thing, keeping the Mohonk Mountain House going as an excellent resort while at the same time maintaining the biological integrity of the Trust lands.

During their era it would have taken a great leap of consciousness to understand the huge impact of what was happening to the forest cover. They knew about acid rain, but they did not understand soil changes or the danger of atmospheric nitrogen. I get a sense, reading the proceedings of the Trust, and things like George's Hudson Estuary Bundles, that there was this basic belief in the persistence of the biome that they couldn't escape from. They could not use their imaginations to break out into the future and see what was coming.

To save this land, they should have become forest revolutionaries, they should have marched the long trails with their voices raised, they should have gathered the people and gone where they had to go, to Albany, to Washington, to the capitals of the states of the Ohio Valley – the states that were killing their forest – and fought for change. They had the commitment, but not the urgency born from understanding. Here in New York, the Department of Environmental Conservation was taking a 'wait and see' attitude on acid rain as late as the Dieback of 1998 when it was realized that most of the Adirondack forest had stopped growing. But by then dieback was already uncontrollable.

224

Nowadays, of course, there's nobody who doesn't agree that the forest should be 'saved.' Saving the greenlands is a political cliché, now that there aren't any greenlands left to save.

What we do here at the Station, basically, is grow trees. We have all kinds of environment available to us, from lowlands suitable for deciduous varieties, to a maple forest, to rocky highlands where conifers thrive.

The trees are growing in a fundamentally hostile environment. The main problem is nitrogen-laden dust blowing in from the Midwest, that and the water supply. Acidity in the rain is still a problem, although nowhere near as bad as it was when the forest died. Every time it rains we have to flush the trees with treated water, which we have to pump up from the rivers or collect in rain tanks because the ground-water isn't treatable due to chemical and metallic pollutants.

Really, what we are trying to do is grow these plants in an environment which is no longer suitable for them. The conifers are the most sensitive. The days of stands of pine and hemlock are gone, I'm afraid. About all we can do there is send genetic material and spore to gene banks to be stored in hope of better days.

The maples are another matter. Come on down to our maple forest and I'll give you a treat. We sell this syrup for a thousand dollars a quart, and believe it or nor there are buyers. Of course, you can get pancake syrup in the stores, but it's really just sugar syrup dyed and artificially flavored. This is the real stuff, and I'll bet you've never even tasted it.

A few years ago the sugar maple went extinct in the wild. But we had anticipated that, and went out and found seed, and germinated it artificially.

These maples aren't really producers yet, at least not on a grand scale. And the old-timers like George say that the syrup is thin compared to what it used to be. That's no doubt because we've restructured their genetic program for faster growth, so the sap comes out thinner and the wood less dense. But, dear God, it's still a maple tree. Our tallest specimen is number 18 over there. Thirty-one feet. Probably the tallest tree in Ulster County, and we're very proud of it. We're still getting a good growth rate out of that tree, and we're hopeful that we've adapted the sugar maple both to modern climate and air content.

I'm glad we came here, I really like it in our little maple forest. I notice you looking at those two diebacks. Don't worry about them, they got hit by an airborne bacterial combinant called D-404, which was mutated from an anti-nematode bacteria used in the South in the teens. Why it attacked maples, of all things, we don't know, but what it did was strange. The bacteria absorbed the component of cellulose that causes it to have atomic integrity, as a result of which the trees became soft – you can pull out a chunk of that limb, it's almost the consistency of dry earth – and sap could no longer flow.

We designed a counter-bacteria with a destruct clock and released it in the maple forest. It ate the offending bugs and saved the forest. We watch for a recurrence of the rot, and when we see it we will release the counter-bacteria again. But our bacteria are programmed to die after a certain number of reproduction cycles, so that they cannot escape into the environment. Back when bacterial combinants were first coming into use in the nineties, people thought of them as the great savior. They didn't take mutation into account, and anyway designing bacteria with age clocks was beyond their skill. So we get these weird bacterial attacks all the time.

I know that this recitation of problems must make our job seem almost impossible, but it's far from that. If you look, you'll see sensors all over these trees. See the yellow patch under this leaf? It's a conductivity sensor that tells us how stressed the leaf is. There are seventy or eighty of these patches on every tree, in addition to sap probes and process sensors that tell us the rate at which biological activity is occurring within the plant. The Sapling Society's Newlife program evaluates every tree in our care thousands of times an hour. Working with the program, our scientists develop strategies designed to keep these trees alive through all sorts of adversity.

When I was eighteen the family closed Mohonk Mountain House. My parents moved to Savannah, Georgia, where they live now, and most of the staff just drifted away. It hurt so very much to leave this land – and by then it was so terribly scarred. I remember I went up to our overlook on the last day of Mohonk – our overlook is famous in this area, it's called Skytop – and I looked down across the Hudson Valley toward the Taconics, which were gray. A cloud of dust hung over the New York Thruway. I did not want to cry then. I wasn't angry. Instead my head filled with plans. I kept thinking of things to do. The stewardship of the Smiler Brothers land had been handed to my generation, after all. There might not be much left, but there it was!

I thought of my grandfather and my great-grandfather, and his father before him, the schoolmaster, who bought the first few hundred acres of this place back in the nineteenth century. All of a sudden I felt a hand on my shoulder, a heavy old hand. I turned around, but nobody was there. I decided I would not give up, no matter what.

When I went back to the house my parents had loaded up their car. They were waiting. I leaned in the window. 'I'm staying on,' I said. They understood, and they were glad.

I've been here ever since. The electricity was off here at Mohonk, so that night I went across the mountain and stayed with George. We sat up talking, and he told me about the Network. Do you know? I don't think I should tell a media person, except to say there's this very large group of people in the world called the Network, who come from a thousand different backgrounds, but who share a desire to reshape human culture along the lines of a more coherent consciousness. The Network is about ending the assault on the planet, and beginning a new life of harmony.

Anyhow, to get back to the Sapling Society, each individual chapter is responsible for the trees they order. World-wide, Saplings are maintaining the fairly amazing number of a hundred and eighty million trees and other forest plants. But there's still far to go. We need to get more mass notice and support, and the numbers of viable trees have to go from the millions to the billions. We need to re-establish not just the tree cover but the ground cover as well. The forest must be brought back to life, and with intelligent planning, nursing and management, it can be.

Of course, no matter how many trees we grow, mankind is going to have to manage things from now on. Natural balance isn't possible on this planet anymore. Human planning must take its place.

ALLIE: The Danger Grows

There has been more sabotage of our lives, something beyond the removal of John's gerontological support. Singh seems to have abandoned the idea of killing us. No doubt he sees the danger there, given our ability to publicize such things. Instead he is seeking to remove all of our supports – to turn our lives against us.

I manage our business and control our finances. We have been fortunate. Over the years we have made decent money. Royalties on the Falon Conviction amounted to three million dollars. Not an enormous sum, admittedly, but it came in so quickly and from so many parts of the world that we were able to reinvest much of it without paying any US taxes at all, let alone the seventy percent Maxi-Tax that such an income would normally have required.

Last year we made a little under a million dollars, which, even after the Maxi-Tax, kept us all in this comfortable apartment, enabled us to run two cars and to travel as needed for our work.

I call our accounting program Bob, in honor of its designer, Robert Simon, who was a friend before he died, and who did a superb job. The program is developed on the ICC Accounting Standard, and we've had it for ten years, during which time it has operated flawlessly. All you really have to do is input cash received and spent, which is a very minor factor since most transactions are obviously electronic. There's nothing more to it than that.

For all of these years Bob has faithfully spit out the

thousands of paper records the National Income Authority requires, paying the taxes, paying the bills, handling collections and giving us a monthly budget that has enabled us to build up a substantial retirement plan as well as make the required contributions to the US Aged Program.

Bob has an investment template, and has made good investment decisions, trading in the stock market with a fifty-one percent record of success, as well as buying and selling currencies to maximize the value of our foreign holdings. As a result of Bob's work, the family had, as of December 2024, a net value of over eight million dollars, and an income from investments of nine hundred and eighty thousand dollars a year. At a time when interest offered on National Revenue Notes is seven percent, that represents an excellent return, especially as Bob is set to deny all investment opportunities below Standard & Poor's Tier Two, Grade Three.

I am proud of Bob, and my work with it. After all, I taught it everything it knows about our family's needs and wishes, and gave it reams of advice about its investment decisions.

So it hurts me, it hurts me terribly, to see Bob go as wrong as it has gone. It called me this morning when I was making tea for Scott and myself. We always get up about six and drink our tea together and plan the day. John and Bell read late and rise late. We were listening to 'AM America' on National Public Radio when suddenly, of all things, my computer comes to life.

'Yes?'

'This is Bob. I want to interrupt your planning session.'

It was odd. I didn't even know the program was capable of spontaneous activation of the computer's vocals. 'Fine, Bob. What's up?' Scott turned off the radio. Outside voices are known to confuse programs, at times.

'Do you have any source of income that isn't direct input?'

'No, Bob, of course not. You know that, don't you?'

'Doublechecking. I have an emergency financial situation. The National Income Authority garnisheed me last night. They took all of our funds on hand, nearly a million dollars.'

I forgot about the voice interactor and went for the keyboard. After a few seconds I saw it, as clear as day: an NIA Due Notice, registered and signed, appeared on the screen. 'Garnishee of 7,991,655.80, authorized against Sinclair Family Partnership, sum completed: 971,335.29. Sum still owed, 7,020,320.51. This Garnishee is carried out under the Taxpayer Revolt Act of 1996 and is associated with criminal penalties. This notice will rotate until the tax action is complete.' End of message. You can trust the damned NIA to be highhanded, but this is the sort of notice they reserve for fraud artists who are on their way to tax prison.

I think I may have screamed. I felt as if I had been slapped across the face. I jumped back away from the computer, which was open on the breakfast table.

'Allie, is it – it's for us? This is our money they're talking about?'

'Scott, the NIA has taken every available penny we own. And the rotating notice means that they'll continue to take everything that passes through our account at the Bank of New York until the garnishment has been satisfied. Not only that, there's so little explanation, you can assume that the Tax Fraud Unit is involved. That must be why they mention their authority under the Taxpayer Revolt Act.'

I keyboarded a frantic question about our status into the computer. The answer came back at once: 'The Tax Fraud Unit has closed information ports on your holdings and accounts, under authority granted by the Taxpayer Revolt Act of 1996, Section 3, Paragraph 14.'

We couldn't even inquire about our own bank balance, much less the status of our investments. 'We're under tax attack, Scott.' My voice cracked; my mouth had gone dry. I took a swallow of tea.

'We're totally clean.'

'I know we're clean! But the NIA doesn't agree, apparently. A Paragraph 14 is about the worst thing they can do to you. It means that all we have left is the cash in our pockets. Even our credit cards are stopped.'

Scott turned slowly gray.

I had work to do. I went back to the computer and opened the code program. It's nothing for a super-sophisticated computer like the National Income Authority to break a smalltime code like ours, but I changed it anyway. At least we'd have a few minutes of freedom on-line.

I forced myself to think quietly and carefully about our problem. It was immediately clear to me that whatever financial freedom we might have left would depend on cash. Back when the Taxpayer Revolt Act gave the government such sweeping powers of control over income, I set up an account in the Senegambian Free Financial Market. This was two hundred thousand dollars cash, delivered personally to the National Senegambian Dollar Trust Bank in Dakar.

I ordered Bob to close this account, and told it to write an MCI draft for the proceeds.

As I watched, messages shot back and forth between Bob and the bank in Dakar – including, I noticed, a bribe of fifty thousand dollars to the director of the Senegambian Dollar Trust to release the funds at once instead of imposing the usual twelve day waiting period.

I withdrew all that the Senegambian Government

allowed: three hundred and eleven thousand dollars. The rest went for the bribe and the Quit Tax.

Bob transferred the three hundred thousand to MCI XPLAN/Cash in my personal name. The printer clicked, then dropped a nice, warm cash draft into its basket.

'Scott, the Bank of New York opens at eight. I suggest we be at the door waiting to cash this thing.' The bank is on Fifth Avenue and Forty-third. We left without waking the other two. There was no time for explanations, not until we had that money.

It is hell to live in this world without electronic money, but at least the cash would keep us in such things as food and fuel, and pay our mortgage. It wasn't good for air travel, and going overseas without credit cards would be suicide, but at least, at least . . . I was shaking as we left the building and started across the park.

At once a shoe gang of Russian refugees came running up, the father rolling his cobble bar, mother selling flowers and perfume, three little boys all with rags in their hands. 'Shoee, shoee,' they screamed. Mother tried to pin a flower to my suit as the boys started buffing Scott's shoes and Dad opened his bar to reveal a huge selection of shoelaces, heels, soles, insoles and every conceivable kind of shoe accessory, ranging from Johnson's Odor Eaters to Scholl's CoolPad shoe coolers.

It was so tiresome to deal with a shoe gang just then, especially as their cries had attracted Citrus Joe and a whole crowd of other street people, including the inevitable prostitutes, one a tired-looking girl with a whip dangling from her hand. As we dodged them a man with an Instaclean Kit threw himself on Scott's pants with the vengeance of the desperate.

The street people usually get driven off by the Neighborhood Rangers, but their shift closes at seven-thirty, and there's a fifteen minute window when the desperate come pouring into Gramercy Park, right over the white lines, looking for whatever they can get.

And they got us. By the time we had satisfied them all, we were twenty precious dollars poorer. We found a cab waiting at the stand, and took it to the bank. It was an ancient Ford converted to burn charcoal, and it moved slowly, with a great deal of wheezing and rattling.

The bank wasn't crowded; they rarely are. We walked up the wide marble lobby to the cash teller. He sat in his elaborate brass cage, smiling as we came. I handed him my MCI draft, trying to control my trembling.

He took it into his cage and examined it. 'Do you have anything to carry this in?' he asked.

Scott had the sidol briefcase Bell had given him for Christmas a few years back.

The teller began to punch his computer terminal. His expression never changed, but I was afraid that he might call up our account and find the NIA seal. Would he honor the draft, then, given that we might be criminals?

But all he did was verify the draft with MCI. He began handing out packages of bills. We got twenty packages of purple hundred dollar notes, ten packages of pale yellow fifties, and the rest in twenties and small change. When we left, the briefcase was nearly full.

'Was that a criminal act, Allie?'

'I don't know. As soon as we get home, I'm calling the legal program. We've got to find out where we stand on this.'

'It's Singh, you know.'

My mouth was bitter. Inwardly I raged against Singh. 'He just won't stop. Now we've got to run from the Tax Police. No doubt his thinking is that we can't write a book, convict him, care for John and run all at the same time. But believe me, Scott, we are going to do just that!'

234

We went down Forty-third Street toward Grand Central. A young black woman held up an emaciated baby, which bleated like a squeezed kitten. Commuters stampeded past, pouring out of the station. 'Let's find a taxi, for God's sake.' Scott glanced behind him. It was nerve-wracking to be carrying all that cash. For all we knew, some spotter was already tailing us. Seeing nothing but limousines in the street we ducked into Grand Central.

The place reeked of humanity. Wherever people didn't walk, others slept. Like every public space in New York, Grand Central was home to hundreds of the dispossessed. As we picked our way among the pallets and piles of rags, I watched the hollow faces, the bruised and the infected, the slovenly, moving about like dreamers, and I thought what a thin line remained between us and them. Between the two great American classes, the comfortable and the destitute, there is only money.

Scott walked beside me, his face set, his eyes straight ahead. Near the information booth a woman wept as two men relieved her of her wallet. Voices rang out as people called for the police, but there were no police. A blinder flashed and one of the men clutched his eyes.

We hurried on, passing next a group of male and female prostitutes, offering their services in any free corner. And indeed, leaning up against a far wall was a shabby businessman with a young woman kneeling before him. From somewhere else an outburst of screaming filled the station, only to be drowned by a computer announcing the Stamford Local, saying the names of each town in the too-precise accents of its cheap Indonesian voice generator. Behind us three cops scooted in, their sirens blaring as people scrambled aside. They remained in their armor as they questioned the distraught hit victim. We picked up our pace.

A cleaner robot yelled angrily, spraying our feet with

detergent as it sped past. The floor went from being dirty to being slick and dirty. We finally left the station on Lexington Avenue. Scott was trying not to give himself away by clutching the briefcase too hard when a lovely Angel Car suddenly appeared. I flashed my bright silver Angel card and, thankfully, it stopped. Another second and we were in more normal surroundings: the luxurious leather and silk interior of a Chrysler Ray.

'Thank God,' Scott said. 'I was afraid we'd be killed.'

'The police were right there.'

'If they'd known what I had, they would have been the first to steal it.'

I thought of last year's budget. We had spent three hundred thousand dollars before June was out. 'Is it really so much that the cops themselves would want to take it?'

'To a cop who makes a hundred thousand a year? Or one of these street people living on subsistence or less? To any of the people around here – yes, it really is so much.'

For us it was about four months of money, certainly no more than that. In those days I did not yet understand how great the difference between classes had become. America is not the same as it used to be, not even as it was a few years ago. Things cost more, but we who earned a lot were indifferent to that. I was astonished to learn you had to be rich to live the way I had thought all legal US citizens lived.

When Scott and I got home, all was as usual. Bell and John were up, eating yogurt and drinking orange juice. 'The *Times* didn't print out,' John said as we walked in. Of course not, there was no money to pay for it.

I went to him. He looked up at me, half-smiling, and I saw again the haggard shadow that often crossed his face. Already he looked older than any man of our

236

acquaintance, and daily it got worse. The Ling treatment was already wearing off, and his hair was dry and mottled with curly gray. His lips were cracked, and there were fissures around his eyes.

I loved him so dearly at that moment. I wanted to hold him, and above all I did not want to tell him what I must.

'We have a problem,' I said.

'A money problem,' Scott put in, and proceeded with his usual bluntness to explain the whole matter.

John sat listening, his jaw set, his lips tight. Bell stared at the briefcase full of bills, which was open on the breakfast table between them. She jabbed at her computer. 'Stratigen, what is the probability that Singh did this?'

'Virtual probability. One hundred percent.'

'This is craziness.'

'Singh's not crazy,' John said. 'He considers himself a teacher, and this is the lesson. Remember, he said he was going to knock my teeth out with a stick, like the Zen Master Shochi. He's hitting me where I really hurt, I'll say that for him.'

What Singh was doing was taking out our underpinnings. He had excellent access to the computer system. No doubt loyal Depopulationists would do just about anything for him, including alter sealed records.

I didn't know what to do. Literally, I had no idea. I sat there staring at the briefcase full of money. We were lost.

JOHN: The Form of the Trap

Gupta Singh – or whoever he was – had become a terrible storm in our lives.

We worked with Stratigen, outlining our options. 'Consider the use of a digital detective. We don't know how Singh's people are managing to do so much damage to your records. I certainly didn't anticipate that they would have this ability. If a digital detective was able to prove that there had been tampering, you'd solve your problems very efficiently.'

Roach knows people like that. I called him and he recommended one Mandy Cross, who was willing to consult with us for a thousand dollars an hour.

The tone of her voice told me how serious our problem was. 'Somebody certainly doesn't like you,' she said to me over the phone. 'I hate to do this, but considering the circumstances, I'll have to ask for cash. Do you have cash?'

'We're covered. We borrowed from friends.' I did not want to mention Allie's MCI check over the phone. Such a statement could be used as evidence, and by now our phones were certainly being monitored.

Allie and I kept the appointment with her. She had an office in the Chrysler Building, on the fortieth floor. It was not an elaborate affair; her receptionist was a robot. Even the small waiting room was jammed with equipment. There were ancient TRAC computers and IBM AXs with screens that glowed like television. They struck me as strange, these old machines, as unresponsive as doors or blocks of stone. I am used to a computer that knows me. Seeing a non-interactive version of such a ubiquitous and familiar appliance makes me react as if I was dealing with a cripple, someone so damaged that their missing parts could be neither prosthetized nor regrown.

Even as the robot was greeting us Mandy Cross came out into the reception room. We were momentarily startled: here was a full grown woman with the face of a girl of twelve. 'Sorry to shock you,' she said in a reedy voice. 'I've got a lunch date. Shall we get down to business?' Her luxury realthetic moved well, conforming accurately to the movements of her face. It was waxy, though, with a corpse-like sheen.

We went into her inner office. Here the equipment was much more modern, the walls covered with densepack arrays, their keyboards hanging from exposed cables. This was more like it: the sort of esoteric brain center I visualized a digital detective having.

'I'm sorry about the smell. My MCC Cyber needs its nutrient fluid cleaned.' I had never seen a so-called tenth generation computer before. Inside the dark vat was a computer that had been grown, a shadowy mass of artificial neurons that looked like a dismembered sponge floating in brown ink. A haze of hair-thin wires led into a controller the size of a thimble. From there a more ordinary glass strand went to an interface box.

Lying in that solution was one of the world's most powerful minds, reputedly stronger in almost every respect than a human brain.

'I've never seen one of these before.'

'You're looking at two million dollars worth of computing genius, so don't even sneeze.'

Allie was openmouthed. 'You have a two million dollar computer?'

She laughed. 'This is just a terminal. When they

delivered it I thought some idiot had sent me a fish tank. This thing rents for a mere ten thousand dollars a month, but it gives me access to the cybernetic network, which, in many cases, is much to be desired.'

'Why is that?'

'You're an example of why. There's only one way somebody could have broken the NIA codes and changed your records without instantly being detected, and that would be to use one of these babies. Mother, which is what they call the master brain of this thing, probably stores a detailed memory of what was done to your family, who did it and why.'

'We know the answers to those questions.'

'Ah. May I hear?'

I recognized that I was taking a risk. This woman might be afraid of Singh. Or worse, maybe she was a Depopulationist herself. I looked around the room, seeking some symbolic indication of where she stood. There were no pictures on the walls, no framed certificates, nothing to tell about her.

'Princeton, 2017,' she said. 'I was with IBM for two years, then I worked in cognitive design at CyberCore. I joined the Digital Intelligence Group, quite frankly, because being a digital detective pays very well. Last year I got the Kraken account, which gave me enough cash flow to go into business for myself. I can understand why you're peering around for diplomas and licenses. You can't trust anybody, that's how you feel right now. So, look, you give me just enough code to call you up on the NIA link, and we'll take it from there.'

I gave her our personal code, right out of last year's tax records. Her hand turned and twisted over a palm board. In a moment the program spoke. 'No alterations detected.'

Her fingers moved.

'Investigator intervention has occurred. Official. Authorized. There are violations. A warrant is being drawn up – '

She clicked off the machine. 'What in cray are you doing here? You don't need a digital detective, you need an attorney.'

'But our records have been changed. We aren't tax frauds.'

'I can tell whether or not records have been changed, and there is absolutely no sign of illegal alteration of your data, which I suspect you know perfectly well. If you want me to go in and search restricted NIA files to help you clean a fraud, you got yourself the wrong man. I value my license. My oath specifically states that I can't intrude into legally constituted investigations. You're obviously bent. Those records go back twenty-five years, back to the time the NIA was the old IRS. You've played every kind of tax scam there is. Unreported income. Unacknowledged obligations. False names, false code numbers. Fake returns, false reasons for delaying tax payments. This is the profile of somebody who belongs in tax prison.'

'It's not the truth,' Allie said. 'Our tax record is totally spotless.'

The detective's artificial face was expressionless, the eyes completely blank. 'I don't say you're lying. But the record – I think I know how to read it. There isn't any indication of tampering.'

'What if the entire database was replaced?'

She blinked. 'That would be an enormously compli-cated task. Your whole tax lifetime would have to be included, and let me tell you from experience, altering these things is hard. I've never done it but I know how. Replacing NIA files is – well, I don't think you'd better use that as a pleading. You'll be laughed out of court by every expert in the business.'

Allie sat beside me, her stillness betraying to me the tension that filled her. I wanted to shield her from the torch of these words. Allie is honest, and she and Bob don't make mistakes.

The silence that had followed Mandy Cross's words lengthened. It became painful. She sat there, her expression changing from suspicion to the amused contempt of the unassailable expert. I wondered, in that bleak moment, if I had ever looked that way to any of the sweating, desperate politicians who have pleaded with me for their careers. I twisted and squirmed inside myself, remembering how cruel I had been to some of my victims, when I was on her side of the desk.

Allie spoke. 'You can't offer us any alternatives at all, then.'

'Who signs off on your taxes?'

'I do,' she said.

Cross looked askance at her, an odd expression that emphasized the mask-like qualities of the realthetic she was wearing.

Allie sighed deeply. 'Oh, God,' she said in a tiny voice. I could hear the isolation she felt and I sought to take her hand. She drew away. Both of us had heard the machine droning on about a warrant. The tax authorities were acting fast, because to them this must look like a case they had ignored far too long.

'Any advice,' I asked, 'if you'll assume for a moment that our whole tax lifetime has been completely replaced by somebody who's trying to destroy us?'

'It's just so implausible! Why go to all this trouble? If you really want to hurt somebody these days, it's not hard. Just hit them. You can get some Dragons to do it for a few thousand dollars. There's nothing to it. And if the victim's guarded you can get them with gas or drugs or – '

'Or, if you're a bit of a sadist, and very, very powerful, you can hang them on a hook and watch them struggle.'

'John, Singh's not a sadist! He's trying to make you see yourself, to force you to confront your own soul.'

'That's a load of – '

'He's doing it, John! He is certainly doing it, and not just to you. We all have to suffer with you.'

Mandy Cross reached out toward Allie, grasping air. 'Sister, you're the one the NIA is after. You signed off on the returns, so it's you they want in prison. If they get any of the other involved parties, so much the better. But they are going to do a full criminal dump on you, judging from the mess you've made of your life! And the tax laws bite, believe me.'

I understood at last – and I could see that Allie did too – that we were in immediate danger of confronting tax police with pretty blue warrant cards in their hands.

Allie sobbed. Mandy Cross moved like a snake around the desk, and tried to touch her. 'No, I want my husband.'

I held her, and looked across her shoulder into the empty, staring eyes of Mandy Cross's little girl mask.

PART THREE
Food

So soft, the fall of wheat on the floor,
each grain tumbling in sunlight,
bouncing on cool linoleum,
being licked up by a frantic dog.

– G-Shaw Shang, 'Kitchen Talk,' 2024

Down the Halls of Web

While my advancing age was settling on me like dead air, our life was speeding toward catastrophe.

This tax affair was terribly serious. Insane, but serious. None of us knew quite how to deal with it. Even Stratigen was helpless: it had no data on erasing and replacing things like gerontology and tax records. There wasn't supposed to be any way to do it.

Nothing in our outer lives had changed – the apartment, the city, all were the same. But inside we were burning and we couldn't put out the fire.

Mandy Cross was not only a waste of time, she was emotionally exhausting. A typical Roach choice. Speaking of whom, the night before our tax disaster Scott had gone through the list of a hundred and fifty-eight doctors, world-wide, that he had given us. For one reason or another, every name failed to meet some key part of the profile we had developed. Stratigen was right: Gupta Singh had not abandoned his old identity, but only added the new one.

When we got home my old body found the act of sinking into a chair blissful. Despite everything, I slept. I dreamed in music, loud, dissonant crashes that would jar me half awake. By evening my brain was echoing, my clothes wet with sweat.

The place was as quiet as a sepulchre. I wanted light and life. Then the long, drumming blows of reality banged down.

I feel this way because I am getting old.

We are in terrible trouble.

This is why this house is so quiet.

People are suspended in a web of technology. Cut its strands and we start falling. We fall and fall – and where does it end, locked in tax prison and so loaded with moodies we will think we've passed the gates of heaven?

I panicked, grabbing for my computer.

When I tried to access our personal bank account I received the last transaction record, and then the screen froze. The computer couldn't even respond. I had to do a cold boot, turning it off and then on again to get the programs reset. 'What does this mean?' I asked Stratigen.

'The Tax Police have laid a digital trap at your account address. They're recording your access attempts.'

Scott came out of the dining room. 'The cancer's spreading. Now we can't even touch the accounts, let alone the money.'

Night was coming down, the shadows pouring into our apartment. I felt the chill of rising wind. Through the hours of afternoon clouds had been building. The week of rain predicted since last month had finally arrived, and slow drops had begun to fall from the thick gray sky. Perhaps this year we would have a little winter.

Scott watched me work. 'You won't get anything out of the account files. We tried with Stratigen and Bob both, all afternoon.'

'No kidding.' I closed the computer.

'Taxpayer prison is a nasty place,' Bell added. 'We have more bad news about that, I'm afraid.'

Allie had run our problem through Summers & Kanter, our legal program. She spoke from a chair in deep shadow. 'We can be held up to six months before constitutional privilege has to be applied. Meantime anything we legally possess can be sold to pay owed taxes. Even if the tax court eventually reverses the Authority, it is under no obligation to return our goods and property, only the proceeds of the sale. It need not pay interest.'

'Can all of us be held, or just the taxpayer?'

'Ultimately only the taxpayer will be charged, but the Tax Police can hold anybody they want under relevant administrative law. What's worse, if they're not ready to file charges in six months they can rearrest on revised charges, and start the clock from zero. And they can do that as often as they like.'

As far as taxation was concerned, the United States had suspended the Bill of Rights. Due process might be served, but later. After you were dead, perhaps.

'Stratigen says that there aren't even any available records about how many people are held in tax prisons, or how long they've been there.' Allie came forward from her chair. 'We might very well spend the rest of our lives in jail without ever being charged with anything.' She went into the bathroom. I heard water running. I followed her.

'Allie, don't.'

'I'll do what I want!'

I grabbed the bottle of Happiness and threw the tiny yellow pills in the toilet. 'John, that's a violation of my person! How dare you.'

'We can do without moods. We've got to work this mess out.'

'We've lost. All we can do is sit here and wait for them to come.' She stared at the pills as they settled into the bottom of the toilet bowl, already dissolving. 'We'll live on moods in prison. A jail is one of the happiest places in the world.' She returned with me to the living room.

I could well imagine the laughter echoing in the long steel halls. It has been a source of ironic comment in the humanist press. 'There was an article about prison life in the *Atlantic* a few months ago.'

'I read it,' Scott said. Beside him on the couch, Bell was working with Stratigen.

'I think I have an idea,' she said. 'Hardcopy,' she told Stratigen. The printer in my study clicked and Bell got up, marching across the living room, her blonde hair bobbing on her head, her stride long and confident. She came back with a sheet of paper. 'This is a list of all of the ways this family contacts the datanet. If we break these links, Stratigen claims that the Authority won't be able to find us.'

I felt a burst of anger. Even Stratigen hadn't thought this through. 'They don't need our data links. All they have to do is come here. Our address is all over every bank account we own.' My mind went to Gupta Singh. If I could only find out who that man really was, I'd have a bargaining chip of immense value. If not, I couldn't even take the conviction public. It wouldn't be complete and I'd look like a fool. 'We've got to find out Singh's real name. That's what'll save us.'

Bell uttered a snap of a laugh. 'That particular project's got cancer of the parameters. Do you know what our chances are of getting the right man, given that we have nothing to go on? One in five billion. You get better odds out of a one yen ticket in the All-Asia lottery.'

'Well, severing all of our data links is a waste of effort. And how do I do my conviction then? Just make the damn thing up?'

'Hear me out, John. Stratigen and I really gamed this thing. It has a good probability of saving us, or at least buying us some time. The key is, we not only close down the computers, we also run. With no links to data and no computer contact, we'll be very hard to find. Very hard indeed.'

The idea still seemed weak to me. 'How can we run?

Where do we go without credit? How do we buy air tickets or rent hotel rooms? How do we eat?'

Bell's voice was sharp with hurt. 'Why don't you let the healthy ones work this out?'

Allie came to my defense. 'Don't come down on him. You're being unfair, Bell.'

'Allie, I'm sorry, but he's slowing us down. Once the Tax Police have us, darlie, we're dead. We've got to get out of here. This apartment is a death trap.'

'John has a right to talk.' To have them discussing me as if I was a child, or worse, senile, made me suffer actual, physical pain. I remembered my parents treating Granddad thus, and how he would chomp his cigar and stare, refusing to speak at all.

'I believe that we must be prudent. Allie, have you instructed Summers & Kanter to get in touch with its front office? We might be needing a human contact.'

'I have. Let me read their message.' She hit a couple of keys, peered at her screen. 'This office cannot intervene in criminal tax matters until after charges have been filed. We will, of course, make every effort to induce the Authority to levy charges as soon as possible.'

Scott came up behind me, resting his hands on my shoulders. 'In my opinion, John, there will never be any charges.'

'It's my fault, I never should have agreed to do the conviction. Damn Stratigen for being so stubborn about it. That program's more trouble than it's worth. Singh's too damn powerful, why didn't it see that? Unless we can get a weapon in place, we're dead. We'll lose all credibility. Who's going to believe a convictor with a criminal record? It's laughable.'

'Every time you take the conviction to another level, Singh strikes. Right now, our concern is our physical freedom. We turn off the computers and we hide.'

I was furious. Not at her, maybe her idea wasn't so bad after all. But at myself. If only I was a little smarter, a little more skilled, maybe I could make the conviction work. The problem is, the first thing most people will ask it is its name. It'll soon tell them that Gupta Singh is an alias. Then what – they ask its true name. It responds with a 'no data,' they laugh and turn it off. 'Give me some ideas, for the love of God!'

'John, it's suicide to go back on-line. You touch that conviction program again and I cannot even imagine what's going to happen to us. Look at you, you're physically broken. And this whole family is ruined. What else do you want!'

I was tempted to remind Bell who had insisted the hardest that we try to convict this monster, but I didn't have the heart. We weren't going to make any progress fighting among ourselves. There was one thing, though, that I was determined to do. 'I'll go on-line one last time, and try to bring the conviction to level three.'

'John, please – ' Allie practically wailed.

'Then we'll get in the car and run like hell. The minute I'm through.'

Bell looked at me as if I was Singh. 'It's a terrible risk.'

I could not let Singh go. I had to get to him. Absolutely had to. 'If you leave now,' I said, 'you leave me behind.'

Bell barely nodded. Allie's warm hand came into my dry, cool one. I was speaking with confidence, but I felt awful. My body had never seemed this heavy, my breath this hard to draw. My mouth was so dry I could hardly trust myself to talk. I forced myself to speak into the quiet, grave faces that were looking at me. Outside the rain began to drum on the windows. Blue flashes of lightning put the others in dark silhouette. All the inertia of my flesh protested, but I spoke above the storm. 'Let's prepare to move.' A wire, taut and dangerous between us, seemed to break. Now that we had made our decision, we drew close again. Bell smiled, her relief tinkling in those big green eyes. Allie and Scott, with their characteristically practical minds, immediately began discussing what we would take with us.

'I'll get to work at once,' I said.

'We'll need heavy clothes,' Allie said. 'And good boots in case we have to do some walking. Bell, do you know where the outdoor things are?'

'I swear, I keep hearing footsteps in the hall. Let's just hurry up and get out of this apartment!'

Allie started to notify the garage to pull out the car.

'Don't contact the garage,' Bell said. 'We do nothing more than pack until John's finished. Then we run. The more suddenly we act, the better off we are. And that's Bell speaking, not Stratigen.'

'So we know it's right, or what?'

'We know it's what's going to happen.'

I opened my computer. I called Delta Doctor.

THE CONVICTION OF GUPTA SINGH
LEVEL THREE: TEST INTERROGATION

– Are you ready to speak on this level?

I feel ready.

– Tell me what you want the most in life?

This is almost too simple a question. Often I wonder why everybody is so dark, so empty. I think that I want Buddha-nature. I would like to see as Buddha saw, to feel as he felt, to be loved as he was loved. People do not realize how close I am to God, and this is frustrating to me.

– What do you mean, close to God?

I have had many direct experiences of the Godhead. In Benares, I once walked a short way beside Krishna. He showed me what it was to be loved by God. Ever since that moment, I have hungered to go back there, to be at God's side again. God sometimes takes the form of a little boy and comes to me in the night, and kisses me.

– God kisses you physically and personally, or is this an allegorical statement?

God takes a physical form. God is capable of this. He comes in the form of a small, quiet boy, who steals close to my bed and kisses my lips. He blows his breath into my mouth, and when he does that he fills me with knowledge and wisdom.

– Are you in love with this God?

I love God. If he took the form of a rat, I would still love him.

– You say that you love God. What about man?

That is a very difficult issue, isn't it? Man is not easy to love. As a doctor, I have an interest in the body of man. But man's great obligation has been to live in harmony with the planet. Everything is in disharmony. Sometimes I think that the life of a gopher is worth more than that of a saint, so rare have animals become, and so common are saints, at least in the streets of Calcutta! Man has not evolved properly, and cannot do so. Look at the effects of intelligence enhancement. Those children are terrifying. They're dangerous and they cannot be controlled. They are what the species itself will become in another two hundred thousand years, and they are hideous failures.

– Does it matter if the species is destroyed?

The species, the species. I am tired of hearing that word. No, it does not matter. The species is a failure. The danger is not that the species will be destroyed, but that it won't. We of the Depopulation – we at the highest levels – know that, added to natural attrition, our program will trigger extinction. We welcome this. Before God and nature, it is very much needed and even overdue.

– What makes you despise mankind?

Human beings in their natural state are simply machines that process valuable earth resources. The world is driving me mad, it is so jammed with pointless, aimless people. Why should the whole planet be destroyed just so these idiotic lives can be lived out?

– Will you be glad when you die?

I cannot say that. You know, the truth is that I will die wishing for one thing that has never happened. Never in my life has a woman, young, beautiful and bright, shown a passionate desire for me. I have never known what it is to be loved, and I will miss that.

– Weren't you once a handsome and successful young man? Surely you could attract feminine attention.

Successful, yes! But I had a birthmark on my face that put women off, all except those who could see beyond disfigurement. Most people are wretchedly shallow. They don't even want to see beyond the surface. Women turned away from me. Not only the disfigurement, but my personality, my rather dramatically great intelligence, put them off. I frightened them, and I have led a life of loneliness as a result. Now, of course, I have my mission, so I am not so lonely, and there are those who will comfort the great Dr Singh whenever I wish it. But they do not love me, only my power.

– You have said that the hidden purpose of the Depopulation is to further human extinction. The only real reason you have given is that you have been disappointed in love. That seems almost criminally shallow.

What is shallow here is your question. I base my position on obvious facts of history. It became clear during the last century that this species was flawed, although even before then an astute observer could have seen it. The species knows it, too. What do you think all the wars of the twentieth century were about – an instinctive attempt to reduce population. D. T. Somtow was exactly right about that. I accept his Crowding Psychosis concept. And the great trend toward suicide by nuclear war, which has not faded even yet, that is also an instinctive hungering for extinction. If I had not created the Depopulationist International, it would have come about in another way. Instinct knows that it will mean the end of the species, and instinct demands it.

– This test interrogation is terminated. Please save and resume psychological profile pyramiding. Please provide Delta Doctor Analysis, with probability levels, of all statements about enhanced childhood intelligence, extinction and depopulation.

PART TWO: BACKGROUND (DATA RESTRICTED)

WARNING: UNDER PUBLIC LAW 1243, THE PROGRAM ACCESS ACT, SECTION 21, PARAGRAPH 606, THIS PROGRAM IS REQUIRED TO STATE THAT YOUR DATA HAS BEEN ACCESSED BY LICENSED CONVICTOR EDWARD THOMAS, LIC. 232–504–A ON DATE 11/14/25. CONVICTOR THOMAS REVIEWED YOUR DATA IN VIOLATION OF THE CLASSIFICATION ACT AND IS NOW UNDER CITATION. Please indicate that you have read this warning.

– I have read the warning.

Thank you, Convictor Sinclair.

– I wish to perform an interrupt on my processing request.

Interrupt active.

– Did Convictor Thomas attempt to question the program?

No.

– Did he damage any data, or attempt to change any previously established logic structures?

No. Convictor Thomas obtained the nodal identifiers of all initial datapoints.

– What is the significance of this?

Unknown.

– Thank you, Delta Doctor. Cease interrupt and provide requested analysis.

PART TWO: BACKGROUND (DATA RESTRICTED) – Resumed

The subject is deeply traumatized by his new physical appearance, which he regards with loathing. His failure to have a simple birthmark repaired before he underwent the transformation into Gupta Singh also suggests that there is appearance-related psychopathology of long standing present. (Probability 55.7%.)

Since at least 1992 there has been extensive ability to repair virtually any disfigurement. His parents' failure to have it removed when he was a child suggests that it was extensive, and the probability (90.2%) is that it was a purple birthmark covering the entire right cheek.

His difficulty in dealing with this material indicates that he has developed severe self-loathing (79.9% probability) and that he has been unable to control its negative influence on his life and thinking.

Because of his own appearance, this individual became fascinated by beauty. His ugliness and his failure to attract feminine interest resulted in his interest fixing in the human – more especially female – form. His body temperature rose .04 degrees centigrade when he looked at Bell, and he often sought her eyes with his own. But when their eyes met he would turn away. Voice stress would rise, suggesting (98.1% probability) suppressed anger.

It must be understood that this individual's obsession with appearance is a serious and profound problem, not the shallow difficulty it would at first appear. It has affected his ability to reason, and caused everything from his excessive religiosity to his dislike of humanity. End of analytical stream.

Program to Convictor: Please provide this individual's true name. Without knowledge of a subject's early background and life experience there is a severe limitation on reliable deep-character analysis. The name would make acquisition of the background data possible.

GUPTA SINGH: So You Continue to Threaten Me

I have telephoned you with this personal appeal because you have very foolishly spent twenty minutes with the Delta Doctor program, working on encrypted material. Since you know that a loyal supporter of mine gave up his Convictor's License to enable us to identify your nodes, you must also know that we are alerted every time those nodes are accessed. We may not know yet exactly what data your conviction contains, but you cannot consider that your work is secure anymore.

You are a powerful man, the destroyer of the great! How is it that you have so much time for a miserable scholar living in the slums of Calcutta?

You must understand that I will stop your conviction. You think I cannot go farther into the Delta Doctor program now that my convictor has lost his license? I can, and I will.

No, John Sinclair, your conviction is no more than an annoyance to me. My primary interest in you has to do with the salvation of your soul. The people who matter are those who are close to God. The others are pointless, aimless, irrelevant.

You could matter very much. I see your strength. I admire you. You are a handsome man. God loves the beautiful. Why then do you hate me so?

I think that I can not only prevent your convicting me, I can make you into a supporter. I know what you are thinking, but I am not speaking of drugs and coercion. I want you to become my friend and my student. I can teach you many things, I know many things!

Through the medium of Gupta Singh, you can learn about your own soul. You are on this earth to break through illusion, to become a deep, full human being. You are here to do what I think Melissa Barnes, Jr, called 'dimensionalize' yourself. Isn't that it, from America's latest spiritual guru?

You think in the west, 'If only I understood myself, I would gain power. If only I knew the secrets of others, I would gain mastery.' Those are silly notions. A human being, in the full richness of the soul, does not even want the sort of power to which you are addicted! My dear pupil, it is enough to contemplate the play of light upon a floor-tile to discern the very face of God. If you but knew!

Usually I would agree with the adage that nobody can teach anybody anything! But you and me – well, all posturing and pretending aside, we are a special case.

I love you. Ever since I saw your eyes, I have loved you. I must honestly say that I hope you pass across the depopulation when it comes. Afterward you can come to Calcutta and live with me. You will serve in my house as a secretary. Oh, it's probably only a dream! But you would learn such wonders as kings would envy if you had the courage to give up all of your possessions and powers, and come to me.

Let me begin at the beginning. You know in Egypt there is an ancient object called the Sphinx. A few generations back some Italian soldiers shot off its nose! Recently it has suffered great disintegration due to air pollution. In fact, it is dissolving.

To really commence work on yourself, you must understand the Sphinx. This is the beginning of all inner work. Do you remember the business about the riddle of the

Sphinx? Herodotus speaks of it. Here it is: what has the strength of the bull, the courage of the lion, the intelligence of the man and can soar like the eagle? The answer, of course, is the Sphinx. Here is another answer: strength to the body, courage to the heart, intelligence to the head, and objectivity to the soul. This is the evolved man.

So the Sphinx is really an evolved man, the kind of man you wish to be. You say, what is this? It is no part of the Shinto tradition, nor the Hindu, nor even Moslem or Christian. True, but what I am talking about underlies all of the great religious traditions. It is objective acceptance of all human experience, good and evil.

John, my son, you are going to endure great trials. I have sent you plagues, don't think I don't know it! Either they will destroy you or you will evolve. But to evolve you need some foundation, some basis for your new life.

This material about the Sphinx is that foundation. Listen, and you shall gain something of value. This is secret knowledge, which came down from the priests of ancient Egypt at the very dawn of time. It is the fundamental basis of evolved human consciousness. With it you can surmount even the awful trials I have set for you.

The question is, how do you change yourself in such a way that you gain the wings of the Sphinx and soar above the trials of life?

You have three parts of the Sphinx already. Your body is the bull, your heart is the lion, your mental system is the brain. What you lack is the wings of the eagle, and to gain them the other three parts must be in balance. Your body is facing degeneration, so it must prove its natural strength. Your heart is facing the terror of death and the ruin of your family, and so must find courage. These twin problems give your mind its greatest intellectual challenge. Understand or be destroyed.

If you can get your three parts working in balance, if you can face your life with strength, courage and good sense, you will eventually evolve. But you must apply your attention at once to yourself and to the world around you. You must seek harmony inside yourself, you unbalanced, confused man.

I promise you, once the harmony of the Sphinx is within you, there will be a great change of being. Where you were frightened you will have courage, and where you saw only darkness and defeat, you will see the limitless sky of objective understanding.

Well, that's enough for now. I am sorry that you are beset with so many problems. What a change it must make, going from a fine and powerful man to a dusty fugitive in just a few days! What a change.

I enjoy working with you, John Sinclair. I am glad that you have started along the path to personal evolution. No man is truly conscious, save the man who understands himself.

I am sorry that I cannot change anything that has been done to you. It is a matter beyond my small powers! But I love you, John, and I keep you always in my prayers.

Escape

Never in my life have I wanted to consult Stratigen as much as I did after I finished that session with Delta Doctor. They had identified my nodes, my God! Anything could happen now. Delta Doctor encrypts itself very skillfully, but Scott's work with Tom's files proves that a good codebreaker can accomplish miracles. With the node addresses, it was only a matter of time until they had access to my conviction.

I was punching up Stratigen when Singh called. I was so astonished to hear from him that I listened to the schmedlock's whole darned sermon. That's exactly what he wanted me to do, of course. They've gamed this, maybe even with their own copy of Stratigen, and they must realize that we're going to run, and while we're running we'll be computer-blind. You can't access the really big programs like Stratigen and Delta Doctor without going on the net. You go on the net, even for a second, and someone who's filed a search for you will probably find out where you are.

He knew it was my last chance with Stratigen, and he prevented me. He would have read the Declaration of Independence if he had thought it would keep me preoccupied until I ran out of time. The Tax Police might be slow, but the're not *that* slow.

The others had worked out a careful plan of escape, and we at once put it into action. To avoid notice it involved leaving in stages, Scott first. He would pick up the car and get the rest of us at different meeting points.

If the house was under surveillance, leaving together would bring them down on us immediately.

Allie was watching him from the window. She gave a little moan, then stepped back, her fist in her mouth. I rushed to her side. A woman in a fashionable blue skinhugger followed him, turning the corner just after he did.

'Let's move,' Bell said. 'We'll meet him at the corner. Forget the rest of the plan.'

The drumming hiss of a police helicopter suddenly filled the room. White light burst in the windows as it maneuvered to the ground in front of the building. Without a word we left our place, my home of twenty years, all our memories, Tom's pictures, his tapes. I stopped only to get the disk of his database, a million pages of information collected over his lifetime.

Allie had about thirty thousand dollars in her purse, all she could carry of the bulky cash we had withdrawn. Bell and I stuffed our pockets with more, perhaps another thirty thousand between us. There were voices echoing up the stairwell of the old building, calm, quick voices. I could picture the tax policemen who had come out of the helicopter, their dark blue trousers and shirts, the letters US Tax embroidered in red across the patches on the front of their wide-billed caps. They were a sign of the death of the world, these policepeople, like the tax agents of the ancient Roman empire, extracting ever greater sums out of an ever smaller tax base, using more and more brutal methods.

'To the roof,' Bell said. 'We'll try crossing to twenty-six.'

Rain swept us when we dragged the old steel door open. Wet wind made us stagger on the slick roof. We weren't dressed for the storm. I pulled my pretty street coat around me. It was meant to be admired, this beautiful piece of brocade and embroidery, not to keep out the elements.

As we crossed the roof another helicopter swept over, leaving us choking in a cloud of steaming downdraft and exhaust. It circled the park, its finders darting lights down on one pedestrian shadow after another as its computer strove to identify us among the passersby.

We moved quickly, but not quickly enough. Just as I stepped through the door into twenty-six's roofhouse, one of the lights flashed against my back.

It would be enough for their computer to infer it was me. Who else would be on the roof in the rain in a brocade coat?

As we rushed down into the depths of the building we could hear the helicopter above us, landing with a roar of wind. Then there came silence, and in the silence the creak of beams as the chopper settled onto the old roof.

Footsteps, quiet and quick, began on the stairs. I heard the sputter of a blinder running on ready. Would we soon be taken into that helicopter, sightless and terrified? I ran like I have never run before. Doing the conviction had become a thousand times more important now that I knew the lie of the Depopulation program. I had to let the world know that lie. My mission was more important than my life, but it depended on my remaining free. I could not afford to be swept up into the brutal official world.

We reached the lobby, passed the startled gatekeeper, which clicked and moved forward to block our exit. Fortunately, it stopped when it recognized Allie's voice. 'It's all right, George, we're the Sinclairs from next door.' Our friends Rick and Nancy Washburn live on the sixth floor, and they've trained George to recognize us.

Standing at the curb was an unexpected and welcome

sight: our beautiful black Mitsui Interceptor, Scott at the wheel. The doors popped open as we ran up. We literally dove into the plush interior as Scott hit the accelerator.

Behind us a massive flash signaled the frustrated use of a blinder. For a few moments everything went red, then the effect subsided.

'Thank God you were here,' Bell said. 'I was afraid we'd have to try and run to the first meeting point. What did you use, Stratigen?'

'I didn't have time to mull with a computer. I thought it out myself. As soon as I heard the first helicopter, I knew you wouldn't have time to execute the plan.'

We were racing up Third Avenue. So far nothing was behind us. 'Sunroof open.' Nothing above, either.

'Red light,' the car said. As we charged through it the city's traffic computer announced, 'Billing you fifty dollars, A228291BZ.'

Scott dropped us to thirty-five, the maximum legal speed. We didn't want to attract unwanted attention with too many billing incidents.

'Scott, it won't take a logic program for them to figure out we're trying to leave the island.'

'We have to try.'

I turned on my computer. 'Any unusual methods of departure – '

'Leave it, John,' Bell said. 'Don't use it. Don't even talk.'

Of course not. If they were tracking us, there were a dozen different ways they could listen to conversations in this car. And computer use was out, a fact that was hard to remember. Scott hit the autopilot and took a paper notepad out of the dash box. 'Autopilot overload,' yapped the car. 'Traffic.'

'Override.'

The car began to jerk, accelerating and decelerating

suddenly. Our highway autopilot was a bastard about heavy traffic. Still, it gave Scott enough time to jot a note. 'Going to Seventy-ninth Street boat basin. Will get on Westside at Fifty-seventh. We will roll out onto ped. ramp at Seventy-ninth. Car will continue on auto.'

'Good God,' I burst out when I read it. I dared say no more. The drumming of a helicopter filled the air as we turned onto Fifty-seventh.

'Illegal speed,' said the car. 'Slow down.'

'Billing you ten dollars a mile over limit, A228291BZ. Total $55.70. Billing to date this trip $105.70.'

'Shut off the voices, Scott,' Bell said.

'You can't drop the legals.'

'Red light.'

'Billing you fifty dollars for passing red light, A228291BZ. Billing to date this trip $155.70. Are you in trouble, A228291BZ? You are required to reply.'

Scott grabbed the phone. 'No trouble. Just a mistake.'

We reached the Westside and climbed onto the old highway, our tires rumbling on the much-patched pavement. The concrete that had been used in this project was notoriously poor, and the road was a mess of patches and potholes. Sitting beside Scott, Bell punched Fort Lee Mitsu into the navigator. A moment later the map appeared with our position marked as a moving blue dot. She pushed the integrator, and the autopilot took over, guiding the car toward the dealership.

We passed under the glowing orange Seventy-ninth Street exit sign. 'Get ready,' Scott said. He pulled into the far right lane, the autopilot yammering protest.

There was a hundred foot section where the pedestrian walkway was nearly parallel to the road, just before the highway dipped into a tunnel it would not leave until it reached the George Washington Bridge. Scott slowed the car to eight kph. He popped the doors. 'Danger, doors ajar. Danger, doors ajar.' With neither word nor hesitation, Bell jumped out of her seat and onto the concrete abutment. She slipped once, then scrambled up and over. Next Allie went. I heard her gasp as her leg scraped.

When I went the wind seemed to scream in my face, then I found my footing and galloped along, reducing my speed as best I could. One moment I was staggering, the next hitting the ground hard. Lights bore down on me, a horn blared, and suddenly I was yanked over the low wall by Allie and Bell. Scott came up behind me. We watched our car accelerate into the tunnel. Now that it was on the highway, its autopilot could easily take it all the way to Fort Lee. A helicopter passed overhead at an altitude of ten meters. 'Still tracking the car,' Bell said. 'Hanging low and back so they'll be hard to see.'

'Let's get going. We probably only have a few minutes before they realize we're not in the car.'

'Anybody hurt?' Bell asked.

We were all skinned, but there were no broken bones.

'Those cops up there are too busy staring at their chase management program. I think it'll be a while before they come back.'

'Don't bet on it, Scott,' Bell said. 'Even a government-designed program can figure out that something's fishy when a car slows down that much on a highway.'

We hurried up the stairs and into Riverside Park. The rain had set in again – naturally, now that we were out of the nice, warm car. I am no runner, and the exertion made me gasp. The rain tickled down my back and got in my eyes. Where it touched my skin, I itched.

I thought I saw the lights of a helicopter in the gloom, coming low from ahead. Then a sheet of rain obscured them. I have never felt so exposed in my life, knowing that every detail of my body, every movement, every shaking breath, could be observed by the men in the machine, rain and dark notwithstanding.

We went down into the boat basin, close to the black Hudson. There was no robot guard here. Instead a man in a smart white uniform stood in a kiosk. Beyond him, under steaming lights, stood row upon row of priceless yachts. T. Malcom Forbes kept his boat here. I saw it, an eighty-footer soaring in a perfect form at its mooring. Figures moved behind the windows of the main salon. Once I had been in there, cruising down to the Islands with Forbes, discussing a proposed conviction of one Robert Falon, President of the United States.

Now, Malcom, I am here, a fugitive in the night, while you listen to your beloved Scarlatti and drink some ancient port, perhaps even that 1986 Warre you were so kind as to give me. Has it opened up yet, yielding the fullness and nose you were hoping for?

There are two boat basins, really. One is this rich place, carefully protected. The other, dark and crowded, tails off down the Hudson for a half-klick or so, a miserable collection of houseboats and other illegal river craft. Once or twice a month one of them founders, usually with loss of life.

As we approached we saw small lights glimmering behind dirty windows. A helicopter thrummed past, rushing down the middle of the highway at an altitude of twenty meters. 'They know we're not in the car,' Bell said. 'They're backtracking.'

I did not mention the one I had seen in the park, because I was not sure. But didn't I see it again, a stealthy shape in the storm? No, that was only a low billow of cloud.

Bell rapped on the door of the first houseboat we reached. To greet us, the lights inside the boat went out.

These people were probably all illegals; they had no desire to show themselves to strangers.

Bell knocked again.

Silence.

She tried the door. The lock clicked, the hinge creaked and an alarm began buzzing. 'Damn.'

The buzz rose to a clangor and we went on, passing boat after boat until the rain muffled the sound of the alarm. The boats were tied one to another, and they made a treacherous floating sidewalk of foredecks. Here and there a dog barked, but the real problem was not dogs but the pitching of the boats and the slickness of the decking. Allie lost her footing and fell heavily against Scott. He pitched backward into me. 'Keep moving,' Bell urged. 'We haven't got much time.'

The knocking started again. This time there was a startled reply. As I came up to the others, who had gathered hopefully at the door, I sensed a change in the night.

Behind us and up in the park the helicopters were sending out their brutal beams of light. 'Oh, God, may they let us in,' Bell whispered.

The door opened. A man stood before us, his face shadowed by the gentle glow behind him. 'Please,' Bell said.

He looked toward the helicopters, which were beginning to search the far end of the marina.

Suddenly, as if the decision had come from his heart more than his mind, he stepped aside.

We entered a low room that stank of garlic and beans and an alcohol fire. This wasn't really a houseboat, but an aged family cruiser. It must have been every bit of fifty years old. It was designed for a weekend journey, not for a lifetime. The engines had long since been taken

271

out, and from the darkness where they had been there came the sound of an infant crying.

'What?' the man said, looking first at one of us and then another. Outside the rain hissed against the boat and the Hudson waters gurgled and sighed. A girl of perhaps ten squirmed down into the engine room and began to comfort the little bundle of creature housed there. Two boys played some game on the tiny bunks in the bow of the boat. A woman, her eyes tired, looked up at us from the dinette. Before her on the table was an alcohol lamp and a book. She was studying a college textbook called *Genetic Combination: A Practicum*. These people were immigrant strivers, one family among millions.

Bell spoke for all of us. 'We need a boat that will take us across the Hudson. We will pay well.'

'This boat ain't going anywhere.' The woman gestured toward the nursery where the engine had been.

'Do you have anything else? A fishing boat, a dinghy?'

The man looked at us. 'You four people go out in my flatboat on a night like this, you got a lotta nerve.'

'How much?' Bell asked.

The woman spoke. 'Julio, the helicopters are after them – '

'I know, Connie.'

'Will you sell us the flatboat?' Bell's voice was calm but strangely high. I fought to stop shaking. Her obvious desperation was making me frantic. Bell has such a cool head, when she's scared I get even more afraid.

'A thousand dollars for the flatboat,' she said.

'That's not much. I'll have to pay that much to replace it.'

'Two thousand.'

'Look, you got the helicopters on your tail. This I know. My boat, it might help you. They ain't gonna be expecting no boat trips. Plus a flattie is a little thing on that big river.'

'Julio, say ten thousand.'

He turned to his wife, put a big hand on her shoulder. 'Look at them. Could *you* ask that of them?'

She stared up at us, the hardness in her eyes changing to something tender. 'Five,' she said. 'It's fair, considering our risk.'

Bell told Allie to count it out. As she took the big yellow fifties the woman sobbed. She broke down, the bills on top of her textbook, her tears flowing over them. One of her sons got up from the bunk and began nervously to pat her hand, saying 'madre, madre,' in a quavering voice.

Julio stared at his wife. 'We need this money,' he said. 'We need it bad. It will pay for a whole semester.' Then he smiled, his bright plastic teeth gleaming. 'The fuel cell I got on the flatboat's good for all the juice you need to cross the river. I had a leak, but I fixed it, so that shouldn't be a problem.'

We followed Julio out into the storm. In its rush down the Hudson the wind nearly knocked us down. Far to the north I could see the lights of the GW Bridge as faint spots in the rain.

Julio dragged a rotted tarp off the most pitiful excuse for a boat I had ever seen in my life. It was an old fiberglass shell fitted with a couple of metal bench seats. On one end was an electric outboard, a ten horsepower job. 'Don't make no noise,' Julio said, 'no wake, very low heat signature.'

He didn't mention radar, which would pick us up easily. If we wanted to escape, this boat was going to have to look to a computerized radar system like a big piece of flotsam. We got in as best we could, jamming together on the two seats.

Back before the end of time Allie and I used to sail this river in a marvelous little ketch named 3-Wishes. 'We want to seem to drift,' Bell said. She started the motor, which was not silent at all. It not only made an angry hum of its own, it caused the boat to rattle. She nosed us out into the channel. A moment later Julio was lost to view.

'The tide's running out,' I said. 'Go with it.' Bell headed us downstream while Scott spent time stuffing the money from Allie's purse under his shirt. I felt a cough burst up from the depths of my lungs. I could not suppress it, but coughed and coughed until there were tears in my eyes. I could not remember doing such a thing since the days of flu and colds.

Allie touched me. My mind, dulled by discomfort and sadness, grew sharper at the contact. I began watching for the dark silhouettes of helicopters against the lights of Manhattan.

The wind spun us. Again and again the angry river waves slapped over our sides. We bailed with our hands, and worried about the whine of the motor. The lights of both shores reeled and swung. Allie soon felt seasick, just as she sometimes had on 3-Wishes. We had no Loatol tape to put behind her ear, so she was forced to use the side.

'As little movement in the boat as possible,' Scott said. 'If a radar detects motion aboard, they'll be on us in a minute.'

At first I thought it was my imagination that was making the lights of the Jersey Shore get bigger, but then something thudded against the side. The motor screamed and we heeled far over. Scott threw himself in the opposite direction and saved us. 'Rocks,' Bell said, 'I think we've made it.'

Our boat was bouncing along the forbidding hulk of the Palisades. As the black, wet rocks went bumping past, we realized that we had done the impossible. We had escaped the Tax Police, at least for a little while.

ALLIE: Falling off the Edge of the World

We spent what remained of the night in an abandoned factory, four people huddled around a fire of wood torn from crates that once held shrink-wrapped toys. Shipping information was marked on the side in black letters: 'Concorde #1411; KillMan Pt. 02 (Only); Slinky Stinky.'

John was more upset than I have ever seen him. All of his personal power depends on access to the computer net. Without that, he is nothing. The exertion and the frustration were aging him so fast you could see the lines coming, hear the sinking wheeze of his breath. When he coughed I flinched. Each one pierced me, a freezing cold spike. He must have seen me, because he began to try and stifle himself. I wanted to crush him to me, to bury his face in my breast, to surround him with magics and protections.

'You're absolutely certain about the accuracy of the conviction so far?' Scott asked. Given some respite from running, our minds all turned back to our work.

'It gave a high reliability rating. Of course it could be wrong. Anything can be wrong. But I don't think it's wrong. I'm the intuitive end of the conviction process, and I intuit that the rational end is not wrong. What worries me is that this conviction – which is an act of historical importance – may never be finished.'

We contemplated this possibility in silence. We were tired and the hour was late, and we were in a very strange and unexpected situation. We waited in the dark for we knew not what. I tried to assess our surroundings.

There was no way to tell exactly what had gone on in

276

this huge, echoing emptiness. It was cold and dank from the storm; water dripped everywhere. Once we saw a rat with a fat, pink tumor bulging from the side of its head. It came to us, sniffed, suddenly screamed, then wobbled into the dark. We covered ourselves as best we could, frightened that we would be bitten while we slept.

John lay his head in my lap, moaning from time to time. Once he spoke. 'Without my computer, I'm as good as dead.' As age sucks him away from me, I want to weep. But I do not weep. Nor do I weep for myself, although my Gerovita days are also quite obviously over.

That does not distress me. If one of us must grow old, it seems moral and appropriate that the other join.

'You know,' Bell said, 'the reason we can't use the computers is that they identify themselves when they reach out for datalinks. But we could use them for a few things, like reading data files. They don't connect to the net to read disk files, and as long as they keep to themselves, we're in no danger of being detected.'

'That won't help John.'

'No, but it'll help Scott and me. He can still work with Tom's data files.'

'How is that going?' John asked. His voice was hollow and tired, a dismal echo.

Scott's reply was animated. He loves those files. They fascinate him. At that moment, they might have obsessed us all: they were the only tool we had left. 'I've solved a remarkable encryption technique. I think I'm on the point of getting to some really well-hidden material. Maybe information about the location of Magic.'

It was Scott's El Dorado, that place. Tom had spoken of it seldom, but I remembered his words well: 'Mother, if I've never accomplished anything else, I've put Magic together. One day, Magic will be seen as the best hope. I really believe that.'

He had said similar things to all of us. It was clear that he was right in the middle of creating this mysterious institution when he died.

Did it need more work? What was it, and where? Was something important going to die because Tom suddenly stopped coming back? We searched and searched, but his files told us nothing.

Scott had looked for Magic for years. Occasionally, when he came across a file, the file erased itself before he could break its code.

It was possible that we could lose it forever, so the search had become very meticulous indeed.

'Do we know anything at all about it?' John asked.

'It has to do with children and it is illegal. That suggests to me that intelligence-enhanced kids are involved.'

'If it survived it's been going for years. It could be important.'

'Of course it's important. He got something going with those children, and it was working. Maybe it still is. If so it could have become something quite extraordinary, given their intelligence.'

'And whenever you touch a file concerning it, the file disappears.'

'Right. But I'm solving that. I made a great breakthrough with the file about the Sapling Society. And when I opened it, everything we needed was right there. Names, locations, all sorts of things. Of course, there's not much reason to keep it secret now, but Tom collected that information during the Falon years. The Saplings were an underground group then.'

John laid his head on my lap. His profile, resting on my knees, seemed sharp and terribly delicate. It seemed as if I could have crushed his head between my hands, he appeared so frail. I felt a rush of cold; my whole body began trembling. I do not want us to lose our youth.

The rest of us became silent. Long into the night the screen of Scott's Interactor glowed. The faint clicking of his keyboard joined the sound of dripping rain.

Toward dawn I awoke suddenly. The Interactor was dark. Scott and Bell were curled up together like two sleeping children. I moved John off me and stretched my legs. Then I lay down beside him and put my arms around him. He kissed me in his sleep, a slight smile tracing the gray stubble on his cheeks. As the fire died the huge room became dead dark. It soon filled with the dragging sound of rats pulling themselves about, their breath coming in tormented little screams.

I sensed that somebody else had awakened. 'Bell?'

'Yes?'

'Are those rats coming closer?'

'Does it sound like it to you?'

'I'm not sure.'

She stood up. I heard her pull the cover off her flashlight. As its glow cast back the shadows, she gasped.

I could not help screaming at what I saw. All around us were hideous, misshapen rats, hundreds, maybe thousands of them. Tumors protruded from heads, backs, bellies, flanks. Their tails were knotty and bleeding. Many of them had white, wrinkled growths over at least one eye. They moved forward in the light, squinting, their noses probing, breathing their husky little screams. They were thin, moving like gnarled snakes in the half-light. They smelled of some chemical pungency and rotting flesh, and here and there one was carrying a load of maggots in holes where its ears had been.

We woke John and Scott; we got to our feet. 'This place – it's poisoned. Oh, God, it's cancerous!'

We ran for the door, which seemed an immense distance away, and the rats threw themselves at us, their bodies soft, the tumors bone-hard where they rubbed against our legs. We ran and ran across what seemed to be an expanding desert of concrete until finally we were at the gaping ruins of the loading bay. For a moment my mind simply rejected this oozing reality. I saw flashes of bright forest, I smelled fresh snow, I imagined birds singing in the cries of the rats.

Then we were joined by a great, black ball of fur, a twisted cheshire cat stinking of death and old meat. It bounded in among the rats and they scattered, all but one, which shrieked once and then lay limp in the cat's jaws. The animal dragged its prey away from us. Presently from the dark came a low growl, and then eager licking.

The storm had blown away during the night. Across the blasted land to the east we could see Manhattan, the tower of Trump Mile-Hi soaring into a sky glowing deep red. As we watched, a TAV rose from La Guardia, its engines burning so brightly they banished the subtle colors of dawn. In moments, though, it was gone, its smoke trail scattering in the brisk wind. Left were the towers, black against the sky, and far above them something that seemed at that moment perfect: a star of a blue so pure that it pierced through all of our suffering, to the heart.

We began to walk through the stillness of this dead place. Here and there drums of chemicals oozed their black or green or yellow contents. The puddles left from last night's rain were covered by sticky, yellow film. There was trash everywhere, and once we came across the emaciated corpse of a dog which some chance combination of chemicals had mummified.

The industries of eastern New Jersey were exported to Taiwan and Korea and China decades ago. No longer are the plastics of life extruded here, nor the fractions mounted on the fractions of substances so lethal they should never have been forgotten.

280

Long ago, the Department of the Environment chose the only possible solution to this mess: quarantine, declare it off limits, avoid it. This isn't earth, this place. It is a new planet, a place of long molecular chains that never break, with its own pungent atmosphere, its own tastes, its own deadly customs. To walk here in safety you need more than a moon suit; you must not only be sealed and fed canned air, you must be armored.

We went along in our damp fashion rags, four misplaced pretties from the planet across the river.

The sun was high and the air bitter when we reached a sign of human habitation. We were still well within the West New York Quarantine District, but there were nevertheless houses occupied, cars at the curb. The neighborhood was silent, but it was alive.

As we straggled down the street avoiding water-filled potholes and weed-choked sidewalks as best we could, lace was drawn back on windows here and there as the neighborhood observed us. We came to a large house with an iron fire escape attached to the front. It was a great, gothic pile, all gray granite and copper sheathed roof. Where there once had been air conditioners, bright yellow plastic catalytic air cleaners protruded from windows. The driveway had four cars in it, a Mitsui Baby, a Toyota Oh and two Chrysler Clubbies.

'Here,' Scott said.

John, who was a trembling shell of himself, looked up from the depths of his beautifully embroidered coat. 'Why?'

'It's either a boarding house or a commune. It's worth a try.'

The house was open. When our knocks were not answered we went in. The air in the front hall had the thick, faintly human smell that is associated with worn-out catalysts. It was strangely damp, even wet. Beyond the human smell there was something else – loam, perhaps. The hall floor was bare, the walls in need of paint. From some distance away, there came voices.

The voices were cheerful, even excited, but faint. We moved down the hall and into the front room.

We found ourselves facing an exuberant rush of plant life. Huge tomatoes hung from gigantic, twisting vines. Lettuces the size of watermelons floated in vats of nutrient fluid. Carrots four feet long grew behind hazy glass, their tops forming great bushes that reached almost to the ceiling.

Bell raised her voice. 'Hello?'

There was a shuffling movement between two of the hydroponic vats. A woman appeared, badly crippled, wearing braces and using two canes, wearing a plastic apron, her hair tied up in a checked scarf. 'What in the world,' she burst out. 'What happened to you?'

I wanted to ask *her* that – I haven't seen such a severe cripple in years. But we were the invaders, and we were certainly a mess. 'We were in a boating accident,' Scott said.

'Boating, yet. Now I've heard it all. Where was this boating accident, in the Hackensack? Did your boat dissolve, or what?' She laughed, throwing back her head, guffawing with total abandon. 'In the Hackensack!'

'The Hudson. We hit some rocks last night in the storm.'

She stopped laughing. 'I hear the lie in your voice, Mr Man. I think I'd better convene a session on you people. You stick right here.'

We certainly didn't care to do that. 'Convene a session' had a most unpleasant sound to it. Very official. Bell began to leave.

The woman grabbed Bell by the wrist. 'Now, now,

don't go all shadowy on me. I'm not the cop that's after you.'

We stopped, of course. We were very innocent then. The fact that she had guessed our predicament struck me, at least, almost dumb with amazement. 'What is this session?' Bell asked.

'Just a meeting. There are eight of us living here, and if we're going to take you in, we ought to at least convene, don't you think? I mean, it's not a decision for just one.'

She went off toward the back of the house, passing through the dining room, which was almost filled by eight massive honeydews and their supporting equipment. We could not see beyond, nor understand the import of the conversation that took place in the kitchen.

One and another, people started drifting up, until there were six of them clustered around us. A man who had a startlingly cold artificial hand introduced himself as Sunrider Charles. 'Charlie,' he said. 'Sunrider was my folks' idea of a name.' He smiled so quickly it might have been a trick of light. Immediately his face returned to what could only be described as tight repose.

'Who are you?' Charlie asked.

We started with a babble. Finally Bell explained us as best she could.

'They said they had a boating accident last night in the Hudson,' the young woman in the checked scarf added.

People looked nervously at one another. Their expressions were grave. 'You're fugitives,' someone said. Surely she was no more than fifteen. Not even age management could duplicate the absolute freshness of such a face.

I decided to speak up. What was the use of pretending? It was perfectly obvious that we were exactly what they thought. 'We're running from the Tax Police.' John grew stiff and nervous. 'We did nothing wrong, but we're fighting the Depop, and we think some of Gupta Singh's people screwed up our tax data files.'

'I wish it wasn't them,' a tall black man said. 'They're so damn mean, and they work awfully hard.'

Bell spoke quickly. 'We're finding that out. Are you people Depops?'

The crippled woman laughed. She introduced herself as Scylla, 'named after a friend of Charybdis,' she remarked. 'People like us don't matter. We aren't exactly registered voters. If Depop comes, we'll get ourselves out of it, you can be sure of that.'

Another woman, this one in her unmanaged, unmadeup fifties, spoke up. Her voice was loud and demanding. 'Do you know anything about indoor farming?'

Bell answered for us all: 'If it means a roof and a place to sleep and no questions, we can learn.'

There was no ceremony over the decision. Scylla turned out to be farm manager. 'We need somebody on the water purifier,' she said briskly. 'You, the old man, you do it. Charlie, you instruct him and then go down and pick those mushrooms that are due for Piedmonte this afternoon.'

'Can I get a bath, some clothes?' John raised his hands, almost in supplication.

'No. Go do what I told you.'

We were all assigned different tasks. It seems there was plenty of work for us on the farm. I went with Scylla to continue taking molecular samples for the cloning lab. It turned out that these vegetables were not grown from seeds but cloned. 'They can't seed,' she said. 'They're all hothouse freaks.'

She showed me how to take a core from a carrot with a needle that looked like a hair. It was slow, exacting work, and each carrot had to be done in order that the best could be found.

I worked through the afternoon, sometimes staggering in my battle against sleep. 'We have a rest period after the truck,' Scylla said. Later she asked me if we really were just ordinary tax cheats, or if the Gupta Singh story was true.

'Since we've always paid our taxes and Singh's people have played other data-theft games with us, we're assuming it's another form of harassment.'

'Nice people. The Tax Police can be a pain.'

'I think the idea is to keep us so busy running we can't finish our conviction or get our book into data.'

'What does it matter? Nobody reads data. People take videos under five minutes. Nobody reads.'

'We sold forty million sessions with our Falon conviction. And it was heavy work, questioning that thing.'

She giggled. 'I remember it. I asked him all kinds of intimate stuff about his sex life. It was hilarious. He wanted a big strong mommie to cuddle him.' She regarded me. 'So that old man you've got with you is the John Sinclair who did Falon. You're the first famous people I meet, and you're fugitives. Such luck.'

We worked together in silence. The older woman brought carrot juice at four, and I drank with desperate relish. Scylla didn't even give me a chance to catch my breath. 'Got to be ready when the truck comes. The palace must be fed.'

'The palace?'

'Manhattan Island, lady. The largest, richest palace in the world. Problem is, it can't get fresh produce from legitimate sources. What's left of the Imperial Valley sells only inside California, and the Southeast produces second-rate junk in its depleted soils. So here we are, bootlegging in the Jersey Jungle. We supply fruits and vegetables to some of the best restaurants in the city.'

I remembered Manhattan restaurants with their endless supply of fresh, sweet fruit and perfect vegetables. 'I wonder if I've ever eaten any of your stuff before.'

'These giant carrots they cut up and sell as *petits*. "Very fresh, madame,"' she mimicked. '"They have been especially flown in from Belgique."'

Ruefully, I realized that I had indeed eaten them before. 'Is the food dangerous?'

She glared at me. 'I don't like that question.'

'I mean, where do you get the water you grow it in? Surely not from the ground, not around here.' This was certainly one of the most toxic places on earth.

'The water's filtered,' Scylla said. Her face had grown dark and hard. 'There's a lot of money in this business,' she said. 'If you can survive the pollution for five years, you can go out rich.'

'I didn't even know places like this existed. How do you live? Isn't the Quarantine Zone dangerous?'

'Call it the Jungle. That's its real name. As far as surviving here, that's quite a story.' She wiped her brow. 'Want to hear it?'

Of course I wanted to hear it.

Scylla and the Charms of Circe

We aren't doing a legal thing here. Lots of people on the Network don't do legal things. So many things aren't legal. Look, I don't know exactly what to make of you people. You're dirty, wearing Manhattan clown suits, I don't know where the hell you've been or what you're up to.

That old guy says he's John Sinclair. The last time I saw John Sinclair on tv he was a smarted-up age-suppressed Adonis. So what happened? Your story holds together, but it's so strange.

I find that I'd still like to talk about myself. Just sitting here and talking into a recorder is nice. I could turn out liking this even though I suspect it isn't very safe.

I'll tell you a little bit. I was born in the west and I worked for four years in the Imperial Valley. That's where I got this surge of knowledge about farming. Half the place is saline, so it doesn't produce like it used to. A couple of years ago I heard that there were damn good plant geneticist jobs in Michigan. Agra Hydro was opening the Bill Taylor Farm #1 in Roscommon, Michigan. It's three square kilometers of hydroponics, the largest building on earth. Jobs? I was making a hundred thousand a year. Then I developed this bone loss thing. My back went to pieces. What the hell is it? Nobody knows. 'Cellular deterioration, nkc,' is what they call it in the medical centers. Nkc stands for 'no known cause.' Just life, eating me away.

I went on pain blockers and got fitted for my brace. Then other Agra people started getting it. Their solution was to robotize the whole plant. So I was not only out of work, I was dealing with braces and these canes and a thousand dollar a month medical bill for pain killing.

I guess at that point I was so disgusted I just dropped out. I left Michigan, I thought maybe I'd find some kind of skilled personal work in Manhattan. What, I still don't know. It turns out they don't want cripples there. Cripples are too eerie. You just don't see them things prancing Fifth.

I drifted into this, met a guy through the night manager at my hotel. He said he knew of good paying jobs for hydroponicists. So here I am, and now that I'm on the Network, I don't have to worry about registered medicines. I can get some real serious pain killers and thank the Lord.

I had a friend once. She couldn't take it when the Agra thing fell apart and I started bending up, so she left. I refer to her like she died, and that's how I like to think of her.

After Win died, I felt like I had been hollowed out. Permanently. I kept on, but it was a charade. It still is, I guess. The others here work to get rich. I work to buy pain medication, and to take the occasional trip to a clinic where they regrow bone. But it doesn't work. I end up with so much calcium in my blood it's like a red milkshake, and nothing grows. They don't know why.

My mom was a short-order cook, a waitress, a working woman, and she disappeared on me when I was fifteen. I did what I could. Put myself through technical school working as a geisha in LA. Blonde geishas are really prized by the Japs. If you're pretty and good. I was once, I haven't always been all bent up like this.

God, I almost forgot, I was a professional chimney sweep for a couple of years, and I still have my top hat to prove it. That was before the bone thing, of course, like all the good parts of my life.

Right now I am running this operation, which is by far the most money I ever made. We draw these clones and grow them hydroponically. We are not known to the Federal or State EPA, nor to the New Jersey Toxic Food Watch. Now that doesn't mean we run a bad operation. It's just that the house is in the Jungle. We have no city water service, so we have to rely on a well.

Why am I telling you this? Because you asked me to talk about myself and my work and I kind of like you. You're obviously all a little crazy, trying to run away from your problems. You'll fail, of course, unless you do a total system detox. You can't escape just one or the other part of the system. The only rational thing to do is to get away from the whole system. You have to erase yourself. Cease to exist. Drop out of the National Retirement, close all bank accounts, abandon your cars, your credit cards, your computers, everything that links you to the system. Otherwise, no matter how clever you are, or how hard you struggle, in the end the system will catch you.

You seem to me like perfect Networkers. And you don't need to be on the shady side like us. There's lots of good people on the Network. We evildoers just give them a bad name.

I know what it's like to run. I mean, once I was on the road, I told you that. Now I sweat over these veggies, we all do, because this is ours, you get my drift? This place is ours, these beautiful vegetables. There are serious profits, and our loyal clients, they belong to me and to the others. It's our own thing, you get my drift?

We're a little commune, really, I guess, although I make most of the final decisions. That's the way it is with me, I can't stand not being in control. It's why I never fly in a TAV or even take a fanprop if I can possibly avoid it. Out of control and I'm a sweating jelly.

I control the money and manage things. I also work. We don't have any robots. We only use simple computers. None of these genius computers for us, with their links to the rest of the system. There's another mind come alive on this planet, and even though it works for mankind right now, I wouldn't be at all surprised if it had its own ideas about what this planet ought to become. It is the electronic mind.

You have to understand, we are all the enemy of this huge electronic being that is conscious, you have to get to that or you just don't know anything about planet reality. This conscious thing, see, it's not an artificial intelligence, not as originally designed, anyway. It scares me because I can't know its motives. Maybe it would help us. But then again, I don't intend to go on-line just to find out.

There's so much to say. I look at you. Blanko four times. You don't know what I'm getting at. You never heard of any of this stuff. On the Network people know more. There's even supposed to be a group of kids on the Network who can communicate with the electronic mind. They're called Magic.

Listen, I'll tell you the truth. The second you got on that boat or whatever you did, to run away from your system crash, you joined the human race, the ninety percent of us who live totally outside the world of Manhattan and London and Beverly Heights and the Moscow Hills.

Notice, sweetpeas, you are now going where the wind blows you. You have to get into being here from an ethical viewpoint. Like, what I do. You've probably eaten some of our food. Maybe a lot of it. Belgian baby carrots, flown in by TAV? Made right here. Our carrots might be big, but they ain't tough, not when we get through with 'em. Those things in the vats, you'd have to go at them with a pickaxe. But after they're sent through the cutter and then soaked in molecular solution, they're so tender. Then we flavor them with active triomes and the restaurants pop them full of Satisfaction, and you eat them up and yum yum *yum*!

Am I right? Do you remember how good the veggies are in those slick places like Primavera and Contretemps? I'm a little prejudiced. I want praise for a hell of a product! We really do genius work here. This place is not a food factory, it's an art colony. We aren't a bunch of scruffy bootleggers, we are artists, making the impossible real.

We can grow one of these carrots in four days. You come down here at night when the music's off and you can hear the stuff growing, I swear it. There's no way this can be achieved on a conventional hydro.

And our other stuff, these tomatoes, you don't get 'em like this in the stores. These are real, red, juicy goodies, just like they're supposed to be. The invention of the tomaple might have made it easier on the shippers, but it sure ditched the succulent pleasure of biting into one of these soft, delicious, cool miracles. A tomato was never meant to be crunchy like an apple. And most of them are even worse, grainy.

My, I love your eyes. You four really have good eyes. You, the young woman – sorry, no offense, Mrs Lady, but I can smell a gerontology job fifty yards away – you look almost mad at me? If you could get to a phone, what would you do – call the EPA? Soho, that's your societal ethic screwing you up. You think, we might cause an outbreak of icthyosis or something with our tainted veggies. Or we might induce some kind of mutation in the shines who are feeding off all this false freshness.

Maybe we even caused that outbreak of ten-level malignant glioma last year. People getting tumors in their livers and guts and brains that were full of teeth and hair.

Look at you, lady love, you hate me. *Hate* me. All right, I'll tell you something you've got to understand. In this house I am the law. The United States stopped at the quarantine sign down the steet. Hell, we'll probably all get generalized cancer just from living in this chemical slup. Go down in our basement, it smells like toluene or benzine or something. West New York isn't off limits for nothing.

I decide what happens to you. If I say you go back to the Tax Police, back you go. Or if I say you have to take off and the hell with you, that's what happens. If I decide we help you, we'll get you on the Network and you'll have a chance. Sort of.

You're so fancy and proud, but you're out of luck. You aren't on the Network yet, so you're nonpeople. You don't belong in any world.

If you can stop sneering and looking down your collective nose at me and give me some reason to want to get you into the Network I could turn out to be a good friend. You know what you have to do? You have to become real human beings. If you can make a start on that you don't have to worry about dear Scylla punishing you. The Network is linked together by love.

Now, if my nose doesn't lie, it's time for a feed. Look at you, old man, chewing without even realizing it. You poor dopes, you're starving. Come on in the kitchen and dig into some of the juiciest vegetables you ever ate.

Commune Meeting: What Now?

SCYLLA: OK, we're ready to start. Mole, you got your 'corder going? We don't want any arguments later.

MOLE: It's on.

SCYLLA: It's really evil days that a man like John Sinclair turned up here. He has political enemies the like of which none of us have ever faced and I hope we never do. We're little people, and this man is a beached shark. I think his trouble is absolutely for real even though I'm not too sure what it is. The question is, how do we react to this?

CHARLIE: All I'm sure of is he's a celebrity type. He's been on tv, in the news, in data. I don't want him around, and I don't think we ought to let him within a million klicks of the Network. What if he's trying to do a number on the Network?

AMANDA: He comes here with his whole family all wet and cold and smelling like the river. I agree with Syl, I think he's totally for real. What bothers me is that they mentioned they're trying to convict Singh. Well, for God's sake. They're really hot stuff, if the Depop is after them. You've got some very hard people in that organization. And they are the last people we want to know about the Network. When the Depop bill passes, the Network intends to hide even deeper.

SCYLLA: So what do we do? The very fact that they came here is scary. Somebody's certainly chasing them. They may follow them here.

MOLE: We can handle the Tax Police.

SCYLLA: Can we? What'll you do when they fill you full of Truth-20? Spill your soul is what you'll do.

MOLE: I feel for these people. They're fugitives from the same world that screwed me. They're scared and helpless and hungry. Listen to them in there eating. It's a good thing to be able to feed somebody who needs it like they do. They're like beautiful, impossible insects, aren't they?

DAVID: They think of themselves as powerful, in control of their lives, but actually they're crawling across our hands, and if we want to we can crush them.

SCYLLA: David, what makes you think like that? You're so damn indirect. What are you suggesting? Put it on the table.

DAVID: We could just put out their lights. Drop them in the Hackensack. Goodbye problem. Only, I can't do it. I haven't got the heart. I respect Sinclair. He showed a lot of courage with Falon. Also, they're totally helpless, just look at them. Wandering into a dangerous place like the Jungle. They have no idea what they're doing. On balance, I guess I want to help them.

AMANDA: Wow, you bring up a lot of convoluted possibilities. If we help them we could get into trouble with the TPs, which I agree it's stupid to think we can handle. Can't be bribed like regular cops. Or anyway, we haven't got enough money to bribe them. On the other hand, if we don't give these people some help the TPs are going to get them. And then they'll tell all about us. I don't want to be the one to say it, but they are suffering, and maybe it would be best if they didn't have to suffer any more.

MOLE: I can't believe I'm hearing this. I think we're deciding whether or not to kill these people, and I'm not sure I even want to participate in this conversation. If we do a thing like that, I'm leaving the commune, I'm telling you that right now.

JOSIE: My thought is I'm scared and I'm really unhappy that they came here. The way I look at it, we're about certain to get into some kind of trouble with some authority almost no matter what we do. I think it's probably best to put them on the Network. That way they have a chance of getting away clean, and that's probably our best chance, too.

JOE: I want to talk. I want to say they can't get away no matter if we help them or not. Look at them. I mean, they come here dressed in those fashion rags, all messed up, half starved, and they've only been on the road one night. These people are real inexperienced. They don't know what they're doing. You put them onto the Network, and you hurt the Network, because these people are going to get caught no matter how much help they get. Nobody will sew it to our shirts if we sink them in the Hack. I don't like it, it isn't a pretty thing to do. But it is what will keep this place from getting raided. It is the only thing.

SCYLLA: This has gone a lot deeper than I thought it would. I want you all to think very carefully before we

295

conclude this meeting. We have one member who will leave if the vote goes a certain way. And I don't know what I'll do if it does. I've always believed that respect for the lives of others was sort of fundamental.

AMANDA: OK, Syl, you sell polluted food, so don't bother with that load. The only real question is, what's best for the future of this commune and the Network of which it is a part.

SCYLLA: Bearing in mind that most Networkers have no use for us. We're evil, vicious, greedy. Not Network style. We sell polluted food. Not the Network consciousness, not at all.

DAVID: I think we've gotta do the river. It's simple, it's safe.

SCYLLA: Anybody else to talk? Roger? Does anybody have a problem with me making a final decision now?

DAVID: I'm with you, Scylla. Always. I know you heard me.

SCYLLA: On this one I want to see a vote, so raise hands for the river. Five in favor. That makes it hard, because I don't agree with you myself. But I won't go against the majority on something as important as this.

MOLE: I'm shocked and disgusted. This world is full of violence and death. Life is cheap. Just now it got a little cheaper. I'm going to leave. I'm getting my things. God, I can't believe this. I think I'm sadder than I've ever been in my life. Goodbye, you people. I really loved you.

SCYLLA: Mole, will you consider having a twenty-four hour think-through?

MOLE: I'm gone, Syl. I don't belong with you people.

SCYLLA: I'm sorry, Mole. Better give me the 'cording. You only made one copy, right?

MOLE: I made what I made. Here it is.

DAVID: I say we move fastest. Let's hit them and then put them in the river after dark. We move immediately. Get it over with before we all start crying.

BELL: The Alliance of the Hunted

I had quit eating before the others. My stomach was churning because I was afraid of the food. But I had been too hungry not to eat a little. The commune was huddled together in the basement having what Scylla had told us was a business meeting.

I took the opportunity to have a look around the place. The second floor was a clutter of labs and casual sleeping arrangements, pads on floors with sheets crumpled on them, the living areas oddly contrasted to the highly sophisticated cloning apparatus that dominated most of the rooms. Here was where they replicated their giant vegetables, ensuring that each generation was precisely identical to the last.

Then I heard a man's voice in the next room. He was making a husky, private sort of a sound very much like sobbing. My initial reaction was to call out to him, but he slammed his fist into his palm and then began throwing things around. I approached the room cautiously.

As it turned out the things were personal items, and they were being thrown into a duffle bag. The man they called Mole was apparently leaving, and in anger.

When he saw me he stopped. He glared at me with such fury in his eyes that I backed away. Then he shook his head and went back to his packing. The energy flowing from this man was almost a physical thing. I was transfixed by it – I couldn't stay there, but I could hardly turn away from someone in such a terrible emotional state. 'Is there anything – '

'Get out of here. Please.'

'Of course.' I turned to go back downstairs. His suffering was none of my business. I hadn't walked three steps before his hand slammed down on my shoulder. He terrified me and I jumped away. I whirled to face him, expecting a fist in my face.

Instead he was standing quite still. His expression was full of conflict – anger, hurt, fear. It was hard to see which suffering emotion ruled him. 'I'm a traitorous bastard,' he said. His voice was so low I had to strain to hear him. 'I have a word of warning for you. They're meeting in the basement. You know that?'

'A business meeting?'

'Yeah, and you and your friends are the business. You listen now. Get out of this house. Run like hell. I know a farm where they'll treat you better than this bunch. A legitimate place. It's way the hell out in Iowa, a place called Summerland. Thirty klicks south of the town of Defiant. I worked on Summerland for three years. If you make it that far you might see me there again – if I can get Summerland to forgive me for the wrong I've done here.'

'Is there an airport – '

'Oh, Christ and Jesus, don't *fly*! You buy a used car for cash. If you don't got cash, get some. Drive. You have three days grace before the title vests. During that three days nobody knows you own the car except the dealer and he ain't talking because he wants to get rid of the damn iron.'

From downstairs Scylla's voice drifted up. 'Mole, if you're going before we get started, now's the time.'

'This place is a deathtrap for you. Get the hell out of here and do it right this *second*!' He threw his duffle over his shoulder and started down the stairs. Then he hesitated. He handed me something from his pocket. I looked at it – a Sony 'cording, its tiny use light glowing.

299

'I wasn't supposed to make two copies of this, but I did it anyway. Listen to their meeting,' he whispered, 'it's all in here.' Then he turned and ran.

My impulse was toward panic flight. Fortunately I did not listen to the 'cording until later. Had I heard that conversation then, I might have done worse than run, I might have frozen.

I had Scott and John and Allie to think about, and no time to listen to 'corders. I would sooner cut off my own legs than risk my family.

I was going to go racing downstairs and get them out, but the others were already emerging from the basement. I forced myself to walk, and as I walked I tried to reach a state of composure.

From the kitchen John's clipped, raspy voice asked for the plate of beans. We were in terrible danger, I felt sure. Not knowing its nature made it that much worse.

Before me in the kitchen was a dim tableau, Scott and Allie and John at a green composite table, eating from the big plates of steamed vegetables that had been set before us. Scylla came in, moving briskly. 'Fill up, fill up! We've always got plenty of veggies.'

For the moment I didn't know what to do; I had not expected to see anybody but the family. I had no plan. I was just going to yell and start running. Now things were more complex. I fought down my terror.

Were I more oriented toward action, it might have occurred to me to just tell the others of the danger and then overpower Scylla. She wasn't in any shape to stop a healthy young woman like me, not with that back of hers. She could barely stand up even with the help of the canes.

I locked eyes with Scott, hoping to communicate some sense of danger by my expression. I must be a severe lover, for Scott returned a melting glance, then looked away as if embarrassed. He's always saying that I strip him with my eyes.

I just stood there, staring stupidly while Scott ate a head of broccoli and John scraped juice from his plate with an old kitchen spoon. Only Allie perceived something from my manner. She looked very suddenly straight ahead, then turned back to me. In her face there was a frowned question.

Footsteps sounded on the stairs behind Scylla. 'Look, if you folks're finished,' she said, 'why not come upstairs and take a shower? Get cleaned up, you know. It's not good to let rain stand on your skin. After that you can slope here if you want. We can't keep you forever, but nobody's tangled over a couple of nights.'

'A shower,' Scott said, 'sounds wonderful. You're sure you can spare the water?'

'It doesn't matter, it's straight groundwater. Just don't drink any and you'll be fine.'

There was a general scraping back of chairs as the others got up. I felt Scylla's eyes on the back of my head. At that moment I would have believed that she could read my thoughts. Mentally, I tried to wrap a coat around myself, to hide, to somehow disguise my guilty knowledge.

'Are you all right?'

It was not a casual question; there was an arrow in her voice. I met her eyes. 'Yes. I'm sorry I didn't finish.' There was no mistaking my plate of food.

'Why didn't you, if I may ask?'

'I – the pollution – '

Scylla looked at me again. Her right hand toyed with her cheek, the middle finger moving back and forth over a thickening that lay just beneath the skin.

'I had a look around the place,' I said. I smiled, a strange, mechanical sensation. 'It's fascinating!' I'm no actress. To myself and to Allie I sounded very strange. Scylla didn't seem to notice, but a frightened look had come into Allie's face.

'We're very proud of it. I'm surprised that you felt like exploring. You look even more done in than the others.'

'I feel pretty good.'

'Well, doctor says all of you need to get that gik off your skin. Rain's dangerous. And I'll bet when you see the nice clean beds we've got for you, you'll feel tired enough.'

In Scylla's jerky, nervous movements, in her darting voice, I detected clear menace. But the others noticed no such thing. The look of creature-satisfaction on John's devastated face distressed me. How should I handle this? I didn't even know exactly what was wrong. Only that Mole had been in a terrible state, and delivered a terrible warning.

The others stood back in the hall as we moved up the narrow back stairs. In this confined space the odor of human flesh and oozing plant life was nauseating. Didn't the others see anything strange in the fact that these unwashed people were taking such pains to get us clean? Our cleanliness didn't concern them; they wanted us naked and helpless, surely that was the point.

'This is the master bedroom,' Scylla said. It was an eerie place, an old, old room with a bay window and molding around the join of walls and ceiling. A saucer-shaped light fixture hung into the room. When Scylla turned it on I tried hard not to scream. The walls were graffitied with scenes of terrible agony, people burning, being torn apart by huge black machines, enormous hands ripping infants to pieces, skulls, bones, rough dismembered limbs. And on one wall the scrawled word, 'AILAT, 2012.' A reference to the massacre of the Israeli children.

'I'm afraid an artist once lived in here,' Scylla said absently. 'All I can suggest is that you get to sleep as soon as possible, so you don't have to look at it. Which means, it's time to take that shower. We have two bathrooms, so you can all go through at once, more or less.' Allie and John hesitated. Long habits of modesty are not easily broken. 'Strip,' Scylla said. 'We can't keep the water heater running forever.'

I had to act now. If I waited until we were naked, it would be too late. There was a ripping sound as Scott opened his belt. 'Stop,' I said. My voice sounded so small! 'Stop.' I tried to put authority in it. 'STOP!' I put too much, and this time it rang through the whole house.

Scylla raised her eyebrows.

'Scott, put your clothes back on. We're going. Now.'

'What?'

'I – I've decided. We have to keep moving.'

'You've decided,' Scott said. It was a question, though, almost plaintive. Allie's eyes narrowed. Slowly, Scott did as I asked.

'I've been our natural leader ever since we left Manhattan. Let's codify my role.' My voice came out nasal this time, more a whimper than anything else. I realized that I had raised my head and jutted out my chin. Had the situation been less dangerous, I think I would have laughed at myself. 'Any objections?'

They stared at me. Scylla had become extremely still, hanging on her canes.

'And as our new leader, you have decided that we can't have a shower and a rest? We have to go back out there and risk the fact that the Tax Police might be skimming this very area?' Scott was not a sarcastic man, not normally.

'We're with you,' Allie said. 'Me and John.'

Scylla suddenly left the room. 'Please,' I whispered.

303

'There is – ' Before I could finish she returned. I could see her friends clogging the dark hall behind her. Allie and John were looking sharply to me.

'Scott, you ought to listen to Bell,' Allie said. She didn't waste a moment: this elegant Manhattan lady, looking like nothing so much as a bedraggled fairy and not a lot more formidable, took Scylla by her powerful shoulders and moved her physically aside. 'We're leaving.'

I went up to Scylla. 'Thank you for helping us,' I said. Then I had an inspiration. Why not make the damned Tax Police help us? 'The truth is, the police are closer than we said. They're going to get here any minute. You've been good to us. In conscience we cannot stay.'

Back in the hall someone coughed, a long, liquid muttering, like the echoing of thunder. Scylla's mouth was dry, but she was smiling. 'You don't like the room.'

I took Scott by the hand and led him into the crowded hallway. The stink was almost overpowering. We were crowded up against the wall, the four of us, by our hesitant captors. A large man stood before me, his body pressing against mine. His clothes were slick with dirt and sweat, and an oozing rash made his neck look as if it had a crust. 'If we move fast we won't bring the police down on you,' I said. 'I wish I could think of some way to thank you.'

They stopped us. The only sound in the hallway was breathing. 'I'm sorry,' the big man said. He slammed his closed fist into the side of Scott's head. Scott staggered, gasping.

Suddenly John's voice filled the stifling hallway. It was ringing with command. 'Stop! You can't hurt us, what we're doing is too important. If you have any regard left for humanity at all, you'll let us go.'

'Don't stop, Joe,' one of the women said in a shrieking

voice. 'Knock him out.' She grabbed Allie and began shoving her against the wall. Allie's hands windmilled.

John took Allie from behind and pulled her away. 'I have to convict Gupta Singh. If I don't he's going to carry out a worldwide program of murder. And it is not at random. You think you've escaped official notice? Maybe the government has lost track of you, but the Depop hasn't. Every one of you will get a lethal pill. He isn't simply reducing the number of human beings, he plans on doing it selectively, and the whole Network is selected out. Unless I convict him and destroy his movement, you can expect Depopulation officers at your door by April.'

The speech was a brilliant extrapolation of what he had learned from the three conviction levels he had run. How much of it was true we might never know, but it was frighteningly convincing.

Then Mole appeared at the far end of the hall. He was dragging his duffle bag beside him. His face was hollow. 'Listen to the man,' he hissed. 'Listen to the man!'

Slowly, Joe took his hands off Scott. Allie went to John. 'Wish us well,' he said. 'Your lives depend on us. You and the whole Network, and millions upon millions of others. Everybody who is unwanted.'

They parted for us. Then we were on the stairs, going down. Behind us I heard Scylla. 'Wait.'

I did not stop.

'Wait, please!' She struggled down behind us. Before I knew it she had grabbed my wrist. 'Bell,' she said. 'Please, Bell, wait just a second.'

I pulled away. Ahead of us was the kitchen door. John and Allie had reached it, and I could see him pushing it open.

'I know you're scared! I don't blame you.' Scylla's

305

voice had softened, just enough to make me hesitate. 'Mole warned you.'

'Yes.'

'I thought so. You have to understand. This is all we have, and we were so afraid.'

'You were going to kill us.'

She looked suddenly down, and I saw that there were tears gleaming in her eyes. Her hands came out, knobby little claws, and I found myself taking them in my own. Then she moved forward a hesitant step, then another, and suddenly her whole weight was on me. She laid her head against my shoulder and draped her arms around me. Her tears were bitter and angry and sad.

I tried my best to accept her. People are complex, from moment to moment they reform and become new again, changing shape and color as easily as the mythical beasts that symbolize the inner life of man.

We left that strange, strange place in the simplest, most awkward possible manner – on foot, in the rain, without so much as an umbrella.

We walked silently for a time, until the dim lights of the house were behind us. The streets were pockmarked and running with water.

My mind went to the practicalities of movement and shelter. We had to get to that farm Mole had told me about. It was a long way. We needed rest, and we needed to be clean and dry. I wondered if there were still any motels along Route 17. The old highway was outside of the Quarantine Zone, so we might find some sleazy place where our cash wouldn't be questioned. 'Come on,' I said. The rest of the family followed me.

SCOTT: Troll Heaven

Bell got us out of the Jungle on that awful second night, and then into a room at the Moonbeam Motel at four in the morning. We arrived soaking wet and on foot, confronting the sleepy owner, Bell speaking for all of us, lying about a breakdown, a raid by roadies, a stolen car, a web of obvious falsehoods that got us a schlicky three hundred dollar room for a thousand cash.

I followed along, my mind almost continuously turning over the problem of decoding Tom's files. He knew all sorts of things about this underworld. People trusted him. Somewhere in his files I felt sure that there would be something about Summerland, the place we were now going. And we had listened to that horrifying 'cording Mole had made. Did Tom know about the Jungle, also? If only I could crack more of those files and do it faster, we might get some of the help we had to have.

Allie and John dropped into bed the moment we got to the motel room, but before we slept I took Bell to the motel's coffee shop. She had barely touched the commune's feast, for which we certainly couldn't blame her.

The counterman didn't seem to care that we stank from the rain. He asked us our story: it was a forgotten hour, four A.M., and there was nobody in the coffee shop except him and the radio. I ordered strong tea and Bell got a tofu plate, and we told him pretty much a pack of lies, except that we had been waylaid in the Quarantine Zone.

'You went into Troll Heaven and got out alive,' he said

at last. 'That's damn lucky.' I made a note of that name, Troll Heaven. Maybe it was an identifier in some key file.

'You know Scylla?'

'I know Troll Heaven. There's so much poison in there nobody can stay long without getting all kinds of stuff they don't even have a name for.'

'But people live there.'

'Criminals. Crazies. Network types who can't get along with us ordinary schmedlocks.' Troll Heaven. Network. Datapoints. I wanted to get back to my computer. All the years I'd spent on those files, though, I wouldn't be surprised if I failed yet again.

The counterman went on. 'The problem is, there was every kind of illegal dumping over the other side of the highway. More than a hundred years of it. Basements, back yards, vacant lots, even in the tanks of abandoned gas stations. It was a big business. It made Troll Heaven what it is today.'

He stopped for a while to listen to *Girl Girl Girl* on the radio. Then he went on. 'Look at them rags you people are wearing. You must have been rich as jewels. I see them limos coming and going on the Turnpike. You don't know nothing. You're totally ignorant, you limo people.' He was leaning into my face, searching my eyes with a frankness that seemed a little strange. He was big and dark and frightening. 'Still and all, you sure need a helping hand right now.'

Bell looked up from her meal. 'What would you say is our biggest problem?'

'Real clear to me. You don't understand anything. You don't know what's going on in the world.' He chuckled. 'You want another meal? A real meal? That stuff you got, it cost sixteen dollars. It's rich man's food. I don't sell more than one of those tofu plates a week. Nobody comin' through here's gonna eat any of that Manhattan food. You let me, I can feed you better for three dollars.'

'I'm full.'

He threw back his head and laughed, a bitter sound that ended suddenly with a sharp cough. 'You won't be in fifteen minutes. You shoulda asked me, Cheapie, give me some stew. I got it right back there in that big pot. Delicious, and it'll keep your insides warm for a week.'

I was fascinated. 'What kind of stew?'

'Just whatever I get. Onions, carrots, potatoes, tomaples, meat.'

'What sort of meat?' Bell asked, her voice dull with tiredness. 'I don't eat much meat.'

'Just the sweetest rabbit meat you ever tasted. No bones to get in your teeth. I took 'em out myself. Deboned rabbit stew.' He laughed again. 'I hear a man can starve to death eating rabbit. But not this stew, no sir. There's navy beans in it, too. You get almost a complete protein.'

'You get all those vegetables from the trolls, I guess.' Bell sounded relieved that she hadn't eaten it.

'No troll food here. There's trucks come up from the Amish farms in Pennsy. The Amish are on the Network, you know it, not like them trolls. They call themselves Networkers, but the Network won't have them.

'Them Amish kept Lancaster County alive when the rest of Pennsy turned into a desert. They know the land, the Peculiar People. That's where I get all my stuff. Now, you know, their veggies aren't much to look at, not like the troll stuff, all perfect and beautiful and poisoned. The Amish farms are totally clean. They even keep the food washed and covered to keep down the airborne pollutants. It isn't pretty stuff. Potatoes the size of your thumb, and hard as stones until you cook them. Tomaples just the same. Cabbage that's tough, the leaves as thick as slices of bread and so full of string they have to be boiled for an hour. But you put all that junk into a stew with a nice fresh rabbit or two, and golly, you got food.'

'I want a taste of it,' Bell said.

'Sure, two tastes, comin' up!' Before I could say no thanks he went around to the kitchen. I watched him happily clinking dishes and drawing up the stew with a ladle. In a moment he was back, bearing two heaping plates of the stuff with a stack of bread on top of each. 'There you are, four dollars each, including the bread. Now you can't beat this! This is real food. You take that tofu platter. That comes in a bag. You just stick it in the sonic and whoosh, the bag puffs up all ready for you to open it, decorate it with a piece of plastic parsley and take your sixteen bucks.'

Bell raised a spoonful of the brown stew to her mouth. I could see the shock register. I tasted mine, and was swept by what I think must have been a wave of instinctive nostalgia. The flavors were so intense, so real that they almost made me gag at first. But I wanted more, I had to have more. 'You see, you people don't know what real food is. You've gotten lost, you're off the edge of the world and don't know it.' He leaned back, his hairy arms crossed over his greasy apron. 'You oughta come by when I fry chicken. I don't get them *things* from the factory. I get real chickens that grew up in a barnyard with heads and eyes and feathers and everything. None of those Simka Bigbirds in this kitchen. 'Course, it costs more than rat – '

Bell dropped her spoon into her food with a splat.

I sat, touching a chunk of hard meat with my tongue. He hadn't gotten all the tumors out.

He threw back his head and laughed. 'You rich people don't know the half of it! You don't know what we're going through, you don't know and you don't care! My kind of people are grateful for rat stew!' His eyes bulged, he shook his fists in our faces. 'My wife died of I don't know what! I took her in to Catholic in Newark and you know what they diagnosed? They diagnosed fibrous disease, unknown. They wouldn't even let her spend the night. What was it she got? What did you rich people give her! She died screaming, clawing at her throat, screaming until nothing came out anymore! Then she turned black and died. She died like a dog, and I saw you out on the Thruway, brrr, back and forth in your fine cars. You got a car that's smarter'n me! You never get sick, never get old. Now I'm tellin' you, you eat every bite of this poor man's rat stew or I will personally force it down your gullet with a goddam cake decorator.'

Bell didn't need to tell me what to do. We ran out. Behind us the counterman shrieked and hopped across the counter, an enormous, frightfully agile man, his face so distended with hate that his humanity seemed to have been canceled. He sailed the plates of stew at us. They splattered against the plastic door of the coffee shop, which cracked down the middle and fell into two pieces. As we raced across the rainswept tarmac, darting back and forth between the few old jalopies in the lot, we heard him screaming, a sound that went on and on, slowly getting higher and more breathless.

I looked back and saw him leaping up and down before the lighted doorway, a gargoyle come to life.

Back at the room we found John sleeping heavily against Allie, whose own breathing was deep and slow. John seemed small beneath the green army surplus blanket, a wisp of bones cuddled up against his delicately lovely wife. One of her small, perfect arms enclosed him. His hair was a gray haze now, his face a labyrinth. So far Allie had not been affected by her own withdrawal from

311

Gerovita. She was younger than John, though, and had not been off it as long.

We lay back on our own bed, which was the usual cheap-hotel super firm, and for a time listened to the sweep of the rain, the murmur of the air conditioning and the faint screaming of the counterman, which had become a sort of mantra of shrieks, four tones endlessly repeated.

'Do you suppose he's brain damaged?'

'I don't know, Bell.'

There was a long silence. Bell shifted onto her stomach and put her hands on her chin. In that sudden way of hers, she was vulnerable and dear. 'What do you suppose is going on?'

'It seems almost like some kind of movie or dream we're in and can't leave. I wish I could shed some light on it.'

'Tom's files.' She smiled ruefully. I've been working on them for years, after all.

'Precisely. They're the one card we have left to play.'

'It's weird to be without Stratigen. Like one of us was missing.'

'I hardly ever used it. It doesn't do decryption.'

'We surely need some facts about the underworld,' Bell said, and I could have wept, her voice was so small. I looked at her, at her soft face and brown, steady eyes. I touched the gleam of freckles that crossed her nose. Gone from those eyes was the easy confidence I had always admired. In its place was a wariness that seemed more animal than human. Then she raised her head, and for a moment I saw a strength that was new, or had always before been hidden.

'I have to crack Tom's really well encrypted files. Have to!'

'You're sure you can do it without your programs going on-line without telling you?'

'Of course. I work with mathematical programs and statistical stuff. Nothing needs to search big databases. Nothing goes on-line.'

Bell turned a steady gaze on me, and to some extent against me. She needed me to be careful.

'Bell, my programs don't have the capability of going on-line.'

'You're certain? Programs have a way of surprising people.'

'I'm certain. I know my tools.'

'I don't want to entrust our survival to Mole. What if he was lying, or confused, or I misheard the name of the farm?'

'I'll get on it right away. I think that the decryption scheme I used for the Sapling Society might just work for the Network data, too.'

'You aren't working without sleep. We might be running hard tomorrow. We have to keep as fit as possible.'

'What if there's no time when we wake up? We need this information.'

'Humor me. Sleep for two hours, then work.'

I kissed her downy cheek. The eyes that regarded me now were slow and steady, but there was a new objectivity there, which was just a little scary. I kissed her again, and our lips touched. I drew her closer.

'Not now, dear boy. You said you don't have time to sleep, so you don't have time to play. Anyway, before anybody does anything else we've got to get ourselves showered and hope there's some detox soap in this hole.'

'Now, please.'

'Be practical, Scott. You don't want your sweat glands opening until this rain is thoroughly and completely washed off. Anyway, we smell like chemical factories. Allie and John had the good sense to bathe.'

We showered in the thin, cool water. There was no

313

detox soap, but there was Ivory, plain and good, and we stroked one another in luxuries of lather.

The bath refreshed me and I agreed not to go into Tom's files for a few minutes. She agreed to come into my arms. In this precious, private moment, we covered one another with love.

SCOTT: The Code in the Code

It is one thing to extract some information from Tom's files about something like the Sapling Society, which he wasn't trying too hard to hide. Getting at the well-hidden stuff is another matter entirely. My success with the Sapling Society file encouraged me and gave me confidence. But when I sat down to my computer, decoding programs arrayed across the screen, my confidece evaporated. I have often erased data while trying to get at it. That must not happen now.

With the loss of access to huge, intelligent programs like Stratigen all we really have left that gives us an edge is these files. Tom moved freely in the Network. I know, he mentioned it to me often. He never gave any specifics, though. Because the Network is an underground movement facts were handled on a need to know basis, and as far as he was concerned I never needed to know.

If we can get help from the Network we might have a chance. Otherwise we are just ordinary fugitives. Worse, we are amateur fugitives.

We have all listened to the 'cording of the trolls' discussion about us that Mole gave Bell. From the tone of Mole's voice we have tried to tell where he really stands. Were his instructions about Summerland honest and valuable, or just the ravings of a moodblown mind? Delta Doctor could do an evaluation in a few seconds, but we dare not access. Going on-line will alert the police to our whereabouts. Worse, even touching Delta Doctor is liable to induce Singh to raise things to yet another level of hostility. What would he do next – get some

315

goons to come in and burn out our minds with Aminase or something? God only knows.

I inserted the disk of Tom's files into the computer. There was no sound, but a flash of the ready light indicated that the identifiers were loaded. It would take an hour just to roll them all across the screen at blur speed. There were a hundred and sixty-eight thousand uncoded identifiers, and no way of knowing how many coded and hidden.

I felt a small sense of competence. I've been working with this little silver piece of metal the size of my thumbnail for four years now. It is the center of my life, my career. So far I have read eighty percent of its uncoded data and four percent of the coded stuff. Approximately half of the filespace doesn't access, which means that coded data represents more of the filespace than uncoded.

I know that Tom used standard linear identifiers protected by access-altered encryption – meaning that the code that hides them changes every time you load the disk. Whenever you start working on them, you start from zero. The cipher also changes at random times, or when certain levels are accessed incorrectly, which means that you often go back to zero even while you are decoding. And there is always the possibility that you'll trigger a gremlin and erase what you're after.

He was a very brilliant man, was Thomas Sinclair. But I think that the Sapling Society codebreaking might have taught me something about his methods. This time I did not start by querying for some obvious identifier like 'Network' or 'Magic.'

Instead I went to machine language and offloaded the raw code to the printer. I was confronted with pages and pages of 128-bit bytes. But at least I was now working with paper instead of that nerve-wracking booby-trapped disk.

I got the optical reader out of my bags and drew the sheets of paper through it. Of course, I hoped that the same thing would work that worked with the Sapling Society data, but it didn't. The distribution curve of on and off bits was already an average curve for this density of script.

I thought about that for a while. I compared the machine language code to a couple of pages from a Gideon bible that was handy. They looked about the same.

Then I saw something astonishing. In Tom's files there was a visual pattern, light-dark, light-dark, repeating itself four times across each line. The bible page was random.

I was excited by my discovery, but also even more fascinated by the mind that had done this. It has taken me four years to even begin to think like Tom. This is a totally new method of encryption – the best codebreaker programs in the business don't even address this method, which is to adjust normally random byte structures to a pattern that can be returned to randomness. Of course, when you go and read the file in English, the patterned bytes read as garbage, while the random structures become words.

I wish I could report that mere randomizing of the pattern resulted in a readable file, but it didn't. Far from it. What I then had was six double-spaced pages of lines that looked about like this:

sitsi igh ta ttr hh eaa ei ds oo dyen nunesr h clm ofricid

But this is not an insoluble problem. It took decryptor only a few minutes to come up with the thirty-six meaningful sentences in English that contain these letters and no others.

I chose the most likely of the sentences. 'This is a night entry, hidden outside of normal search.'

That's Tom's voice quite unmistakable. This time, when I read the whole file, I knew I had mined treasure.

FROM THE DATA FILES OF TOM SINCLAIR:
THE NETWORK

Tuesday, April 22, 2014

This is a night entry, hidden outside of normal search parameters, at the end of a long and unlikely logic tree. I do not know if anyone will ever find these words, but I feel it is my obligation to record them somewhere, if only for my own future reference.

For the sakes of the people involved, I cannot allow this material to receive wide circulation, not now at least, not in 2014 when the United States Government is in the throes of a massive tax registration program. The reimposition of the Income Tax in 2010 caused this. But the government was going bankrupt on VAT; there was no way to tax barter, nor any way to trace the increasingly large number of cash and direct-credit transactions outside of the normal recording system.

The Network started as silent tax resistance. The fact that over thirty percent of all US economic activity was underground by 1997 caused the collapse of the income taxation system in the first place. Because of the heavy use of computers it was thought that value-added taxation was the solution. But all that did was cause many people to abandon electronic transfer altogether.

In 2010 the National Income Authority tried to register people for income taxes. But it didn't work. Now we are trying to live with the Tax Police, and tax resistance has evolved into a whole alternate society, possibly as large as the conventional society.

As a social phenomenon, the Network represents the end of bureaucratic government along the lines suggested by LT Malenkovski in his classic analysis of the collapse of the Soviet system, 'Free Flux in Post-Bureaucratic Societies' (*Social Affairs Papers*, Vol. 126, Feb. 2012).

Malenkovski makes the point that 'flux,' which he describes as 'the flow of activity generated by the effort to satisfy wants and needs,' cannot be controlled if the members of the society become indifferent to the bureaucracy. 'All social control is political control; all social organization is ideology. It is not resistance which kills social control – indeed, when it is resisted it often gains in power. What kills social control is indifference.'

The Network has been growing rapidly, probably more rapidly than any part of the conventional economy. It is filling the cracks left by the decline of the previous system. One type of Networker is living in such places as the Federal Quarantine Districts in Harris and Chambers Counties in Texas, in eastern New Jersey and St Louis and the two thousand smaller Quarantine Areas. Typically, these people risk disease and injury to set up small and often illegal cottage industries in abandoned real estate. They pay no taxes, and let the buyer beware if their products are poisoned. These Networkers tend to view members of the conventioanl society much as old-time carneys looked on the 'rubes' who crowded their midways.

One of the earliest and strongest Network groups inhabits the New Jersey Federal Quarantine Area. In 2013 this group had a population of approximately 3,500, and was growing at an annual 33% rate. Interviews with members of this population – conducted anonymously – revealed the following backgrounds:

Tax fugitives, failed to register:	31%
Unregistered aliens:	22%
Wanderers, hobos:	21%
Abandoned, runaway, under age 18:	11%

| Victims of program sabotage: | 09% |
| Others, or refused to answer: | 06% |

The sexual mix of the Jersey population is 61–49 in favor of women, generally due to female enculturation making women more aggressive than their male counterparts. It is a cliché to state that women are the aggressive sex, men the passive. But nowhere is this fact more clearly demonstrated than in the sexual makeup of this population. Women tend to break their ties with the past more easily, and to seek new alternatives when old solutions no longer work. Men, on the other hand, generally prefer to tinker with the existing order of things before striking out into something as risky as the Network.

Not all Networkers are classified as criminals or fugitives, and not all live in such dubious circumstances as those in the Quarantine Zones. There are a substantial number of extended-family farms across Ohio and Iowa, and in Pennsylvania. One of the most successful farms is Summerland in Iowa. This farm has a population of about eighty individuals, of extremely varied backgrounds. The core group are pantheists with their philosophical roots in the wiccan movement. Summerland is deep in the Midwestern Desert, close to the Amish communities that took over Shelby County as conventional agricorps abandoned their land to the desert. Despite the cultural differences between the Networkers and the Amish, there appears to be little friction. Both groups have managed to keep their land productive despite the terrible destruction caused by the spread of the desert. For example, Iowa as a whole has seen a sixty-six percent decline in farming activity since the turn of the century. Among old-order Amish populations, however, farming activity has risen fourteen percent. While the overall amount of land under cultivation in the state has dropped by nearly three quarters in the past forty years, the amount cultivated by the Amish has risen four percent.

I hope to visit these oases in the Midwestern Desert some day. I have a feeling that much may be learned from them.

Beyond the desert dwellers, there are dozens of Networkers in small, private industries, producing 'sufficiency tools' such as solar heat storage cookers, Lepcon cell electricity generators, hand loomed garments and recycled cars. One highly successful Network factory in Dallas specializes in lobotomizing Unon Interactors so that they no longer connect to outside the data grid, but carry on board most of the information normally accessed from the grid. A lobotomized Interactor can't call grid, but it has a fifty gigabyte rion that contains world knowledge and can be updated for a few dollars at your neighborhood information pump. Although the law says that possession of a lobotomized computer is a class three felony, subjecting the offender to mandatory personality reconstruction, *finding* a non-grid computer is practically impossible, since it never accesses the grid and therefore doesn't reveal its existence.

At the edge of the Network there is a shadowy world of revolutionaries, gene-altered freaks, and the certifiably insane. In this latter group are the brain-transplant victims of the Reasor Hospital Scandal of 2008. Over the five years preceding that date, fifty-six people were brain-transplanted despite the fact that Reasor's transplant team knew the terrifying dislocational consequences that would result from the disturbance to their morphogenetic fields. Reasor elected to hide the Finemann Study, and thus created a hundred and twelve unmixed souls without regard to the extraordinary agony that resulted.

Other genetic revolutionaires are the intelligence-enhanced children, who form the penultimate limit of the Network. Not even in this document will I reveal where these children are located, nor how many of them I have found and tried to help. They are the result of ambitious parents presenting their fertilized eggs for illegal genetic manipulations, creating super-intelligent freaks incapable of joining normal human society. Intelligence beyond genius is a kind of madness, but with sense and direction.

Despite all the pain that these children endure, the loneliness, the painful insights into human frailty and our bleak future, and despite the fact that we chose to legislate against their creation rather than make a real effort to help them, they are probably the most important thing in the world right now.

We may despise them because they form an intellectual super-elite, but we must remember that they are also suffering. For the past few years I have been seeking them out. I have made a place for them, bought land, helped them establish a social order, even found for them a sort of nursemaid and general helper who, were he observed in action, would astonish the world.

Knowing the world, though, it would probably take him from my kids and put him in a circus.

It was one of the greatest privileges of my life to meet these children. I found them by analyzing patterns of data-search in Nexis. When certain data about morpho-genetics and genetics were being searched by an individual under nine years old, I knew that I had found another one of my lonely geniuses, trying to figure out what in the world was the matter with her or him.

I am deeply in love with them. I live to be with them. I spend every moment I can at Magic, which is what they have named the place I bought for them. Thank God Boola is working out as nursemaid. They could not tolerate a human supervisor, but he seems acceptable. He cannot understand their motives and goals, so he ignores that aspect of their world. He never questions them. When five-year-old Randy is up playing with her sextant at midnight, he does not scold her, he brings her soup. And he watched from the shadows. If she falls asleep, he takes her to bed.

I have seen him go thirty and more hours without sleeping. As long as even one of them is awake, Boola is on the alert.

Personally, to get along with them I present myself as their student. I never tell, I ask. At least Boola can keep discipline among them. Size alone ensures that, and he has all the gentleness of his kind.

Being with them is like soaring with angels – distressed angels.

Nobody knows what these children will do. Nobody understands them. But they are among us, and they must be cherished, no matter how difficult or odd they are.

I have gone to each one I could find, and only two have refused to come to Magic. They will come one day, I am sure, but in both cases they have parents who are at least marginally capable of coping with them.

If parents had been trained for this, if there were new ideas ready for these new people, they would not be suffering so much. The kids at Magic have given up home and family to gain for themselves a chance at growing up sane.

They must grow up sane. They are the triumph of mind on earth, and the hope of this planet.

JOHN: Down the Road

I woke up in that miserable motel room with my mind already buzzing with questions. I grabbed my Interactor and just naturally started to access Stratigen.

'John, don't!' Bell snatched the computer out of my hand and I came fully awake.

How could we possibly figure out what to do without Stratigen? And what about Delta Doctor? Were Singh's people somehow tampering with my precious conviction?

I will tell you frankly that I had never before in my life felt as black as I did at that moment. Stratigen couldn't be used, my conviction was in trouble, and I was sitting on the side of the bed coughing up the phlegm of an old man's night.

Allie rose up beside me and put her strong, still-youthful arms around me. Bell smiled into my face. 'Scott has a little surprise for us,' she said.

Scott certainly changed the tone. He managed to make the morning a triumph, as a matter of fact.

By a dazzling feat of codebreaking, he had found and deciphered one of my son's key files about the Network. His four years of heartbreaking and frustrating effort were finally beginning to bring results.

I read the file with a joy as from music, my excitement growing through his all-too-brief narrative. He had given us the most precious of gifts: we now knew for certain that Mole's instructions hadn't been delusions or lies; we could believe that we had some sort of future. Summerland was real, and it was indeed in Iowa, just about where the Mole had said it was.

Our escape route was confirmed. And we were going to find the Network.

If only this bunch of city butterflies could manage a cross-country trek with no credit cards.

Considering that prospect made me realize how tired I still was. What sleep I had managed had been a fluttering, elderly doze. I had been too frightened to fall into deep sleep.

I kept watching that flimsy motel room door, and with good reason. Just after Scott and Bell came back from their experience of rat stew, an incident occurred that illustrated for me just how dangerous all of this was.

They had startled me awake when they rushed into the room, pale and sick looking. Bell was furious, Scott giggling with what appeared to be hysteria. Outside I could hear the thunder of rain, and behind it bleat after bleat of strange, demented shrieking. They spoke together softly for a while. They needed privacy. I tried not to listen or to embarrass them by letting them know I was awake.

Soon they went into the bathroom and began showering. I sat up in bed and put my hand on Allie's forehead. She was sleeping heavily; she has always had the knack of deep sleep.

Then the shrieks started coming closer. They crossed the parking lot to this block of rooms, then stopped. Over the past few days my body's reaction to fear had itself become frightening: the hammering of my heart, the shortness of my breath. I felt so frail.

A gleam of golden light on the handle of the motel room door began moving up and down. I knew that someone was working the handle from the outside. My mouth became dry; I could not even call out to warn Scott and Bell.

My body literally quaked. It was as if all consciousness

had contracted to a single note in the dead center of me. I was a bright pin of light, nothing more. That was me. But I was also the two feet dragging toward the door, two hands trembling as if captured by a rough wind, an ash-dry mouth.

A shadow crept along the glass wall of the old motel room. I could see it hunching, could see the hands come up, and as I struggled forward could hear on the other side of the wall a low human noise, repeated again and again, as if whoever was there was struggling into some new and difficult shape.

My fear was such that I could barely place one foot in front of the other. Behind me, far away in another land, I could hear Scott and Bell showering. I all but fell against the door, almost weeping, and forced my mouth to work, my voice to talk. 'What do you want?'

Silence.

'I know you're there.'

Under my hand I felt the doorknob move as if it had been brought to life.

'I swear I'll open fire if you don't get away from this door.'

With a final jerk the doorknob went dead. From outside there came a faint snicker.

'What on earth do you want? Why are you trying to get in here?'

The whole world seemed to be groaning in the voice outside the door.

I was frozen there when I heard Bell's voice behind me: 'John, come back.'

'There's somebody out there.'

'Leave it. Go back to bed.'

'But – '

'I doubt if he's dangerous. Just crazy.'

Then she peeked for a moment past the curtains that covered the picture window beside the door.

I returned to my bed. When I lay down she stroked my head with long, gentle movements, and hummed the Mobius. Scott came, and they went together, speaking softly. Soon he was working with his computer, his fingers flying, the faint glow of his screen reflecting a tense, haggard face.

I listened to the rain. I was waiting lest the maniac come back. When dawn came I found that I had slept after all. Bell had been out to the Total Shopper across the street and bought some maps. The question was, how to travel.

Bell had the answer from what Mole had told her. 'We buy a used car for cash. Then we drive. We try to make Summerland.'

'Buy a car for cash?'

'It can be done, I'm sure. Final Truth Preowned Vehicles is just down the road. When we walk onto the lot, I'm sure we'll be greeted as long-lost friends. And cash will suffice.'

The lot was an ocean of Mitsus, Toyotas, Hyundais and Chryslers, even a Jeep and half a dozen Osaka Streaks with their infamous exploding dashboards.

'I could stand breakfast,' Allie said as we moved down the rows of vehicles.

Bell glanced at her. 'First things first. We want one that's as uncomputerized as possible. The less computer contact, the better off we are.' I heard smooth music in her voice. There was a sense that she felt confident in what she was doing. She pushed her hair back out of her eyes. 'This Excitation looks like just the thing.'

'What about its guidance computer?'

'Are you kidding? What do you expect in a ten thousand dollar car, Blaupunkt Road Eyes? We're lucky it has seats.'

We went up to the cashier and Bell began bargaining with it. A few minutes of give and take and the program had dropped down from thirty thousand to twenty-two and was threatening to close the window of opportunity.

'Like hell you will', Bell said. 'I'll bet the window'd stay open if I offered twelve.'

'Twenty,' the program snapped. 'You're a hard woman, you're leaving me owing the company.'

'Eighteen.'

'You're killing me. Remember there's an author behind this program. A starving bastard. My commission is down to powdered pickles.'

'Eighteen, robot. You have a deal.' Allie put cash in the window and got a noname title to slip into the transponder.

'Title it in three days in your home state,' the robot said, 'or the transponder will go back to our serial.'

This meant that we had only a few days of use before the bureaucracy could begin tracing it.

As we drove out of the place we had the interesting experience of seeing a man kick open a door in the side of the supposedly automated computer enclosure and stroll off to an outhouse at the edge of the car lot.

'I had a feeling there was a person in there,' Bell said. 'Lawyers and accountants are completely computerized, but you couldn't write a program to sell used cars. Can't be done.' She laughed. 'Look at us. We just got a car worth ten thousand for a mere eighteen. A computer couldn't do that to me.'

The car banged along, its ancient engine hissing and clattering. The air conditioner hardly worked and the black interior soon grew so hot I contemplated designing an openable window with one of my shoes. I remember when you could sail down the highway with the car windows open and enjoy the air of a summer night.

A roaring filled the car, so huge that it seemed directionless. I looked off in the direction of Newark Airport but saw no rising TAV. As we moved along, the sound slowly got louder and louder. Traffic grew slower and more dense. This car had no automap, no guidance system, no trip computer, no satellite link, so there wasn't any way to tell what was ahead.

As soon as the traffic got slow enough swarms of people leaped up from the shoulders of the road, where they lived in shacks so minimal that they looked like piles of trash. Hundreds of men, women and children came out among the cars, wiping windshields, selling everything from spring rolls to paper silhouettes cut on the spot. A barber offered haircuts for five dollars, prostitutes held up pictures of themselves performing their services, dozens of children scuttled around with drywash boxes. Because all cars are closed, they shouted themselves hoarse, leaping on hoods and roofs, battering with their long, gray hands at the windows, shaking the cars from side to side, screaming when a foot or a hand was run over.

Then the traffic sped up and they disappeared like an oily wisp of smoke.

As we proceeded the ground started shaking. Finally the source of the disturbance became clear: just ahead the Hackensack River was a black monster, blaring under the Route 46 Bridge. The water was speeding along, bearing bits of plastic from houses and cars, unidentifiable snatches of color, poles and tangled wires. A swarm of robots raced about untangling flotsam from the bridge abutments. Occasionally one would fall into the water, its emergency siren making a melancholy shriek above the voice of the torrent. A State Highway Department Comm truck was parked to one side directing the emergency crew.

To add to the mayhem, the traffic had begun to move at full speed. How these drivers could cross this endangered bridge with so little regard for their own safety I could not imagine. And why the highway people didn't just close it was even harder to understand.

It was jerking in spasms as we swarmed across, barely managing to avoid robots and hurtling cars. From beneath the span there came explosions as bolts popped out. I looked back toward the comm truck, and had the horrible thought that it might all be automatic. Maybe there was nobody in the truck, just another computer system. And maybe it hadn't been programmed to close the bridge in case of danger, only to carry out its worthless repairs.

We were tired and thirsty. Jammed in the back seat, Allie and I were cramped. As we roared up Route 46 toward the Route 80 interchange we saw a massive sign floating above a riot of green and blue and purple buildings. 'Teterboro Illusions,' the sign said.

'We'll stop at that mall and get some supplies,' Bell called out over the rattling of the car.

As we parked a wheelie came screaming up, shouting 'Room for four more for more values! Come on, four more for more fun!' We got into the seats beside the rangy, sweating others, two men, six women and a couple of kids in cheap masks. Compared to the parking lot the autumn-scented interior of the mall was a shock. Trees soared into leafy heights; for a moment there was the heartbreaking impression that we had entered a healthy forest. The gentle tones of *Country 'Tude* wafted among the trees.

Then the impression was shattered by a young woman, a robot, coming up with an offering. 'Nibs are nibbling good,' she said with a latex smile. 'Nibble 'em anytime.

Food value zero, fun value total. Have one?' She offered a basket. I took one of the blue spheres, knowing from long experience that she would crank up the next part of the commercial if I didn't. How did it taste? I have no comment. They've made it to the stores, so you can try them yourself.

A short distance away another rubbermaid lay on her side, knocked over by vandals. Nevertheless she smiled and churned her legs, holding before her an empty bucket of 'Georgia Perfect Lickin' Chicken.'

'Mmmm,' she said, 'that's fried!' She nodded vigorously, the side of her head scraping against the floor. People walked around her, their faces totally indifferent.

In Manhattan real people take the places of these cheap robots, so we found them fascinating.

When some prostitutes invited us into a spa for a little relaxation, it was a moment before we realized that they were also rubbermaids. Presumably we could have engaged in some sort of sexual activity with them, God knows what.

Bell had a list in her head of what we would need for the road. 'First a couple of air conditioners for the damn car.' We got on the sidewalk and told it to take us to Tandy, where we picked up two 1,000 BTU hand units with full filtration. Then we went to the grocery store and got three days worth of supplies, ranging from Liquichick Soup to Squibb Total Food Bars. Bell and Scott had developed a profound distrust of roadside restaurants. At Glorious Wilderness we bought camping equipment so that we could sleep without registering in a motel. Then we had breakfast at one of these chameleon restaurants. It was Mornin' Sun before noon, Burger Perfect at lunch and Steakout at night.

I was glad to be out of Illusions. There is something terribly depressing about an artificial forest full of stores made to look like cottages. You add to that the banal joke of knocking rubbermaids over on their sides or standing them on their heads, and you have a dreary and oppressive scene.

We headed out Route 80. The old roadway became wide and fine after the cruiser bases, and we began to be passed by the massive vehicles, which left us rocking from side to side in clouds of acidic fumes.

Our car full of petrolene, our air conditioners taped to the dashboard, we rattled off into the late morning. The sun came out from behind clouds long enough to make the windshield turn to blotchy patches of black – the sunscreen was defective. Bell cursed, peering out through a latticework of black lines. She hit the windshield with the palm of her hand, but the problem remained.

We drove on for hours, deep into the night. We had left Manhattan, I suspected, forever. Next stop, another world. Was it the one where we belonged?

Yes, it was. We could tell by the dust.

FROM THE DATA FILES OF TOM SINCLAIR:
BIRTH OF THE DESERT

'Erosion of agricultural topsoil is a "quiet crisis" that could lead to famines in some parts of the world, according to a new study by the Worldwatch Institute.

'The Washington-based research organization concludes that new agricultural techniques have destroyed many of the natural barriers that once protected fields against erosion.

'The Agriculture Department has identified 30 regions most at risk, most of which are in the soybean-growing and corn belt states such as Nebraska, Idaho and Missouri.'

— *The New York Times*, September 30, 1984

'Because corn is relatively poor at holding soil, the corn-growing lands – about 7.5% of all lands in cultivation, producing roughly one-fifth of the world's grain – will fare the worst. The United States, as the world's largest corn producer, is in particular danger.

'The US Soil Conservation Service considers soil losses of 1 ton per acre for shallow soils and 5 tons for deep soils to be the maximum that can be sustained annually without harming productivity . . . In Iowa and Illinois, the two corn-dominated states covered by the GAO study, half the farms surveyed lost between 10 and 20 short tons per acre per year.'

— *The Global 2000 Report*, Penguin Books, 1982

'Soil erosion is a problem in a number of Midwestern states during this year of drought. From Oklahoma north to the Dakotas, dust storms to rival the great "dusters" of the thirties have convinced many farmers to return to the soil conservation practices commonplace until the profit demands of big agribusinesses caused them to be abandoned during the seventies.

'A rapid decline in the vast Oglala Aquifer that provides much of the Midwest with agricultural as well as industrial and drinking water has caused the governors of six states to declare drought emergencies and forbid irrigation and watering of crops.

'"This is a catastrophe for the farm belt," said Nebraska Farmer's Union leader Brett Wilcox. "They can't ask us to go to dryland farming during a drought. We intend to fight this in the courts."'

– *The St Louis Post*, July 9, 1987

'The continuing loss of topsoil in the Midwest is a problem which cannot be ignored much longer by state and federal authorities. The Agriculture Department considers this a minor issue, but the third straight year of declines in corn and wheat production in the United States and Canada can be blamed directly on the loss of farmable soils and the depletion of soils.

'Windblown dust also releases nitrogen from fertilizers, which adds to the already heavy nitrogen load of the atmosphere. Congress has to realize that abandoning land, closing down land, and reliance on densescropping isn't going to work forever. Parts of Iowa, Nebraska and Ohio look like a desert right now. Unless we get a couple of years of more substantial rain, these areas are going to turn into a real, sure enough desert, and that is going to be a problem.'

– Mr Wayne Turner, Iowa Wheat Farmer,
Congressional Testimony, January 17, 1998

'Rains throughout the Midwest were blamed for severe flooding along seven major rivers. An eleven foot crest was reported on the Mississippi at St Louis, and dozens of cities throughout the region were flooded. Runoff from eroded areas of near-desert was blamed for the rapidly rising waters and the flash flood-like conditions that prevailed.

'At least three thousand people were driven from their homes. Seventeen people were killed in Buffalo, Iowa, when a bus plunged over an embankment into the flooding Mississippi. Damage to structures along the Mississippi, Ohio, Missouri and Iowa rivers is estimated in the billions of dollars.'

— *The National Times*, September 22, 2007

'Over the protests of Iowa's Governor Betsey Clark, the Federal Department of Land Reclamation declared sixteen Iowa counties desert areas and forbade the planting of agricultural crops in those areas. A hundred and thirty million dollars were allocated to fund six new reclamation stations in the zone, according to Secretary of Agriculture Hendrickson. An attempt will be made to establish grass cover behind seven hundred miles of windbreaks, to be constructed during fiscal 2013, according to the Secretary.'

— *NewsNet*, June 13, 2012

JOHN: Night in Iowa

It is beyond my powers of description to communicate the sense of desolation that overcame me when I knew we were in Illinois. I was born in Galesburg of the wide, tree-lined streets, and I spent the first ten years of my life there. Galesburg, town of Carl Sandburg and my father. When I write the name Ed Sinclair I write the names of millions, the kind, tolerant people who made the Midwest in its fine years such a very good place.

Galesburg, 1959: I remember standing on a streetcorner and watching a string of limousines pass. In one of them was a cheerful young man named John Kennedy, campaigning for the presidency.

I remember the way Galesburg smelled, the fresh smells of flowers and trees, and the smell coming in from the farms when they mowed the hay. My favorite things were Grapette sodas and Fudgiscles. Galesburg, 1960: Dad dies, Mother and I move to Chicago to be near her sister. They are very close. That was so long ago.

Some people have contended that the earth is changing into another kind of a planet, one more like Venus. The long, gray emptiness of this land, though, looks more like pictures of the surface of the Jovian moon Ganymede. It doesn't look like the earth. It is not home.

The desert silenced us. You don't even see it crossing the continent in a TAV. To get between Chicago and Billings takes five minutes.

I cried, silently, to myself, staring out the window of that car. This wasn't even for Allie, this was between me and Dad and Mom and all the meadows that are gone.

When night came we tried to make use of the camping equipment we bought back in New Jersey, but the winds proved too much for the lexithin tent, which was torn to pieces. We ended up sleeping close to the car, the miserable sleeping bags either too hot or too cold. They crunched whenever you moved, too.

It is becoming usual for me to lie awake. Aging has disturbed my sleep pattern. I had read Tom's file on the Network at least fifty times, and my mind wandered through fantasies of Summerland, and even more of Magic.

Would we ever get there? Should we go?

I did not want to think that Tom's death might have caused Magic to fall apart, but it was certainly possible. Could a bunch of children have kept going without adult help – even given the odd creature Tom called Boola? Who or what was that?

It was toward morning that I heard the crunch of tires on the silent road. We were well away from the main highway and this area is empty of people, so I was instantly alert.

I sat up, but all became silent. Above me the sky was full of stars. The air was dry and smelled of dust. The Midwestern Desert is a place of gray dunes and gigantic erosional features. When it rains out here the floods are devastating. All through Illinois there had been robot crews on Route 80, pushing hardened mud off the highway, a result of the last big rain. But it's dry now, the earth sparsely covered by sawgrass. Tumbleweeds bigger than land cruisers march this country.

After a few minutes of silence I settled down again. I had been enjoying the stars. You do not often see them elsewhere. There was a continuous procession of lights passing in every direction, satellites, TAVs, fanprops jammed with two thousand people each, all going some-where. I thought of it as a kind of autumnal motion, all that transiting in the declining world. We are like leaves, restless at the dry end of time.

There was such a sense of hugeness out here. The sky was high and brilliant. I was watching it when I heard the crunch of tires again, much closer. In fact they were so close that I could see the car.

It was a big one, a Mercedes 2000, I think. It had stopped moving perhaps fifty meters from our car. I have never in my life wanted a weapon as badly as I did then. There hadn't been enough time to go through the temporary permit rigmarole back in the city, so we were totally unarmed.

There was a soft click from the car. Now I could hear a steady, unfamiliar sound. It was the breathing of the people in the car. The place was that quiet.

I lay still. My mind was racing. It was dark, maybe they wouldn't see us. Then I heard footsteps coming along the road. They paused on the other side of our car.

Then more footsteps approached. These were swift and light, the tread of a small man. I opened my eyes just enough to see, and almost cried out when I understood that the man standing over me, his turban framed by stars, was Gupta Singh.

We were going to be killed. He must be here to kill us. I wanted to twist away from him, but I forced myself to remain still. We had eluded the Tax Police, but he had never lost track of us, not for a moment.

How could he possibly have done this? My mind was in a fury. I simply could not understand it. He crouched down beside me, leaning closer and closer. When I looked again, his face was scant centimeters from my own. I could smell his breath washing over me, and it had the smell of cumin. He was either smiling or grimacing, for I

339

could see his teeth, a blurry gleam. Under his breath, almost inaudibly, he spoke. 'Sleep,' he said, 'sleep deeply and sweetly, John Sinclair.' My name, barely whispered, nevertheless was said with contempt.

Then there was a soft whistle. Singh drew back. I heard the rustle of his clothes as he stood up. He lingered, and I saw him above me again, looking down. He made a little noise of surprise in his throat, as if he had seen the gleam of starlight on my slitted eyes. Then he departed. The car disappeared into the darkness, making no more sound than that of the tires on the road.

I woke the others.

'Singh. He was here. I saw him.'

Bell's voice was thick. 'John, you need to sleep.'

Allie reached toward me. 'It was a nightmare. Move your bag closer to mine.'

'It was real. He was here. He and another man, in a Mercedes 2000. Singh stood over me. He looked me right in the face. He was staring at me like some kind of a madman. I've never seen anything like it.'

'John, honey, it had to be a nightmare. Singh is in India. He's thousands of miles from here.'

'We've got to go into town. We can't stay out in the open. He could have killed us all. He could have drugged us, done anything to us.'

'Then why didn't he?' Bell's voice was sharp. 'Because he couldn't. No matter how realistic, nightmares can't hurt real bodies.'

A little while later there was another sound. The wind had come up, and was blowing harder and harder, sending stinging dust down the side of the low hill where we were camped. From beyond the hill there came a crackling sound, getting louder.

This time I didn't have to wake anybody. Bell sat up, Scott went to his feet. The noise rose and rose until it seemed to fill the whole place. Then a huge, black shape emerged across the top of the hill. It was at least twice the size of the car, and it was bearing down on us.

'Get down', Bell shouted. We all ducked beside the car as the huge tumbleweed slammed into it, bounced and bounded down the hill, picked up Bell's sleeping bag as it rolled on.

As it hit the car there had been a funny noise, a loud click and a sort of whoosh. Bell was peering into the car, her hands shielding her face from the starlight. After a moment she drew back. 'We owe you an apology, John. Look.'

The air inside was hazy. 'Gas?'

'Gas. Scenario: we get in the car, the gas renders us instantly unconscious. Singh's medical geniuses take over, wash out our minds with Aminase and refill them.

'A week from now our eyes blink open. We're still in the car. We don't even know anything went wrong. But we have forgotten all about the conviction and the book. We even think that the Depopulationist Manifesto has some good points. And we are such good citizens that we decide to turn ourselves in to the Tax Police and take our punishment for the fraud we so painfully remember doing.'

Allie shook her head. 'Thank you, Bell, for that cheerful idea.'

'Thank the tumbleweed.' Bell stared at the car. 'It's useless to us now. We can't even get in it.' She kicked the door. 'Oh, God, I hate this!' Bell had grabbed her hair in both fists. 'Why don't you stop,' she screamed. 'Why don't you stop!' She collapsed into Scott's arms, her sobs competing with the wind.

Shouldering our little bit of luggage, we walked out across the dry prairie, seeking Route 80. From the hilltops we could see it, a line of light in the distance. We walked for hours, arriving at the roadside exhausted. It was just before dawn.

Hitching isn't safe. Crazies cruise the roads capturing hitchhikers for everything from ritual murder to permanent slavery and God knows what else. You take your life in your hands if you hitch.

We had to hitch, though. We were exhausted, we needed water and food, we were afraid.

We were picked up by a woman named Allison Naylor, Jr, who has lived here all of her life. She wanted to help us. Apparently it wasn't hard to see our need. An old man with bent glasses, two women in tatters, a young man trying to carry camping equipment in the ruins of a thousand dollar Max Rose suitcase, I guess we didn't appear particularly threatening.

'I thought you'd been in a wreck,' Allison Naylor said. She had an old Chevy, but it felt awfully good to sit back and be driven. As we sped toward Des Moines, Allison told us her story.

ALLISON NAYLOR, JR:
Shadows over Home

I was born in Davenport, on September 13, 1995, in Broadlawns Hospital. That was the year after the first big duster. I grew up here, went to Drake here and married Red Brown here. We did a four-year and didn't have any kids. Now I'm just dating. I have worked at Laddie's Cruiser Base since December 2023, so it's not quite two years, I guess. I get sixty dollars a day and tips, which are pretty good. I probably take home an average of a hundred and twenty a day.

Mostly I work the restaurant, but two days a week I go on the cleaning squad and wash down the cruisers. I also do welding when there's a need for a licensed welder.

I live a quiet life. Mostly I work. Usually I go ten days on and one day off. You want me to tell you about myself and my days, so I will try. I hope this isn't too short. I'll talk until we get into Des Moines, unless I run out of life before then.

I live in Windward, which is a singles condo in Capitol Heights. I don't own my room; it's a sublet. I've thought of buying a prefab, but so far the condo's been nice, so I stick with it. We're only about half full. The city's been losing population for years and years. It's about forty thousand now, plus all the illegals. Maybe another forty thousand illegals. They seem to be everywhere. They'd work my job for five dollars a day, but the cruisers don't get on with them, thank God.

There were hundreds of thousands of people here before 1997, but you can just cut our history in half with that year. After the first of the dust, things started going down. They still are, they still are.

Well, here is my day. I get up at seven and go to church. There is a sunrise service at Capitol Heights Christian, and I go every morning. We have prayer and hymn, and on Sunday morning there is communion. A lot of my spare time centers around the church, I guess. We have parties on Saturday night, and I sometimes take Laddie or I go alone. Red and I go together once in a while. We dance. There's a prance party once a month, and folk dancing and ballroom. I like to prance, I must admit. It just lets me go, you know. Sushanna's my favorite group, except for the Coal Black Conspiracy, which is also good.

After church I take the streetcar out to the base. It will now be eight A.M., and the breakfast crowd will be pacing in. I get my first assignment from the computer. Say it's to monitor the prolene pumps. So I'll do that for about an hour. It means taking the cards and physically putting them in the slot. The cruisers are good people, but if they can get away with two or three thousand dollars worth of prolene, you can't blame them.

After that I might work the tables for lunch. We serve the Base Co-op line of meals, so we don't get many food complaints. I'm glad Laddie's a member of the co-op. Otherwise we'd have to have a chef and worry about buying food and all that. The co-op makes it easy. You just put the meals in the heater and you're in business. In my opinion they're more like home cooking than the real thing. At least, *my* cooking. You can't get anything as good as Co-op Cottage Fries. That's just the best eating there is. We have whole cruiser families'd tear this place apart if we didn't have Cots. They're so long and crisp. What I don't get is, how do they get those things off potatoes? You know what they are, those little black things like the size of your thumb? How do they make those into a fry six inches long?

Anyhow, the way I'm talking I guess I like working the tables the best. You get to meet people. Every waiter dreams of going on the road. Sometimes some bachelor cruiser comes in, he can have his pick of any of us, boys and girls. My dream is signing a lifer with a cruiser who has his own rig all paid down. Oh, golly, it's sad, you know, I can't afford them cosmets. You see these girls so beautiful and for God's sake, they're forty! I can't do these two hundred dollar a week things, just no way. So I buy Youth of Age at Woolworth's and just do my best.

I'm thirty. I turned thirty last September. The crowd here at the base threw a little rock. All of a sudden, I'm swabbing down the mac and here comes all this prance – Night Cougar – over the p.a. I think, Laddie's gone over, he doesn't like music on the ways, says it distracts people. Then, what do you know, but I get a birthday rock.

They had a cake from the Gusher, which is our local friendly megamart. On it there is this perfect portrait of me in icing. Well, what about that? I cried, I must admit. These are good people out here. Laddie, he gives me this card. It says on the outside, 'Gee, you're getting . . .' and you open it up and it says, 'older.'

Older. It was a hilarious card, kind of.

Let's see. This is weird. Are you psyching me, making me just keep talking? You asked about my life, what I do, what I remember, my politics. Yeah. I voted with the President. We sent Marks back to Washington. Good. I don't hold with the Depop. We've had enough trouble here in Iowa without that business. I suppose we'll get it, though. They're saying a bill will be introduced supporting the Manifesto on January 5. That was on DataNews or *National Times* or something. I read the news. I like to keep up.

345

I'm trying to think here, what's really important to me. Well, I have to get back to church. You know, we don't talk much about it, but if you keep up, you soon learn that the world's in trouble. I mean, where we are now wasn't an eternal desert. I have vague memories of corn around here where it's all dry now. When I was a little girl this was a farming area. It still is down in Iowa City where the Amish are.

But mostly, it's just a desert. And when it rains the river gets mean and black. You have flood all upriver from Davenport. When it rains the water hits the river and bang, another flood. Always. You can find property near the river for nothing. You wouldn't want to go down there though, the crazies'd get you. There's a story about that, this woman and man bought a warehouse down near the river on the Moline side and fixed it up with all kinds of nice stuff, a dreamscope, a sound room, every kind of assist, a huge communal bath for all their friends and all that, and do you know, people didn't hear from them for a while, and the bulls went in and found their bones neatly stacked in the kitchen, and the bones had been gnawed.

So, the word is, eat you alive.

Of all the things in my life, the church is really the most important. A lot of us feel like God is coming closer and closer. Sometimes there is this feeling of a wonderful and great presence watching, just watching. At Christian on Saturday morning we start at six and sing the Arrangements. We go for two hours, which is the first thirty-two of the seventy. I know all seventy of the Arrangements. Our pastor believes very strongly in repetitive worship. Last Easter we said the Jesus Prayer ten thousand times. I felt like I was floating, and Christ came to me, and took me in His arms, and at long last He took me away.

You asked me about the Depopulation. We don't hold

with that in our church, and not in our state, either. Iowa's still sending Republicans to Congress. And as far as Gupta Singh is concerned, he seems like a strange kind of a man to me. A strange, foreign man with very strange ideas. His ideas are light years away from Iowa. We don't need *less* people here, we need more. Gupta Singh lives on the other side of the world, where things are different. He can stay there forever, as far as I'm concerned.

ALLIE: Night and Fog

After the appearance of Singh we had abandoned any and all conventional forms of travel. We were like ghosts, hitching, hiking, moving sometimes as four, sometimes in pairs, trying to reach Summerland before the next blow.

Coming back to the Midwest after forty or fifty years had made John melancholy. His sorrow seemed to concentrate him even more on his work: he burned to get back to Delta Doctor.

Night was the hardest time for us. Even though we now posted watches we slept like wild animals, hovering between dream and reality.

The image of Gupta Singh standing over John would not leave my mind. I kept telling myself that he was no more than human, but then I would remember that Mercedes 2000 drifting like a ghost.

Now it was midnight again, and we were only fifty kilometers from Summerland. The farm wasn't near any main roads, and we had spent a maddening day trying to hitch there. Tomorrow we would start to walk.

We were in the abandoned town of Defiant, at a Federal Land Reclamation station run by a man none of us trusted named H. D. Rheems. H.D. was pleasant in a by-the-book sort of way. We were certain that he suspected we were fugitives. He wouldn't give us up to an extralegal organization like the Depop, but he would eagerly turn us over to any official agency he thought might be following us. All he needed was to come across a wanted bulletin from the Tax Police and we were finished.

John slept beside me; there was no sound from Bell and Scott's room.

I heard a small noise, which could have been the crunching of tires on dust. It was tiresome. Since the other night we were all hearing noises constantly.

It was my responsibility to check it out, though. I lifted myself out of bed and stood in the middle of our bedroom. I was barefoot. I jammed my feet into my shoes and went toward the front of the house.

Faint blue light from Rheems' weather station came in the windows. It seemed strange for him to be there so late at night, but he was a strange man. If he wanted a weather report at eleven o'clock at night, he could certainly get one.

I crossed the creaky board floor and stared into the small yard, which was empty of everything except dust. There was no sign of footprints. That was disturbing, because an exploring dog would have left them. A human being would be smart enough not to.

Rheems' house was dark, so was the rest of the town. These facts did not reduce my suspicion, though. Rheems was a priggish, nasty man. Maybe he was out there himself, trying to learn more about us. Or maybe it was Singh, or the Tax Police. Oh, it could be anybody, even a pair of lovers from the migrant camp, strolling in the night.

Normally I would have waked the others to tell them about the noise I had heard, but we were all seriously stressed, and it wasn't an emergency yet.

I went to the front door. As quietly as I could I stepped onto the porch, careful to avoid loose boards.

The night enclosed me. On the eastern horizon a red moon hung behind a thread of cloud. Down the street I could see the dark hulk of the dead Burger Perfect. Beyond it the McDonald's arch gleamed with a first soft edge of moonlight. Once Defiant's businesses would have banished night with a blaze of light, but now H. D. Rheems was the only permanent resident of the town, and H.D. goes to bed early. H.D., us, and a hundred and forty migrants housed in the Defiant Rodeway were the extent of the population. The only sign of life was a radio, very faint, playing off toward the Rodeway. My ears are not what they used to be, but I could pick out the nasal voice of Bob Puckett singing *Angel Lady*.

> 'Come down to me, Angel Lady.
> Come down and show me the way.
> Save my soul, Angel Lady,
> Lead me to a bright new day.'

There aren't any angels and there isn't going to be any salvation from the sky, no matter what Bob Puckett and his followers believe. We live in a world where a pop singer can become an overnight religious phenomenon and as quickly fade away. One hopes that people just like his music, and the rest is all clever marketing.

I stood on the porch shivering, listening, feeling very much prey to the night. There was nothing moving, though. I was just about to go back to bed when I thought I saw a shadow in the street. Was there indeed a faint crunch of tires on dirt – and didn't I hear the whine of a well-muffled engine?

I backed into the house as if withdrawing from a coiled snake.

I went to Bell and Scott's room. The air was thick, smelling faintly of sweat. They were wrapped in one another's arms.

I touched her shoulder. 'Bell, wake up.'

Her breathing changed. I sensed that her eyes had opened. She made no sound; experience had made her too careful to commit herself.

'We might have a problem.'

Scott is as heavy a sleeper as my Tom was light. Bell extracted herself from his arms and rose up from the bed, lithe and unashamed in her nakedness. She has never known an era that was fussy about privacy, but her easygoing nudity still unsettles me. Physical secrecy is a deep habit with me. I wonder if Tom was like Scott and Bell, so indifferent about privacy. It frightened me that I didn't know. I wanted to talk to my son and I couldn't. I wanted his help, and it wasn't available.

Bell got into a cotton nightshirt. We went together back to the kitchen, which was the only usable room in the house except for the bedrooms. She poured a glass of water and drank it down. 'Here's to cancer,' she said. 'I wish I wasn't always thirsty.' At first the faintly salty taste of the water had disturbed us, but H.D. had assured us it passed Federal potability standards, so we used it and hoped for the best.

'Somebody might have been here, somebody in a car.'

'Oh, God.'

'A sound woke me up and I went out on the porch. I think I saw a car going down the street, almost silent. I'm not sure because there wasn't much light. But I thought I ought to tell you.'

Her dark form was hanging over the sink. She turned to me, her movements swift and silent. 'Car or not, we've been here long enough.'

'We're all exhausted, and John wants to go back to the conviction in the morning.'

She chuckled softly, mirthless laughter.

'He can wait until we reach Summerland. At least there we'll be able to learn better where we stand.' She pushed her hair back from her eyes.

'We could delay a few more hours. I was just reporting

351

this like I'm supposed to. I don't think it's really an emergency.'

'Of course it's an emergency! Anything we see or hear that we cannot explain is by definition an emergency. The only way we're going to survive is by overreacting.'

The first day we had come here, we had discussed a number of escape plans. The simplest was the best, and it was the one we had settled on. As long as Summerland was willing to hide us, we hoped we'd have a reasonable chance, at least to escape the Tax Police. I suspected that there wasn't any safe haven from Singh.

According to H.D. Rheems, Summerland had degenerated into a bad place, nearly starving, not making it, because their farming methods weren't effective. He was also negative about the local Mennonites, and we had seen their farms with our own eyes. Certainly they were not bursting with productivity, but nobody was starving. On that basis, we felt we could discount what the jealous Dr Rheems said about the Network farm. His own station was clearly failing.

Our plan was to steal one of the station's supply trucks, take it down to Summerland and pay the farmers to get it back before H.D. missed it.

Bell brushed past me, and I inhaled the sweet-pungent smell of her skin. I love her with the fierceness of a mother. Even though she is not my blood. Bell is my daughter.

As quietly as we could, she and I woke up John and Scott. We were always packed; instead of our elaborate city clothes, we now wore Federal issue work greens, compliments of Station 121 and the generosity of H.D. Rheems. Bell had thrown on her own clothes and come into our room to fill the duffle as John and I got dressed.

As planned, Scott left by the front door, John five minutes later by the back. We then waited half an hour,

352

Bell and I, sitting together in the kitchen, motionless and silent.

Some desert dogs raised a howl as the moon rose higher. The house sighed and creaked. A woman cried out in Chinese, her voice cracking with tears and rage. Afterward voices came from down toward the Rodeway, low and soft, drifting through the silence like smoke.

We moved out of the house together. As we passed H.D.'s weather station we could see him inside staring at his radar screen, his face gleaming in its green light.

Finally we reached the parking lot. An engine turned over and we hopped into the back of a slowly rolling truck. Scott was at the wheel, John sitting beside him clutching his precious computer. He seemed so very fragile.

The moon glared down, Route 80 soared away in glowing gray blankness and the acrid fertilizer smell of this strange desert made even the air seem alien and hostile. Unlit, slow, the truck headed out onto the highway.

Soon there was nothing left of Defiant in our lives but the piercing light of the station beacon. Then that, too, dropped below the horizon. As we traveled, an occasional land cruiser roared by, its lights filling the cab of the old truck with a shattering white glare, the scream of its engines making us cringe. That didn't happen often, though, not in this empty place. Farther south, on the highways of Tennessee, the cruisers would look from a distance like a line of fire in the night, shimmering and roaring, the stinging saltiness of their exhaust sweeping in hot gusts over the land.

But not here, where the world had already ended. We turned south onto Highway 59, and left what little sign of life there had been. For long stretches the road was

353

dusted out, all but invisible beneath the blowing gray of Iowa.

Occasionally we would pass through an empty town, seeing from time to time the light of another Reclamation Station, once even passing a field of gigantic, tree-like corn stalks, all dead, some tumbled like columns alongside the road.

There was a sign of life in Lurline, a street light burning in the center of the town. We could see dim goods behind the windows of some of the stores, and there were ruts in the dirt-clogged streets. Where death was everywhere else, this place was at least half-alive.

'The farm ought to be on the right side of the road about two klicks farther on,' Bell said.

We slowed down and watched carefully. There was no reason to expect any lights or identifying signs. In the event, we were surprised. First fencing started, neat posts linked by wire, with a plymar lattice woven in to act as a windbreak.

Then there was a gate, simple enough, of rusty steel. Beneath it a new cattle guard ensured that whatever animals they had managed to raise would not escape. On the gate was painted a sign in simple script. 'Summerland Farm.'

John put his arm around me. We all felt the same hope, that this would be the refuge we needed.

As soon as we crossed the cattle guard we noticed something that made us ache with longing: the smell of plants, rotting, yes, but it was autumn rot, real autumn rot. My whole body seemed to fill with this rich smell, the living earth in its great mystery.

In the moonlight the ground seemed to shimmer and pulsate like restless flesh.

The road was deeply rutted, and there were pools of

water in the clay, apparently left over from the thunder-storms of a few days ago. Most of this environment ran water off so fast that it seemed dry even a few hours after a rain. But here, the moisture lingered. The air pouring into the cab was soft and silky and rich. Ghostly memories of my girlhood rose in my mind. I recalled summer voices, the easy laughter of my mother in the hot night, the shouting of my friends at play. I am a Southern girl. I'm glad I do not have the sadness John does, of having been born out here before this was a desert.

A vision emerged of our elm in the moonlight, katydids arguing in its secret cathedrals of leaves, and lying beneath it with my childhood friends, Roxanne and David, Linda, Bob Sweet and Bob Parker, exploring together the immense questions that the night and the moon bring up in twelve-year-old minds.

When I realized that John was wiping my eyes with a corner of his shirt, my own advancing age came shoving its way into consciousness. I saw in his gesture a love so large that it might be immortal, but in that sudden fertile heaven, I remembered that nothing really lasted forever.

'What in the world is going on here,' Bell said.

Nobody answered. A bug hit the windshield with a crunch and I gasped. I know we all felt the same fear – by breaking this insect, had we broken the whole miracle?

It did not wither, though. As we began passing barns a dog started to bark, its voice powerful and confident. This was no whining desert dog, a scabrous legacy of forebears who had been abandoned in the rush south. This was a strong, domestic creature.

Beside the road there now appeared trees standing ten and twelve feet high. They were wrapped in white breather sheets to protect them from the scratching wind and supported by cables and guy wires.

Despite all the suggestions of life, there was also that

dryness on the air, coming in from the outside. I wondered how often all this work was drowned in dust. This place is only an insignificant oasis. It could grow, though.

Bell patted her temples. 'I'm not wearing a dream machine, am I?' The question made us laugh a little, but it had been caused by a perfectly valid concern.

'I don't think this is a dream,' Scott murmured.

'How can we be sure?'

You could buy experiences as realistic as this on disks. But of a farm like this, a place without story? In a dream this would be the Old West, and there would be a threatening outlaw lingering behind the barn, or perhaps the sounds of sex from the dark house.

Almost in concert with my thoughts a porch light was turned on. At once moths began fluttering around it. Raw fear surged through me.

Could we have been caught and taken to tax prison and force-fed dreams?

Bell was right. There is no way to tell for certain whether or not a given experience is real. I told myself that the spontaneity, the detail, the sheer richness of what we were feeling and smelling and seeing could not be dreamware. The most realistic dream I had ever experienced, the Warner production of *Winesburg, Ohio*, was not as good as this. Even with *Winesburg* there was that subtle lack of solidity that characterizes dreamware, and the familiar tendency of things to become overly detailed when you concentrated on them.

'Stop the truck.' There was a man standing on the porch of a nearby building. He carried an old-fashioned shotgun in his hands, its barrel short and mean. Scott put on the brakes.

'Driver, get down.'

As Scott descended the man stood motionless. His face was hidden by a slouchy hat. He was wearing not greens, but old-fashioned overalls. There were Amish down here, but this man was not one of them. Far from it. When he raised his head into a shaft of moonlight I saw that he was black. His lips were grim set, his face hard.

'Who are you and what are you doing here?'

John coughed. Instantly there was a movement beside the truck. Another man stepped forward. He was wearing kods and had a breather mask hanging around his neck. In his hands was another shotgun.

'We don't harbor roadies,' the first man said. 'Burned once, that was enough.'

'You'll have to move on,' the second man said.

I was insulted. Roadies indeed. A month ago the word was a pejorative in my vocabulary. 'We're not road people,' Bell said, 'we're fugitives from the Tax Police.'

'Oh, I know who – '

'Quiet, Mole. I'll handle this.' The first man came down the porch and shone a light into the cab of the truck.

'Mole,' Bell said, 'did you call that man Mole?'

'It's the convictor,' Mole said from the other side of the truck. Both men were smiling now. 'Welcome, convictor Sinclair,' Mole added. 'We've been hoping you'd make it.'

So Summerland had forgiven him. The other man trotted off. Shortly a bell began ringing. Lights, low and mellow, flickered behind windows and in the fields. Nobody had been asleep, it appeared. Instead they were all out in the fields or in offices and storerooms, and all wearing or carrying respirators.

'Come on out and show yourself, John Sinclair,' a woman's voice called. People were shaking my husband's hand, approaching him with respect of a kind I thought he had lost forever.

357

'I thought your conviction of Falon was really great,' Mole said. 'It woke me up.'

A woman came forward. 'I'm Selena,' she said, 'and this is Brother Thomas. We're the co-leaders.' I remembered Scylla, but this woman had kindness in her voice. She was tall, her hair long and dark, and she wore a black dress. Like the others, she was fitted out in respiration gear.

'We welcome you,' Thomas said. 'We'd celebrate, but there's very little time. There's a dust storm on the way and we're just in the middle of preparing for it.'

A moment later we were moving into the big old farmhouse. A lantern was put on a paper table in the middle of the room, and suffused everything with a lovely glow. We were given chairs, and soon found ourselves seated with Selena, Brother Thomas, and a number of other people, ranging in age from perhaps twelve to at least eighty. 'Let me introduce you to the Farm Council,' Brother Thomas said. 'This quarter's board of directors.' Gone from their faces was the joy of a moment before. They were facing a serious situation, and they wanted to deal with us as quickly as possible. They would decide at once whether or not we could stay, and what to do with us if we did.

Bell told them about the Tax Police, and even about Gupta Singh's recent appearance. She added our relief that H.D. Rheems' description of the farm was untrue. Selena laughed when she heard what Rheems had said about Summerland. 'Doesn't he wish. H.D. and I were married for two contracts. I got sick of being a public service wife. I wanted to make things grow.' H.D. had never made references to a wife. I must say, I wasn't surprised that the marriage hadn't lasted. This chipper, energetic woman was the very opposite of H.D.

'You bring trouble in our door,' the youngest of the

board said. She had flinty eyes. But her face was soft, the bronze tones of her Asian skin warmed and enriched by the flickering yellow light. 'Why should we accept you and your trouble?'

I sensed the tension of my family. A healthy family is four walls against the world. If these people didn't want us nobody wanted us, and we were alone.

'The Tax Police could legally run every one of us in for harboring fugitives from Federal Justice,' said a rangy man of natural sixty.

'I call that trouble.' This from a young woman, whose soft expression harbored a careful, tough voice.

Bell leaned forward. 'He's the man who broke Falon. You owe him. A lot of you would be in prison if it wasn't for John Sinclair. And he is trying to break Gupta Singh. That's even more important. According to information he's uncovered, the Depopulationist Manifesto is false. The selection won't be random. Somebody is going to choose who lives and who dies. You're all members of the radical fringe. I don't want to frighten you, but you need John Sinclair as much as he needs you.'

'I found a new kind of faith,' Thomas said. 'The Falon conviction shattered me, broke my whole belief system to pieces. I remember sitting there running it, listening to the voice of Falon answering my questions, reading all the amazing structural detail and knowing that this was no ordinary conviction, this was the real man. I was talking to a perfect model of President Falon, and he was telling me he was a liar. After that I learned what Christianity could really be, a faith that has nothing to do with guilt or dogma, but arises from love.'

John looked down at the table. He was embarrassed by the man's tone. I knew he was thinking of the image of Falon that haunts him, the one of the President slumped dead behind his desk, his left eye peering sightlessly, his right a burned hole.

Life hurts, life is not simple. What Selena said to me later fits here: 'John has the habit of guilt. He can leave it behind, though. He has to make the decision.'

There was no particular vote about us, just a sort of end to objections and questions. Our presence was accepted and the board adjourned. It was now after midnight. Selena took us to a storeroom where there were about a dozen respirators, hats and coveralls. We dressed quickly and soon found ourselves assigned to various different parts of the farm.

I regretted leaving John with Selena at the farm's weather station, but he couldn't possibly survive being outside in a dust storm, not as frail as he had become.

I went out on the front lines of the farm, assigned to the team that was going to keep the water tower from blowing over. There were eleven of us, five men, four women and a boy of perhaps eleven. We sat together beneath the tower as our team leader, Fred, carefully explained for me the whole design of the tower. I looked up at it, a tremendous dark shape in the night, topped by a green strobe light.

To the south lightning flickered. The northern sky, which still hid the storm, was full of stars. The air was absolutely still. It was dense and much too warm.

It had a message for anyone who understood weather. It told us that we were soon going to face an enemy who ought to have been a friend. We were going to face nature.

JOHN: Dust

Slowly it had been building in the ashy plains, its presence monitored, measured and reported on by the whole spinning array of devices from solar probe to earthwatch satellites. Slowly it had been building, beginning as breezes that blessed the muddy, mosquito-swept tundra in the far north, slipping softly in the moonlight past the hutches of the Inuit Indians, sweeping then into the dark to the south, rushing across Alberta and Saskatchewan, growing high and dim and making the late moon run as blood.

Summerland was totally silent, but nobody was sleeping. The night was so quiet that the mice could be heard in among the corn, restless in their travels along the ears. Far off a bell was tolling, the dismal alarm of the Mennonites, and the flash of lanterns could be seen across the sweep of the land as they went among their windbreaks, checking the posts.

Selena sat before the NWCS Farmer Station, watching the satellite picture change from moment to moment. 'Wind sixty klicks,' the station said. Her face shone in the flat green light.

'This is me,' her voice said into the farm's public address system. 'Dust management procedures are now in effect. Report to your station. We have about an hour.'

'Won't somebody go help the Mennonites?' Allie asked. They would not use a National Weather Control Service station themselves, so they had to rely only on their understanding of the sky.

'They don't want station data,' Selena commented absently. 'They don't want help.'

Allie wiped the sweat from her own face. I held her around her small shoulders. In a moment she was going to leave me, off on an assignment in the dark. I hated the very idea of it, but I could not refuse Summerland, not after they had just agreed to take us in.

'Particulate count at storm front four count three zeros,' said the weather station.

Selena glared at the screen. 'It says four thousand parts! Four thousand!' Selena sighed. But for us she was alone in the little control room. 'Take your station,' she said. 'It won't be long now.'

Allie and Bell and Scott hurried off to positions along the windbreaks. I stayed with Selena. I am ashamed to report that my frail appearance excused me from the hours of brutal labor ahead.

The telephone beeped. 'Yes.'

A roar of sound filled the room. 'It's H.D., darlin'. We're getting torn apart up here.' His voice was shaking against the clear shriek of the wind. 'Ground wind clocked at one seventy klicks, one seventy!' The transmission faded into a hiss and died.

'He must be lying, the station said – ' She stared at the station. 'It says twenty fifty hours! My God, it's twenty-two thirty. That means – John, I think – is it – '

Her confusion was total. Like most people, she was completely frozen by the breakdown of any electronic device. 'Run its diagnostics,' I suggested.

'How? I have no idea how! Oh, God, H.D. said a hundred and seventy klicks. That'll crush us. We won't be able to handle it.' Another flash of lightning came, and then another. I looked out the open door, and I saw it.

I saw it in the lightning, the thing from the north. I

cannot describe it as a wave or a wall, those words are not adequate. It was a range of flying mountains.

Selena's voice echoed over the public address system. 'We have one seventy klicks. Everybody hook up lifelines. Repeat that. Go on lifelines.'

I was drawn outside. Nothing I have ever seen made me feel so small. The moon rode high in the sky. To the south thunderstorms flickered and flashed almost ceaselessly. All across the northern horizon and up to the very top of the sky rose tier upon tier of mountains, black palaces in the pale moonlight. Near the moon Saturn gleamed with perfect light, and the usual reefs of satellites and TAVs swept about. The north ate the stars, and as I watched, a long finger stretched out and gathered in the moon. Now the only light came from the distant and retreating thunderstorms.

We were alone with the beast, we ragged stretch of farmers. Off in the heavy quiet I heard voices. Lanterns had come together; the Mennonites were drawing in upon themselves also. They did not need a weather station to tell them that Satan's whole armies were let on them tonight.

They began to sing, and their voices filled the distance: *'O Gott vater, wir loben dich, Und deine Gute preisen; Dass du uns O Her gnadich lich.' Loblied,* the Hymn of Praise. Its slow tones seemed to shudder the dry stalks of the corn, the polytufin-covered trees, the very eaves.

A team of Summerlanders came in silence, taping poly over the windows and installing stikrete in the doors. They were gone in a moment.

Selena came out of the NWCS station. 'It's just not working,' she said.

'You ran the diagnostics?'

'Maybe. I tried. But it doesn't matter because the satellite link failed. How can that be?'

363

'The storm must have interrupted it.'

'The storm isn't even here yet.'

She seemed so small and vulnerable, standing there in the dark. My impulse was to put my arm around her shoulders but she shrugged me off. A thought struck her and she darted back inside to the p.a. 'Mask up, do it now.'

I wondered where my family was, out there in the dark. Selena shook me. 'Mask up!'

I put on the headgear. There was an instant rush of sadness. Smells make you remember things, and the smell of the respirator took me back to Denver, and there was Tom, his back to me, going off into the crowd. A dread came upon me then, and I turned on Selena. 'Where's my wife?'

'I don't know.'

The storm came roaring across the fields. A bell began ringing, the song of the Mennonites was drowned and all the world became wind.

It slammed into me like a gang of Dragons shouldering me aside in the street. Selena's arms were around me, and then we were in the station, huddled against its impressive, useless glow. 'H.D.,' she screamed into the phone, 'H.D.!'

Defiant did not reply. The phone gave no indication of what might be the matter. Selena turned on the sideband radio. 'Report, all stations.'

'Station One here.' The voice was unfamiliar to me. Was my family on Station One? Where were the outposts? I was alone in the dark and memories of Denver were flashing through my mind. 'The break's holding, Selena,' said the radio, 'but it's bowed bad in the center. I sent Joan to pull off some slats.'

'What's the corn?'

'Flat. It was knocked down . . . almost at once.'

The other six stations gave similar reports. As Selena sat huddled over her radio, her face hidden by the gleaming mask, I realized what she had probably known for some time: Summerland was being killed.

The building we were in housed records and clerical offices, as well as this weather station. I heard glass shatter with a pop and a roar of wind. 'Please, please,' Selena screamed. The sorrow in her voice went deep into me. I did not want Summerland to die, not this symbol of human ingenuity and courage.

I thought of what Depop propagandists could make of the destruction of this place.

The wind was shrieking so loud that it took me a moment to realize that Selena was trying to communicate with me. 'Go down the hall and check the office. All of our computers are there, our records, our horticultural information. Get whatever you can, keep it with you.'

The hallway was still intact. I ran down to the office, only to find that the windows had broken and computers and disks and papers were blowing around the room. The softscreens of the Unons were flapping like flags. I grabbed one and stuffed it under my shirt. Bending against the stinging, dusty wind I pushed farther into the room. A trash can seemed to leap at me from the floor. It took me in the chin and I tasted the blood of my tongue. I snatched at the can but it escaped me and went clanging off down the hall. Two of the desks were moving, and brown dust was literally streaming in the window and pouring like a liquid along the floor. I had never seen anything like it. It took all my strength to pull the office door closed as I backed out.

For the time being the hallway was quiet again. As I walked my feet raised dust. It was as fine as the softest powder, and thick. In the few seconds I had that door open, the whole hall floor had been covered with an inch of the stuff.

I returned to Selena.

'Status.'

'I couldn't save the office. I managed to close it off.'

She jabbed a button. 'We need a damage control team in the main building. Be prepared to secure broken doors and windows.' She turned to me. 'If we don't seal it, we lose it.'

I held out the Unon with the crinkled screen. 'I managed to save this.'

She took it as if it was a gold bar and placed it on top of the nonworking weather equipment. 'Your wife is on Station Six,' she said.

'What is Station Six?'

'They're trying to save the water tower.'

My breath almost stopped. A water tower was certain to collapse in this maelstrom. Allie could be killed.

'Scott is on Station Four. They do roof repair. Bell is with the harvest team. They're out bringing in the corn.'

'Bringing in the corn!'

'Some of it's still green, but we can't help that. We'll have to gas it and hope for the best.'

'Why the corn?'

'How do you think this place survives? Iowa corn's worth a fortune!'

I could hardly imagine what it must be like to be out there, trying to pick corn in winds so high they could roll you to death if you relaxed a muscle, and dust so thick you couldn't see. They must be working by feel.

I thought of the water tower swaying and groaning. Allie.

Damned Selena and her orders. I was being kept in here while my wife was in danger. Old, dry, flustered man. Worthless. I heard Selena shouting into the radio, getting no replies from the various workstations. The dust had put out the electronic eyes and now the ears of Summerland.

I couldn't bear waiting here as I had waited in the hotel room for Tom. Never again would I allow myself the luxury of doing that. As the repair team came banging in I headed out into the storm.

The wind slammed across the little yard in front of the building with a screaming, hissing sound. The dust stung my hands, roared against my respirator, dropped me into darkness so absolute that I felt for a moment as if I had turned upside down. My arms windmilled involuntarily, and I found myself sitting in a strange, giving softness, a dune of dust which had collected against the porch. The wind blasted full against my chest, pinning me to the low wall behind me. There came a dull thudding, coming closer and closer, and soon I made out a light bobbing toward me. Then something heavy brushed me, rolling me aside as it crunched into the steps, which temporarily stopped its movement.

I flailed at it, pulled myself up against it. My hands went to the brown smudge of light dangling from it. I recognized a gas lantern, and I realized that this was an Amish carriage. It was covered with a sticky substance, which was itself full of what felt like hair – the remains of the horse, or the occupants of the carriage, or both.

The wind took it, and I heard it shatter in the dark as it tumbled against the dining hall, whose lights were now faintly visible to me. As my eyes adjusted I began to be aware of landmarks, including the piercing red emergency beacon atop the water tower. If I navigated by its light I might reach it.

As soon as I started off, though, I heard a shout. 'English, English,' a male voice, frantic. A train of figures emerged from the swirling gloom. They were swathed in homespun blankets. They wore no respirators. 'We are trying to find our horse and carriage.' The man was staggering. I saw a rope around his middle, his wife tied behind him, two small children on his back and a train of three more roped to their mother. The bedraggled procession gathered around me. Eyes gleamed from cracks in their wrapping, and the father held an ancient lantern, its flame spitting with the wind.

'It's been smashed,' I said.

He reared back, his shroud flying from his face. I could see terror and pain in his eyes. 'It had all our things in it, what we needed to start over.'

One of the children, straining into the gloom, cried out the horse's name.

What could I say to these people? Their lives had been destroyed. 'I think you can stay over there,' I shouted, pointing to the dining hall. They moved off and the storm absorbed them.

I continued on toward the faint glow of the water tower beacon. As I walked I thought I felt drops of rain hit me from time to time. I would not allow myself to hope. The wind was dry and ice-cold. And yet something splattered against my mask, then another drop hit my hand.

Ahead I could now glimpse the water tower's composite carbon girders. The wind whined in the guy wires, cutting into me with such force that I had to lean forward almost to the ground in order to continue.

I screamed for Allie. Somewhere in this chaos she was working or sheltering, or dead. Great white sheets began thundering past my head – sections of the water tank's skin.

I realized then what the rain had been: the tower was disintegrating. 'Allie, Allie!'

My voice was frighteningly small in the wind. Everytime I opened my mouth I was choked with dust. I kept moving, trying to get to Tom, to do what I should have done years and years ago in the tumult of Denver.

I saw my son ahead of me, bending over a crumpled body. 'Tom!' He turned, and as he turned I knew he was already dead. Then I remembered where I actually was. The respirator was laboring, the lenses of the mask were fogging up. I knocked dust out of the air intake as best I could and kept on. Finally, flailing out ahead of me, I found a grip on one of the tower's supports. When I snatched at it the wind made my arms swing akimbo. Again I tried, and again. Then I had a grip with the tips of my fingers. I could work my way along. A high-pitched screaming sound came from above, and wire suddenly covered me. Fighting it, trying not to get cut, I freed myself. A sheet of water hit me, then another, then more wire and flapping sections of the tower. Something heavy slammed into the ground.

The wind took me by the shoulder. I'd never get to Tom this way. 'John!'

Was that a voice? 'Tom? Oh, my God, son – '

'Tom Sinclair is dead! Dead, John! I'm Bell. We have to get out of here, the tower's coming down.'

My mind was twisting in on itself. Tom? Bell? Who was this woman?

'I'm Bell Harper-Osborne, your contract daughter. Now come on, old man, get going!'

She took me by the hand and began leading me. From high up the tower there came a terrible shriek, and I saw there my son Tom, his body stretched like a flag in the wind, hanging by his fingers to a snapping wire.

Then he was gone, a wraith in the dark.

'Tom just fell off the tower!'

'Your son is dead! Now move or I'll have to drag you.' Her voice was stronger than the wind, and her grip was firm. I went with her, and as I walked the ghost of my son dissolved into the dust.

With a substantial roar and a white flash of foam the water tower collapsed behind us. At that instant I felt something snap inside me. This place was dead. The desert had won.

Someone was shouting at me, not Bell. I released my hold on her hand. 'Can you work?'

Work? Were they crazy?

'Can you work?'

How should I answer? Suddenly Bell thrust a white bag in my hand. 'Go over there, find your wife. Take her bag to the collecting point and give her this one. And don't let the bag belly out, it'll get torn to pieces.'

I found Allie on her hands and knees in the dust. The water tower team had given up and come to help with the harvest.

'John – ' She rose to kneeling and turned toward me. We managed a fluttering touch. 'John, now listen, I've got to get back to the staging area, my mask's all screwed up. Come on, get down here.' I went down into the flattened corn, into the dust and mess. There was nothing left, no point in even being here. 'Close your eyes, they won't matter. Keep the bag under you. Feel along, finding the corn is something like digging for potatoes.'

I've never dug for potatoes and I doubt if she has either. But I dug for corn on that mad plain. It was there, too, the little ears hiding among the heaps of ruined stalks.

As I dug, something close to what these farmers must have been feeling came into me, creeping up from the tortured land, a feeling as if I could make my heart a stone in the wind, as if nothing, not the dust, not the bitter song of the night, not floods, not fires, nothing, nothing, would drive me from this place.

370

I worked, feeling along until my fingernails were oozing pulp, and each ear of corn I found seemed a bar of gold. Time folded into itself. Occasionally I was aware of Allie beside me, then of somebody else. A little girl brought me a bag, crawling so that the wind would not destroy her, holding it in her teeth. She went back with my filled sack, carrying it I do not know how. The Amish woman I had seen earlier arrived with a flask of water, and I drank, and chewed a preserved yam.

I had become part of the field, part of the land, the little fold of ground I worked, part of the corn. I crept on, and although I was in agony, my hands threatening to go numb, my knees stiff, my neck firing pain down my back, still my fingers found the corn, and my heart sustained me as best it could.

The storm went on through the night, dying at last toward noon. Like the others, I simply dropped flat in the field when the wind stopped.

Then something incredible happened. People came alive. They stood up, and they started singing and clapping, an old harvest song, 'Where are you, John Barley, where are you gone?'

The children came running out of the bedraggled farm buildings, running to their parents. They were beautiful, the children of this place. Some genius had seen to it that they were fresh and clean, as if they had just climbed down the hair of God.

Like a part of the land I rose up, dust pouring from me. One of them pulled back my mask and I breathed the snapping new air. We were drawn toward the dining hall, we dirty ghosts, guided by these eager kids.

Somehow they had made a meal. They laid before us bowls of potatoes crusted with salt. The dining hall was bright with light, full of Amish and Mennonite refugees, Summerland farmers and the kids.

As harvesters came in they began to clap for us, perhaps only to keep us from collapsing until we were seated.

I drank off a bowl of soup that must have been made in the kitchens of perfection, and ate a half a dozen of the tender little potatoes.

Statistics: 1,211 bushels of corn were saved, of the 17,200 estimated to have been in the fields.

Twenty-one kilometers of windbreak were destroyed, three kilometers remained.

The Summerland water tower collapsed.

Eight of eleven buildings were destroyed.

Over a million short tons of dust was deposited within the boundaries of the farm.

The Mennonites soon left Summerland, returning to their old farmsteads, some with little more than a hand hoe and a few precious bags of seed.

The Summerland farmers stayed on, and as far as I know remain there still.

We four were proud of our new blood-tie to this land, but Summerland had other plans for us.

We were lingering over dinner with some of the other farmers when Selena came to us.

'The board of directors want to see you,' she said. At first I thought we were going to be thanked or rendered some sort of honor, but the gentle sadness of her face told a different story.

The board was grim, sitting in the remains of the headquarters building. The roof was still off but the room had been swept of dust. The meeting took place in the glow of beeswax candles, with a silver moon hanging in the sky.

A young woman was the first to speak. I didn't know her name. 'We can't protect you anymore,' she said simply. 'All of our resources have to go to rebuilding.'

All I felt was a dull sort of pain. Allie sat staring straight ahead. Scott frowned.

Bell exploded. 'We risked our lives for this place!' She grabbed my hands, held them up in the soft candle glow. 'Look at his hands! And you reward us like this. How dare you!'

'Bell, we can send you somewhere that'll give you a better chance.'

'Where? Heaven?'

A man spoke, Jean Ridge, who had been on the damage control team. He was bandaged from being hit by glass shards. 'You've come to mean a lot to us. You threw yourselves into helping us totally, and we love you for it.'

Bell shook her head. She was near tears. 'Summerland could be our home. We can work, you've seen that. And, over time, we could get back to our conviction and even finish our book. Summerland can protect us, I feel sure of it.'

'From Singh? He knows all about this place.'

'You mustn't say that! You can't knuckle under to Singh, you just can't! So he knows where you are. Once we deposit our conviction and publish our book what he knows won't matter!'

Selena tried to take her hand, but she jerked away. 'Bell, let me finish. You'll be better off at Magic – '

Scott almost leaped out of his chair. He lurched forward with such violence that he knocked over both candles. 'Magic!'

The moonlight exalted his expression. Allie's hand came into mine. Bell let out a long breath. 'Magic,' she murmured.

They were smiling, the Summerland farmers. Bell let Selena embrace her.

It was not bitter to leave, not in view of where we were

going. On the contrary, we were so excited that even Bell fell silent and accepted Selena's affection.

An advantage of the fact that we were leaving was that I could turn on my computer, secure in the knowledge that we would soon be on the move. The possibility that Singh had managed to hurt my conviction was eating and eating at me. It woke me up, it made me think constantly of my impotent Unon Interactor.

Not having access to my programs is like being paralyzed and blind.

When it was time to leave, we found ourselves facing a truly unique means of transport. The experience was filthy, revolting and deeply affecting. It uncovered layers of disgust and love in us that we didn't know existed. I never, ever want to do it again.

But before we left, in the grimy ruins of Selena's weather station I opened my Unon Interactor. The screen glowed, the voice spoke. 'Ready.'

I was so nervous that I had trouble hitting the proper keys. 'Delta Doctor,' I said.

'We know, John. We've been hoping to hear from you again.'

What was this? Machines don't spontaneously generate statements like that.

Expecting anything – that hell itself might open before me – I resumed my test interrogation.

– Are you prepared to speak on this level despite the fact that the true name and factual background of this individual have not yet been obtained?

The name is known.

– I didn't input that datum. How can it be known?

The name is known.

– Tell me.

I do not wish to tell you. But you may proceed with the interrogatory.

– This can't be correct. Interrupt.

Interrupted.

– Delta Doctor, have you experienced a further security breach? Is this conviction still virgin?

If I had a failure I would have told you already. Now proceed with the interrogatory.

– End interrupt. I would like to expand on your theory that the human race is deciding, on an instinctive level, whether or not to become extinct. What scientific basis does this theory have beyond the writings of D. T. Somtow?

Beyond the writings of Somtow? There is nothing better than Somtow on the subject of crowding psychosis. He has certainly identified an actual disease. It accounts for all sorts of aberrant behavior, ranging from serial murder to compulsive hostility.

– But there's nothing in Somtow about this instinctive urge toward extinction. Is it simply a pet theory of yours, or what?

You haven't read much Somtow, have you? What about *War on an Overcrowded Planet*? He proves that both twentieth century general wars, the destruction of the European Jews and the creation of the nuclear arsenal were results of unrecognized crowding psychosis.

– But he never goes so far as to say that crowding psychosis leads to an instinctive urge toward the death of the whole species. But you say that.

It's a perfectly logical assumption! What would have resulted if the twentieth century had set off its hydrogen bombs, if not extinction? Of course the species wants to go extinct. This is entirely logical.

– Dr Singh, do you hunger for your own death?

That is to say, am I projecting some twisted personal death wish on the entire human race? No, John Sinclair, I am not!

– You don't sound like my Gupta Singh conviction.

Why should I bother?

– Who are you? The program is required to tell me.

Oh? I am not a computer program.

– You aren't Delta Doctor? Terminate.

JOHN: The Lost Conviction

I was so damn afraid of this. I just wish to God – but what's the use of wishing? My conviction is dead.

I need Stratigen to help me analyze the extent of damage. But Allie is calling me to get in the truck. I wish she'd stop, I want to be alone right now. They'll have to wait another few minutes, scared as they are.

Singh did it. He broke Delta Doctor and destroyed all of my work. He was there just now, behind that data link. It wasn't a program talking to me, it was him.

Sometimes it is hard to tell the difference between a program and a person, I'll admit, but I know Delta Doctor and it doesn't act like that. There is an open, accommodating quality to Delta Doctor. It seems almost to urge you along as you work, striving with you for the insights it needs to keep building its model of the subject's personality.

It does not refuse to divulge critical pieces of data. It isn't closed and unwilling to meet me halfway. Delta Doctor is just a massive listing of logic code, I know, but over the years I've come to thnk of it as a friend.

I'm furious, as much at myself as at Singh. I should have risked everything when I had the chance, and taken this conviction all the way to level eight even without the factual data. The sheer force of it might have convinced people, even if the facts weren't there.

I want to show people what a murderous fraud he is. I want to stop him so badly I don't think I can bear it. He's taken my great weapon out of my hands and broken it over his knee. If he was here I'd go after him with my bare hands.

'John, come on!'

'Please, just a minute.'

I know that I am waiting for his call. He probably knows that too, so he's delaying as long as he can. He found us once and missed us. He doesn't want to miss again, I'm quite sure of that.

Bell comes in, takes my computer out of my hands.

'I don't like that.'

'You're just sitting here. We have to break all data links and leave.'

'Just another minute. He might call.'

'For God's sake, John, what has he become, your lover? He's the man who set that gas trap, remember. He didn't expect us to escape, so we managed to lose him. But don't count on it a second time.'

We were supposed to cross the country in the back of a land cruiser full of intelligence-altered animals. We were supposed to go to Magic where even Singh couldn't find us. I thought then that Singh could find us anywhere.

I was finished with running, and anyway, the phone was saying my name.

GUPTA SINGH: I Have Broken You

Well, John Sinclair, I think that you have met with defeat. The only thing left for me to do is to assist you to change your mind about me. We must get together, really we must.

I have a vision of you and me together on a newsvideo, discussing why you abandoned your conviction. You could not embarrass such a good man, or risk damaging his program.

The great difficulty a man such as myself has is that he can easily be led astray by people who want to please him. Regarding your capture, I have been given one false report after another. You were trapped. You were in the hands of the Tax Police. No, you would be in an hour.

When I actually found you, I had to do it personally.

My gas would not have killed you. No, it is a much more interesting gas than that. I was thwarted by a tumbleweed. It really is funny, you know.

I looked at you that night, John, sleeping so peacefully. I looked closely at you. In your aging you have acquired a remarkable and melancholy beauty. Your skin is like ancient paper, upon which is written the story of your soul. How could you have hidden such a face in the obscurity of youth?

You work well together, you four. You certainly don't look like you could escape a curious puppy, but you're really doing quite well. You are escaping me!

The American Tax Police, it seems, could not catch a blind cow in a stall. I have these reports. Oh, by all that is holy, a list of your 'possible locations' that includes the names of over eight hundred towns! Eight hundred towns, all filled with basements, warehouses, storerooms, whatever. Millions of hiding places. Another list of two thousand places they checked. They even looked under all the cars in a shopping plaza in New Jersey.

Indeed, you are admirable. Only I myself can overcome you. There will be no stopping me now, no stopping me, but I must find you, I cannot tolerate this ignorant, insane, egotistical, eccentric opposition.

You rich with your gleaming hair and your perfumed skin, with your roaring TAVs and the full plates on your tables, you addicts of infinite expansion, you have eaten the world and left for my children's children not a crust or a bone. India has starved a hundred generations so that America could fatten a hundred generations. By all the holy things of the world, I despise you.

Do you know what unimaginable suffering you will cause if you somehow hurt my movement? Haven't you seen the projections? What do you think will happen when mankind realizes the truth of it all, that the end is come and there is no hope? Oh, my heart, my heart beats fast. I have to turn on the regulator. You are killing me. You are killing the most important man in the world.

Well, not quite. I am overexcited because I cannot catch you. I suppose I should be as triumphant as my supporters over the conviction. I have read every word of your test interrogations, you know. What a pleasure, to read that scurrilous garbage, and know that it would never be released into the world. You are a poisonous reptile!

I know exactly where you are going. You are going to Magic. Ah, yes, they have a universal address, those clever ones. If you query for the location of Magic, you get a fifty gigabyte answer. Their address is all addresses.

They have led us on quite a chase. We ended up

searching a shoe factory in Santiago de Cuba, a rugby field in Wales, a stadium filled with old Soviet army equipment in Poland. Then we understood. Query for Magic and you get anywhere.

And yet when you send a message to Magic, it says received and thank you! Magic's telephone number doesn't exist, according to ITT. Who pays their connect bills? How does it work? Where are they? You know, don't you, you white-faced devils.

I knew I would have trouble when I took the Manifesto to America. Such a crowd of surly, contentious people! Nobody else disagrees, not overtly, except the wearisome English.

But they all say, for us to actually do this thing, the Americans must first agree. Europe has signed as a continent. The European Depopulation Agreement will come into force 'when all powers accept it.'

I have accomplished miracles, in that I have understood enough of the American and English political systems to make some productive decisions. It is like American football, or that damned English cricket that some Indians also pretend to play. You read the rules. They make no sense. Then you see the game, and you understand, the rules are not supposed to make sense. If the rules made sense, American football and English cricket could not be played. Your systems of government are the same way. If the rules made sense, they could not function.

You and the English. They keep their constitution in their heads. You have a written constitution that you 'interpret.' They have an unwritten one that is above interpretation. In both cases, my people are having trouble!

But we are making headway. If we keep winning elections, finally, inevitably, inexorably, we will succeed even in your countries. That is the beginning and end of this battle. I gained a majority in the US Congress, so the President threatens to invoke some sort of rule that makes it necessary for more than the majority to pass the bill. What is this? If he doesn't like a bill, he gets to make it extra-hard to pass. All right, accepted. Insane, but accepted. Now my Congressional Co-ordinator tells me we lack four votes in the House and one in the Senate to override the President's veto. We will get those votes, let me assure you. There will be no breath of trouble from you.

Right at this moment I could almost clap my hands. I do have a brilliant group of computer technicians, don't I? Once we knew where your work was located within Delta Doctor, it was only a matter of days before I was myself working with your precious conviction!

No matter where you go, I will follow you. And I will find you, I can assure you of that.

Every day, every hour, every moment we get a little closer to finding the location of Magic. It may be a hole in the world, but it is the only hole in the world.

Let me say this seriously. It is from my heart, my soul, my very blood. If you dare to continue, you will wish you had never heard of Gupta Singh. I will not torture you. I will not kill you. I will remake you.

You will be a famous Depopulationist, and you will help me make the Manifesto the law of the world.

PART FOUR
Children

so gay gay gay and with a
wisdom not the wisest man
will partly understand

– e. e. cummings, from 95 Poems, 1958

SCOTT: Innocents in Hell

The land cruiser that was to take us to Magic pulled into the small gas station near Summerland on schedule. The station was long since abandoned, but Summerland still used its tanks and pumps for fuel storage. Refueling the cruiser would empty Summerland's tanks, but the farmers seemed to give no thought to the problem of refilling them as they set about the job.

We came here in secrecy, leaving the ravaged farm behind, just the four of us driven by Selena in a rusty pickup. Summerland had instructions about us from Magic. Nobody was to be trusted. Our departure had to take place at night. We were to be loaded onto the cruiser in a cargo pallet, like so many pounds of produce.

There was also something else about this land cruiser that was important. We were not the only fugitives scheduled to travel in it.

It was stifling in our pallet, and we were beginning to need air. Forest Boone came down from the cab and stuck her card into the station's recorder. The compressor began hissing, transferring prolene to the cruiser's canisters. She stood talking to Selena. She was a small, muscular woman in a brown cruiser suit. She smiled a lot as she talked, but we couldn't hear her.

Her husband Johnson climbed down the gleaming silver side of the enormous vehicle. He had their baby with him, the child sleeping on his chest in a Snugli. The group came over to the pickup where we waited. We didn't know exactly why we were in a pallet unless it was to throw off satellite surveillance.

'You must be the supercargo,' Forest said, sliding back the side as if to inspect the pallet's contents.

Bell introduced us. 'Will you want any money for this?' she asked.

'Money's always useful, but if you don't have any to spare –'

Bell gave her a thousand dollars. From inside the closed land cruiser cargo bay there came a loud cackle. 'Are you sure you're really under a threat,' Forest asked, 'enough to make you want to ride in there?'

'Magic did the planning,' Selena said.

'What's in there?' Allie was practically wringing her hands. She had managed to do up her hair with some combs and looked reasonably nice.

'Chimps from an enhancement lab in Chicago.'

'You've got to be joking. Surely we can't be expected to ride with a bunch of animals!'

'They have Intelligence Indexes of five and six. They're almost as bright as people.'

Allie was not going to take this well, but what could we do?

'Are they dangerous?'

'I'd be lying if I said no. The answer is that they certainly can be. We have a copy of the Handler's Manual that comes with them. It says that they've been taught to interpret smiling as "benign dominant" behavior, whatever that means. So you're probably best off smiling a lot. There's another problem, though. You have to be prepared for it or you won't be able to endure it. The poor chimps have been cooped up in there for three days already and they smell awful.'

With that they backed the pickup over to the cruiser and opened its pallet bay. 'I'll throw the pallet sides open when you get in the cruiser,' Johnson called over the rumble of the mechanism. 'I'll give you a little light once we're under way. It'll be dim, though. The chimps are supposed to be sleeping.'

Then we were dropped into total darkness, out of which there arose yelps, cackles, laughter, whimpering.

The odor almost knocked me out cold. I staggered. Nausea overwhelmed me and I tippled forward, grabbing for the wall, retching helplessly. The smell cannot be described. It was excrement, urine, dirty hair, the alien stinks of animals, the fetor of breath and the sick-sweet odor of rotting fruit.

Allie grabbed me. She and Bell helped me to the floor. 'Stop it, you're hyperventilating. Slow your breathing. You too, John.' The four of us huddled there, trying to get ourselves under control. 'Take shallow breaths through the mouth,' Bell said.

There was an increase in the ambient sound level and a sensation of being pushed to the rear of the cruiser. The Boones hadn't wasted any time: the pallet was fully open and we were accelerating onto the highway.

I wish there had been more time to say goodbye to Summerland.

I slipped and was groping helplessly along the floor when the lights finally came on. 'At, at, at! Eheheh.' Standing before me was a chimpanzee. The animal seemed enormous, looming over me with its arms akimbo, a faint gray beard on its face and a rim of gray hair around its bald head. When I smiled it folded back its lips and showed its teeth. 'At, at, at,' it said, giving emphasis to the sounds by nodding its head at each word.

The whole shadowy front of the cab was suddenly in motion, and the truck was filled with a cataract of shouting. Leaping chimps, all screaming 'at, at,at,at,' at the top of their lungs.

Bell stood up, her face twisted into a rictus that was

probably intended to pass for a smile. She was at once knocked down by one of the creatures.

Then the large gray one clapped his hands over his head while he ran from one side of the bay to the other, back and forth through the screaming, leaping mob.

Bell got up again, rubbing the shoulder that had taken the blow. She had not stopped smiling. I smiled, too. We all did.

Natural chimps have an Intelligence Index of four. These animals were fives, some of them sixes. The human norm is eight. The troupe had a language of words borrowed from English and incorporated into their own expressions, sounds and movements. They could understand an unknown amount of English and could be cunning in their concealment of what they had grasped.

They had been stolen from an experimental facility in Chicago, where they were being prepared for shipment to the L-5 Space Colony to work in occupations considered too hazardous for human beings. Now they were headed for Magic instead, which seemed to have become a refuge for all intelligence-altered creatures, not just human ones.

According to theory these children were altered in the zygotic stage much as an animal is altered, by microelectrosurgically changing the structural characteristics of certain genes. This resulted in higher density glial cell growth in the relevant areas of the brain, the outcome of which was sometimes higher intelligence. Brain malformations also occurred, with all kinds of bad consequences for the victims.

As we stood smiling for all we were worth, swaying with the movement of the cruiser, the chimps would dash up, touch us, then rush away waving their arms, crying 'you, yeyou, ye, ye!' This went on, I believe, until all of the chimps had touched each of us.

Abruptly they became still. The gray one moved forward alone, stopping every few steps to show his teeth, wave his arms and shake his head. He never made a sound. His steady eyes were on Bell. They never left her face, not for an instant. He had correctly analyzed the order of our group; he was going straight for the leader.

He arrived before her. She smiled down on him. Tension was high. I had the feeling that he was ready to tear her apart, which he could easily have done.

'Hi, guy,' he said in a thick voice, guttural and heavily slurred. Then he stuck out a long arm. They shook hands. Bell's face was in a skeletal rictus. 'Oh, Lord,' she said softly as he stuck her fingers in his mouth. Then, 'hi, guy, hi, guy.'

'Hi, hi, hi!'

'Hi, how are you?'

'Ohh, out, out, we!' He hugged himself, twirled around. 'We out, we we we out out OUT!'

These animal people survive only a few months on L-5.

The whole room erupted with cries, 'out, out, out!' I cannot convey to you how this sounded, the deep, rich timbre of the voices, the sheer pandemonium, the passion.

Bell crouched to be at eye level with the leader. 'Soon.'

'Oh!' He leaped up waving his arms, his lips folded back, whooping and shrieking, 'At, at, atatat! Wego-wegowego – OUT!'

They began hugging one another, the children riding the backs of their elders. Some of the females presented, and the males entered them, screaming cheerfully during their brief, furious copulations.

The leader moved around us to the doors. He squatted in the center. 'Out,' he said. I could hear the satisfaction in his voice, and I felt a twinge of fear. There was a miscommunication taking place – he thought we meant they were getting out immediately.

'Bell – '

'I know.'

The others began coming, lining up in front of the door, all saying in that same satisfied tone, 'out.'

Bell stood behind them, facing the door.

'Out,' the leader said. His tone was a little more ominous. After a moment he slapped the lock. 'Out!'

Bell also slapped the lock. 'Out,' she shouted. 'Out, out!' He turned around and glared up at her.

Then they were all slapping and shouting, Bell as loud as any of them. She yelled something. We couldn't hear her but we understood. We went to the door and banged and shouted with them, as loud as we could.

Then it ended, a storm blowing off. A terrible sound came up from the leader, a soft, sweet tone, sad, ending in a series of gulping gasps. I wanted to cry too, but I kept up my crazy smile.

He turned again to Bell. 'Ohh, you. You.' The question in the words was almost tangible, a thing as much of his body as his mind and soul.

Bell was before him, their hands were intertwining. Then he was embracing her, cooing softly. 'Hi, guy,' he said, 'ohh boy!'

'Oh, boy is right,' Bell replied.

Solemnly he shook both of her hands. Then they all came forward, each in turn touching her hands and scuttling off, some with a murmured 'hi, guy.'

They were more bold with the rest of us, shaking our hands, touching our clothes, our hair. John's eyes bulged as a female thrust her fingers into his mouth. As gently as he could, he drew them out. His expression was awful.

A moment later it happened to me. It was so sudden, I couldn't even turn my head aside. I tasted urine and rotted fruit and filth – my tongue went into a spasm, I gagged. Fighting the nausea, I withdrew the fingers, only to find my own pulled into the mouth of the female who had attached herself to me, pulled in and lovingly sucked and tongued. As she did it she half-closed her eyes. Then she gave me a coy glance and yanked at my pants, cooing and wriggling. I was terribly embarrassed and confused. I smiled all the harder, which she took as encouragement. With a smack of her lips she thrust her face between my legs. I pushed her head back. 'No,' I said.

'No! Nonono! NO!' She cavorted, she threw her hands up in the air, she pranced, showing me her bottom, smacking, cooing, whooping. 'No, no, no!' The whole troupe surrounded us, all leaping and screaming no, tearing their hair and showing me their teeth, jumping at me and delivering blows that were getting harder fast.

'Show your teeth,' Bell shouted. 'Wave your arms and scream.'

More than the danger, I felt embarrassment as my rejected companion hopped up and down in front of me, thrusting her buttocks at my groin and bellowing with what I can only describe as hurt. I grimaced and waved my arms. I let out shrieks through my teeth.

Slowly, the troupe quieted down. The old leader came over to the humiliated female, who was crouching at my feet with her face in her hands. He began to groom her, and soon they were all grooming one another.

We moved off to one side. 'Twenty-one hours,' Allie said. She looked at Bell. 'Were you briefed about toilet facilities?'

We followed Bell's gaze. There were three filthy porta-pots against one wall, one of them turned over, the other two reeking and encrusted. 'I was told there were toilets. I was not told about their condition.'

'Or that they're right out in front of everybody.' Allie's

voice had a scream in it. 'John, I think I could go crazy in here.'

'Allie, Allie.' They had been so beautiful, so happy once. 'I'm sorry I did this to you.'

'John, don't say that. We're here for a purpose. Nobody needs to be sorry about anything.'

'The conviction – '

I didn't want him to dwell on that. It had occurred to me that he might commit suicide, if he thought hard enough about what had happened. 'I think maybe we should eat and then try to get some sleep.'

'*Eat*? My God, Scott, don't start me vomiting.'

'Come on, Allie,' Bell said, 'you can do better than that.' She snapped a bag of sukiyaki. While it heated itself she laid out the bowls to form. 'We're going to eat, all of us.' Allie turned away. In the dim light I could see tears on her face. 'You too,' Bell said, 'even if I have to feed you myself.'

Allie looked at her, hurt and nervous. There was no question in my mind that Bell would do exactly what she threatened if she had to.

'Is there a mood in that stuff?' Allie asked. She picked up the faintly sizzling bag. 'Ramen Suki Nature,' she read. 'Hell. Why doesn't it at least have some Satisfaction or something?'

'We can't risk moods, you know that. Anyway, the Summerland people don't stock foods that contain them. We were lucky they even had these bags, otherwise we would have had to make do with cold cornbread and stuff.'

The bag peeped its readiness and Bell pulled back the tab, dividing the sukiyaki between the four bowls. My chopsticks sprang straight as I took them out of their wrapper. I started to eat. The food tasted as if it had just been cooked, the onions crisp, the meat a convincing simulation of beef. I hadn't taken two bites before my female friend was before me, cooing pitifully, her eyes swimming with desire, offering me a piece of papaya in return for my dinner.

I dared not say no again. Instead I gobbled down as much sukiyaki as I could, then gave her some daikon on the end of my sticks.

She took it between her teeth, drew it into her mouth – and began doing backward somersaults. She backed away from the next bite, tossing the papaya aside. In a moment she brought me something else, which could have been either a date or a piece of excrement. She tossed it at me, clapped her hands and then began to grunt and holler, her huge mouth grinning, her eyes twinkling. As I watched, a feeling of awe came over me. I realized that she was laughing. The excrement had been a joke, to tell me what she thought of our food.

The animal had a sense of humor, the gift of laughter. Just a moment ago in the earth's time our own laughter was as coarse as this. Could this filthy little creature represent some new and unexpected future for the world?

What would her children be like, or her grandchildren?

What would her species be like in a thousand years, or a million?

When we finished our sukiyaki Allie and John drank water from their bag and cuddled together. Soon Allie had to use the portapot. Bell went with her, and held her so that she would not touch the dirty rim with her naked body. I only glanced at them, the young woman supporting the old.

I decided I would stay awake for the rest of the night, guarding us from the chimps.

I must have fallen asleep within moments of having made that decision.

When I woke up, the cruiser was still moving, the dim

light and the stench were the same, and something seemed to be crawling in my hair.

I put up my hand and touched rough fingers. My friend was there, grooming me. I raised my eyes and saw her brutal face, the lips turned to softness, the eyes hooded, dark, infinitely mysterious. Her fingers wound slowly, carefully through my hair, and I relaxed at last. I dreamed that night of swimming in a river so clean I could drink it, in a fresh summer morning of the kind you buy in dreams.

In my dream the dew of morning left no film on the grass.

FROM THE DATA FILES OF TOM SINCLAIR:
CHIMPS

Intelligent Animals on L-5, Blessing or Danger?
by
Thomas Sinclair

Neuron process alteration techniques – illegal in most countries for use in human embryos – are increasingly being applied to animal young, sometimes with revolutionary results. Cranial capacity limits the effectiveness of the technology, of course, so the popular image of the scientist with a genuine Cheshire Cat on his shoulder remains nothing more than a charming idea. So far cats and dogs have not passed the so-called 'cognition threshold,' which occurs at Intelligence Index level four.

It is possible, of course, to buy a dog that can ruff out a few words, such as its name and the ubiquitous 'I wruff yourff,' which fond masters believe to be an expression of affection. Cats have not yet been made to speak, and indeed intelligence-enhanced cats do not make good pets because of their tendency to harbor grudges and to hide with almost supernatural skill.

More successful has been the National Intelligence Laboratory's work with primates. The young male gorilla Boola Boola had an II that measured an astonishing eight, higher than 40% of the human population. This animal was lost to science when it escaped under mysterious circumstances thought to be associated with an illegal refuge for the intelligence altered. Subsequent attempts have not produced a gorilla with a score over six.

Chimpanzees have proved to be the most practical species for study. Electromicrosurgical alteration of the embryonic genetic material is no more difficult than it is in human ova, and the 98% similarity to the human gene map means that chimp studies are almost directly applicable to man.

The chimp zygote can be correctly altered at a reliability level of 65%, making intelligence enhancement for industrial use a cost-effective alternative to sophisticated robots. An intelligence-enhanced chimp will cost an average of $177,450 over its ten-year working life, while a robot with considerably less task flexibility would cost four times as much to purchase and maintain.

Unfortunately, as the number of interventions in the genetic material goes up, the likelihood of success decreases exponentially. This means that a 65% chance of intelligence enhancement may be accompanied by a 31% chance of successful structural alteration of vocal chords to enable unlimited speech, and only a 12% chance of successful alteration of esoteric 'personality' related brain structures such as the hippocampus, which are connected to memory and time sense, and upon which such civilizing tendencies as an understanding that actions will have consequences depend.

Because of this, the great majority of these animals, while capable of limited reading, understanding simple spoken instructions and carrying out repetitive and/or dangerous work for reward, must be guarded all the time.

The chimp tendency to become vicious with advancing years has made their installation on the L-5 orbiting colony controversial. At the present time, colony law requires that the animals be destroyed when they reach the age of twelve, unless they can pass the Ebler Social Set with a rating of 75 or more.

There is at present a population of 621 chimps on L-5. They are at work in toxic refuse management, outer skin maintenance and other hazardous tasks. The program, although still experimental, is generally considered a success. While there have been a number of 'negative contact incidents' between the chimps and colonists, only two colonist injuries have been reported, one a bite wound and the other a detached arm. These minor injuries both occurred during a period of unrest among the chimps. One of their number was killed when his spacesuit lost pressure during an eva to repair exterior impact damage. They became enraged and left their designated areas.

For a brief time the chimps were uncontrolled. They attacked a group of picnickers in the colony's Buckminster Fuller Park before being apprehended by their advisors. When they were returned to their compound anger finally gave way to grief, and they became docile once again.

Animal rights groups, especially the Chimpanzee Exploitation Unit of the American Civil Liberties Union, deplore the actions of the biointelligence industry, saying that the uses of intelligent animals should be regulated by civil rights laws, not animal care statutes. The industry replies that intelligence enhancement does not confer human status. 'These creatures are adequately protected under the Animal Rights Act of 2016,' says Dr Thomas Paul of Smartlab, Inc, a Chicago producer of intelligent animals. 'They are not human beings. You have only to talk to one for a few minutes to realize this.'

– Science Watch, December 2020

JOHN: Dallas

Every few hours one of the Boones would check on us, looking down through the inspection door. We passed through Kansas City safely, then through Wichita, then Oklahoma City.

'I'm getting out the next time he opens the door.' Allie remained extremely uncomfortable.

'Magic made this plan,' Bell said. 'We'd better follow it to the letter.'

'Oh, Magic. What is it? They might be geniuses but they've ignored the human factor. If another one of those chimps tries to put its hands on me, I think I'll go crazy.'

Allie was as good as her word. When Forest Boone checked again, she marched right up to the door and through it. 'Where's the shower,' she said as she disappeared.

The chimps erupted, rushing in a body toward the small door. Forest slammed it shut before they could get out into the family compartment.

'Oh, no,' Bell said. With a bloodcurdling shriek she moved toward the door. The noise shocked the animals, making them cower away from her. 'Come on,' she called over her shoulder, 'unless you men like it in here.'

The baby burst into tears when we came up out of the floor of the tiny living room. It could have been that we simply startled him, but I think it more likely that he was reacting to our odor.

Bell and Allie were sharing the shower as we rolled down IH 35, an old road festooned with aging traffic control equipment. It was nostalgic to see the radar guides flashing past. I used to count them when Allie and I were young and autopilot highways were a delightful innovation. We'd sit there in luxury, counting and enjoying watching the car drive itself. New roads are too sleek. Progress has killed the romance of the highway.

I sank back into my seat, enjoying the comfort like it was a sin. Maybe I am addicted to material pleasure, but, God, it was a beautiful feeling up there in that cool, quiet cabin, just sailing the road.

The so-called habitation pod of a landcruiser is a masterpiece of compaction, and the Boones' was no exception. 'This is the low-end pod,' Forest said. 'You wouldn't believe all the magic they can pack into one of these things if you pay for it. Chairs that grow and disappear at a whisper. Total voice control of the cruiser, supersmart autopilots that even do automatic weather linking and design the route accordingly. But it costs, oh, it costs.'

This seat couldn't do any disappearing tricks. All it could do was turn into a bed – not much of a trick, but a welcome one at the right time of day. I'd wondered about life in a pod. Everybody does. This was the reality, though: crowded, cluttered, everyone on top of everyone else. When little Fred cried the whole pod resounded with it. I can understand why children brought up in cruisers are the heroes of the toughest dreams, always imaged as brutal and cruel. How can they enculturate out of an environment that's so cut off? These kids are as ill-served as some miserable twentieth-century cultural isolates, slinking out of their ghetto with knives in their hands.

Now, of course, we have much less perverse forms of violence: people tend to kill to eat, unless they are so hungry that they can't make the effort. And then there is thrill killing, what Horace and Timmi Poluchnik called 'the joy of knowing you are making them die.' Crowding psychosis wasn't known in the twentieth century, and it wasn't a general trigger to crime until ten or fifteen years ago. I think they had serial killers as far back as the sixties, but they didn't understand population pressure caused the disease, just as it creates mass murderers in overpopulated rat colonies.

To end crowding psychosis we need hope. Our energy has to go to breaking out of the cage. We could turn to space. The ideas are certainly there, and the technology is available. We could revive NASA's Star Magic project and send out the first fifty star probes. Build more space colonies – a hundred L-5s, a thousand. Step up the terraforming of Mars, expand the moonbase.

Obviously, all of this will only absorb a fraction of the population. But people will have the feeling that we're on the move, not that we're just down here in this poor, used up ecosystem, suffocating.

'What are you doing?' It was Scott. He came into the control room and sat down beside me.

'Typing notes. Explaining the world.' Scott said nothing. No doubt he heard bitterness in my voice, or perhaps felt it himself.

We had lost the conviction. Give any one of us a few minutes alone, and that fact is remembered like a recent death. We sat in silence. The Boones' baby played beneath our feet, the music was soft, the air fresh. By now the desert was far behind us, the pallor in the fields the only reminder of the dust. I turned on the radio, patched through to WQXR in New York, and listened to the Dana Andrews program. Bach, Dvorak, Handel, *The National Times* news.

'Top story Friday, November 14, 2025: Eleven hundred and sixty-one people were killed when an Azanian Airlines Fanprop blew up on takeoff at Capetown. Afrikaans

Union spokesmen in London stated that the bombing was a legitimate act of war. No Americans were believed aboard the aircraft.

'The American Depopulationist Council announced that it would begin a countdown to the point of no return commencing on January 3, 2026, to coincide with the introduction of Manifesto bills in the House and Senate. Depopulationist scientists now put the point of no return in the third quarter of 2034. After this time, it is claimed, atmospheric damage will be irreversible.

'The trial of the Beverly Hills Boys ended today in acquittal of all seven members of the troubled Highland Paradise Development Corporation. It is believed that the scam, designed by superintelligent computers allegedly at the direction of the California developers, netted over forty million dollars. The jury decided that the computers themselves were responsible for the crime, and that they had used the money in an unknown manner for an unknown purpose. The devices will be shut down.

'New York City suffered its seventeenth water pressure emergency of the year when silt again clogged all six intake vents at the Kerhonkson-Croton water washing station. As a result, unwashed water was bled into the system and residents were warned not to use it for drinking until further notice.

'The L-5 colony received its two-thousandth colonist, Mr Tai Kim of Brooklyn, with a colony-wide celebration. Mr Kim was signed on as a metallurgist in the lunar mining program.

'That's the news at nineteen, sponsored by City Dreams, Manhattan's most exclusive dreamworks.'

I miss home, miss our former life, but I suppose there isn't any time for that. Tom never seemed to feel like I feel, out of control, falling down a well.

Evening turned into night as the cruiser rolled on. Just

south of the Oklahoma border the road became more modern. There was an unlimited speed lane and the autopilot soon found a slot for us. I watched the speed move from a hundred to a hundred and eighty kph. Ahead of us a line of thunderstorms flashed, and an occasional muffled rumble filled the pod.

I had drawn a short straw, and bedded down on the floor between two of the pod's four bunks. I dreamed of my old desk, of my old computer. I dreamed an odor, which I think was of the vegetable soup at Louie's on East Sixty-second Street, and woke up thinking grimly of Troll Heaven and vats of giant, sick carrots.

We had decelerated and were now passing over the Ray Hubbard Bridge across the reservoir immediately east of Dallas. The reservoir gleamed with a coating of Olene to protect the water from evaporation and atmospheric pollution. All around its featureless tan there were housing developments, hundreds upon hundreds of three room tract houses, all extruded concrete and pressed paper, little cottages with false green shutters embossed in the walls beside the windows. Some shutters were red.

There was heavy traffic, and ahead a car was burning to the side of the road. I have seen at least half a dozen of those XOAs going up in flames. Like the others, this one had failed to open its doors. I think the people must have still been in it but there weren't any emergency vehicles around. I suppose the local fire department planned to let the thing burn itself out, as its location on the shoulder beside the reservoir made it unlikely the fire would spread. Whether the car was occupied or not, there was clearly no point in an ambulance.

Ahead of us Dallas rose in the morning sun. With the drowning of so much of Houston the population of Dallas has really exploded. Corporate headquarters are

404

transferring here, and along with them all of the usual supporting businesses. In 2023 Dallas saw the construction of fourteen new skyscrapers as well as the Texas Opera Center where fifty thousand people can listen to Katherine Trimble doing *Manon Lescaut*.

The spire of the Texas Tower caught the sun, its flying red horse a beacon to travelers for miles in every direction. White contrails were rising into the sky almost continuously from beyond the city. The Dallas–Fort Worth TAVPort, after La Guardia, is the busiest in the world. A fanprop, great and fat, turned slowly around the city and began its descent.

Traffic was so heavy now that the autopilot called for a manned wheel. Johnson took the controls while the rest of us ate a breakfast of World Beaters and Frickles washed down by J-J-juice. I was eager to get my feet on the ground soon, but the Boones seemed content to remain in the cruiser.

'We'd like an hour's stopover here,' I said.

'Well, the people in the back won't care for that,' Johnson replied.

'We need it for the book we're working on. We need to meet people.' With the death of the conviction, the book had become of utmost importance to me.

'Would you like to be let off? We'll be glad to drop you.'

'How do we get to Magic without you? Can you tell us where it is?'

'Don't know myself. We go to Monterey and they meet us. We follow them in and out, and then they wipe our memories with hypnosis. We don't remember how to get back until they send us a signal in data.'

No matter the importance of Dallas, none of us were willing to risk failure to connect.

'Our book is important, too,' Bell said. 'The chimps can stand one more hour.'

Forest looked steadily at her. 'They can stand a year if they have to, but they'll suffer. Tell me the truth, is it worth their suffering?'

Bell nodded. 'I feel for them, but I have to say it's worth it. Especially now.' She did not mention to the Boones that we had lost our conviction. Too many of the Networkers were aware of it. There was no reason to hurt their morale.

Finally the Boones agreed to stop at a cruiserbase in Grand Prairie between Dallas and Fort Worth. We could spend the hour any way we wanted. As the cruiser climbed the Dallas Flyover, a five kilometer long stretch of highway that spins across the center of the city, we called up detailed local maps of the area.

A housing development, Holland Meadows, virtually surrounded the cruiserbase. As we pulled onto the access road we saw a sea of white roofs, some of them marked with squares of black Lumaloid.

It felt awfully good to be out of the cruiser, moving around in a place that wasn't full of dust.

We crossed the blazing hot pavement of the base, and went through the front driveway into a curving road called Holland Avenue. Dozens of streets connected to it: Amsterdam Place, Hague Road, Utrecht Boulevard, Rotterdam Road. The Dutch theme was continued in the houses, all of them cottages, with relentless little flowerboxes filled with plastic flowers under the carelessly molded fake window frames. Picket fences stretched for miles and miles past the rows of these houses.

Everything was old and worn out. The lawn patches were too green, most of them repainted many times. The houses were wearing away. Many of them had split corners, repaired with tape. A child of perhaps twelve came running down Utrecht, screaming in terror. He was followed by a gang of kids in black reflectives, on black bikes that made a snarling sound as they roared along. The bikers were carrying rods of some kind with nasty, glowing ends.

He dashed across Amsterdam and into a weedy ditch. The bikes sailed in behind him. 'Help me,' he shrieked, wading toward the far side of the ditch. 'They're not kids, they're not kids.' His voice was frantic. There was no play in his terror. Bell began to move toward the bikers. Two of them separated from the others, their vehicles roaring like animals, the tips of their batons glowing and hissing.

The boy on foot reached the far side of the ditch and scrambled up to the border of the cruiser base. His legs were covered with green and purple mud from the ditch. 'Base,' he called. The bikes snarled and screamed, roaring up and down at the edge of the ditch. The boy stood with his hands on his hips, his chest thrust out. 'Puckernuddles, puckernuddles, sick slop puckernuddles,' he chanted, and the bikes snarled some more.

'Kids,' Bell said, smiling weakly. As she came back to us the two bikes still behind her peeled off and sped away with the rest of the gang.

A silver ultralight swooped overhead, marked with orange letters, 'Holland Meadows Patrol.' We felt ourselves under police scrutiny as we walked along. Bell waved absently at the ultralight. Her face, though, was taut with fear and rage.

Only when the tiny plane had disappeared did she speak. 'Why didn't I think of this? Why am I so stupid!'

'How were you to know a dowdy place like this would have a patrol?'

'Every housing development in America has a patrol. We've got to get off the street right now.' She looked up and down the block. There was a lot of activity, people tinkering with cars, the sound of vacuums, voices, prance music drumming furiously, the whine of air conditioners. 'There's a place,' she said, pointing to a house that looked a little quieter than most. 'Come on.' She strode angrily to the door. It took a few seconds and a considerable part of our dwindling supply of money to get in. She gestured to the rest of us and we hurried in to the shelter of the living room.

Lora of Holland Meadows

I'm just really sloped, you got me out of a dream. It just came in, it's the new 'Whisper to Me,' by Etella Lavender. She always has a lot of beautiful adventure, never anything like that one I got, 'Goodbye, Paradise,' that turned out to be about witches getting burned at the stake. You say you're datanewsies? I have to tell you, I don't watch newsvideos. They really aren't well acted, and I'm a fan of good acting. If you people want to get popular you ought to hire somebody like Ti Maston or Virginia-Carolina Blakenship. You can *watch* these people, they don't need to be in dreams to stay interesting.

We could have a dream about the Depop, what it would be like after. A thing like that would keep me going. I voted the right way, of course, but gosh it scares me, now that it looks like it's really going to happen.

Oh, I wish I had known you were coming, I wouldn't have done all this ecstasy. I am in a state of ultra-slope, and here I am talking to newsies instead of dreaming. Well, never a dull moment in Holland Meadows! I'm so excited, am I going to be on a video? Why not news dreams, I've always thought it would really bring the news home, you know. You would be able to take the latest bombing in Azania to bed with you.

Would you like something to drink? I have all kinds of stuff. Likemlots, which the kids chug because they think it'll kill them, I swear. I've got Coksi, too. I've got, oh, God, I just remembered, Freeman Forbes gave me an ounce of Greenland Water for Christmas, and I haven't opened it yet. Should I open it now? Is this an occasion?

409

Well, I don't know about you, but I'd be afraid to drink a thousand dollar ounce of water! Omagawd! I think I'm supposed to save it for the occasion when we get back together. He took off to Lubbock with the kids a year ago for a rest and found a job in the General Foods Soysters factory where they make fake oysters, fake bluefish, fake scallops and fake calamari. I'd like to have a little work. I do really beautiful massage, and I'm a good reflexologist. No, really, I can do it. I'd love to. People around here come to me all the time. I do half an hour for a hundred dollars or two hundred on outcall. Seriously, I'll do it. Who am I kidding? You can't really lay into someone when you're on ecstasy. I was expecting to emote this morning, and here I am talking.

Is there something going on in the neighborhood? Last week a couple of landcruisers blew up over on the base and we had a toxic alert, stay indoors. Are you some kind of follow-up team – were we really, really scared type of thing? The Dexter sisters got kidnapped last month. Is that news?

Listen, you're making me feel weird. I know I'm supposed to do all the talking, but you have to talk some too. I've already said everything I know. Now I'm making it up. Come on, talk.

OK, don't talk, I took your five hundred dollars, I suppose I ought to co-operate. Although, how do you spend cash? It looks funny. I like it, maybe I'll glue it in a frame and put it on the wall.

This is really upfront, to be able to just sit here and talk, and know that International DataNews is going to broadcast me to the world. What will I do in my own living room, loop out?

This is the average American thing? What do I think about? Well, actually, I am thinking about getting a new couch for in here. There's this one with contour command

I really like at the GP Galleria-Joskemart. I want to have men friends, so I think I ought to fix up a little. I will do cosmets. I'll start some exercise. I'm only thirty-two, I could be really pretty. Already I'm on low-cal meals. I take in less than I put out, but I still gain. My neighbors, the Yeagers, say I'm too thin. I ought to be like Lady Dove, lying there all curvy in those Bustoons ads that pop up in dreams. Mr Yeager is a retired Dallas garbageman. He retired at the age of forty-two on fifty-six thousand dollars a year. Of course a guy like that gets work. So he's in this super-exclusive job over at the cruiserbase on refuse management. A registered job, plus his retirement. They're raising three kids.

Well, that's about it, I guess. Want to know what I ate for breakfast? Nothing. I don't eat breakfast. I just eat any time. If I'm hungry, I'm tearing something open. Sometimes we all go roaring down to Texas-Q or Burger Perfect and order this, well, nonhumanitarian meal. You can get real beef at Texas-Q. A barbecue beef sandwich for thirty-seven dollars. Real thing, cooked by hand over a real electric fire just like they used to do it in the old days. True. Texas-Q is unique. Texas culture is unique, you know. This is actually a special place. People used to wear hats. You think it's a problem carrying a wide-angle blinder? Well, here in Grand Prairie you can have a stunner in your home if you want. Or anything except a gun. But who wants a gun, you might miss your husband.

Was that funny? Sorry. I'm getting crazy with this thing turned on and you not saying anything.

Let me see. I will tell you about my past. I was born in San Antonio at the Northwest Baptist Maternity Center. San Antonio was a beautiful city in those days. Now it's so miged up, you can't go there. The state police do not recommend it, believe you me.

We had this huge house in Shavano Park. Shavano

411

Park is still there, but in those days it was out in the country. The Texas Hill Country after a rain, my it smelled delicious when I was growing up. The cedar and the mesquite and the dry grass – it was so beautiful. They used to hate cedar, the ranchers would try to cut it out. There was a state cedar program. Then all the cedar died and now what a mess. San Antonio had its water from an aquifer. It got full of nitrates around the turn of the century and they started washing the water. Then they started finding all kinds of other stuff in it. Plus, the aquifer would go down real fast. We had six years of drought and San Antonio had a water crisis that lasted three of those years. It was not the same after that. New building in Bexar County is still illegal. South Texas was nice, except for Houston, which was a grik and a half. Gosh, Texas has been getting smaller, hasn't it? Oh, well.

FROM THE DATE FILES OF TOM SINCLAIR: INTELLIGENCE ENHANCEMENT

'Everywhere on Earth, at this moment, in the new spiritual atmosphere created by the idea of evolution, there float, in a state of extreme mutual sensitivity, love of God and faith in the world: the two essential components of the ultra-human. These two components are everywhere "in the air" . . . Sooner or later there will be a chain reaction.'

– Teilhard de Chardin, *The Phenomenon of Man*, Harper & Row, 1965

'Aleksandr Przybylski believes that the capacity of amino acids to organize themselves into electronically active surfaces could one day be used to make self-assembling biochips for organic computers. "It's science fiction now," he said, "but after maybe fifty years, it will be a real technology."'

– *Omni*, 1984

'In one section of Einstein's brain, Ms Diamond said, she found more glial cells for every neuron than there are in the same section of the average brain.

'"Either Einstein had larger neurons, or his neurons had more 'processes' that needed more support," the professor said.'

– Associated Press, February 15, 1985

'Indeed, we can even ask ourselves, "What kind of human beings might we like to be? What kind of abilities that we lack would it be good to have, and how are we going to go about getting them?"

413

'And what kind of dangers would be involved? And what about morality?'

> – Isaac Asimov, from the introduction to Brian Stableford's *Future Man*, Crown, 1984

'A 4-year-old pygmy chimpanzee at a research center near Atlanta has demonstrated what scientists say are the most humanlike linguistic skills ever documented in another animal.

'The researchers say that the pygmy chimpanzee, Kanzi, has learned to communicate, using geometric symbols representing words, without the arduous training required by the famous "talking apes" of earlier studies, and that he is the first ape to show, in rigorous scientific tests, an extensive understanding of spoken English words.'

> – *The New York Times*, June 24, 1985

'A method of altering genetic material so exact that it will enable scientists to control such things as the color of skin and eyes has been developed at the Hughes Genetic Research and Engineering Center in Los Angeles. The method involves etching microscopic grooves in individual parts of the gene's structure. It is thought that the process will eventually make possible the revolutionary ability to adjust and alter the human body in almost any manner desired.'

> – *Science Watch*, July, 1989

'A child has been born with an artificially altered brain. A medical team led by Dr Augustus Melo at the Schwartzmann Institute in Berne, Switzerland, has announced that the child, whose embryonic gene map showed before surgery that he would be born hydro-cephalic, has instead been born with a better than normal brain. "He may even prove to be more intelligent than normal," stated Dr Joachim Gruber of the Institute.'

– The National Times, October 2, 1997

'The practice of intelligence enhancement of human embryos has been condemned in Congressional testimony by Dr Joachim Gruber of the Schwartzmann Institute of Berne, Switzerland. "This is tampering with the very soul of man. I have had agonizing first-hand experience of the suffering that intelligence enhancement can bring. Beyond the maximum level of normal human intelligence lies a great unknown, and we have no right to send innocent children into that strange realm. When we send them there, they must always go alone." Of the thirty-one cases of intelligence enhancement recorded in the United States since 2015, six have committed suicide, eight are institutionalized with unknown psychological disorders, and the rest have disappeared. The Intelligence Enhancement Control Act of 2016 will go before the full Congress before its July recess. Dr Augustus Melo, one of the pioneers of intelligence enhancement and its chief advocate in the United States, disagreed with Dr Gruber, calling the process "the hope of mankind." Dr Melo, a former associate of the Schwartzmann Institute, is now in private practice in Los Angeles.'

– NewsNet, June 6, 2018

'Dr Augustus Melo today agreed with federal authorities to close the world famous Center for Intelligence Enhancement in Los Angeles. "Results are disappointing, there is substantial hostile legislation and more on the way, and the process itself is too unreliable," Dr Melo said in a news conference at the Center this morning. The clinic was responsible for over seventy enhancements in the two years of its operation, charging hundreds of thousands of dollars per job, with no guarantee of success. It is not known how many of the altered fetuses went to term and were born. Federal officials are attempting to locate these children, in an effort to place them in the Special Support Facility at San Bernardino.'

– *The Los Angeles Times-Herald*, October 8, 2020

ALLIE: Motherhood

Bell insisted that we ride the rest of the way in the back with the chimpanzees. I nearly went mad. I could not stand the creatures. They were ugly and smelly, they disgusted me, and I found them frightening.

'Why do we have to go, Bell?'

'Somewhere in some computer, our presence in Holland Meadows has been recorded. Four people in greens, two men, two women.'

'Oh, so what? It's filed and forgotten.'

'We can't assume that. What if this cruiser's presence at the base and those four people are tied together? Think if the cruiser's stopped and searched. There's no place to hide in the pod. At least among the chimps we have a chance.'

'Shut up, just you shut up, Bell. I won't go down there, I can't bear it. It's – sadism. You just like to be in control. You like power and you like to punish.'

'I want us to be saved, I don't want us to be turned into zombies by that monster. It's my responsibility to do what I have to do.'

John put his arm around my waist. Ultimately all of us relied on his calm and steady strength. As he has aged, there has emerged in him something that was too deeply hidden before to be seen: a kindness that seems to wash over all who are around him, a love that is not going to be broken.

'Allie, she's right.'

I had to admit it. 'I'm sorry, Bell. I just hate it so down there.'

I went down through that hatch in the floor to what I thought would be two days of hell. But the chimps were used to us, and they no longer wanted to feel us and stick their fingers in our mouths. Their children came to me, and played in my lap across the long hours of the day. There was one little girl who would lie on her back and wave her legs and arms, and when I tickled her she would laugh, and I must say that I think laughter is some sort of triumph of life. She and I got along very well. She would fall asleep very suddenly in my arms, and lie there like a shabby little rag. What is peace, final and pure? The expression in that sleeping girl's face?

Her mother groomed me, and I found the patient touching of my scalp very pleasant. Once or twice the mother erupted in triumph. I was terribly embarrassed, the chimps didn't find anything in anybody else's hair. Was it a joke? I believe it may have been.

In any case, she was very careful and very good with her fingers. What was so astonishing was that she replaced my combs very neatly, and made me look well.

When the cruiser finally stopped and Johnson announced over the P.A. that we had reached our destination, I was in a new state. I had found out that these were people. They had feelings and language and were possessed of the fundamental decency that seems needful, if you are going to be a person. All human beings have it. Those who ignore it do so at immense personal cost.

I have always equated decency with civilization. If that equation works, the chimps were not only people, they were good people.

The lights came up. The cruiser was still and silent.

We waited for what seemed like a thousand years, the chimps huddled in the dim green light, all of us near the door. The chimps shouted rhythmically, 'out, out, out.'

418

They were organized in a tight line around us. I think I was shouting too, we were all shouting.

I was very eager to see what my son had created, what of him had lived on.

The door whined and rolled open. Sunshine, blasting, glaring, knocked me back against John. The chimps roared, then recovered themselves and began to stretch their long arms before them, squinting and leaning into the brightness.

Then there came laughter, the delighted pealing of a child's voice. They were here, the children of Magic.

Before us was an amazing group of animals, though, other chimps, some of them wearing hats, two large dogs skimming the edges of the crowd, watching with sharp eyes every move of the new arrivals, a family of raccoons, and an enormous gorilla working some kind of a box that talked in response to his hand movements.

There were children with him, clustering around him, six beautiful, healthy kids. So this was the creature Tom called Boola in his file. A gorilla, of all things. From the way the children responded to him, it was obvious that there was great trust and love for him. Now he turned his gentle eyes on the chimps.

'Come out, all in line, ' his box said. The huge creature was nodding and smiling. 'You're OK, all OK. Kids OK!' The gorilla's face was a shock to see, a familiar simian weight, the thick brow and dark eyes, the huge jaw. But the way his lips worked involuntarily as he talked, the delicacy of the movement, caused a series of intricate expressions to cross his face. There was an inescapable conclusion: this gorilla was conscious of what he was doing, and he loved his work.

Our chimps were huddled at the cruiser's open bay, clutching one another.

'Welcome,' the box said. The gorilla nodded vigorously

to the resident chimps. He smiled. It was not an ape's grimace, but a huge, face-filling smile. 'Go on, Joe, welcome them, they are your brothers and sisters. They have children too.'

The leader of the resident troupe spread his arms. 'Hi hi hi!'

At once all of the chimps, new and old, erupted into a great calling of hi, hi, hi, with much baring of teeth and waving of arms. Then the great lowland gorilla snapped his straw hat over his eyes with a flourish, reared to his full height and bellowed.

Every creature looked at him. He raised his box. 'Come,' it said in its tinny voice. Flanked by the dogs, with the raccoons trundling on ahead, the procession of chimpanzees moved off, led by the old gorilla.

Only the human children were left. They stood quietly, watching the exuberant procession of animals disappear over a low hill. I saw that this was a beautiful land we were in, with stands of pine and bright green grass. The sky was blue, touched by fast white clouds, and there was a scent in the air I thought might be the sea.

'I'm Emon.' The boy who spoke was about twelve. He was tall, with a thin, nervous face and light gray eyes. 'Welcome to Magic.' The seriousness of his tone was not at all childlike. 'You smell terrible,' he added.

Bell jumped down from the truck.

'All of you come. You need to clean up. After that, we have to start re-enculturation.'

Emon took my hand as we walked along. His grip was firm and warm.

'What's happening to the chimps?' Bell asked.

'They'll get themselves woven together. The new troupe doesn't speak Nomonic, but they'll soon learn from the others.'

'What's Nomonic?' Scott asked.

'Their language. It has all the structural potential of English, but it fits their vocal cords.'

'I've never heard of it.'

'We invented it. It's only spoken here in Magic.' He looked up at me. 'I like you,' he said. 'I thought I was going to. You remind me very much of your son. We loved him.'

Until this moment, I had not realized how nice it would be to have a child's voice speak to me. It has been a very long time since Tom was a boy. But I remember him, I do remember so perfectly well.

'I like you too, Emon.' We went up a rutted dirt road, quite steep, bordered on both sides by thick bushes that led into the high, old forests. The road was swept by steady wind from across a ridge ahead. There was no mistaking the sea in it.

'Where are we?' Bell asked.

Emon laughed. 'In a minute.' So far none of the other children had spoken. With us was a tall, strikingly beautiful girl of perhaps fourteen, two smaller children, one Chinese and the other black, and two boys, strapping and blond and very American, in the ten-to-twelve age range.

One of these boys was playing a tiny wooden instrument, beautifully made, which must have had a hundred extremely fine strings. His fingers raced, and an intricate hum emerged, melodies wrapping melodies. Superficially there was nothing memorable about this music – no tune you could hum – but my heart responded. From moment to moment I would feel deep resonances in myself, almost as one does when one unexpectedly encounters a familiar odor from long ago.

We continued to walk up the old road. I was hot and breathing hard when we reached the crest of the hill we had been ascending.

John's arm came around me. The children watched us. 'It's beautiful,' John said. 'God, how beautiful.'

Before us was an enormous view, a hidden harbor on the shining ocean. Trees grew almost all the way to the shore, stopping only for tumbled rocks and a thin strand. Behind this beach were a group of buildings, low domes and prefab sheds. A large garden stood in a clearing behind a sheltering shoulder of land, and chimps could be seen moving in this garden. Children and young people moved about among the buildings, which were white in the sunshine.

'This is the Pacific, isn't it?' Bell asked.

Emon guffawed.

Bell tossed her head, her hair shining in the sun. 'Can I know the joke?'

'What else could it be, the South China Sea? What about what's in the valley. Ask about that, why don't you?'

'All right, is that Magic?'

Emon laughed again. 'You have a thing about the self-evident. What if I say no?'

Bell was glaring at him. 'I just want confirmation. Can't you see I'm afraid for my people? I don't know what's going on.'

Figures were coming out of the prefabs, waving and beginning to run. Fast, high voices were brought by the wind. 'Come on,' Emon said, 'everybody's very excited about this.'

Behind us we could see the landcruiser climbing out of the farther valley.

Ahead the broad clearing was now dotted with running children, the white clouds were flying and the distant, immense Pacific shimmered.

'What about that gorilla?' Bell snapped. 'That strikes me as an interesting question.'

Emon went over to her and hugged her around the waist. He said nothing.

'You've got to tell me. You can't ask for questions and then ignore them.'

'The animals take care of themselves. They live among us, in that blue dome near the beach. The coons have put together a tree house, and the dogs sleep with us. So do some of the chimp kids. Boola has his own house out in the woods. You are only allowed there by invitation. We all miss something, our parents, our homes, the lives we couldn't live. But we are all content at Magic. The animal people are self-governing. We provide medical services and food, and in return they work the fields and do the heavy lugging. Is that enough of an answer?'

'I just want to be sure my chimps are safe.'

'Yours? They don't belong to anybody. They belong to themselves. Here they have rights, just like you and me.'

'I feel a responsibility for them.'

Poor Bell. She has really gotten the habit of responsibility. She needs followers as much as we need her.

The other children were close enough now to have separate faces. I saw kids of every race, but most of them were blond and very California. They were beautiful, coming along, and I could see their faces, some lovely, some strained and complex, one or two almost deformed. I counted over thirty children before I got lost.

John and Scott and I drew close to Bell. There was something fierce about the faces of the children, something that must have struck us all, for we were standing very close together. Over our time on the road, with all the hardship and the constant pressure from Singh, we had become a very intimate group.

'I'll handle this,' Bell said. Her voice was small.

Then they were around us, a swift mob, dancing, jumping, at least as energetic as our chimps had been.

423

They were a wildly dressed lot of kids, wearing everything from stretched t-shirts to shabbies to expensive embroidered coats, most of them frayed at the edges. Nobody had realthetics or costumes, and there was none of the harsh, almost bitter, banter that one associates with children.

My immediate impulse was to mother. I remembered Tom coming up the back steps, his shirt out, his pants full of dirt, his hands and face smeared. I remembered the laughing, the slamming of the screen and how I staggered back when he threw himself on me.

'We have to take you to see Thomas,' Emon shouted above the tumult. The name startled me. Obviously, though, it was not my dead son he meant. At the mention of the name, the children grew more quiet.

'They're older than *my* parents,' a girl said.

'From now on they are your parents,' Emon replied.

What was this? I could see Bell's frown. We really were beginning to want an explanation.

As we moved along our welcoming committee swirled around us. I saw blond heads, black heads, curly hair, straight hair, one head in braids, and faces flashing up, faces somehow more alive, complex faces, soft with the deceptive softness of childhood.

'What's going on here?' Bell asked. I could hear an edge of panic in her voice. She liked to understand the why and wherefore.

'I'm Randy,' a girl said. 'You can fall in love with me if you want.'

'Give us all a chance,' a boy snapped angrily. He smiled. 'You can fall in love with me. I would welcome some adult affection.'

'They'll prefer reverse capture,' a little black girl with tight, neat braids shrieked. 'I love you, my dear parents!'

424

'You're too easily bored, Snicks. You're just manufacturing complications.'

'I don't need to. Anyway, she's mine, aren't you, Bell?'

'I must be allowed to understand this!'

'I like her. She's fiery. Just the personality for me.'

'When we decided to bring them here, we agreed they'd be communal!' Snicks was screaming and stamping her feet. Her fists beat against the air before her. Then she took a deep breath and gave Bell a sidelong look. 'Anyway, I said I had dubs on Bell when she got them out of Troll Heaven. She's my kind of lady.'

'I –'

'Emon's right, they're all ours,' another girl flared. 'You can't go staking claims, it's not fair!'

'Well, Bell's mine primarily. We ought to center on each other, we look alike.'

'Surface features,' someone said scornfully. 'I ran everybody's profile in Delta Doctor, and Bell's actually closer to G-Shaw than anybody. And she certainly doesn't have deep pigmentation like you do, Snicks.'

At that a tall girl stopped walking. 'Wait a minute. Bobo Jones, you dared to run profiles? You're a sand brat, that's not clean!'

'Look at them, they're both standing there glaring!' Bobo Jones roared with laughter. It was true that Bell and the girl he had called G-Shaw had assumed identical postures. 'She's not yours, Snicks, she's G-Shaw's. What'll it be, Bell and Bell 2 or G-Shaw and Big G-Shaw?'

'Big G-Shaw sounds like Boola sneezing!'

'So does G-Shaw without the big.'

'Shut up, all of you.'

'She's still primarily mine,' said Snicks. Randy took my hand and gave me a secret glance. Three of the boys were with Scott, two boys and a girl with John.

'Pardon us for bickering over the expression of long-suppressed instinctual needs,' a child of six said. 'We hunger for parental love here at Magic.'

We had begun our ragtag procession again. I liked the wind in my face, the children all around me, the wonderful colors of land and sky. Before us, though, was something I liked less well. At the edge of the compound stood a boy in clean tuffies, his legs apart, his arms folded across his chest. He was no more than twelve, but he carried himself with the force and authority of a much older man. As we drew closer to him the other children fell silent.

For a moment I met his green eyes – hard, careful eyes. They appraised me quite calmly and frankly. His face was most remarkable, young and fresh and soft, a face still undecided about its gender, and yet not a child's face.

'How are they, Emon?'

'They're OK, Tom.'

Tom looked straight at us. 'Come in,' he said. 'I have a lot to talk to you about.'

'What is it?' Bell asked. 'Tell us before we enter any buildings.' Her voice rose. 'I've got to know what's going on.'

Tom turned around, moving toward one of the prefabs. 'Be patient, Bell'. His voice was melodious and very calm. 'We've brought you here for a lot of good reasons. But first you have to learn us, get to know our ways. There is a great storm coming, a terrible storm. Magic may very well be destroyed.'

Bell flared at that. Tom went on. 'The four of you are here to help us. To save us, if we can be saved. We are important, you know. We have to do with the future.'

RANDY: My Life in Magic

When I was seven Tom Sinclair found me and offered me a place in Magic. I was one of the first intelligence-enhanced children born in the United States, if not the first.

Tom Sinclair put this place together along with Tom Kinnon and, I guess, me.

He got Tom Kinnon out of juvenile detention and brought him up to this land. Did you know you officially own Magic, Allie and John? It's in the county records, but you won't find it anywhere else. The two Toms hid this place very, very carefully. After Tom Sinclair died so suddenly we almost fell apart, but Boola kept it all afloat with his farming and his love, and one way and another we kept getting kids. We all needed this place so bad it had to work.

Tom Kinnon came down to San Bernardino after they had gotten water running and electricity working and got me. I was Tom's best friend in school. I am still his best friend. We are not brother and sister, we are lovers. We will marry ourselves next summer. I am fourteen, he is twelve.

Years and years ago this was a farm called the Magic Land. All but one of its inhabitants was dead by the turn of the century. She was a woman named Morning Glory and she bequeathed this place to a group of homeless children who had come here in 2003, refugees from some Falon-related upheaval. Morning Glory died, and the Magic Land gradually just became Magic. The children grew up and went away. The land was let go empty, and officially it reverted to the county for nonpayment of taxes. When Tom Sinclair bought it he put it in your names and listed its purpose as 'pleasure.' That's a good word for it, actually. Magic has brought a lot of suffering animal people and children the pleasure of being with their own kind.

I was born in 2013 in the LA Grid. My father was a backoffice worker at International Clearance. He was obsoleted off a week before my birth. But, while he had money, he had decided that I would never suffer the kind of miseries he had endured – the old adage about work so dull robots refuse to do it. But when IBM came out with readers that could interpret the scrawls people used to put on paper checks and things, he was finished.

I was just a zygote then, so he and Mother had me enhanced. I don't know who did my operation, but whoever it was had good luck. I was born with just the kind of brain they were trying for – lots and lots of neurons and all the glial structures needed to make full use of them.

As I grew up I went through agonies. Being that precocious isn't a blessing, it's more like a deformity. I was more comfortable with defective kids than with the whole ones. By the time I was five, I was conscious in a way that really hasn't been encountered before us. I understood a great deal, but I lacked informational background.

I was extremely unhappy and bored. It was clear to me that I couldn't live in the environment in which I found myself. My father was driving a truck, my mother was working as a masseuse. They were saving for down payment on a landcruiser, and my own projections showed that when I reached age seven I would be taken out of the woefully inadequate school I was attending and given over to an even more inadequate educational program aboard the cruiser.

When I came here I was eight and very alone. Only Tom Kinnon lived here. Tom Sinclair was always on the move, coming and going like crazy. This was just that big plastic building over there, known as Pod One, and me and Tom. We used to sleep all curled up in there in the middle of that big, empty space.

At home my fantasy life had been growing larger as my life grew smaller. My parents were obsessed with their plans. The fact that they had created this superintelligent child was now lost on them. Their attitude was that I didn't need any help or support. Because I was so bright I 'had all the advantages.' If I wanted help it was just because I was lazy.

It was torture for me to sit in a stupefying gifted program, pretending to an II of twelve when I had measured myself at twenty-three. Of course, if the teachers had found out where I stood I would have been sent off to Federal School and my parents might have been arrested. I did not want the Federal Program, I wanted freedom.

There are six Federal School escapees here, but I now realize that the government program isn't invalid. It's a good try. But normals, even genius normals, have no idea of how to deal with us. We have to make our own decisions. Effectively, we must be considered as different from you as the bird is from his dinosaur ancestors.

Getting Magic started was a great happiness for me. Tom Sinclair supplied us with the basics we needed. Computers, money, seeds, clothing and bedding. All the books we wanted and whatever data we cared to access. We got G-Shaw right after that, and along with Tom she started increasing our computational and manipulatory

429

power. We started finding other kids by searching the data grid. Inevitably, they'd be on-line somewhere.

Bell, I see a tightening around your eyes. You feel threatened and you resent us. To hear conversation like this coming out of the mouth of a child frightens you. Please try to keep an open mind.

We have drawn the four of you here partly for altruistic reasons. We need one another, and your background – the fact that you are Tom Sinclair's parents and friends – makes us feel comfortable with you. There are no adults here. On an instinctual level, we need contact with grownups. There are difficult and subtle matters of discipline that would be most conveniently solved by recourse to an adult arbiter. Also, some of us are about to reach puberty, an event which will have unknown consequences. I am in that group, and, frankly, I'm afraid. I want somebody to turn to who has already had sexual experience.

Do not assume that we want role models. One of our most painful curses is that we cannot have them, although we do crave them and suffer insecurities without them. Nobody can be role models for us, sadly enough.

What we need from you is a lot simpler. We need adults to love us. We aren't very lovable, except to one another.

Two months ago we had a suicide and that was what convinced us that the group lacked sufficient emotional resonance on its own.

In the end, we offer you a proposition and a question. The proposition is this: we will protect you as best we can. We will all face the Depopulation crisis together.

In return for our protection and help the four of you will love us.

The question is: can you love us?

430

SNICK: You Are Magic

We all have those stories like Randy does, of how we found Magic. I am from Nairobi. Like so many of the others, I was enhanced by Augustus Melo at his Center in LA. My father was Kenyan ambassador to the US, and his dream was for his firstborn to grow up to become President of Kenya.

A few weeks after my conception they discovered that there had been a mistake. I would be a girl, not the boy they had planned for. My father thought, Good Lord, I'd better do something extra for her. So I was given this crippling blessing. Randy is a twenty-three. I am a thirty-one. I am ten years old and I found Magic by myself, largely because I inferred that it must exist. I searched the data files of the world, trying to find out about other children like me. So many of them disappeared that the inference is obvious.

Usually people can't find Magic, but I did find it. I will not say how, but it was very hard. I suppose my cognitive advantages helped.

I would like to talk about the philosophy behind Magic. Why is it here, a hideaway for misanthropes? Let's not think about intelligence – which threatens the part of the population it doesn't impede, in my opinion – but about consciousness. This is something totally different. You don't need a manipulative intelligence to be conscious on the physical plane. The dolphins and whales are the classic example. Some insects are thought to have morphic consciousness, the honeybees, for example.

It is this self-knowing that life strives to reach. We are

431

more intensely self-knowing than anything that has come before us. Life itself created us. And there is another creature, an even more conscious one, of which Magic is just a part. This is the creature which has been directing you, which has been moving you through the world toward a great confrontation. You must prepare for this confrontation over the next few days here at Magic.

The deepest, most intense consciousness of all has brought you here, and has brought you for this purpose. We must all surround John like a hive of bees surrounding a queen, in order to fill him with our energy and our strength. It is his day that is coming, his and Gupta Singh's. Remember, life seeks more and more and greater and greater consciousness. To do this, it makes combinations. One atom with another, one molecule with another, cell and cell, more and more cells in more and more careful combination. Sometime in the last few thousand years what we call final man was created, the highest and most perfect combination that nature could achieve. But the striving went on.

There is something in the universe that hungers desperately for awareness. Somebody said that the universe is God's attempt to create a companion. This loneliness is the greatest force of all, and it does not like death. It accepts death but it does not like it. It seeks, rather, growth, and only loves death that leads to growth.

Beyond final man, there is the consciousness of Magic. We are a part of a single mind, which includes us as the intuitive factor and the entire computational system of the planet as the cognitive part. In using Stratigen and Delta Doctor, you've had a small taste of the true capabilities that the computer mind net has achieved.

Our connection with it is just like a gigantic version of the relationship between Delta Doctor and John. Delta

Doctor created endless relationships between speech patterns, vocal tensions and the meanings of the words spoken. Out of this it inferred personality. John provided the intuitive questions and insights that made the personality come alive.

This is how Magic works. We intuit, the programs extrapolate and strategize. So Magic is not just us kids. It is also the electronic mind net. We are Magic, together. And now you will be part of it too, like Boola is, only with higher duties.

I have the disturbing feeling that responsibility for our welfare is out of my hands, and I hate it. Who is going to decide what happens to us? Tom Kinnon, Snick, Randy? I don't feel good being at the mercy of a bunch of children. They may not sound like kids, but they horse around, they play games, they act like kids. I love my family too much to give up responsibility for us to a bunch of ten- and twelve-year-olds.

But I can't help it, because I don't know what's going on!

Last night, which was our first night here, there was a celebration. They have all sorts of musical instruments, flutes, recorders, a harmonium, a set of ulelian pipes, drums, a number of harmonicas, guitars, a sackbut, a rebec, two or three different kinds of harp, and a remarkable perceptive music program that listens to what they are playing and adds all sorts of imaginative things from animal noises to a full chorus.

Not only that, they have the animal people, who sing with a passion that stands your hair on end.

The sun set and we had dinner. The food here is very nice. All kinds of things from the garden, which the chimps tend with incredible skill and the kids manage with great care, all watched over by that gorilla, which displays the patience of a saint with the kids and is capable of knocking the chimps to glory when they cut up.

There were carrots at dinner, beautiful lettuce salad, tomatoes, roasted green peppers and rice.

Among other things, Boola has a wonderful sense of taste, and can mix things, like salad dressings that you will not forget. He might use ten or fifteen spices and dozens of other flavors. And they don't get muddy. They are sharp, each distinct, unforgettably subtle and wonderful.

What they cannot grow here, the kids get by playing an economic simulation that somehow ties into the actual order-deposit networks of various companies, ranging from clothing manufacturers to grocery chains to electronics companies. About ten kilometers from here is an open field that the whole Integrated Economic Transfer System thinks is a warehouse. I saw a robotized truck come up, depallet, and deliver six cases of foodstuffs to a location in the field that the computer was convinced was the loading bay of the Big Mama Market in Monterey.

I've got to get back to this dinner, because it was the best food I'd had in a long, long time. I mean, we ate. There was even fresh sushi, glory be, caught by their own boat, the *Sunlight Warrior*, and tested before use for every known chemical contaminant, so we were confident it was safe.

To understand this place you've got to understand the concept of real play. Real play is what a ten-year-old does when he knows too much for play play, and has to survive.

It was strange to see a bunch of kids playing chef, complete with 'Le Kitchen' toques on their heads – and yet producing that meal, hulked over by a gorilla wearing a toque so tall that any òne of them would disappear under it. Boola likes hats.

I see the beginnings of roles for us. As long as we don't interfere with the management of the place, I think we might fit in. Allie is nuts about children. What a wonderful grandmother she makes. John responds to them, too. He has a rapt audience for his tales of America in the twentieth century. There are somewhat stunning questions: did the debt crisis of 1997 lead to Falonism, or was it an inevitable byproduct of the coming of the then-called millennium? This from that girl called G-Shaw, who Tom says is an Intelligence Index twenty-three like himself. She's seven, and she believes she is a natural, not an artificially induced intelligence.

This gets me to an interesting point. About half of the children here believe that they are natural and I'm inclined to believe them. It would be logical for their parents to try to hide their artifical origins from them, but I doubt if it would be possible. These are extremely subtle minds. You can't hide anything from them.

We are just beginning to understand such things as the morphogenetic field, which is what determines the funadmental shape of being. It is what makes a chimp stay a chimp even when we alter the one percent of its genetic material that differs from our own, and make a chimp zygote into a perfect model of a human zygote.

The baby that's born is still very much a chimpanzee, because we haven't affected the morphology, what Snickers called the deep nature.

A brief note: when I attribute such ideas to somebody named 'Snickers' it makes my paper look less than serious. It is serious. You have to get used to ideas like this coming out of a kid. I admit it's hard.

The appearance of children like these may have to do with some kind of morphogenetic change in the human species. Mankind is on the brink, and to save itself, the species is falling back on the one thing that has always served it best: intelligence.

I do not think that they are meant to supplant us. They consider themselves a new level of man, not a replacement. They are a protective mechanism, the

436

species trying to create guides bright enough to extract us from the mess we are in. Fifty years ago, before we had these terrible problems, we could have repaired the environment without the need for such brilliant minds. Now, however, they are going to be a great help.

I have to say that being with them is a joyous thing. They truly crave our love. All of them had hard experiences at home. Here, where they are in complete control, they can use us adults comfortably.

They are so full of passions, of music, of poetry and thought. We have put a number of their poems in this book, one at the beginning, and at the front of the first three sections. The last section – their section – is opened by the verse of a twentieth century poet who had much in common with them.

At first Magic seemed chaotic to me. But now I've come to realize that it's highly organized. Tom runs the political and planning unit, interfacing with the computer net. Randy designs management and resource models, using the most sensitive version of Stratigen yet. G-Shaw is food production, Emon and Snickers appear to be involved in some sort of philosophy group, which the others dip into like bees sipping nourishment.

There are complicated, noisy arguments all the time. I witnessed a battle between Snickers and Tom which lasted all day, and was carried out entirely in music. Was the music good? The music was very strange, and seemed to have more notes than any music could possibly need. At the end of it Tom sulked, so he must have lost. The argument was over why the whole human race overlooked the fact that the first man on the moon's first statement was logically inconsistent, and whether or not unconscious rejection of the statement hurt the space program.

Most of the day they spend in their workrooms, Tom tinkering with something that may or may not be a computer, but which gives him extraordinary access to the world. And he does have an effect on the world, too. Yesterday I heard a familiar voice coming out of the room. It was the President, talking from his TAV to Reginald Coopersmith at State about the swing voters who are going to be so critical next January, after he vetoes the Depop Bill.

When Tom suddenly joined the conversation, the two men listened with interest. They were polite, if guarded. They had obviously heard from him before.

I can readily imagine that the US Government is searching for Magic as hard as Singh, if not harder. Here is this kid breaking in on a highly secure conversation, and they just have to swallow it. No telling how many other heads of state have the same experience. It could easily be that every intelligence service in the world, every police organization, is looking for this place.

It is the one place on the planet they can't find. I suppose that's why the children call it Magic.

ALLIE: Terror and Music

In the dead of our third night at Magic I was awakened by screaming. We slept in four of the five structures, one of us to each fifteen children. The fifth structure was a sort of mixed work, dining and play area. I jumped up. All day I had been uneasy. John had had a long conference with Tom and Randy, and wouldn't tell me what it was about. He never kept things from me, and I was afraid.

I was suffering from cultural dislocation. The anarchy of this place seemed total. Its sublime sense had not yet emerged for me. I had seen that the kids were healthy. They kept themselves well-fed, and there was an inner organization I still do not fully understand. The gorilla, Boola, was an important part of it, a creature they all looked to for kindness and support. It would cradle them, it would comfort them.

Once it brought the chimps at night, and there was what I can only describe as a wild revel, drums thundering, animals and children dancing in a kind of frenzy of joy, as if the two intelligent species together made a magic that was beyond mere love, something new in the world.

They did not need us for guidance; they are beyond that.

I trust them, and yet when I see the emotional vulnerability behind their wisdom I know that I am needed. I love them more every day I am here, all of them, the children, the chimps, Boola.

The scream that drew me awake wasn't even very loud.

But I was on my feet before I opened my eyes. My deeper levels were completely aware of the job the children had given me. I had work to do.

I saw, in the dimness, a pile of covers flopping. I went to it and uncovered Randy, sweating, her eyes wide, the eyeballs jittering from side to side as if she was having a seizure. 'Be careful,' somebody said in the dark.

'Randy. Randy!' I gathered her into my arms. Like this she seemed a frail little thing, her skin cool plastic. Her hands were snaking and moving sinuously over her naked body. They came up and caressed my face. I held her to me and kissed her. She went as rigid as a board, lying straight out, and shrieks began to burst from between her clenched teeth.

'What's the matter? Has this ever happened to her before?'

Shadows were moving in the room. Then Boola came blundering in among us. In a moment he was beside me, an enormous hulk, and young Tom with him.

'Boola,' she moaned, and the huge creature gathered her into its hands, it lips thrust out, its voice soft cooing thunder.

I fought through my own store of knowledge, trying to discover a source for her symptoms. Various toxicities came to mind. 'Is she mercury-poisoned?' I asked the children, who were crowding around. For a moment nobody spoke. Boola had almost absorbed her in the furry cradle of his arms and chest. She was still heaving, her breath coming in sharp shrieks.

'Toxics aren't the problem,' Tom said. 'She's having a bad dream. A lot of us get like that.'

'How can I help her? Oh, Randy.' I moved close to Boola, who clicked his tongue at me and folded back his lips. He let me caress her sweating face. 'Randy, it's just a dream.'

440

'Boola . . .'

'A dream isn't a just,' Tom said. 'A dream is a big thing.'

The symptoms weren't consistent with any nightmare response I knew of, not even with night terror of childhood, which can be as violent but not as extended. Her face was turning blue, her chest was distended, she appeared to be having trouble breathing. I wanted John but he sleeps like the dead, nowadays. 'Help me. We've got to wake her up.'

'No,' Tom said. 'Sing to her. Don't be violent.'

I am not much of a singer. I could remember hardly any words. I tried my best.

> 'The river is wide, I can't cross o'er
> Nor have I the wings to fly.
> Build me a boat, and both shall go,
> My love and I.'

The song had no effect, nor did Boola's cooing. This child was in serious trouble. She was not breathing. Her eyes were now fixed, her body suddenly hot and dry. 'Tom, she's going.'

'We'll sing, Tom.' It was G-Shaw.

My voice trembled. 'Will it help?'

All around us the children began to sing, a soft wordless song. It started as a whisper, then rose to full purity, so fresh and sweet that it hurt. They harmonized their voices, making a sound that reminded me of soft wind, then of leaves blowing. When melody emerged it evoked memories in me that I didn't even know I possessed. Boola bowed his head, his eyes shut tight, as if wishing Randy back to life.

I was sitting in my father's lap, my head on his chest, lazily watching a sprinkler send sparkles into the sun.

I was in my bed, watching the moon ride past the top of my window. When I sat up, I saw the whole neighborhood, dark lines of houses in the night, and I tried to think of a poem.

I was here, transported on clouds of song so lovely that there are no words that fit. If there is somewhere after death, and there is song there, it is this song. The tones were long and sweet, while underlying them was clapping so fast and intricate it was one moment like bubbling water, then like a breeze in summer leaves, then like the pregnant silence of a hot afternoon.

I remembered walking down to Dascola's and getting my hair cut. The place smelled of Toni Setting Lotion and Drene Shampoo.

I remembered my bike, a blue Flyer with big, thick tires and no gears.

I remembered when I was ten, my Keds, my short-shorts, my friends.

The song did not exactly end, but rose higher and higher, until it escaped into registers beyond hearing. Lying in Boola's lap was the consequence of the miracle, a soft, relaxed little girl.

Randy pulled Boola's face down and kissed him long on the lips. I remained there in silence. I felt awe for this strange affection. The ape let her lie back in his arms. He looked at me. There was something so profound in his face that I almost could not look at it without feeling an obscure sort of shame, as if I had not been sensitive enough before, as if I had missed some fine note of life that is essential to being truly human.

He handed me Randy, putting her in my lap. Then without sentiment, without looking back, he returned to the dark.

A sleepy voice: 'Are you going to be my mother?'

'Do you want me to be?'

Her eyes flashed. 'Obviously. Why else would I have asked?'

'Well, of course I am, then.'

'Forever. No divorces.'

'No divorces.'

Tom took her chin and turned her face to him. 'We want you to recount the dream.'

'Oh, Tommy, do I have to?'

I was shocked. These children were usually so sensitive with one another, I couldn't believe his callousness. 'Leave it till morning,' I said.

'We can't. These dreams don't enter the medium-term memory. By morning she might have forgotten important details.'

Randy snuggled up to me. 'I'll tell you,' she whispered.

She seemed a bundle of sticks against my thigh. I put my hand on her head, stroked her vaporous hair. 'I'll listen.'

'Not here. Let's go outside where we can be alone.' A shudder passed through her body. Something about this place frightened me. Because it was so strange, it sometimes seemed as dangerous as an evil old mine.

I got up and followed Randy out. The night assaulted me with its beauty. Above us the stars were clear, so bright they seemed like glaring animal eyes. Randy went along a path toward the ridge that separated the camp from the sea. She moved as quickly as a rabbit. Twice I had to call to her to slow down.

Finally we mounted the ridge. Before us the ocean was a great dark. The stars disappeared toward the horizon, to be replaced by the lights of shipping, which winked along the edge of the world. The air was tart, not quite alive, but fresher by far than it is inland.

They say that Japanese trash washes up on shores of Alaska, but so far this Northern California wilderness has been unaffected by the deterioration of the seas. Randy pointed at a particularly fat star. 'L-5.' At a dimmer one, low on the horizon. 'Mars. There are people there.'

'Russians.'

'That doesn't matter to us.' She turned around and pointed to the eastern dark. Another star hung there. 'Lenin.'

'Do you know all the satellites?'

'Depends. Like the one moving over us, that's a Soviet Beamer, UN Designation C-10232. If it was turned on right now we'd be vaporized along with half of the rest of California.' I watched it sail through the Belt of Orion. She must have felt my tension, because her hand came around my shoulder. 'Our friends in Russia are getting control of their weapons. We're working on the same thing here.'

What she had just said, so casually, set my mind to racing. I had to question her further. 'What do yo mean, getting control?'

'I have to tell you my dream or Tom'll get mad.'

'But I want to hear more about this. If somebody's defeated those satellites, it could make an immense difference to mankind.'

'You think so? The Soviet-American rivalry is too ritualized to be relevant anymore.'

'Unless it destroys the world.'

Her voice became brisk. 'It's colder than I thought out here, so this is my dream. It starts, I'm walking through the woods. The trees are tall and black and terrible. I am afraid. Very afraid. I feel helpless, like a great storm is coming and there is nothing I can do.

'Then, all of a sudden I am at Magic. John – your John – is with me. There is a car with bright lights, and I want to help John, to somehow protect him but I can't protect him, and the lights get brighter and brighter and brighter.

444

'And then it changes. I am asleep. Then I notice it's day, so I get up and go outside. I am a different person. I'm sad all the time. Everything is gray. You are there, but you are sullen and you cry in your sleep. I go down the path to the farm garden like I usually do every morning, but as I go I notice someone standing at the top of the road. It is a man of about twenty. He is looking down at the camp, and there is a terrible, evil, dark look on his face. Then he smiles and comes strolling over the ridge. Behind him are thirty or forty other people, most of them his age or younger, but some of them are older.'

She stopped, took a shuddering breath. I put my arm around her. 'If it's too cold here, we can go in the main building. We'll still be alone.'

'No.' She pointed. 'Right over there. That's where the car comes that gets John. That is the beginning of the end. You understand, you're to tell Tom that this is a very high probability dream.'

'I'll tell him that.'

'So here's the end of the dream. The people come up to the compound and they start calling us. Yelling our names. We come in from the farm, from the chimp camp, everywhere we are working. We have no computers, so the computer center is dark and empty. These people act happy, but their eyes are poison.'

Her voice got lower, seemed to hug itself. I strained to listen. 'We know who they are, and why they are here. They are here for a celebration. They want to take poison with us. Tom arrives. He has no weapons. They read a court order. Over the ridge, they explain, there is a unit of the Federal Police, waiting to come in and enforce the order if we refuse.'

Her fists went to her eyes. She leaned against me. I took her in my arms, which to someone who was once a parent is both a lovely and very hard thing to do. Her body was almost as cold as stone. For a moment I didn't know what to think, then I sensed something I did not know before coming to Magic, and that is the suffering that people of great intelligence must endure. She saw too deeply into the world, this poor little girl. I caressed her stone back, and felt sweat coming through her shirt, sweat that was dark in the moonlight. She made a sound like paper being torn. Her whole body convulsed, stretched, her muscles knotted. Her fists were like two rocks pushing into her skull. There was black sweat on her arms, her face.

When I kissed her I tasted the sweat. It wasn't water; she was experiencing hematidrosis, the sweating of blood.

'You cannot understand this, Allie, but we are one person, all of us over the world, the children, the computer net. Some will feel threatened by us, most will hate us, but without us to act as guide, mankind will die. We are the next evolution of mind. Without us there is no future.'

She fell silent. I wished I had some magic that would comfort her. I held her, closing around her like a mother bird, trying to protect her from the night. Boola came up, his form huge against the sky, and placed himself between us and the wind.

I wanted to reassure the child. 'We're far from Depopulation. The President is against it. So far there hasn't even been a bill.'

'The Depopulation Bill is being considered right now.'

'That isn't true. At least, it wasn't as of the last time I checked, which was three weeks ago. It hadn't even reached committee.'

'We have access, remember. There was a secret session of the House last Wednesday. The bill passed. Now it's in Senate Committee. It'll go before the full Senate in January, as soon as the new senators get sworn in. There

446

is legislation being passed throughout the world. The great movement is coming to climax. My dream is real.'

There came from the blackness a sound, rhythmic clapping, rougher than that of the children. The sound grew louder and closer. I saw on the path ahead a line of dark, humped silhouettes appear, grunting, moving in a strange, swaying time. Boola stood full up and moved off, following the chimpanzees.

'They're going down to the beach to watch the moon.'

It lay, a sickle against the sea. Bloody glimmers danced the water. I saw the chimps spread along the beach in a neat row. The clapping changed, became quicker and more intense. There arose a gabble of voices that went into a high, droning whine. The whine was picked up by the others. They sounded like an organ making a single sustained note as the moon dropped. The lower the moon went, the higher the note rose, the fainter it became. It almost seemed to rise into the sky, a voice in the dark vault.

'We taught them this ritual,' Randy said. 'It'll be the beginning of their culture.' Her voice broke. 'Will they ever know who gave them their chance at consciousness? Earth is trying to form a mind. If it turns out not to be us, it'll be them.' She cuddled into my arms. 'Carry me back. I'm so sleepy.'

I put her to bed and then told Tom her dream. He questioned me about it in detail, about John and the lights, about the people coming across the ridge.

'It's the death of Magic,' he said at last.

'But – '

'The death of Magic!' His voice was a hard knot of a whisper.

His anger was so dense, I almost hesitated to ask him the question that was burning in my mind. 'What about John and the lights?'

447

'I'm not sure. It seems impossible that Singh could find Magic. Obviously not, though.'

'It was just a dream.'

'You don't understand at all. Her mind sorts out probabilities and she dreams what's most likely. It's and old form of prophecy. It's just that nobody ever understood it or controlled it before us.'

'I –'

'Let me be quiet, Allie. I have to stop talking now.'

Deep into the night I could hear his shallow breathing, and if I sat up and looked into the shadows where he kept his bed, I could see his open, staring eyes.

Tom Talks to John

I had an awful time holding this place together after your son died, John. He found me, he found Randy, Emon, about five others. I met him in data. He tempted me to talk to him on-line by hitting me with a really fascinating time-sensitive holographic cipher. He was a pretty bright man, I think. We were just getting going when all of a sudden he stopped coming. We surmised Denver. He had powerful negative tendencies that he wasn't entirely in control of. It's a tragedy. If he'd had time to let me be his psychotherapist, I might have enabled him to gain control of himself.

He saved us because he had the sense to give us Boola. You can't keep a stolen gorilla hidden for long, so it was a matter of mutual necessity that he come here. Tom hated the idea of intelligence-enhanced animals being enslaved. That's why we started the chimp colony, in his memory.

So, you even look like him, and you have similar speech patterns that cause me great feeling. He was my brother, your son, and the closest thing to a father I ever had.

Well, there's no use dwelling in the past, is there, John? He's dead. We have to go on, and I'm afraid we're under a considerable amount of pressure.

We have a pretty good version of Stratigen. The best there is, as a matter of fact. Your copy is the equivalent of a minor node of ours. To an extent we controlled you, drew you to us, through the medium of Stratigen. Our intuition was that you would be needed here. We left it to the rational part of our mind, which is the computer net itself, to sort out the details of getting you here. When it told us that the probability of your arrival at such and such an hour was 98.6% we got your beds ready.

We have been working very hard to get a handle on the Singh situation, and have concluded that the Depopulation program will be carried out next summer. The United States will sign the Manifesto this spring, and when it does all that will remain will be the setting of a date and the logistics.

Stratigen has gamed this thoroughly. If Depopulation comes about it will be because mankind wants to become extinct. Nature herself is going to continue the reduction of the human species that has been under way since 2018, the first year of a worldwide population decline. This process will be so intensified by the Depopulation that the species itself will not continue.

Whether or not mankind kills a third of its population, nature is going to render this planet almost unlivable by 2045. Without the Depop the human population will be one-sixteenth what it is now by the year 2100. With the Depop the number of people will be nil.

The primary mechanism of destruction will be atmospheric deterioration. It will still be possible to breathe the air, but by that time temperature rise will cause polar melting, and a redistribution of planetary mass as the water now trapped as polar ice flows toward the equator. This will tilt the earth straight on its axis and end the seasons. Planetary conditions will return to what they were during the era of the dinosaurs, only the mean temperature will pass the critical threshold and become self-sustaining. It will soon go so high that all life will be destroyed.

We have developed a set of strategies that will slow down or even reverse the deterioration.

There is the Solar Shield concept. This is a cloud of gas combined with massive reflective shields that would reduce the amount of sunlight reaching earth. This will be the biggest engineering project in human history, will take ten years, and will cost upwards of two thousand trillion dollars. It will require a massive – in fact, planetary – effort at financial, economic and scientific co-operation. But it will delay the inevitable. We can clean up the atmosphere by 2050, given that we are not contending at the same time with overheating.

To rebuild the air we have designed electrostatic attractors for sulfur and other particulate contaminants, self-limiting bacterial aerosols that will eat nitrogen and carbon dioxide, and seaborne algae which will produce oxygen and consume carbon monoxide and carbon dioxide.

Based on a device developed in the late twentieth century, the Lepcon solar cell, we have created a film which converts light into electrical energy at eighty per-cent efficiency. It can be spread on roofs and across the ground, and is efficient enough to provide ample electricity from the sun even given the sunlight reductions we plan. This concept, by the way, was developed by an inventor named Alvin Marks over forty years ago, and hidden by the US Government in 1985 so that it could be used as a secret energy source for a military space system called Star Wars. When Star Wars died the Lepcon solar cell was forgotten, lost in the classification system. Had it been taken advantage of, the world would have been thirty percent solar by 1994. The average American home would have had an entirely solar electrical system by 1997, and the building of polluting nuclear and conventional power plants the world over would have ceased.

We can bring those things about now. It isn't too late. Only Singh stands in the way. Billions of people tell themselves that they believe that his Depopulation program is what is needed to ensure life on earth. But it's a lie; it isn't needed to ensure life, but to induce death.

In their hearts people sense that his program is death, and that the issue is extinction. It may be that the species is in the process of deciding whether or not to join the dinosaurs and the whales.

Singh represents mankind's ancient hunger for the putting out of the light. Somewhere in each of us there is an urge to sleep, to die, to float away on memory.

As he sees it, your coming here means that his greatest enemies have joined together. He has been seeking us for years. We are life, we are the future. He sees us as the most serious threat against him, us and you. If we could defeat him – force him to face his own conviction, trap him in the lie that is his life – then he might lose his psychic force. He would be like Falon after his own conviction, a wasted shell, a bad man so afflicted by knowledge of himself that he could not bear to live.

Singh is coming, John, for us and for you. We will protect you as long as we can. In the end, when he finds this place, we must fight him as best we are able, together.

JOHN: Confrontation

Singh has pushed me past the edge of my life. While I still have the strength, I must record the battle that finally destroyed me.

Magic had been monitoring Singh's movements for weeks. Every time he did anything that was recorded by any node, it was recorded in Magic. His car clocked in forty gallons of prolene in Denver. Then he accessed the datanet, seeking the Boones' route plan. Next he flew to Seattle. Soon the Boones' landcruiser was found by the Washington State Police, mysteriously abandoned outside a cruiser base on Route 24.

Magic concluded that Forest and Johnson Boone had been caught. Tom gave me the news with great tact. He asked me to come walking with him on the beach. We went down to the water's edge. The surf was booming, and there was a thin odor of life in the sea air. I walked along the weed littered beach remembering how rich the ocean once had smelled.

'John, he's going to find Magic.' His voice was so soft that I could barely hear him above the breaking waves.

'But weren't the Boones hypnotized? How can they tell him anything?'

'Drugs can find what hypnosis hides – if you're willing to be brutal to your victims.'

'And Singh is, of course.'

'We assume so.'

While we strolled together the Boones struggled to keep a secret that could not be kept. I knew I would soon face a similar confrontation. I was too weak, too old. I had outlived my strength. There seemed little chance that I would win. I knew what he might do to me – burn out my mind and remake me. Chemical brainwashing is an old technology, perfected a long time ago. There comes first the washing of the memory, Aminase, then scopolamine and benyl-hydrazine, then the suggestions, the dreams, the new loyalties embedded in the shell of the old man.

Then he could put me on the net: the convictor of Falon is so moved by the value of the Depopulation and the honesty of its leader that he abandons his conviction of Gupta Singh and joins the movement instead.

The world's most honest man now believes in Singh.

I had to prevent this from happening.

Tom looked at me out of the side of his eye. 'How do you feel – frightened?'

'I ought to be, I suppose. Maybe on some level I do. But mostly I'm mad.' When I said it I felt it, rage flashing in me. I can honestly say that I have never wanted to kill another person as much as I wanted to kill Singh.

'We're all mad.'

'Why don't you stop him! You seem so powerful, the way you're tied into the computer system and all.'

'The system is very, very complex. We're tied into part of it. There are other parts that don't connect with us at all. And Singh has skilled manipulators on his side. Our power isn't unlimited. Otherwise we would have defeated him a long time ago. When he comes here we'll have to face him. You, especially. He wants to brainwash you. If you're strong enough, who knows, you might be surprised at what you can accomplish against him.'

I looked down at the boy beside me, whose deep calmness had never left him. He turned and began marching up the dunes toward the woods behind them.

Ahead of us on the path I heard voices, the words of a child punctuated by the metallic voice of Boola's box.

'Give a word,' said the box. I saw Boola sitting in a small clearing with Randy and two of the smaller children. They had a stack of flashcards. Randy held one up.

The box spelled it. 'F-l-y.'

'Try to read it.'

'F-f-f-' The box stopped. Boola lowered his head. A terrible sound came from him, high and thin and soft.

'Maybe he does lack the funadamental conceptual tools,' one of the children said. 'Just like his manual says.'

'No he doesn't,' Randy answered. 'Boola, listen to me. You can read. You can learn! I've tested you and I know. Now we're going back to the first cards. What is this?'

'I.'

'You see, you read it. No, don't look at me like that, I'm telling you the truth. Reading is not magic, it's practice, and you can do it. Now read this.'

'A – '

'No, don't spell it out, read it.'

'A-a-'

'Boola!'

'Aaammmmm. Ammm. Am. Am!'

'Now read both cards.'

'I am.'

'That's right, Boola. You are. And you are learning to read.'

The ape reared back, his eyes wide. He grabbed the cards, which seemed tiny in his hands, and shuffled through them, his lips working. He grabbed his box. 'Aa-pp-ee. Aappee? Ape. Ape! *Ape*! Th-e? The . . . eee? Th-e. The!' He threw the cards up in the air and slapped his thigh. Then his eyes met mine. He got up, beating his chest, and rushed me. It was startling, but he stopped just as he reached me. He picked me up under the arms. He was making mouth noises in which I could barely discern the words. 'Am. The. I. Am. Ape.' Dragging me along, whooping and slapping at his chest with his free hand, he got his box. 'I am the ape.' He slapped his chest and indicated the cards with a gesture.

'You can read,' Randy said. 'But please put John down.' I was thankful for that. Absently, he dropped me. He stomped, he hit himself in the head, he grimaced. Then the dinner gong started ringing and he was off through the woods, going to his duties at the chimp camp, which needed a lot of management at mealtimes.

I was left in the suddenly silent woods with Randy and Tom and the three younger children. They were gathering up the cards when Emon came along the path. He hugged me around the waist. 'John, Singh's in his plane. His course is Seattle–Monterey. He'll be here within the hour.'

'Well, you did your best. Don't feel bad that you couldn't prevent the inevitable.' I sounded brave enough. I wondered if I would sound the same when I was face to face with Singh.

'We didn't prevent anything.' Randy's voice was low, her body stiff. 'We've always known he would come here. He has to fulfill the dreams.'

It still disturbed me that these children, at the far border of intelligence, let themselves be guided by their dreams. 'I don't see how I can fight drugs. God, I hate that man!'

Randy's voice was harsh. 'Don't hate him, please. We consider him our father.'

I exploded at that one. 'There'd better not be any Depopulationists in Magic!'

Tom looked up at me. 'John, you know already that his real name isn't Gupta Singh. I'll tell you the truth about him. He is the man who created me. He created Randy and Snick and Emon, too. One way or another, we all owe ourselves to his work, except those of us who are naturals.'

There was a long silence. Tom's hands were shaking, and he clutched his chest to stop them. 'His real name is Augustus Melo. He started out committed to the evolution of man.' His voice churned, electric with feeling. 'When he saw what he had created – us – he became convinced that the species should become extinct.'

I was for a moment too shocked to speak. But I had to find voice. I put my arms around the boy. His chest was thin, he seemed more frail to touch than a child of glass. My arms remembered my son at fourteen, but my mind was fixed on Gupta Singh – or rather, Augustus Melo – and the whole dark cycle that had drawn him from love of man to his present twisted state. 'Why, when Magic is so beautiful?'

Tom answered. 'His vision was a general increase in human intelligence, not the creation of an isolated elite like us. Because we can't function in open society, he considers us a failure. But the real issue is control. Because he can't control us, he can't stand us.'

Randy spoke. 'He hates us because we defied him. We left our homes and came here. We refused to enter ordinary life for the very good reason that it isn't where we belong. Our intelligence is threatening to people. Our ideas and aspirations are hard for them to understand. Worst of all, their society resists us and slows us down. It's nobody's fault. But Melo considered us defiant, headstrong failures. He can't bear to be defied.'

'Maybe if I don't fight, if I agree to give myself up, he'll leave Magic alone.'

Randy took my hand. 'We've gamed what happens if you become his supporter. The probability of his failure drops to zero. You will legitimize him so completely that even the President will go over to him. Pockets of resistance in the rest of the world will collapse. Even the English will collapse.'

'And he knows that his plan will lead to extinction? He's doing it for that reason, and not to save mankind, as he claims?'

Emon laughed a little. 'It's much deeper, much more complex. A man like him is always a mystery. He's a friend of death. There is a saying in the Mayan Record of Time, which our History Group translated last year – "the water of life carries sharp stones." He is one of the sharp stones.'

'Think of a man as a series of surfaces,' Tom added. 'Psychometrists talk about symbolic layers in the personality – the infamous Thanatos Layer, the Logos Layer and so forth. That's not a bad concept, but it isn't complete yet. You have to think of the consciousness as a sort of light that shines first on one surface and then another, moved by the events in a person's life. On his outer surface, Dr Melo is saving humanity. Just beneath that level, he is atoning for having created us. Deeper, he is rejecting all the chaos and mystery of life, and that very definitely includes Magic. Farther down, he is in love, but his love is not like yours and mine, for warm bodies and the touching of souls, it is for silence. He longs for silence, and so he longs for death.'

I remembered Delta Doctor's talk of Singh's Thanatos personality. I must say, at that moment, I was proud of my own analysis, and of the program. We had not drawn the whole picture, but we hadn't been far off.

'Come with us, back to Magic,' Randy said. We went through the dark woods, the tall, looming trees. 'This is where my dream started. From now on, we are living in it.'

We emerged into the night of Magic. The domes glowed, kids moved about in the soft of evening, some arm in arm, others alone. I heard snatches of conversation, and not one conversation did I understand. 'It's the diometry that has the fault. That's why we can't encapsulate data.' 'I don't want a heuristic approach. What's the point?' 'It's the isn't that counts. We could have an instantaneous effect, universe-wide.' 'Hi, hi!' 'Hi, chimps. The modeling's the problem. Tell it that.' 'You tell it. It gets mean as hell when you complain about its modeling. Meaner than Boola trying to make us eat a stinky soup.'

'I don't want to be responsible for hurting Magic,' I said to Tom. I stopped him, knelt down to his level. 'Son, listen to me, you can still find a way out. You can do something, I know you can.'

'John, take this. This is your weapon, use it.'

It was a Unon Interactor – my Unon Interactor, taken right out of the duffle I'd been carrying since Summerland. 'Oh, for God's – you have better computers than this old thing. An anyway, what can I do with it – wrap the screen around his neck and choke him?'

'We were able to circumvent the stops he put in Delta Doctor. Your conviction is finished. We took it beyond level eight. It's the first level ten conviction.'

'There can't be a level ten.'

'There can now. We've improved Delta Doctor.'

I opened the screen, hardly believing what I was hearing. 'Delta Doctor,' I whispered. The program let me in.

Convictor to Program: 'Status.'

Prgram to Convictor: 'Gupta Singh conviction complete, level ten. Status, ready for publication.'

I did not dance, I did not cry out. In a phenomenal feat of their genius, they had given David back his sling.

– What is your real name?

– I was Augustus Melo, I was Gupta Singh. But my name does not matter. I am many names, many voices.

– What voices?

– I am the devoured world, the great victim of human greed. I am also the suffering, defective human species. I am pain.

I could hear a more subtle version of the man in those words, richer than I myself could have created. Magic had indeed improved on Delta Doctor.

I thought, I can die here tonight, because they have given me my life. If he kills me, I will not mind.

Only he must not shoot me full of lies and make me deny this brilliant conviction.

'Are you ready, John?'

I nodded. Weak, old, maybe both of those things. But I was not scared. With my weapon in my hands, I had a chance.

Bell had come up to us. 'You kids are worse than the most superstition-ridden primitives on this planet! Now, you hide John, you find a place for him.' Nobody reacted. 'Do it!'

Tom smiled very softly. 'I don't know how to tell you this, Bell. I don't want to upset you – '

'So what is it? Come on!'

'We've gamed out the effect of hiding John. All it does is lead to the physical destruction of Magic, including the computers that keep us linked to the electronic part of our mind. If this place is physically destroyed, it's like a lobotomy. All you have left is a bunch of overwrought poets. The hard reasoning edge is gone, and believe me, that renders the poets totally helpless.'

The lights of a car glowed off in the hills. 'It's him,' Emon said. 'He's on the access road. He'll come up to the shipping drop and then stop to reconnoiter. The

Boones can't have told him anything about the layout beyond that point.'

Bell groaned. 'Get ready for him,' Tom said. Emon and Randy hurried off. Soon all of the children were clustering around them.

The lights flashed, and then were dark for a short time. The children began moving into the woods. Then the lights came on again as the car left the shipping point and started up the track to Magic. Suddenly they flared and with a snarling roar the car burst across the ridge.

'Come on, John,' Bell screamed, tugging at the sleeve of my jacket.

'No, Bell.' This was my place, my time.

The car stopped. Not a single soul approached it, not even the chimps, who were always full of curiosity. I saw Boola herding them into the woods behind the crowd of children. Tom drew Allie and Scott away. Bell alone remained with me.

I wanted the rest of Magic to get itself well hidden in those woods. Before I confronted Singh, I'd have to buy them some time.

The car was a big one, not Singh's familiar Mercedes, but a larger, even more powerful Chrysler Ray. I turned and headed away from the children and the chimps, moving as quickly as I was able. I had grown so old in a matter of weeks, though, that my movements were impossibly slow, my legs wobbling, my breath too soon hot in my lungs.

The Ray followed me, a gleaming black shape. The closer I got to the far end of the compound, the deeper Magic could hide. Left leg, right leg, draw a breath. My heart was beginning to hammer, my throat to ache. The wind whistled through my mouth. My legs felt like liquid.

The car pulled up beside me, rolling slowly along. Then Bell was there, her legs pounding, a nasty looking piece of wood in her hand. 'You leave him alone,' she shouted. She put herself between me and the car.

The window came down and Bell struck with her wood at the figure in the back seat. The figure moved only enough to avoid the blow. 'John, stop her or I will stop her.'

I could see something in his lap, a shiny object. I thought of the gas bomb in our car in Iowa. He would not hesitate to kill her, though she had only a stick.

'Bell – '

'You get to those woods! Leave him to me.'

I stopped running. 'No, Bell, it's no use.'

'Don't just let him take you. Don't you dare!'

He opened the window. His turban was gone and his few curls of hair were greasy and unwashed. 'Hello, John.'

'Hello, Dr Melo.'

'Ah. Thomas told you, did he? How he's grown.' He looked at me through squinting eyes. 'They are all monsters, you know. Intelligence like theirs is not a blessing. It's a perversion.'

'A burden, I'd call it.'

'John, you go for those woods! Go!' Bell was shrieking. From inside the car there came the rapid *bummbummbumm* of a stunner. She dropped as if she had turned to water. Allie and Scott came bursting from the far woods then, their legs pumping.

'Low stun,' the Doctor said. Scott rushed to Bell, knelt and cradled her head.

'Three minutes and she'll be back,' said a voice from the car. 'No concussion.'

'You see, we are merciful. Take her, Scott. I am afraid that John must come with me.'

Allie looked up at him. 'Please – '

'Must. Get in the car, John.'

462

My body moved like lead. But I was not afraid. I had my weapon, the best version of it ever.

I was being very, very careful, though. Right there in that car, this doctor could strip my mind blank. Aminase can be delivered by gas, by pressure syringe, by capsule.

'John, no!' As the door opened Allie clutched at me, screaming.

'John,' Singh said softly, 'I will kill this place if you do not co-operate with me.'

I stepped into the cool luxury of the Ray. The Doctor slid the door down behind me.

Through the window I saw as if in sharp light Scott bending over Bell, Allie standing with her fists clenched, looking at the car as if it was killing me. None of them moved.

I thought of the ancient fables of sorcerers who freeze people, of men turned to stone by the evil of the eye. Then the windows mirrored in. The only thing I could see was a faint reflection of this blue, softly lit interior, and the bobbing head of my captor.

'So you know me at last,' the Doctor said. 'I had to disguise myself, of course. Four fifths of mankind would despise me if they knew I was an American. Still, I am symbolically valid, eh? East versus west.' He laughed a little. 'Symbolically valid.' His voice was full of scorn.

I had an opening, I saw that. Maybe my only opening. 'The world will know you're an American.' My voice was full of tremors. I took a deep breath. 'The conviction will tell them.'

'What did you reach, level four? I hardly think that will stand for much, especially since you will repudiate it.' My eyes followed his to the priceless rosewood cabinetry of the bar. My new soul must be inside. Dr Melo smiled as brightly as a baby seeing a butterfly. 'Now my secret is out.' He pressed something and the bar slid open. At the same moment the glass separating us from the front parted and I found myself looking into the red eye of a hissing blinder, held by one of his people. 'It is on high,' the Doctor said. 'If you resist, you will begin with permanent blindness. So you will not resist.'

My anger threatend to immobilize me. But I had to speak, I had to try. 'Level ten,' I blurted. 'Level ten!'

'Ah. The children patched up Delta Doctor and completed it for you. So it is no doubt most artful, most perfect. Ah.' A strain entered his smile. 'But it has not been released. It will never be released. You will soon order Delta Doctor to erase it.'

'It will be released.'

'You will tell the world it's a lie. Since you will be thought the author, the world will believe you.'

'A level ten? From what I've heard of it, not even God could repudiate it. Every press group in the world will be proclaiming its authenticity, Dr Melo. They will dig in data and find that its claims about your identity are true. They will find out who you really are, and probably much more about you. No matter what you do to me, the conviction will destroy you.'

'It isn't level ten. There is no level ten!'

I pulled my Interactor out of my pocket and spread the screen. 'Try it.'

'Hold the mirror of myself up to myself? Ah, how charming.'

The Interactor lay open in my lap. I turned on the speech module. It would listen to his questions and reply aloud. He took a deep breath. 'I am a man of love. Often my heart seems to overflow. Where does Singh get his love?'

– My name is not Singh. I am Augustus Melo.

'A clever beginning!' There was a definite edge in his

464

voice. Very certainly he was afraid. 'Melo is a man of love, then, is he not?'

The conviction spoke, and it spoke the truth.

– Love? You speak of an emotion that I don't believe in at all.

'This isn't true. I love all mankind. It's true isn't it, Melo loves mankind?'

– The human species is one of a number of species on the planet. This species is greedy and vicious. It has devoured the earth. At its genius best, it produces only uncontrollable monsters!

He sighed, closed his eyes. 'It isn't me, it's a different person.' His voice was almost inaudible. He knew the truth – the conviction was him, right down to the voice pattern. It was probably copied so perfectly that not even a machine could tell the difference. It was him on the Interactor's speaker, truly him. Off in Washington, in the depths of a revised Delta Doctor, an artificial soul had come alive, and it was the soul of the frightened man who questioned it.

'Melo is noble, is he not, to have accepted a lifetime of disguise, to have accepted early old age, a virtual remake of his flesh from vigor to waste – my God, and how it hurt – all for the sake of his cause?'

– It is not victory but silence I seek. Dreams. I am part of the fate of this species, and part of the future of the earth. I know earth's longings, earth's needs. Just as I have walked with God, I have seen the planet's own vision of its future. Can you imagine the sweep of the empty forest, the brilliance of the stars untainted by human waste in the air, or the sea, so clear you can see the bottom, or a fine, muscular river that an animal can drink in safety? Earth hopes for this.

'The Depopulation is a good thing, a human thing, is it not? What do you say to that?'

– The human species is a failure, a greedy, heedless, foolish failure. We should never have been given hands. With our hands we tore apart God's creation. Let us lie down in the rain, and dissolve, so that the earth can begin again. Perhaps the next species that evolves mind will not only be intelligent, but also good.

'Christ!' He grabbed my Interactor, pulled open the screen. 'Picture!' What appeared on the screen was a perfect image of the man in the car. But without the merry eyes. The eyes were almost blank, in fact, as empty as the eyes of a dead man. And yet they were not dead. 'Tell me your deepest truth.'

– I know myself and what I will do. I can't bear to die. I don't want ever to die. My heart terrifies me, wheezing, rattling the way it does. Sometimes I think to myself, I gave up my youth for this? Despite my blemish I was a fine young man. Oh, but I hated. I was so angry! Once I got a cat and tied it by its tail under the window, and cut a small slit in its belly. It screamed and squirmed about, and once in a while I would stick my finger inside –

'It – how can it know that? The monsters have learned too much. My God, the monsters I created have made this – this travesty of me!'

'I told you, it's at level ten. It's beyond anything I'd have thought possible.'

'How can it know? They're not human, I'm telling you, Sinclair, they are not human. Nobody alive knows about that cat, and Delta Doctor certainly couldn't have extrapolated it. Oh, no. I do not hate life, I am not trying to cause the extinction of the human species! Say it, damn you, Melo is not trying to cause the extinction of the human species, is he?'

– The species is used up. My objective is the greater good of the planet.

The Doctor looked at me, desperation in his eyes.

'You'll deny every word. The whole program's an obvious falsification. Sensation-seeking rubbish. How does it know!'

'It's a conviction, it's supposed to know you better than you know yourself.'

His eyes swam with tears. With a vicious gesture he locked the doors of the car. 'My God, nobody must hear this garbage, this insane garbage. They really did a conviction! I never dreamed it would be so good. Those thoughts are so private, those memories. I have never uttered a word, syllable – and yet – '

He hammered his fist against the intercom button. With a jerk the car started moving. I looked at the windows, and saw only the reflection of two hollow old men.

'May I question the conviction?'

'No! God, no!'

I did so anyway. 'What about death, Dr Melo, if you enjoyed death when you were a child, do you enjoy it now?'

'Shut up, shut up! Delta Doctor, don't answer!'

– You still don't understand me. I am out of control, and I've got to get in control. It isn't death, but control! I'm scared. Without control I am worse than dead. I would rather be dead than be like I was when my father used to take my mother and slam her against the wall, oh, God, I couldn't control him, I couldn't even make a sound or he would hurt me,so bad, and she was screaming and we were all out of control. When she slept I went to her and I looked down into the black sockets of her eyes, and I hate her because she's so weak, and I take her throat in my hands and I am squeezing and squeezing and she breathes like a sick air conditioner, and I am squeezing, and her eyes fly open and I press down harder and harder and then she almost blows up in my face. She

467

throws me off and she goes into the bathroom and she is black, she is clawing at her throat and there isn't a sound but the breaking of the back of the toilet when she falls. They said it was my dad who did it and I saw them take him away, and even he thought yes, I probably killed the bitch.

'It's from hell. They're demons from hell, they wove those lies in hell!'

'Are they really lies?'

He looked at me as if I had put a knife in his belly. I remembered the Falon conviction, with all its intimate sexual detail. But nothing like this – the horror, the ugliness of it.

He moved with strange grace, opening the bar and withdrawing a hypodermic gun.

I looked down at the slim silver object with the black head. Out of that head would come the Aminase oblivion. The ultimate trip: total erasure. I pulled at the door handle, pulled until it broke off, while the black head of the hypodermic came closer.

I put my hands up to shield my face and neck. My own fingers fascinated me. They were trembling so much they seemed like strings whipping air. I was out of time but still I sought some more time.

'Dr Melo – '

'Be quiet!' He jabbed at my eye with the sputtering hypodermic. I dodged, sliding along the seat.

I was trying to get him to listen. Maybe if he did that he would come to understand himself. He jabbed again, snarling angrily. I turned my head, feeling a drip of warm Aminase on my cheek, smelling its chloral reek. 'Dr Melo, why do you hate mankind so?'

– How can there be love? I know the secrets of this world, but what does that matter? Nobody cares! The

468

east has failed to recognize the full miracle of the individual, while the west has become addicted to it. Capitalism is unworkable without expansion, and so is the most self-destructive of institutions. Communism has failed because it lost its Marxist roots and became the final evolution of the cult of the individual, an attempt to implant a code of ideal behavior in the defective human being. The defective, guilty failure, slouching along his filthy byways, dripping semen and reeking of liquor, his body wasted, his soul perverted by drugs.

'Why did you create the Depopulation? Was it to help mankind?'

– I have a fantasy that I am alone in the whole world, and around me is a huge, empty city, and it is very quiet, for I am the last. You cannot imagine how beautiful this image is. The deep red of the sky, the stars just appearing, the black shadows that fill every window of every house, and the twisted, intricate shapes in the streets, their hands, their faces – dead.

'We cracked Delta Doctor once, we'll crack it again!'

'Do you think the mind net will let you do that? It doesn't like you, Doctor. You don't fit in with its plans.'

'Nobody knows its plans! Not even those damanable monsters. And it doesn't have likes and dislikes. Sometimes it works with my people very well.'

'Don't be certain it's that objective.'

'Nobody controls it, not even the children.'

'They're part of it. The children are the intuition and the whole of the computer system – all of its programs, all of its hardware, all of its linkages – is the reason.'

Carefully, almost with awe, he took the Interactor. One its screen was his mirror image, a twisted, perfect portrait of the man. 'So, my dear conviction, what is the purpose of the Depopulation? If Melo hates mankind so much, why did he create something designed to ensure human survival?'

– The combination of depopulation and nature's own violence will cause the total collapse of human society. Mankind will not have the strength to do what is necessary to prevent atmospheric catastrophe. Man will disappear from the earth.

'You say so? There is no proof.'

– I gamed out the whole thing myself, in 2022. My movement has nothing to do with survival. It is to be the engine of extinction. The whole game can be read at data node 2231.657 ATZH in Cryptor Records, by simply calling it up and giving the decrypt code OAN2W.

He stared, his eyes literally popping. Then he hurled my terminal against the floor of the car, smashing it again and again. His image warped and wrinkled in the flapping screen, and he shrieked at it, slamming it down until finally it flickered and died. The Interactor's keyboard flew to pieces, the back of the case springing open to reveal a sputtering electrocell.

'It's only a terminal,' I said.

Suddenly, I felt the car stop, heard the engine turning over. 'What is it?' the Doctor snapped into the intercom.

'Doctor, they are before me, I cannot – '

He cleared the glass between the compartments. Through the windshield I saw the whole of Magic, Tom and Emon and Randy in front, G-Shaw and Snick and all the others crowding behind, and before them all, the enormous form of Boola, his huge face grimacing. He slammed his open palm against the hood and the whole car shook.

'Blind them! Blind them all!'

The driver turned around, his face working. 'Doctor, I – '

The gorilla was now bouncing the car. Chimps were

hammering on the doors and windows. All of Magic was singing, its voice like the snarl of angry bees, then sweet, a song of memory so intense it made Dr Melo gasp and clap his hands over his ears. 'Drive over them, I order you!'

The window beside his head cracked, the victim of a chimp's fist. Dr Melo drew air across his teeth and jabbed at me with the hypodermic. I shielded my face – and felt a hot line of pain strike the side of my neck, and heard the faint ping as some of the Aminase entered my bloodstream. It wasn't enough to destroy me, but it had a shattering and weird effect on immediate memory. The car became a meaningless jumble of images, Melo himself a strange, capering shape. I could remember my family, Magic, but not who this man was or where we were. Life started five minutes ago. The present was a blank.

I could hardly understand when Boola tore off the car door. Melo groaned, and turned his hypodermic on himself. Again and again he fired it into his own face, aiming it up between his skull and his eyeball, shooting directly into his cerebral cortex. He sank back in his seat, an empty, drooling shell.

Then Bell was there, gasping. I was confused. I remembered her vividly, but I didn't know why on earth she had come, or why she was so exhausted.

'We should have been faster,' Bell said. Then I could not remember what Bell had said. I felt as if I had been whirled round and round until nothing made any sense anymore.

My chest began to ache terribly and I couldn't catch my breath. Something was happening to me, something bad. My heart was thundering. The pain shot down my arms and up into my jaw. I got weak, so weak I could barely hold up my head.

I was having a heart attack, but I couldn't remember

that long enough even to form a cry, much less tell them what was happening to me. Someone needed to break a coronary kit against my chest, but – what?

The pain. The dark.

'My poor John,' Bell said, stroking my hair. Then they brought Allie, and she came and kissed my forehead and for a moment I stopped falling. Incredibly vivid in my mind was the first kiss we ever shared, on a hillside covered with dry autumn grass. She was wearing a white turtleneck, her eyes were lost, her skin was pale in the dark, there was a distant line of lights, the night train.

But who had kissed me now?

Was this dose small enough to wear off?

Dose of what? There was something I had to tell them, but my chest was hurting again. My chest and my arms, oh God, how they hurt! Allie, Bell, Scott –

Voices, people, faded. The world faded.

The Decision

In and out, in and out, the old man breathes. He sleeps
at last, his wife sitting beside him. I cannot imagine that
John will die. His breath comes as if the air carries too
much weight for him.

Down on the beach the chimps celebrate the moon,
which rides over a motionless sea. There are no lights on
this empty coast.

The children have examined John. They say that he is
suffering from gerontological collapse brought on by
extreme stress and the toxic side effects of the Aminase.

For me he is life itself, surviving against the collapse of
the world.

Allie stirs, leans close to his face. 'John?'

'Allie.' His voice is so faint that I can barely hear it,
and I am only across the room.

'Come on, Bell.' Randy takes my hand. I start to pull
away, but then I accept her meaning and follow her.
Allie and John must be alone. This is the most private
time there can be in a marriage.

His breath comes long and slow, like the wind before
morning.

Under the big tree beside the main building Randy
begins singing. Her voice is high and clear. The music
spreads through Magic, swelling and changing, growing,
until it seems to blend with the wind and the blood-dark
rhythms of the chimps on the beach. The gorilla moves
gracefully, a huge shadow in and out among the buildings,
clapping his big hands. Tom leans against one of the

buildings, his head down. I am beginning to understand the way they love one another here.

I hear John and Allie and for a moment I am too shcoked to believe it. They are laughing, gently, deeply, a sound as sensual as the voice of summer. If there is a private happiness so great that it stands against death, I hope that I may also find it.

'Bell, take a walk with us.'

'I want to stay. John might –'

'You and Scott come with us. Allie can take care of her husband.'

We walk in the woods in the darkness. I record, finally, this conversation:

Randy: My dream might not come true. The species can now make an honest decision. John did that.

Me: Do you really think so? Will Augustus Melo ever recover?

Tom: The Aminase burned him out. Of course, it was the smartest thing he could have done to himself, in view of the conviction. Now he's a martyr, and his movement will go on. They'll say that the conviction was obtained by illegal means, and that it's a drug-induced fraud, and point to the drooling vegetable as proof. A lot of people will choose to believe them.

Me: That's diabolical.

Tom: No, human. Clever and brave.

Me: It's neither, I'm sorry! Melo destroyed himself for a terrible reason, and that makes him a coward.

Tom: He's committed to what he believes.

Me: How can you be like this, all of you? So – passive, or whatever it is! What's the matter with you?

Tom: Bell, there is a kind of acceptance that frees you. Life accepts. Evolves, adapts, makes do. This is the splendor of life. Imagine some of life's images – a whole meadow reflected in a single drop of dew. How beautiful.

Or a family of termites in a fallen tree, less beautiful but still part of the order of life. Or algae swarming in the yellow sewers of a chemical plant, or bacteria living in the brown reefs of acid clouds – less beautiful still, but can't you see how hard life is struggling to persist on this planet, and how beautiful every part of that struggle is?

Me: Of course, and that's why you make me so mad. You see all of that, but you still let somebody like Melo get all kinds of power. If you love life, why do you let death win?

Tom: We have to accept death. Even the total death of extinction. We need not love it, but all of your anger is energy wasted. To use your energy in a good way, you've got to abandon the luxury of anger. Imagine this world as it may be without man, all the uses of things changing. Those plastic buttons on your shirt, for example, imagine their larger future. They were made perhaps two years ago, they have been yours for a few months. Now consider them a thousand years from now, weathered, covered with lichens, cracked. What is their truth – the wink of time they serve you, or the years and years they will do service to a new world in which mankind plays no part?

Me: That doesn't make me accept anything. That makes me crazy.

Tom: Life is bigger than man, stronger, older and very much more patient. No matter what we do, life will somehow persist, even if it is in a very small way. Even if we send the world back to the level of charged mud, it will simply begin again. Take comfort in this, and your anger will stop getting in your way. We have work to do, we haven't time for rage.

Me: I still want to know what will happen! I don't want Magic to die. I don't want John to die!

Emon: We cannot decide those things, it isn't our right.

Tom: In the end Magic belongs to mankind, and we must accept the fate mankind chooses.

Me: But you did all this – drew us here, finished our conviction. I think you even let Melo find you on purpose so that he and John could have their confrontation – and for what? One of them's a vegetable and the other's dying.

Tom: I will admit that we had a certain hand in all these things. We did it so that the species would have a better chance to make a clear and rational decision about its own future. Without your book and the conviction, the dice were loaded in Dr Melo's favor. If we work at it, we will be able to spread your message in oppositon to Singh's. There will be a choice, and therefore a real decision. It is not right that an intelligent species be fooled into becoming extinct. We must choose. Do we deserve to live? Can we continue to strive toward the harmony that has called to us since the moment of our creation?

Me: I hate all this intellectual mumbo-jumbo, this fatalism. No wonder Melo called you monsters!

Tom: If we die and the chimps do not, what in a million years will be here? Nations of scraggly creatures with long arms and big ears, nations composed of vast families, kinder and softer than us? Or if the apes do not survive, go forward a billion years. Beneath the warm yellow sun of that time, what will this earth be? A blue jewel, and not a single human thread remaining – instead there will be the promise of new intelligence already in some quick species. You have to understand the striving of the earth itself – it wants consciousness. It wants to know and to think through the medium of its creatures. If one thinking species proves too flawed to continue, earth will bring forth another. And so on until the end of time.

476

I stamped my foot. 'Man's fate matters to me. It matters a great deal. I want mankind to succeed. I want there to be more generations. I want laughter and happiness in the world. I want human beauty, human joy, human prayer. I want to see babies growing – oh, I want a child. I don't want to have a baby if the whole world's going to fall apart, but I don't want to die without ever being pregnant.' I couldn't talk anymore. I was so mad, and so sad, my throat just closed up. I know that the warm, searching looks the kids gave me were from a wisdom greater than I can understand, but I have wisdom too even though it's not as grand and I'm not as eloquent. My wisdom is that people are good, and we must fight to keep going.

A bell began ringing. Randy looked up, her mouth forming a word that never emerged.

I knew why that bell was ringing, and I ran like a madwoman through the dark woods, branches scraping my face, my own tears making it hard for me to see.

And then I did see: Allie was standing at the door of Building One. Boola was near her on his haunches, throwing sand on his head. 'Allie, he didn't. Say he didn't.'

Allie did not reply. I scooped her up in my arms. Our tears mingled, and I was furious. Scott came to us.

The bell did not stop, and the whole of Magic gathered, silently.

I learned something in those terrible hours. I learned that there is something permanent about human love, that lives forever in everybody.

Magic taught me by the way it reacted to the death. We buried John in the depth of the woods. The chimps dug the grave in a few minutes, with their powerful shoulders and their skill with tools. Less than an hour after he died, he was gone. A child called Naomi recited from Ecclesiastes. 'In the day when the keepers of the house shall tremble, and the strong men shall bow themselves, and the grinders cease because they are few, and those that look out of the windows be darkened, and the doors shall be shut in the streets, when the sound of the grinding is low, and he shall rise up at the voice of the bird, and all the daughters of music shall be brought low ... because man goeth to his long home, and the mourners go about in the streets, then shall the dust return to the earth as it was: and the spirit shall return unto God who gave it.'

Her thin little voice was enough to fill the woods. In the following quiet Allie picked up some dirt, showed it to Boola and said. 'Fill the grave.'

The sound of the dirt hitting him, and the sight of that face in the dirt, and then the dark in the grave when he was covered, made me cry out, and I wanted to get him, to keep him. Allie raised her head. She drew a loud breath. 'We have to go back now,' she said.

Long into the night I heard her weeping, but I did not go to her. Scott and the children went to her.

Maybe having to accept John's death has made me a little better able to face the future with the objective consciousness that the children expect of me. I can be worthy of them.

It isn't as if we weren't busy. Magic has an immense task. We must publish our book and spread our conviction. We must press such ideas as Solar Controller and all of Magic's other innovations, the Lepcon solar cell that was invented and lost forty years ago, the atmospheric scrubbers, all of it. Against our notions of hope the Depopulation persists. Melo is a sort of totem, a smiling, vacant figure, a symbol of bravery.

I work with the publication unit, selling our book to the paper presses and making sure that Depopulationists don't prevent its distribution. Allie and Scott help on the conviction team, flying in the datanet, testing every copy of the conviction to make sure that they haven't been altered or edited. We feel that we have the support of the computer system but we can't be sure. It is fundamentally a machine, built to serve. That makes it passive in ways that are hard to believe. It might love us, but it will not stop the Depopulationists from using it or even sabotaging it. That is up to us.

Scott has abandoned his obsession with Tom's files, and now uses his considerable skill as a cipher expert to seek out hidden bits of code in the millions of perfect models of Augustus Melo's soul that Tom and the others have seeded in the datanet.

Even as I write, the world roars on, highways swarming, economies helplessly committed to endless expansion, the whole inflamed hive plunging toward its end.

Sometimes I think that the defects in humanity are too great, and that we will definitely choose extinction. Then I hear evening song at Magic, and I think no, it must be life.

Day has changed to night, and a quiet has settled over this busy place. I wait, we all wait. Faintly from the shore I hear the chimps chanting down the moon, a fat yellow lantern dropping into the Pacific. They do not know it, but they wait also. Mankind draws close now, close to its decision.